TEAM SPIRIT

IAN MAYFIELD

Published by Four Limes Books

For information contact: ianmayfieldauthor@gmail.com
Cover design by Pixel Studios
Cover image by noskaphoto
ISBN: 978-0-692638-61-3
First Edition: 2016

10 9 8 7 6 5 4 3 2 1

WEEK ONE
TUESDAY

Halfway up Gravel Hill more fire engines overtook them, sirens blaring like panic-stricken elephants. Sophia frowned as she watched them go past and then said, 'That's four.'

There was no response from her companion, who kept driving at a sedate forty.

'Are you all right, Nina?' Sophia said.

'Mmm?'

Sophia waited. They'd just come from visiting a ninety year old woman, violated in her nursing home bedroom, little better than catatonic despite the best attentions of the care staff. Occasionally, even in this job, it got to you.

Nina became aware that some sort of response was expected, and twitched her head as if to snap out of a daydream. 'Sorry, guv. No, I'm all right. Personal stuff, that's all.'

Sophia nodded. 'My door is always open, you know that.' A pause, then the corners of her mouth jerked up into a smile. 'Figuratively speaking.'

Nina looked across and grinned, appreciating the joke.

Always open because it didn't exist. An 'office' which consisted of having a bigger desk than everyone else. Intimidating though she usually was, there were times when the guv'nor was almost human.

They reached the roundabout at the top of the hill and the moment passed. Sophia's attention was caught by something through the trees.

'There.'

Nina followed her gaze away to the left and saw it: a column of black smoke rising from the valley.

'Petrol station gone up?'

'No, it's all houses down there.'

Three police cars, one unmarked, leapt raucously from the third exit and crossed the roundabout. They disappeared in the direction of the smoke.

'And what's this got to do with us?' Nina asked, pulling out after them.

'Mr Heighway didn't say.' Sophia lifted the phone in her hand and looked at the text message again. 'Just that he wants us on the scene and we'll see why when we get there.'

It wasn't hard to find. Down Ballards Way, left turn into Chapel View at the bottom, smoke billowing into the sky, high and violent like the pillar of cloud that guided Moses. The house was halfway along. Flames gushed from the windows, into which the fire crews were already training their hoses. Smoke billowed from the roof, filling the air with an acrid stench. Inside the house burning wood crackled and banged. Ahead of them the street was blocked, a logjam of red, white and flashing, strobing blue, emergency personnel hurrying and leaping over snaking hose, stringing out tape to keep spectators at a safe distance. Four paramedics emerged slowly, carefully from the garden, two stretchers their burden. An adult body and a small child's, wrapped in plastic, what could be seen of them a ground, charred mass, like half-cooked burgers. It dawned on the two women that the smaller figure wore an oxygen mask. It was still alive.

But they weren't what drew the eye. That privilege was reserved for the thing on the lawn.

'Jesus, Mary and Joseph,' Nina said, and crossed herself. Sophia just stared.

Planted in the flowerbed by the front garden wall, simply fashioned from two sturdy pieces of timber, was a cross. It was six feet high. And it too was in flames.

Copper or not, Detective Sergeant Kim Oliver thought, you could tell a major crime scene a mile off. As the car in which she was travelling crawled eastwards in the rush hour jam on Croham Valley Road, she lost count of the police vehicles and the uniformed and plain clothes officers who'd swarmed into the area to knock on doors. They contributed to the jam not only by blocking the road but also because their presence made everyone slow down to see what was going on. Kim sighed and caught a glimpse of herself in the wing mirror. She noted the bags under her eyes and wondered how much longer she would last. She'd come back on duty at seven that morning after a session with a rape victim that had lasted well into the previous night; now she faced an extension to the working day of unknown length to which she would have to gear herself.

The driver of the car was tired too. Detective Constable

Marie Kirtland had been up most of the night nursing her two-year-old through an ear infection. Her left hand drummed on the wheel; her right held a burning cigarette from which she seldom took a drag but frequently tapped the ash out of the rolled-down window. Neither woman spoke. For now, all that needed to be said had been. Any utterance would smack of frivolity.

Marie gave a relieved sigh as at last they reached their turn and she was able to swing the wheel left and lean on the accelerator. She took a final puff, blew the smoke out through her nostrils and threw her stub out of the window. Kim, who'd given up six months ago, would normally have frowned on Marie smoking in the confines of the car. Today she forced herself to be tolerant, even though she herself was gasping for a fag and fighting a battle of none too strong will.

'Just round here, yeah?' Marie said in her broad Lake District accent, and flicked the left indicator without waiting for an answer. They were coming to a wide green bordered by modern semi-detached houses and bungalows, snuggling among blossom-filled cherry trees. Another street turned left, Chapel View. Marie took it.

Several patrol cars and a couple of dog vans hugged the pavement outside number 84, along with a mobile incident room trailer and a boxlike red van with FIRE INVESTIGATION UNIT written on the side. In front of the charred shell of what had once been a house a cordon of blue and white striped tape, patrolled by a PCSO, kept the public away while the forensic and fire investigators finished their work. Officers went about their business or stood around the trailer in conference or awaiting orders. A couple of dozen onlookers, mostly children, loitered in front of the parade of shops across the street. Some of them were talking to television news crews, an outrider for one of whom, hefting a video camera, was taking stock shots.

They tried to take it in. It was bizarre, disturbing. This should be an inner city estate, with a history of crime and tension. It wasn't. This was a suburban street of green lawns, of second and third cars and grass verges, of comfortable semis that sold for upwards of two hundred grand. The eye turned as if drawn by a magnet to the burnt-out house, then to the obscenity on the lawn. Another world had come to visit.

As they parked, Detective Chief Inspector Sophia Beadle eased her bulk down from the trailer. She came over, looking at her watch.

'Traffic?'

'Yeah,' Kim said. 'Backed up right the way into town.'

'Any news on the victims, guv?' Marie asked.

Sophia looked grim. 'Mother didn't make it. The little boy's still hanging on.'

She brought them up to speed. Not surprisingly, the fire investigator's initial impression was that it had been started deliberately, and had spread throughout within moments, overwhelming the occupants before they could react.

'You wonder,' Kim said, 'what sort of sick scumbag would want to...' She broke off, grimacing as if from a nasty taste. She repeated, angrily, 'You wonder.'

'Do I detect a shift from impartiality, Kim?' The DCI's clear, china blue eyes fixed her in their field of vision. There was no humour in them.

Kim was undaunted. 'Yes, I'm afraid you do.'

Sophia's nod contained many things, but not approval.

Arms folded, Marie was looking at the cross. Charred white now, it acted as a garish signpost to the blackened spectacle beyond. She said, 'The Job's shown me some things, but... phew.'

'The Ku Klux Klan used to use a burning cross as a calling card,' Kim declared.

Marie digested this for a moment. 'I don't suppose anybody saw it put there?'

'No witnesses so far,' Sophia confirmed. 'Except to the effect that it wasn't there up to twenty minutes before the fire.'

'Par for the course.'

'But there is a suspect.'

'Who?'

'The babysitter.'

'You're joking,' Marie said.

'Name of Deborah Clarke,' Sophia went on. 'Sixteen, school leaver. Looks after the kid while Mrs Benton's at work, collects him from school and watches him until she gets home.'

'So she's got a key?'

'Yes. At the moment we have to fancy her strongly, because she appears to have done a runner.'

They waited mutely for her to explain.

'Our only witness of any worth, Mrs Blissett, who keeps the newsagent's over there, served Mrs Benton at about twenty past four. Five minutes later Debbie Clarke came in, apparently seemed a bit het up. She used cash to buy several bars of chocolate and a Basildon Bond notepad, and then according to Mrs Blissett she ran out of the shop and headed off' - she pointed back the way Kim and Marie had come - 'in the opposite direction to her home. Ten minutes after that the house went up like a Guy Fawkes bonfire.'

'Coincidence?' Kim said.

Sophia shrugged. 'We know she must have gone down

Croham Valley but we lose her once we get to the main road. Obviously the house-to-house is still going on and we may get something further from that. Nina's also checking with the bus garage in case a driver remembers her getting on a 64.' She gestured vaguely with a pudgy hand.

'Where do we come in?'

'Your job for now is to talk to the sitter's parents: Andrew and Charlotte Clarke.' She gave them the address. 'Expect a hard time: the PC who went round got sent away with a flea in her ear by the father. Find out,' she added, as they turned to go, 'if Debbie's been been back there or if they have any idea where she's gone. They say not, but the father's attitude may mean he's hiding something. All right?'

Ballards Way was a long, wide residential street, much used nowadays as a rat run between the two main roads it connected, but still affordably affluent. The Clarkes' house was a pebbledashed four bedroom semi with sizeable gardens front and back, a short gravel drive and a garage. A Japanese maple grew on the front lawn. The timbers of the house and garage were painted crimson, echoing the tree. There were two cars in the drive, a white VW Golf and a silver Volvo. Kim and Marie crowded into the red parquet porch and rang the bell.

There was movement behind the frosted glass pane and a man opened the door. He was fortyish, suited, blond, his florid, rough complexion suggesting he might keel over from a heart attack at any moment. There was a strong odour of tobacco on his breath when he spoke.

'If you're press, go away.'

'Mr Clarke?' Kim said. They showed their warrant

cards. 'Kim Oliver, Marie Kirtland, Croydon Special Crime Unit. Somebody told you we'd be coming?'

His faint frown was a look they'd become inured to over time, the look you got when not one, but two women in plain clothes turned up on the doorstep, both claiming to be from the police. One of them black, to boot. Once again Kim felt some uneasy pressure. Not for the first time, she wondered disloyally whether her colour was the sole reason Sophia had appointed her to the team.

Andrew Clarke said, 'Yes. Come in.' He held open the door with grudging disdain, like the doorman of a Mayfair club on ladies' night. They were shown into a large sitting room, furnished in autumn browns. Sliding patio doors gave onto a well-kept lawn with a young cherry tree at the bottom of it. A petite, greying brown-haired woman sat perched on the edge of a settee, smoking. She looked up, as surprised by who she saw as her husband. Andrew Clarke said, 'It's the police, Charlotte.' For the police's benefit he added, 'My wife.' They'd guessed as much.

'Mrs Clarke,' Marie acknowledged. 'May we sit down?'

'I suppose,' Charlotte Clarke said, ushering them with an apathetic wave to any seat of their choosing, 'there's no point asking if you've found Debbie?'

'Not yet,' Marie said. She paused for a moment before launching in. Kim sat, inclined forward, listening. Both had guessed that they might get more out of the Clarkes if Marie did the talking. She began, 'Can I just ask you again if you're sure your daughter hasn't been back here?'

Andrew Clarke greeted the question with a huge and deliberate sigh, and let himself flop back into the settee, flinging his arms up in a show of exasperation.

'We're sure.' Mrs Clarke took a deep drag. 'We've checked

and double-checked her room; we've been watching out for her constantly...'

'And you've tried calling her?'

'Frequently,' Andrew Clarke said. 'Her phone goes straight to voicemail.'

Marie nodded and turned back to Mrs Clarke. 'Did you notice anything missing when you searched? Clothes, makeup?'

'No.'

'How could you tell?' her husband cut in. 'The state she keeps that room in, who knows what she's got in there we don't know about?'

'She'd have had to pack,' Charlotte Clarke said. 'Her suitcase is still up there. All that's gone is her tote bag, and she took that with her when she went to collect Robin.'

'Mrs Benton's little boy?'

Charlotte Clarke nodded. Kim expected her to ask after the Bentons, but instead she said, 'She has that instead of a handbag, like a lot of girls her age. Asking for trouble really: they're a pickpocket's dream, nice and loose. But she will insist.'

'Pretty roomy, those bags,' Marie said. 'Sure she couldn't've stuffed some things in?'

'Not her toothbrush,' Andrew Clarke grumbled. 'I checked.'

'I saw her pick the bag up,' his wife said. 'I'd have noticed if it had been fuller than usual.'

'What did she normally carry?'

'Not much. Her purse, her mobile, a jumper. That's about it.'

'Leaves a bit of scope, though, doesn't it?' Marie said. 'By your account the bag'd normally have been *very* light, so a couple of extra bits wouldn't've noticed.'

'You've got a bit of a bee in your bonnet about this bag, Miss Kirkwood,' Andrew Clarke interrupted again.

Marie ignored the *Miss* and the mangling of her name. 'Let me explain, sir. This was almost certainly arson - well, you know that from the officer who came before. It's looking as if fires were set inside the house, but there's no sign of a break-in.'

'Are you accusing my daughter - ?'

'Nobody's accusing anybody,' Marie said firmly. 'But the fact remains Debbie left the house a few minutes before the fire and may have been the last person to see the Bentons. It goes without saying she may be - '

'A vital witness, yes, so we keep being told.'

'Now,' Marie resumed, having waited for him to vent, 'is there anywhere she might've gone? A friend's, possibly?'

'Tch,' Andrew Clarke said.

'Boyfriend?'

'No.'

'Any brothers or sisters living away from home? Other relatives?'

'She's our only child. I've rung round everywhere,' Mrs Clarke said. 'No-one's seen her.'

'The friends you *know* of,' her husband put in. 'She has so many. Chopping and changing all the time. We gave up trying to keep track long ago.' He shrugged and said, as if it explained everything, 'She's at that age. What can you do?'

'Well, you could tell me if she kept an address book or diary.'

Andrew Clarke waved a dismissive hand, as if the sheer effort required to conceive of such a thing were beyond human capability.

'Teenage girls generally do,' Marie prompted.

Charlotte Clarke thought for a moment. 'I think I've seen something,' she said. 'In her room somewhere.'

'Could we try and find it, please?' Marie requested, with solemn sweetness.

They accompanied Mrs Clarke upstairs to Debbie's bedroom: a private territory her mother seemed reluctant to violate. A brief search produced a black leather bag, and from it a small navy blue diary. Kim leafed through it. 'Crumbs. You were right about her friends, Mrs Clarke.' The addresses section was full: Debbie seemed to have scribbled things both on the diary pages themselves and on scraps of paper and Post-its stuck in between them.

'My wife and I can enquire round these friends if you like,' Andrew Clarke said from the doorway.

'Thanks for the offer, sir,' Kim replied, abstaining from grinding her teeth, 'but this is an official police investigation, OK, so really we've got to do it. Providing you're prepared to let us have the diary, of course.'

The Clarkes looked at one another, then at their visitors. Andrew Clarke said, 'If you think you can find her any quicker, why not?'

'Thank you,' Kim said.

'Anything else you think might come in handy, just feel free.'

She suppressed a smile at his sarcasm. He wasn't about to say so, but what he wanted was to get a look at this diary of his daughter's he hadn't known about. Kim said, 'Anyway, based on my own past experience as a sixteen year old girl, I doubt many of the names'd mean that much to you.'

Andrew Clarke at once took exception to what he saw as the inference in her remark, but the detectives, aided by his wife, calmed him down. Back in the sitting room, they were able to confirm Debbie's description, what she was wearing and anything about her that might help to trace or identify her. On request, Mrs Clarke gave them a recent portrait photograph, taken on her sixteenth birthday. She was wearing an off-the-shoulder sky blue party dress, and was carefully made up with neat blonde hair pinned back to frame her oval face and show off a pair of gold stud earrings. She looked very pretty; she would, Kim thought, be recognised and remembered. That, at any rate, was something going for them. They noted the resemblance to her father in the blue eyes, the nose, the jawline.

Kim put the photo in her bag and frowned at Marie. It had always seemed cynical to her, using people's help and goodwill before turning on them like this. But there were still unpleasant questions to be asked, and if they'd come straight out with them earlier, certainly they would not now be in possession of Debbie Clarke's portrait and diary.

Marie said, 'Just a few more things.'

'Fire away.' Andrew Clarke waved a petulant hand.

'We need to know where you both were between three and half four.'

Charlotte Clarke closed her eyes, and appeared to be praying, but an outraged smirk was spreading across her husband's face. 'Oh, so that's it? You think we're in on it?'

'That's not what we said, sir.'

'That's not what she said, Andrew,' Charlotte Clarke muttered, almost inaudibly.

'You think I'm the Croydon chapter of the Ku Klux Klan, do you? Or Charlotte, perhaps?'

Kim looked up.

'She didn't *say* that.'

'Then why do you want to know?' Andrew Clarke scowled, as if it had been them, not his wife, who'd made the denial.

'Standard procedure, sir,' Marie said. 'We have to account for everyone's whereabouts so we can eliminate them.'

'Or accuse them of bloody arson. I'm phoning my solicitor right now.'

'Andrew, really!'

'That's your prerogative, sir,' Marie said.

'It is, isn't it?'

Kim said boldly, 'Are you afraid of what we might ask?'

'No. I'd just rather my legal interests were represented in a more tangible manner. In fact I don't see why I should tolerate your continued presence in my house.'

'If you'd like us to leave,' Kim said, standing, 'we'd be glad to continue this later on at the station.'

'With your solicitor if you prefer,' Marie added.

'You can't order me - '

'For God's *sake!*'

He broke off in mid-rant, his mouth agape. He looked at his wife. She was sitting bolt upright and staring, white-faced, ahead of her.

'They're just doing their *job!*' Charlotte Clarke shrieked. 'Do you think you're helping anyone, yourself, me, least of all Debbie? Will you stop wasting valuable time and just tell them what they want to know instead of pumping up your ego with this stupid bluster.'

Recovering from his shock, he rounded on her. 'No-one speaks to me like that in my own - '

'Well, maybe they bloody should once in a while! If you don't want to tell them, I will.'

'Charlotte!'

Ignoring him, she turned to Marie and Kim. 'He was at work. That's all.' She laughed, skirting hysteria. 'That's where this criminal mastermind of a husband of mine has been all afternoon: hard at work behind his desk at Nationwide, with about twenty staff to vouch for him.'

'Is that right, Mr Clarke?' Marie asked him.

He hesitated. 'Yes.'

'Which branch?'

'No, not at a branch - head office.' He recited a City address. 'I, er... I left soon after Charlotte rang. At about... five past five.'

'And you say there are people who can confirm that?' With prompting, he was able to supply ten names, which Marie wrote down. 'What about you, Mrs Clarke? Whereabouts were you?'

'I was here,' Charlotte Clarke said. 'At home all afternoon.'

'Anybody else can corroborate that?'

'I'm - I'm afraid not.' She frowned. 'Debbie was here until just before three, but obviously then she went off to get Robin, and I haven't seen her...' Realising what she was saying, she tailed off and gulped down a deep breath. She said, 'After that, apart from the policewoman, I've been on my own until Andrew got in.'

'Which was when?'

She looked at her husband. 'When was that, dear?'

Andrew Clarke glared at his visitors. 'I drove like a mad thing... Must've been about quarter to six. I didn't stop to look at my watch,' he couldn't resist adding caustically.

'I see,' Marie said.

Kim said, 'And nobody rang you, Mrs Clarke - I mean

before we called? Nobody like that what could confirm you were in?'

Charlotte Clarke shook her head. 'Sorry.'

There was a pause.

'So,' Andrew Clarke said, 'are you going to put the cuffs on her?'

'No, sir,' Kim said. She waited a moment, then added, 'That's about it, I think. We won't disturb you any more for now.'

'What happens next?' Andrew Clarke said, as they prepared to leave. He held his hands by his sides, clenched into worried fists.

'We'll keep you posted, of course, sir,' Kim said.

'Is that *all*?'

'Feel free,' Kim took a business card from her purse and wrote Marie's name and extension on it, 'to call one of us any time.' She handed it to him.

'One more thing, Mr and Mrs Clarke,' Marie said. 'Once the machinery's in place, sooner or later the officer in charge of the enquiry'll likely be paying you a visit. I thought I'd better warn you.' She paused. 'It's possible she'll want to get you on radio and TV, do an appeal. Er - make it worth Debbie's while by not threatening to skin her alive if she does come back. That sort of thing. Can you do that?'

'Yes,' Charlotte Clarke said.

'You bet your life,' Andrew Clarke said.

Kim took a perverse glee in saying, 'I really wouldn't come the heavy father bit, Mr Clarke. If she's in hiding, a bollocking in front of five million viewers isn't gonna bring her running.'

'Thanks for the advice, officer,' Andrew Clarke said, through gritted teeth.

'What'd you think?' Marie said outside, noticing Kim looking smug. 'They in the frame?'

'The mother ain't.'

'How d'you figure?'

'She didn't say a word about the Bentons, like ask how they were, not once,' Kim said. 'Even when I fed her a line. She just doesn't give a shit. Take it from me, if she'd been in on this she'd've been falling over herself to express concern, throw up a smokescreen. Seen it before, million times.'

'Point,' Marie nodded. 'Him?'

'Him I dunno,' Kim said. 'If he is, he's a bloody good actor with his all piss and wind bit. On the other hand...'

'What?'

'Might be nothing. I know that cross must've been on the news and all,' Kim said, 'but *he* was the one what brought up the Ku Klux Klan. We never did.'

'Fuck,' Marie said, mulling this over for a moment. 'What d'you want to do?'

Inside the trailer, Sophia Beadle listened to their account and the impressions they'd gathered, then asked to see the diary. She took one look at it and made her pronouncement on their next actions. It didn't surprise them.

WEDNESDAY

On her first day on the beat, Larissa Stephenson had discovered the mouldering body of a tramp under a pile of dry leaves and newspaper at the back of a garage. Three weeks later a nervous caretaker, hearing her footsteps inside the vacant office premises she'd entered to investigate an open door, had drawn the obvious conclusion, locked her in and dialled 999. It was not her fault she'd been issued with a dud radio that night, and so had to remain there until the area car arrived a few minutes later. With her track record established, it was inevitable that the relief should bestow upon Larissa the handle 'Lucky', by which she'd been known ever since.

It was a fair reflection, she had to admit. She was one of those people who attract disaster to themselves like piranhas to a ripple. If there was a virus to catch, a bone to break, a fragile object to drop, a wrong turning to take, a date to be late for, a practical joke to be the brunt of, it seemed Lucky seized the opportunity with both hands - smashing it to smithereens in the process.

But such incidents were speed bumps along the generally smooth and happy road of her life. At twenty-two she was a well-adjusted, intelligent woman, popular and outgoing. She was strikingly beautiful, a quality for which she believed she had her mixed lineage to thank. Five feet six inches tall, slim, shapely, her long, black, silky hair, cinnamon complexion and luminous brown eyes complemented startling Indic features that somehow arranged themselves to give her the look, almost, of a young Audrey Hepburn. She'd achieved straight As in three A Level subjects, but had deferred going to university and joined the Met straight from sixth form. Four years on, despite the occasional mishap, she'd developed into an outstanding bobby.

This had not gone unnoticed by her superiors, by whose grace she was now embarking on a new phase of her career. Yet even this seemed to have come about by virtue of her luck. Last Christmas, she'd been first on the scene when a call had come in about a jumper at the NTL transmission tower on Norwood Hill. Lucky had climbed out onto the girder to which the man was clinging, and persuaded him that plunging to his death from a height of four hundred feet was not a good idea. She'd received the expected mix of praise and reproof, some local media attention, then a commendation, and thought nothing further of it until, several months later, there came a summons from Chief Superintendent Linighan, her station commander. No less a body than the Royal Humane Society had got wind of her actions on the tower, and were proposing to award her their Silver Medal. As if this were not enough to put her off her stride, she'd then found herself on one side of an unnerving interview. What, Linighan had asked, pretending neither of them were aware that her personnel file was open on the desk in front of him, were her career goals? Was she aware that the opportunity was open to her to obtain detective experience in a plain clothes unit? What would she say to a secondment to Special Crime at

Croydon, of whom she had no doubt heard great things?

Lucky said that she would be very interested.

A few weeks afterwards, she was interviewed by DCI Beadle, the creator and current commanding officer of the Special Crime Unit. And here she was, about to set out on her first day in plain clothes, as what had once been known as a CID aide but now, in keeping with the Met's sleek new 21st century image, was called a trainee investigator.

She'd thought a lot about what to wear. PCs on crime squads tended to be given free rein to dress as they pleased; but Special Crime was CID, and CID had the reputation of being rather smarter. She opted for a light grey trouser suit, ribbed white top, sturdy black beat-pounding shoes. Underneath, why the hell not, a matching cream silk bra and panties set she'd just bought herself at House of Fraser on a shopping trip with her friend Juliet. This was a day to feel good, from skin outwards. Breakfasted, dressed, she took a last look at herself in the hall mirror, sighed and opened the front door on a bright New Addington morning.

There was a tall, pale young man hovering on the pavement by the hedge, watching her. Lucky flicked a polite smile in his direction as she marched down the path. ''Scuse me,' he said, hurrying over as she closed the gate, 'didn't you used to go to Edenham?'

She stopped rummaging for her car keys and looked up at him, puzzled. 'Edenham? Yeah, that's right.'

'I remember you. You was really brainy.'

Lucky shook her head, uneasy. 'Sorry, I don't - '

'Don't remember me, yeah? No reason to, really. Prosser. Micky Prosser.'

Light dawned, dimly. 'Oh.'

'Remember now?' He grinned, pleased with his success. 'Your name's Melissa or summink, innit?'

'*La*rissa,' she corrected him. Not knowing why, she added, 'My mum's Bulgarian.'

'Really?'

Vague memories were crystallising about the name and face. Michael Prosser. He'd been in her year at school. Streamed at fourteen with the ablest pupils like Larissa, he'd blossomed - if that was the word - into an underachiever; not a major troublemaker, just the sort who sat sniggering at the back with his mates, aggravating teachers and generally being thick. He seemed about as interested in the ethnic origin of her name as he had been in his schoolwork.

Conversation stopped, stalled by the acute embarrassment of meeting someone you haven't seen in years and didn't particularly know or like in the first place. Lucky, never at a loss for long, said, 'So what you doing nowadays?'

'I'm a machinist at Carter's, over on the Purley Way.'

'Yeah?' She was mildly mystified. Purley Way was several miles away on the other side of the borough. New Addington was hardly *en route*, unless he lived up here, and she'd never seen him around before. She asked, 'Making what?'

'Car components. Wing mirror motors, seatbelt housings, stuff like that.'

'Right.'

Prosser said, 'So what do *you* do?'

Lucky dreaded this question. Coming out as a copper tended to have the same social effect as loudly announcing that you had the clap. It was bad enough close friends knowing; it was the last thing she wanted to tell a total stranger. She gave him her stock response. 'Civil servant.'

It sounded so boring it worked nine times out of ten. Prosser said, 'Home Office, yeah?'

'Sort of.'

An awkward silence fell again. Lucky jangled her car keys.

'Well,' she said, 'better get going or I'll be late.'

'Me and all,' Michael Prosser said. 'See you around.'

'Yeah, right,' Lucky said, having no intention of seeing him around and praying that he wouldn't ask for a lift. 'Nice running into you.'

He raised his hand in a perfunctory wave and went back to the bus stop. Lucky drove away and didn't think about him again.

As a coherent picture emerged from the confusion of the firefighting, Sophia Beadle was able to act. It was established that Doreen Benton, a widow of forty-four and a first-generation Guyanese immigrant, had died in the fire and that her six year old younger son Robin was gravely ill at Croydon University Hospital, suffering from up to ninety per cent burns, many of them full thickness. So disfigured were both of them that it had been far from certain they *were* Mrs Benton and her son; in the end it had taken dental x-rays to confirm it. Sophia had given to Sandra Jones the task of contacting Robin's elder brother Luke, an archaeology student on a field trip in Greece.

Forensic were of the opinion that there had been no forced entry. The fire investigators' initial report stated that the fire had been set using four home-made chemical devices, probably with delayed action triggers, unsophisticated but effective, the sort of thing a five-minute web search would tell you how to build. Meanwhile the cross had been identified as fashioned from two lengths of two by four pine, almost certainly cut to order at any of several dozen timber merchants and DIY warehouses in the Croydon area. The crosspiece (three feet long) had been fastened to the upright (six feet) with five six-inch nails. A hole had been dug in a flowerbed, and the cross planted in it before being doused in white spirit and set alight.

As to who had done all this, the search for witnesses was continuing. But as the count of shaken heads on doorsteps increased, so hope diminished. It was as if the fire, the blazing cross, had come from nowhere.

The Clarkes had confirmed that Debbie had her own bank account and debit card, but although Kim had asked Nationwide to flag it, so far it hadn't been used. She had an email account, which they'd managed to access, but other than spam it had seen very little traffic in several months; as practically everyone under the age of twenty communicated through Facebook, Instagram and text message nowadays, this was no surprise. Debbie hadn't backed up her phone contacts to the cloud; Kim and Marie had therefore spent yesterday evening tracing the names in her diary, comparing numbers with the call records, stopping only when it became too late to ring people. The call records themselves showed no activity after the time of the fire. Kim had left several voicemails but the phone was still either off or out of range of a cell tower. Today one of them would have to see the borough archivist and obtain back copies of the registers for Riddlesdown High School, which Debbie had left last summer, on the grounds that many of her former classmates would remember her and might still be in touch. But a pattern had already developed. They'd spoken to several school friends whose names were in the diary, who remembered her as a bright girl and expressed surprise that she hadn't continued to A Levels; but she had not, to their knowledge, kept in touch with anyone much after leaving. Those who had heard from her reported that she had said little about what she was doing now. No-one knew of a boyfriend or other secret ally. All that had come out of the exercise was yet more names to chase. It was beginning to look as if Debbie had achieved that state most sought after by fugitives, and disappeared off the face of the earth.

They'd both felt the need to escape. Even at this early hour the urgency and buzz of a major enquiry pervaded the office. Sophia had been in since six, delegating actions to the uniformed PCs she'd borrowed from early turn. A couple of hours later the rest of the team started to appear; many of them were instantly summoned, actioned and shooed out again. On the DCI's desk was a mountain of reports and printouts, through which she was ploughing doggedly, casting impatient glances at the two technicians who were inputting data to the HOLMES computer as fast as she could throw it their way. Exhausted though they were, Kim and Marie had felt guilty, and made their getaway to the canteen. Their work was now spread out across a table there. This was a constant source of antagonism between coppers and canteen staff, who tended to respond to the former's complaints about egg yolk on witness statements with remarks along the lines that if they didn't like it then they shouldn't bring paperwork in with them.

'These new names,' Marie said, a last, desperate attempt to get their unwilling brains working again.

'Oh, give it a rest, Marie,' Kim sighed. 'Casual encounters at parties and clubs. First names is all we've got for most of 'em, dead vague descriptions for about two. I mean where do we *start*?'

'Morning, fellow members of the finest crimefighting force this side of the Thames.' They looked up. Detective Sergeant Gary Harper, the extrovert, handsome and tragically married blue-eyed boy of the local Major Investigation Team, breezed in and marched past their table on the way to the food. Gary was bagman to Detective Superintendent Noel Heighway, Sophia's boss; he acted as his driver, collator, organiser, PA and general gofor. Kim and Marie felt wary.

'Morning,' they said, faking brightness.

'Could have another go at the inventory from her room,' Marie said, after he'd gone by.

Kim exhaled through pursed lips. 'Yeah, s'pose. Summink we've missed.' She reached for the list. Marie brought her chair round and looked over Kim's shoulder. They read in silence for a few minutes.

'Fuck all,' Marie said eventually. 'Nothing you wouldn't expect in any kid's room her age.'

'Hang on a minute.' Kim was flicking backwards and forwards through the stapled sheets. 'Here. Don't you think this is weird?'

She pointed. Marie squinted at her own appalling handwriting. '"Newspapers",' she read. '"Pile of old *Daily Telegraph*s". Is that weird? Tory household if ever I was in one.'

'Did you see the room?' Kim said. 'Not a great reader, our Debs. Hardly a book in sight, apart from one or two school textbooks she must've never gave back. So what's she want with old newspapers?'

'Maybe she did some redecorating.'

'She's still got My Little Pony wallpaper.'

'Press cuttings then. For a project or something.'

'Maybe.' Kim wavered, then a new resolve slipped into

her eyes. 'There *were* cuttings taken out of one or two, I'm sure.'

'Gut feeling?'

She thought for a moment. 'First thing we should do, go back to the house and get them papers; then we can find out... Library'll have a back file, won't they?'

'Just look online.'

'Hard copy. Online edition ain't gonna tell us what she cut out.'

'Long shot,' Marie said.

'Got any other ideas?'

'Finish my cereal first.' She dipped into it. By now it was soggy.

They returned to their notes and their breakfast.

'Hey,' Marie said suddenly. 'There's a really peculiar one here. What's this, "thrall"? Can you read that?' She pushed the diary across, finger on the page.

'Looks like "thrall",' Kim agreed. 'Her writing ain't that desperate. Looks like there was a number, but it's been scribbled out.' She held it up to the light and shook her head. 'Pretty thoroughly and all.'

'Like she didn't want anybody to be able to read it.'

'Maybe Forensic can do summink.' Kim was still squinting at it.

'What does thrall mean anyway?'

'You say Thrall?'

They turned. Gary Harper was standing behind them, plate of eggs and bacon in hand, a look of keen interest directed at the diary.

Kim said, 'You know what this is?'

'Not a what,' Gary said, 'so much as a who. Name came up in connection with a job I worked a few years back. Your

Sandra Jones was on the investigation as well, I seem to recall.'

'And?'

'They're an extremist neo-Nazi group.' He saw Kim's expression and added, 'That's to say extremist even by those standards. It's an acronym: stands for - let me think – something something Racial Action.'

Marie wrinkled her nose. 'See what you mean,' she said. 'How were they involved?'

Gary hesitated. 'Young black guy knifed and kicked to death outside his parents' house in Battersea. Word on the street was this Thrall lot did the deed, but the one bloke we collared was peripheral at best. He never put his hands up to it, never named names, case was about as watertight as a rusty bucket, and the jury acquitted.'

There was a long silence.

'Doesn't make Debbie look too good, does it?' Marie tapped the name on the page.

'Your guv'nor should know about this.' Gary glanced ruefully down at his breakfast. 'Better get Gloria to stick this on a warming plate. Finish your Weetabix and let's go.'

'Wait a minute,' Kim said, hand on his arm. Beside her, Marie saw it trembling. 'What else can you remember?'

'Kim?'

'This was Mark Watkins, right?'

'You remember it?' Gary sounded surprised.

'I'm black,' she retorted with sudden vehemence. 'Course I fucking remember it, and Carruth. The slag what got off.' She was shaking all over now. 'And I tell you another thing I remember. Mark Watkins was tarred and feathered.'

'Oh...' Gary said quietly.

Marie asked, 'What's tarred and - '

'Summink else they used to do to black men in the American South,' Kim cut her off. 'The ones they weren't putting burning crosses outside their houses. Gary,' she said, after pausing for some deep breaths, 'you're brilliant. I love you.'

He looked at her. She was ashen-faced, but there was a glint in her eye. He picked up the mood shift and grinned. 'That mean you're buying me lunch?'

'If this ain't a coincidence,' Kim said, grabbing the diary, leaping up and taking his arm, 'I'll get you a seat at the Lord Mayor's Banquet. Come on.'

Slowly, Larissa Stephenson raised a hand. A polite, not diffident hand.

Detective Chief Inspector Matthew Summerfield regarded her with a mixture of approval and weariness. So many new aides started out timid as mice, so afraid even to twitch that they'd sit on what might - sometimes, not often - be a vital contribution. Not this one, though. Trouble was, this one was Special Crime and that, in his estimation, meant lippy cows. Summerfield's view of women in the police was not an emancipated one. He yearned for the not so long gone days when he'd been able to reach for a WPC to deal with a child, or a difficult female witness or suspect, or a difficult *any* kind of witness or suspect. Now they'd even dropped the W from WPC and what was *that* all about? Equality? That was a laugh. Catch a woman kicking in the door of a crack house or bringing down a scrote with a running tackle; *real* policework. Support. Making the tea. That, as far as Summerfield was concerned, was a plonk's place, not shuffling in as a CID bloody aide, if you please. The addition of this one meant Special Crime now had eight of the bitches. He wouldn't mind except that they had a tendency to nick investigations right when they got interesting, and for some god-unknown reason Heighway almost always went along with it. As a result, Special Crime weren't exactly welcomed with open arms at the CID morning briefing and generally stood at the back out of glaring range.

He picked her out in the shadows and said, 'Yes, constable?'

'Doesn't make sense, sir.'

Summerfield resisted the temptation to make a crushing remark, largely because of DI Schneider's presence. Special Crime usually sent two people to the briefing, one being the on-call officer from the previous night and the other either Schneider or DCI Beadle. He was relieved Beadle wasn't there but on the other hand, Zoltan Schneider had a way with his tongue, when he wished, that was the verbal equivalent of a deep paper cut. With him were Detective Sergeant Wallace and this new plonk. Summerfield had forgotten her name already.

'Can we enlighten you?' he asked her, regretting the sarcasm as he sensed Schneider staring at him from behind his glasses.

She stood up straighter and his gaze shifted automatically to her bust. Bit young for him, this one, but a nice pair of tits on it. She said, 'Chomba lives on the other side of the estate, right?'

'So we're told.'

'And he was in his flat when it was raided five minutes after the exchange?'

'Yes, he was.'

'That's what I can't understand, sir. We're charging him with dealing based on what's on the CCTV. I've done car patrols on Shrublands, so I reckon with these timings he could just about've made it if he was driving, but he'd've had to go past the cameras. How come they didn't see him?' She shrugged. 'Doesn't add up.'

'I don't know, constable,' Summerfield said. 'Maybe the clock's off. There *was* crack found in his rubbish bin is all I'm saying. As we speak, minds greater than yours are pondering this same mystery. If they resolve it, I'll make sure you're among the first to know.'

For a moment, as her eyes flicked downwards, he thought he'd achieved the demolition without Schneider's intervention. But she recovered quickly. She looked him in the eye, said, 'Thank you, sir,' and looked down at her notes, indicating she'd said her piece.

Schneider remained impassive, but Summerfield was annoyed to catch the surreptitious wink shot to the young plonk by DS Wallace. An annoyance dwarfed by the horrid realisation that the low buzz of conversation among the assembled detectives had been triggered by her contribution. Coppers don't exactly appreciate it when one of their own gives their favoured suspect a free alibi, but neither do they want a case that won't stand up in court.

Hardly daring to look, he cast his eye towards the back of the room, where Zoltan Schneider stood smiling humourlessly at him.

'Sorry if I spoke out of turn in there, sir,' Lucky said to Zoltan as they waited for the lift.

The DI tilted his head. 'Out of turn, Larissa?'

'CID briefing's like an up-market version of parade, am I right?' She looked away. 'It's not meant to be a debating society.

I should've realised.'

'On the contrary,' he said. 'If we didn't say what we thought, we'd never get anywhere.' He put his hands in his pockets. 'I think Mr Summerfield will have taken your remarks on board.'

Lucky, not reassured, gulped.

'Don't worry.' The hand on her shoulder belonged to Detective Sergeant Helen Wallace. 'What Zoltan's trying to say, and won't because he's a DI, is sod Summerfield. You did well.'

They exchanged grins. 'I didn't hear that,' Zoltan said.

Lucky blinked, glancing uncomfortably from one to the other. She was beginning to feel overdressed. The man who'd turned out to be her DI was kitted out more like a college lecturer, with a hairdo to match. Thick, black and unruly, with strands of it jutting out in all directions like solar prominences, the hair went some way towards cushioning the shock of the open-necked blue and grey cotton shirt, brown corduroys and Hush Puppies he wore, but not far. He was small for a copper, just clearing five eight in her estimation, and slight of build. Zoltan Schneider didn't even look like a policeman, much less an inspector. With most detectives, however outlandish they looked, Lucky had always just about been able to picture them back in uniform. Not this one.

But the authority he sacrificed by his appearance was more than made up for by the man himself. He had a way of looking through his thick glasses, a dry, sardonic way with words, and a strange half-smile through his wiry beard that made Lucky unsure whether he was laughing with or at her. The minimal research she'd been able to do through the grapevine had revealed his reputation as a brilliant interrogator of suspects. She guessed that to get at all close to him you needed the thickest of skins.

Any idea Lucky might have formed that Zoltan Schneider could only be one of a kind was quickly dispelled. *None* of the team looked like coppers. For a start, most of them were women. There was only one other man in the room, a tall, rangy individual with a big nose and a set of face that suggested someone had put cold rice pudding in his shoes. He wasn't wearing a tie either. The women, similarly, seemed to have dressed for comfort or according to personal whim. They were all preoccupied. An anaemic-looking blonde in her thirties sat, headphones in ears, hammering away two-fingered at a computer keyboard as she transcribed an interview. At a corner desk a young black woman had her head down, phone in one hand and flipping through what looked like an archived case file with the other. Two women, one pale and exotic, one small and dumpy with a sharp nosy face, were talking intently; whether about work or not it was hard to tell. Distracted by their entrance, the pale one glanced over and held Lucky's gaze just long enough to make her uncomfortable.

The woman Zoltan led them over to was short but massive, almost impossibly so even for a copper, her rotund form stretching the material of her dark green dress. She turned at their approach and pushed shut the drawer she'd been rummaging in. As it had during the interview process, her smile brought Lucky up in a more direct way than Zoltan's sarcasm ever would. Sophia Beadle's eyes were the purest, deepest blue she'd ever seen that didn't belong to a baby, but there was nothing babyish about the way the smile stopped before it reached them. Lucky understood, abruptly and unmistakeably, that she, not Zoltan, was the guv'nor.

'How'd it go?'

'Fine,' her DI replied in a laconic way which conveyed that he would tell her more when Lucky wasn't listening. 'Made her mark.'

Again the smile. 'Welcome to the team, Larissa.'

'Ma'am.'

'"Guv" will do. We're pretty informal around here, as you may have gathered.'

Before she could stop herself Lucky blurted out, 'At Gipsy Hill people called me Lucky.'

'Lucky?'

''Cause I'm usually the one nearest to a 999 shout five minutes before end of shift.' She deflated mentally. She'd had a job and a half living the nickname down, and it seemed she wasn't going to get away with it here either. Oh, well. Handles had a knack of following you around in the Job; she'd merely pre-empted the inevitable.

Reading her discomfiture, Sophia smiled again, this time with real warmth. 'Well, we'll put "Larissa" on the duty board for now. If people want to call you something else and you're OK with it that's up to you. Right - Helen.'

The DS looked up. 'Guv?'

'Anything major on?'

'I can save the world any time.'

'Good.' Sophia indicated Lucky with an open palm. 'Can you show Larissa the ropes? Introduce everyone, take her through procedures and our current caseload, a guided tour of the office, the building and then hop in a car and whizz round the ground. That should occupy you both for most of the morning, barring a crisis.'

Helen made a face. 'Some hopes.' She grinned at Lucky. 'Come on. This over here's where the magic happens.'

'Go back and do a thorough search of that bedroom again,' Sophia had decreed. 'Don't take no for an answer. I'll think up some excuse for a warrant if necessary, but I want to know what Debbie's involvement with these people is.'

'What about Carruth?'

'Since Sandra is familiar with that case, I've put her onto trying to track him down.' Sophia's faint frown conveyed that Kim's disappointment was noted. 'You two have an in with the Clarkes, so I'd like you to stay on them for now.'

And so Kim and Marie were back at Ballards Way. Andrew Clarke wasn't there. He'd gone to work 'to keep occupied', leaving strict instructions to his wife to ring him if there was any news. 'Nice. Leave *her* to do all the worrying,' had been Marie's opinion, expressed without too much consideration as to whether Charlotte Clarke was out of earshot. Kim had been careful to persuade Mrs Clarke that they were on her side, and had obtained her acquiescence to the search without difficulty. To their secret relief, she'd declined the offer to bear witness to their actions.

Which was probably just as well. Kim and Marie conducted their new search with a vigour and thoroughness that would have astonished DCI Summerfield. They rummaged again through drawers, cupboards and the wardrobe. They shook out the bedclothes and felt the duvet and the mattress for suspicious lumps. They tapped walls, the ceiling and the window frame looking for concealed niches. Shifting the furniture piece by piece, they checked behind, under and if necessary on top of it. Finally, with the aid of a claw hammer, they turned back the rug and lifted floorboards. There, in a dark, dusty space between the joists, they found what they were looking for.

In an old square biscuit tin was stashed what could have

passed as Hitler's junk mail. There were books and magazines bearing apoplectic titles like *White Rage* and *Manifest Destiny*, covers splashed with violent graphic images of fists and flags and marching feet and idealised studies of white male youths. There were badges and booklists and printed lists of web addresses, posters advertising rallies and a talk by a notorious right wing revisionist historian.

There were also a large number of press cuttings.

'Looks like our Debbie's a right little Nazi,' Marie said.

Kim said nothing. She held her teeth clenched as she searched through the tin, handling the contents as though they were crawling with maggots. Suddenly she stopped and pulled something out. It was a small thin red notebook, spiral bound, the sort you could pick up in WH Smith's for a quid. Kim glanced at it and handed it to Marie.

At first it looked empty. But, a third of the way through, a folded piece of newspaper fell out. The subject of the clipping didn't surprise them, but two of the three words written in biro along the top margin meant nothing.

THRALL   *Porter*   *Quaife*

They arrived back just as Gary Harper was leaving. Catching sight of them, he looked like the man whose lottery scratchcard is about to make him extremely popular in the pub.

'Those cuttings from the *Torygraph*,' he said, grinning. 'I think we've got something. They're all - '

'We know,' Marie said, walking straight past. Kim smiled, patted him on the shoulder and followed her.

' - to do with the Watkins murder,' he finished, limply

and to himself. 'Well,' he added, watching them disappear inside. 'Thank you, Gary. Not a Cumberland sausage.'

Lucky had lived most of her life in the London Borough of Croydon, and all her working career had been spent at Gipsy Hill just over the boundary in Lambeth, so she already had a good knowledge of the ground the team had to cover. But Helen Wallace used the tour wisely. Like any good copper charged with looking after a new recruit, she showed her the places she'd have call to be familiar with, introduced her to people she would, in one capacity or another, get to know well. They spent time at hostels and sheltered housing, at the council social services department, at a Hindu luncheon club, at the Women's Centre at Woodside Green, which Lucky had never before had occasion to visit but from where, after wary beginnings, many of the team's calls and leads now came.

And Lucky got to know DS Wallace. Helen was a tall, thin, plain woman in her mid-thirties, short brown hair clinging in curls close to her head. She had wide hazel eyes and a bow mouth that cracked easily into a warm smile which suited her West Country burr. Lucky, who found it easy to talk, revelled in her company, in the prospect of a colleague she could get on with, who wouldn't look down on her because she was a humble PC.

'I think the medal clinched it,' she caught herself boasting in response to Helen's 'what brought you to Special Crime?' enquiry. 'So then the Chief Super says to me, "What do you say?" I'm thinking, "I say stop treating me like a five year old who's just been given a sweetie, you patronising over-promoted git."'

'I presume that's not what you actually *said*.'

'No.' She was enjoying herself. She'd never dared tell the story to anyone above her own rank before. But this was Helen ('sod Summerfield') Wallace, who had a healthy lack of awe towards authority. Lucky or not, she didn't think her remarks would be the final hurrah for the briefest CID service in the history of the Met.

Helen nodded. 'You said...?'

'I said, "Thank you, sir," then went down to the canteen and said it to *them*.'

Amid the laughter, Helen glanced at the dashboard clock. 'Crumbs, is that the time? We'd better head back. It's nearly lunchtime.'

'CID eat lunch?'

'On the hoof, normally,' Helen admitted. 'But it's your first day. Break you in gently.'

'Right.' Lucky thought for a moment and then said, 'Would it be OK, d'you think, if I go home for lunch? Only,' she fingered the lapel of her jacket, 'I feel a bit overdressed.'

'Sure. New Addington, wasn't it?' Helen, stopping for a junction, subjected her to a careful once-over. 'You look fine.'

'I don't fit in,' she persisted. She glanced across at Helen in her sensible skirt and sweater. 'I mean from what I can tell you're all more or less casual. Even the DI.'

'Sophia's policy is we dress as we like, within reason,' Helen explained. 'We have to feel comfortable, and convey that to the people we talk to, who're often very upset. Power dressing is hardly the thing.'

'I'll bear that in mind,' Lucky said earnestly. 'It's just not what I was led to expect.'

'By whom?'

Lucky shrugged. 'The Job.'

'You've hit the nail on the head,' Helen smiled. She concentrated on the road for a moment, making sure the way ahead was clear. 'How much was it gone into at your interview? What we're about?'

Lucky opened her mouth to reply, but stopped and thought. She tilted her head and shot Helen a sly look. 'Let's pretend I know nothing,' she said. 'I want to hear it from somebody who isn't quoting the press release.'

'We're guinea pigs, really,' Helen said.

'That much I gathered.'

'It's basically one upshot of the G20 protests and the death of Ian Tomlinson a few years back,' she explained. 'And what came out of O'Connor, about the heavy-handed way the demo was policed, our tendency to overreact to every tiny thing, most especially about the us-and-them attitudes in the Job.'

'I thought we were all your friendly local bobby?'

'That's the public line,' Helen said, 'but the Commissioner knows it's at least partly true, and that hurt. So one of the things he did was hold strategy workshops with senior ranks, trawling for ideas. Sophia was one of the ones who came up with something.'

Lucky assumed an intent expression.

'She told him the public perception of us as clodhopping Neanderthals with riot shields isn't the problem, it's a symptom. What it basically boils down to is unprofessionalism.'

'We're professional.'

'The perception again,' Helen pointed out. 'The quasi-military structure. Think about it. You recruit somebody, call her a cadet, send her to Hendon to march up and down the parade ground. Then you give her a rank and a uniform, train her to stand to attention and salute senior officers and address them as "sir" and "sarge". Are you getting my drift?'

Lucky shrugged. 'So? Nobody complains about the army doing that.'

'The army don't deal directly with the public. We do.'

'Good point.'

'So, having been trained basically to be a soldier, our recruit is then told she's part of a service, not a force, and sent out on the street. But it doesn't matter how polite and professional you are or how much customer awareness training you've had,' Helen said with feeling, 'people won't trust a plod with a pocket book out there any more than a squaddie with a gun. It's too late. The battle lines have already been drawn. We even *call* them civilians.'

'So we shouldn't be surprised if they get upset when we go around giving the impression we think they're a lower life form.'

'Right.'

'So what makes *us* different?'

'Apart from cosmetically, not a lot,' Helen said. 'We're partly a behavioural experiment, I suppose – to see if our internal culture affects the way we do business. So the atmosphere in the team is informal. The dress code, or lack of, you know about. We don't use rank, except occasionally when talking to other units, for convenience.'

'Not to the public?'

'Give your rank if asked,' Helen said, 'but generally just name and station will do.'

'Gotcha.'

'More fundamentally, we stick to standard CID procedure except that the cases we get – in theory, at any rate –

are thoroughly screened, so we can spend a lot more time and effort on them. Sophia doesn't have to have one eye glued to the overtime budget.'

Lucky grinned. 'And all the women?'

'Refreshing, right?' Helen shared the joke. 'Seriously, the official line is it just turned out that way; we happened to be the people Sophia wanted for her team.' She paused and inclined her head towards Lucky. '*Un*officially, word is the Commissioner leaned on her to have a female bias for appearances' sake. Something he'd never've got past the Federation. Where d'you want dropped?'

'Sorry?'

'You wanted to go home and change. I'll drop you off.'

Lucky nodded thanks and looked out of the window. They were on Lodge Lane, heading up past the fire station. 'Take King Henry's Drive,' she said. 'Sure it's OK?'

'Absolutely.'

'I left my car at the nick, though.'

'No problem,' Helen said. 'You're shadowing Nina Tyminski this afternoon. I'll get her to pick you up around oneish. It's on the way anyway.'

'That's lucky,' Lucky said without thinking.

The two women looked at one another and giggled. So Helen had overheard. The secret was out. But it didn't seem to matter.

The bathroom window hadn't been shut properly, she noticed, glancing up at the house as Helen drove off. Her mother was a sous-chef at a country hotel out beyond Westerham and wouldn't have left for work until about ten, which didn't leave much opportunity for a burglar. Not that, in New Addington, that bothered them. She made a mental note to secure the window.

Even after four years in the Job, she'd never settled to the stiff restrictiveness of uniform. It was a throwback to schooldays, to rebellion against the tyranny of uncomfortable, unflattering ties, jumpers and skirts. Kicking the front door shut behind her, she headed for the stairs, removing her jacket and top as she went and draping them over her arm. Something she'd done since her early teens, this, undressing on the move, when she was alone in the house. It gave her a sense of adventure, a vague thrill of wickedness, and it also meant she could get into something comfortable that much quicker. On the landing she paused to unzip her trousers and take off her socks, then gathered the whole lot together to toss into the laundry basket that stood just inside the door to the master bedroom. When younger this had been the climax of the adventure, never sure as she was whether her father might not be asleep, arrived home unexpectedly from his business travels.

Now he was gone for good, and the Stephenson inner sanctum lay still and quiet, forever imbued with the awe it had inspired in her as a child. She ventured inside, into the gloom where she'd watched dust sparkling like stars in the shafts of sunlight that fell through the half-drawn curtains. Briefly she stood before the wardrobe mirror, to look at herself in the silk underwear. Not bad. She smiled nervously, conscious of the presence of her mother in the fittings and furnishings of the room, turned away and went out.

Her own room was different, smaller, homely and untidy; east-facing and stuffy now from its warming in the morning sun. The paintwork was chipped, dirty, the wallpaper pitted and torn from a transient population of old posters and stickers, torn down and replaced over time to mark each stage in a young girl's maturing. The walls were almost bare now, apart from the framed certificate and medal from the Humane Society and the accompanying Met commendation. One purple velour curtain hung loose from several of its rings. On top of her tatty, both-back-legs-missing green wardrobe, the soft toys and dolls of childhood spilled out of black plastic sacks; she could never bring herself to throw them away. The carpet, threadbare in places, was covered in unwashed socks, books, magazines and pieces of paper. Periodically her mother would nag her to tidy the place up, but by and large she respected her daughter's need for a bolthole. This room held no awe or thrill for Larissa; it was her own, comfortable, safe, to do as she liked in.

There was no room for a dressing table. What passed as one was a freestanding table mirror balanced on the window sill over her bed, surrounded by old shoeboxes full of cosmetics. On the sill, too, half-hidden behind the curtain, was Weezle.

At school she'd been hopeless at anything creative, until Mrs Langton, her art teacher, had introduced her to pottery. No-one, least of all Lucky, could have said she had a flair for it, but it attracted her, the busy rumbling of the wheel, the warm clammy feel of clay under her fingers. Most of the grotesque distorted vessels that were the fruits of her labour had long since been consigned to oblivion, but Weezle survived. He'd been made one winter afternoon when Lucky, fed up because her foot kept slipping off the pedal, had scooped up the wet clay and stomped off to a workbench to see what could be done with it. The result was ragged, but it had four legs and a pointy nose and a slim body that bulged in the middle. Mrs Langton had thought it was a badger; her sister, a hedgehog; others, a stoat. Lucky had settled for Weezle.

She smiled hello to him and clambered onto the bed, wondering whether to touch up her warpaint now or go and have something to eat first. She didn't see the face until she tilted the mirror up to catch the light.

'I understand you're holding my wife.' Andrew Clarke had leapt up the moment he'd seen the door open, and Kim Oliver emerge into the front office waiting area. Now he loomed over her, feet apart, fists clenched by his sides, face and voice those of a man against whom an unforgiveable outrage, an odious crime, has been committed. Kim was not impressed.

'She's here of her own free will, Mr Clarke.'

His gaze wavered, as if he realised they'd stolen his thunder, allowing his wife to phone him knowing full well he'd come straight here. But he recovered quickly. 'With the tapes running, eh? I'm not stupid, you know.'

'It's completely informal, sir,' Kim said. 'We're in an interview room. If you'd like to come through.'

'Informal, indeed,' he grumbled, following her. '"Helping with your enquiries", more like. We all know what that means.' This got no response so he changed tack. With a mirthless chuckle he said, 'It's all a joke, isn't it?'

Politeness demanded a reply. Kim said, 'What is?'

'This.' He indicated her with a nod. 'I know the police are image-conscious now, but this wheeling you in as the token black officer - it doesn't fool anyone.'

Yeah, but one thing about us token black officers, Kim thought with fire in her heart, you can't tell when you've pissed us off. See we don't blush.

'Hi, Kim.'

With exquisite timing Jasmin Winter, who was blacker than she was, came round a corner and disappeared into a lift before Andrew Clarke's jaw had completed its downward arc.

'Sorry, sir,' Kim said, with a blink. 'What did you say?'

Sophia Beadle ushered him to a chair beside his wife and said, 'I apologise for keeping you waiting so long. I'm glad you've both come in.' A stern glance nipped in the bud any retort he might have made. 'Some new evidence has come to light which drastically increases Debbie's importance to us.'

'What evidence?' Andrew Clarke burst out.

'I'll come to that.' Sophia stirred. 'We thought it might be best to talk here, away from distractions at home. So you can think more clearly, as it were.'

Kim, sitting down beside her, thought you had to admire the guv'nor's talent for bare-arsed bullshit.

'Is it all of us you suspect, inspector,' Andrew Clarke said, 'or just Debbie?'

'You're here because you, as her parents, should know her better than anyone,' Sophia answered, unruffled.

'And what gives you that idea?'

'Well, for one thing she's an only child. In my experience that often leads to a closer bond between parent and daughter. How well do you get on, would you say?' The query was put effortlessly, yet stingingly, like flicking an elastic band.

'I don't see how that has anything to do with the fire,' Andrew Clarke said, 'unless you think we *all* had a hand in it.'

Sophia stared at him for a moment, weighing up her choices. 'Let me tell you what I do think,' she said. 'We found this in Debbie's bedroom.' The tin was on the table and she pushed it towards the Clarkes.

'You searched my house *again*?' Andrew Clarke's pupils contracted.

'I said they could,' Charlotte Clarke told him. He glanced at her and made a short sound of disgust.

'Have a look.' Sophia stirred her tea. 'It's all right,' she added, seeing them hesitate, 'we've checked for fingerprints.'

'Whose did you find?' Andrew Clarke said, but a vicious nudge from his wife diverted his attention to the contents of the tin. Sophia and Kim watched as they took out objects and scowled at them. Andrew Clarke said, finally, 'Where did she get this filth?'

'Did either of you know about any of this?' Sophia asked.

'Evidently not, as she seems to have gone to inordinate lengths to hide it from us.'

Kim blinked.

Deliberately, Sophia folded her arms. She said, 'Inordinate lengths, Mr Clarke?'

He wilted under the unwavering blue stare. 'Well...'

'I merely told you these things were found in her room.'

Charlotte Clarke said, 'Andrew?'

'Well, they'd hardly have been in plain view, would they?' he snapped.

'Really? Do you make a habit of searching your daughter's room?'

'Not as much as you seem to.'

'Mr Clarke,' Sophia said warningly.

'If you must know,' Andrew Clarke said after a moment's hesitation, 'my wife told me what you'd found when she rang me. So I'm sorry, but there's nothing nefarious about my knowing.'

Sophia glanced at Charlotte Clarke, who nodded, eyes downcast. Her husband added, 'And if things are going to continue in this tone, I really don't think we want to say anything further without our solicitor present.'

'Sorry, guv.' Kim, despondent, joined Sophia at the office window, to watch the cab containing the Clarkes pull away and merge with the traffic on Park Lane. 'I did let Mrs Clarke know where we'd found the tin. She asked what the noise was. We had to tell her about the floorboards.'

'Not to worry,' the DCI shrugged. 'Would have been nice to have an ace up our sleeves, that's all.' She smiled at Kim in a way that seemed to convey underlying disappointment. 'So what do you think?'

'My opinion ain't changed.'

'Active involvement? Him and the daughter?'

'No way to tell, at this stage.'

'Well,' Sophia said, 'you've spent plenty of time with them by now. What do you suggest?'

Kim screwed up her face in thought. 'Might sound a bit extravagant,' she said, 'but would it be possible to set up an obbo? Not round the clock, just low-level, part-time. See if any interesting faces come to visit.'

Sophia turned to her desk, pulled up an expenses spreadsheet on her computer and studied it for a long moment. 'I can probably justify a couple of hours a day,' she said, in tones that suggested she'd really rather not. 'During the evening, when he's at home. You and Marie. Take turns.'

'Thanks, guv,' Kim said. She hesitated. 'I dunno about Marie, though. Her being a single mum and that.'

'She's also a copper,' Sophia said. 'She knows the score.'

'Yeah, *she* does,' Kim said. 'But childminders don't work nights. Also the Clarkes might make her.'

'But not you?'

'Guv, I might as well be invisible.'

The DCI stared at her.

'I know how people like them think,' Kim said bluntly. 'Far as they're concerned, we all look alike.'

Dubious, Sophia conceded the point. 'All right, get someone else. If no-one's up for it I'll try and borrow a body from CID, but if *that* fails,' she levelled her clear blue stare at Kim, 'you're on your own.'

Her colleague and best friend Sandra Jones had once said of Detective Constable Nina Tyminski that it was as if she'd been standing in the right queue when God was handing out the parts, but had then lost the assembly diagram. Sandra had got away without being thumped because she was Sandra, but the remark had nonetheless hurt. Nina was under no illusion that her best point had always been her face: snow-pale, elegantly fashioned like fine, angular china with its close-set, arresting violet eyes; carefully fringed with darkest brown hair. But from the neck down something had gone wrong. Stooped shoulders, small breasts over a deep ribcage, a high waist, narrow hips, knock knees and an odd, scampering walk on tiny feet that had to make an outward turn in order to keep her balanced. She was painfully aware of all this, and dressed accordingly. An enforced mistress of disguise, she'd turned her choice of wardrobe into an artform. The things Nina could do with black defied even Sandra Jones's powers of description.

Her mother had long insisted that Nina's corporeal state was a question of bad posture, and had campaigned long and hard to get her daughter to deportment or drama or dance classes, or *anything*. Partly to annoy her, Nina had joined the police instead, and they'd taught her to stand sufficiently to attention and march in a straight enough line to pass out of Hendon. Sod balancing books on her head; she'd worry about arthritis and back trouble when she was fifty.

She felt uncomfortable about her current journey, and at the same time silly. For all her physical shortcomings she knew she was still a looker. But so, even more so, was Larissa Stephenson. Nina was needled by the charm, the ingenuous enthusiasm, the elegance and above all, the Mediterranean beauty and flawless figure she had always coveted. Here, her primeval instinct said, was competition.

Also mildly disconcerting was the question of where everybody was. Unemployment was high in New Addington, but even though it was the middle of the day the place seemed deserted. The only human being she'd seen was a bony-looking youth who'd been jogging across the roundabout as she turned into King Henry's Drive, presumably using it as a short cut to the tram stop. She glanced at the inside of her wrist where she'd written the house number in biro; it wasn't a given that this was going to help. New Addington was a town planner's laboratory and a postman's nightmare. Numbers could run alternately, or concurrently, or not at all where a tower block leapt up from the concrete with its own floor-by-floor scheme, or they could even start again from scratch where the developers had built terraces with bucolic-sounding names, Oak Bank, Brierley, Applegarth, trying to make the place sound like paradise, as if they were fooling anyone. But she found her destination without too much difficulty and parked outside, a malicious impulse keeping her in the car. Like its surroundings, the house displayed no sign of life. She tooted the horn. Presumably Larissa had been told to expect her, and would be out soon enough.

After a minute nothing had happened. Blank, shut windows stared back at her. Sighing, she unclipped her seatbelt and got out, in her baggy black cardigan and long black skirt looking like a demented rook scurrying up the path.

She'd got halfway when she heard a wooden clatter, and Larissa appeared from the side of the house, pushing a gate to behind her. She'd changed since the morning, and now wore a plain white sweatshirt, stonewashed blue jeans, desert boots and a grey fleece.

'Hiya,' she said.

'I was just going to knock,' Nina said.

'Yeah, I heard you beeping.' Larissa had stepped onto the lawn and was peering up at the house. Nina felt annoyed.

'Nina Tyminski,' she said.

The Mediterranean beauty turned to look at her. 'Larissa Stephenson,' she said, shaking hands. 'Most people call me - '

'Lucky.' Nina grinned in spite of herself. 'I heard.'

'News gets around, yeah?' Lucky crossed to the front door and pushed. Satisfied, she turned to Nina and said, 'OK. Let's go.'

Furious at her own irrationality, Nina was still smarting at that five minutes later as they headed towards Shirley. What right did *she* have to give orders? Lucky was the new girl, she should sit tight and absorb the wisdom. Of course, Nina fumed, stealing a glance in the mirror, that's what she *seemed* to be doing, *now*.

The cinnamon-coloured face was open and attentive but the eyes were cold, bleak and lost. She wondered why she'd ever thought of the kid as ingenuous; it had certainly worn off fast. Welcome to Special Crime.

Being fair, she was hardly in the best frame of mind to judge. With a twinge of shame she concentrated on the task at hand. 'D'you know De Montfort Court?'

'Old people's home, yeah?'

'We're on a follow-up visit to Violet McMinn, age ninety, assaulted and robbed in the early hours of yesterday morning. The intruder got in by forcing the bedroom window.'

'Not burglar-proof?'

Nina shook her head. 'He beat her severely about the arms and torso, then swiped several items of jewellery and ornaments including a pair of brass candlesticks, one of which he sexually violated her with.' She looked in the mirror again to see if this was having any effect, but Lucky's expression was impassive. 'The result of all this, she was so traumatised we couldn't get anything out of her when we saw her yesterday.'

'Was she hurt badly?'

'Bad enough. However, she's wheelchair-bound and very frail. The doctor thought it was best for her not to be moved, so they're looking after her at the home. Which is why we're going there and not the hospital.'

Lucky hesitated. 'You said "he".'

'Good point.' Nina caught herself being impressed. 'Inconclusive. No semen deposits, just the candlestick, which we know about from swabs of verdigris the FME got from the vagina. CSI lifted some size twelve footprints off the carpet. Faint denim imprints on the sill, looks like he parked his bum on there and swung his legs over.'

'What's outside?'

'Concrete path.'

'Course.'

'Which at the moment leaves us with just Mrs McMinn. Apparently she's now lucid enough to talk to us...'

The heavy sigh that escaped Lucky caused Nina to take her attention off the road for a second. But again the dark eyes gave nothing away. Strange girl. Give her credit, though: keen as mustard. She'd picked up on every point of what Nina had abstracted from the report. She was beginning to understand why Sophia (rumour had it) had headhunted her.

Which reminded her. Nina, who devoured gossip like peanuts at a party, said, 'This medal, then.'

Lucky looked surprised. Understandable, Nina thought with a fleeting pang of remorse: sudden friendliness from this misassembled crone who'd been giving her a hard time from the moment she'd stepped through the gate. She smiled and said, 'All mine.'

'I hear you talked down a suicide from the Norwood mast.'

'Yeah.'

'How'd you do it?' Nina smiled back. 'If it's not breaking a confidence.'

'I don't want to sound bigheaded.'

'Course not. I won't tell anyone.'

Lucky smiled again and brushed a hand in front of her face. 'I said to him,' she replied, choosing her words cautiously, 'look me up and down, and did he really want to chuck away a world when there were girls like me in it to chase after.' She flinched as she saw Nina's expression start to change. 'It was the first thing that came into my head.'

Aghast, Nina heard herself laughing. 'It's all right,' she said, tapping Lucky on the knee with her gear hand, 'I don't believe in hiding my light under a bushel either.'

'I dunno about that - I'm not vain,' Lucky said. 'But when you're sitting on a girder with half a mile of fresh air under your arse you get a very clear perspective on sin.'

'You a Catholic and all, then?' Nina giggled.

'Bulgarian Orthodox,' Lucky said. 'Much as I try not to be.'

She stared into her lap, and Nina was still trying to work out what that meant when the Mini breasted Spout Hill, trundled down into Shirley village and the building she was looking for appeared on the right. She said, 'Let's go to work.'

'You know what gets me,' Nina broke a long silence on the drive back afterwards, 'why we always feel so guilty.'

'Guilty?' Lucky said.

'Don't you?' Nina tried to inject a lighter note into her voice. It came out as a squeak. 'I mean we're there to detect. What's to feel guilty about?'

The question hadn't been intended as rhetorical, but even as she repeated it the answer came to her in fragments. It was the terrible fear, the knowledge, that though they might detect the perpetrator of the crime against Mrs McMinn, nothing, absolutely nothing, they did or said could take back what had happened to her. This was a woman who'd lived through a century during which the world had changed beyond recognition; who'd battled, loved and mothered through a world war, a depression, the collapse of an empire, the Cold War, man on the moon, the opening of the atomic and electronic ages;

who'd witnessed it all, and come through adversity and triumph with a lifetime of achievement to mark against her name. But for Violet McMinn, an invaluable treasury of experience had been indelibly tainted in one hellish moment; what should have been final years passed in quiet, proud dignity obliterated by the senseless act of a slag with no regard for that worth.

Some time since the previous day she'd fought and suppressed the demon in her head, and greeted them with the stoical calm bred into so many of her generation. Her blue eyes were the only part of her now that was not lucid: they stared bleakly beyond the two policewomen and into purgatory. She gave calm and courteous answers to their questions, made her statement, and seemed to reach into Nina's heart and see the ill-defined revulsion that lay there. She understood that there was only one thing they could do.

'Just catch the evil little toerag,' had been her parting words.

Easy to say.

'Maybe it's losing control,' Lucky said, interrupting Nina's dark thoughts.

'Control of what?'

'Sometimes you can't master the disgust. You think you're feeling it worse than the victim, and that's why you feel guilty.'

'I guess what it boils down to,' Nina said, after a pause, 'I just wanted to get out of there. No, worse, I wanted it never to've happened. I couldn't handle it.'

'That's it exactly,' Lucky said with sudden sharpness. 'You're meant to be tough, not feel like that. That's the victim's prerogative.'

Nina looked at her in surprise.

They got back to the office just as Zoltan Schneider said into the phone, 'Right, guv. Yep. I'll get it sorted.' He hung up and called across the room, 'OK. One volunteer for obbo tonight. Don't all leap up at once.'

Nina, who'd just finished booking in, raised her arm and walked over to her desk without looking at him. She sat down and glanced up to find the DI smiling at her like a crocodile.

He said, 'You feeling all right, Nina?'

'I said I'd do it.'

'It's only for a couple of hours.'

'Fine.'

He waited. Nina wiggled her mouse, waited for the screensaver to disappear and started typing in her password.

'Don't you want to know what it is?' Zoltan enquired.

A taxi's clattering diesel engine woke her and she sat up with a start, cursing under her breath. She looked at the dashboard clock. Twenty to midnight. 'Shit!' she said aloud. How many times? How often had she been told, had it hammered home again and again by the instructors at Hendon and every guv'nor since, never, never fall asleep on obbo? She scrabbled around for the log, peered out through the windscreen into Ballards Way, and said again, helplessly, 'Shit!'

Then she stopped, and sat back. Her short-term memory had just kicked in, reminding her that she had not, after all, committed the cardinal sin. The rostered two hours had finished at half past nine and she'd spent some time unwinding, wondering about the prospects as regarded going home. She must have unwound too far. Heaving a sigh, she peered across the street to the Clarkes' house, roof tiles thrown into sharp relief by the light of an almost full moon. The house itself was in darkness and the two cars were both in the drive, Mrs Clarke's Golf in front. Halfway up the side wall a red pinpoint of light showed that the burglar alarm was on. No-one was coming in or going out tonight.

She drove home to Addiscombe. The house was still; presumably everyone was asleep. She let herself in and crept upstairs, closing the bathroom door before switching on the light to take out her contacts, remove what remained of her makeup and brush her teeth. This done, she tiptoed across the landing to the bedroom.

In the moonlight she could make out a shape under the bedclothes. The painful knot that had been drawing ever tighter about her stomach loosened. She stood for a moment in the darkness, listening to the slow, even rhythm of breathing. Satisfied, she undressed, found her pyjamas folded on the chair by the window, put them on and climbed gingerly into bed.

'Mmm?' a voice muttered.

Nina said, 'You awake?'

'You've just got in.' There was a stirring, and an arm extended to encircle her waist. She was kissed, the prickle of encroaching beard growth stinging her lips.

'Yeah,' she answered, belatedly. 'Just this minute.'

'Where've you been?'

'Obbo,' she yawned. 'Tell you about it in the morning.'

'Tell me about it now,' came the affectionate wheedle. A twinge of irritation stabbed through her before she could stop it. Hard to believe she'd once found that wheedle endearing.

She sighed.

'I just need to know you're all right.'

Nina said, 'What time were Mum and Dad home?'

'Dunno.'

'What d'you mean, you don't know?'

'I didn't hear them.'

'I tried to ring, let you know where I was.'

'When?'

'Couple of times. Went to voicemail.'

'Must've left my phone when I went out.'

'You went out?'

'Yeah.'

Nina frowned in the dark. 'Well, if you went out you *won't* have heard them come in.'

'No, s'pose not.'

'Why'd you go out, anyway?'

'I got bored, rosebud. Rang Terry and went up the Cricketers.'

'This late? On a weeknight?'

'No, we had a couple of pints and then went back to Terry's for a game of darts.'

'They've got darts at the Cricketers.'

'They keep falling out the board.'

'Not if you throw them properly.'

'Somebody hasn't switched off yet...' The hand pinched her waist where it held her, paused and began a tentative foray onto her belly under the pyjama top. She took hold of the wrist.

'I'm tired,' she said. 'Sorry, darling. Night-night.' And she leaned over and delivered a kiss on the forehead, before turning over and drawing the bedclothes more tightly around herself. She was asleep in moments.

The hand was withdrawn, and nothing more was said.

Wrapped in a blanket, Larissa Stephenson sat propped in a chair in a corner of her room. Moonlight slanted in through the open curtains and spotlit the bed in a yellow glare. Every now and then the branches of the apple tree in the garden would move in the breeze, thrusting shadows in.

Lucky didn't know how she'd got through the rest of the day, only that she'd had to. The initial horror of the visit to Mrs McMinn had turned to overwhelming relief that at least she hadn't had to pretend to be cheerful. Nina Tyminski, she believed, had guessed nothing. She had some preoccupation of her own which was dulling her intuition. If only the others would be as easy. She felt they might. Carry on as normal, as if nothing had happened. At any cost, no-one must know.

But someone did. He was out there, dancing his mocking dance among the shadows of the tree, leaping through the window, throwing himself uninvited across her bed, her haven, sneering at her in the moonlight. She dared not draw the curtains. Then she would have only the dark. In both worlds lay horror.

The chair was hard, and the pain still gnawed in her abdomen like a parasite. But at last exhaustion overcame her, and her eyelids drooped closed as her body sagged. In a nervous sleep she dreamed of a vast dark room where her mother and father were, of the hallowed kingdom where dust motes flew in the sunbeams, and which would never again hold such terrors for Larissa as her own company.

THURSDAY

Detective Constable Jeff Wetherby had been walking in and out of the building for seven years now, and his provincial sensibilities still failed to be impressed by it. Jeff played to a fine pitch the lugubrious Yorkshireman who revelled in grandiose Victoriana and the mossy ruins of old castles. Croydon Police Station, five storeys of rectangular 1980s functionality on one corner of the town's busiest intersection, was neither of those things. The only remotely romantic features it possessed were the address - Park Lane - and the traditional blue lamp by the entrance, transplanted from the late, unlamented old Victorian station across the road, long since demolished.

On his way in Jeff paid the architecture as little attention as he did most mornings. Following the familiar routine, he showed his pass to the security guard on the barrier and parked in the first available space. Once indoors, he stepped into the empty lift and pressed the third floor button.

'Hold the lift!'

The issuer of the plea was a woman in her late twenties with skin the colour of ripe chestnuts. High, prominent cheekbones gave her face an impish character accentuated by a sharp, triangular chin and fiery brown eyes. Her long straight black hair was tied back with a polished wooden clip carved like a bow; a few strands she'd teased forward into a thin fringe. She had a classic hourglass figure, broad shoulders and hips and a slim waist, although her short legs made her look thicker set. She wore a man's grey houndstooth sports jacket over a mauve t-shirt, black cotton trousers and black leather shoes. A pair of large black plastic earrings rested as daintily as such things can against the hollows behind her jaw. Slung over her shoulder was a large black bag, and a briefcase was tucked under one arm. She was Detective First Class Jasmin Winter, on a year's attachment from Amsterdam. Jeff had fallen for her almost the moment they'd met, on the team's first day of operation six months ago. Jasmin did not - he believed - know this. He'd been careful not to let on, to keep his adoration secret, afraid to be anything more than friends in case knowledge sparked her to any word or action that could be construed as denial. Working together didn't make life any easier.

He blurted, 'Eh up.'

'Hi.' Jasmin's face bunched into a smile that transformed it into a second sun. His stomach churned. Pleasantries over, the smile disappeared and an expression of intense earnest transformed the coal-dark eyes. She said, 'You remember Mrs Abernetty - the assault we worked a couple of months ago that turned out to be a domestic?' Her English was measured, accented, American-taught.

After a brief guilty second's recollection, he answered, 'Aye.'

'We maybe were right in the first place,' Jasmin said. 'I spoke with Nina in the canteen. I think she has something.'

'Should see a doctor about it.'

'Huh?'

'Nothing.' He mumbled, wishing his mouth would stay shut on these occasions when it, and he, knew he hadn't the slightest chance of impressing her. It was impossible, anyway. In six months she'd be on her way back to Holland, and he would never see her again. He should drop it. But the knowledge only added to his sense of helpless urgency.

'You are a twit,' she said affectionately, in that way of hers which never gave away whether she'd understood or not. Balancing her briefcase on one raised knee, she scrabbled about inside and handed him some crumpled notes. From the state of them, they'd been scribbled over breakfast. He took them, adjusting his focus to Jasmin's huge, unruly handwriting, and skimmed through her resumé of the attack on Violet McMinn. Into his mind came recollections of the other incident, recollections that were sketchy and would need to be confirmed by a look at his own notes. Maureen Abernetty, a housewife in her fifties, had complained to the police of being sexually assaulted by a burglar, a claim which, supported by her husband, she'd later withdrawn. The assault had supposedly been committed using an African statuette, a holiday souvenir, which the intruder had then stolen. Jeff and Jasmin had been forced to end their investigation after the Abernettys admitted the whole thing was the result of a domestic row, a fumbled attempt by Mrs Abernetty to get back at her husband for hitting her, and that the statuette had in fact been broken in the fight and then thrown away. It was a conclusion that had not felt right to either of them, but there was nothing they could do.

'Mm-hmm,' Jeff said, handing the notes back as the lift opened on their floor.

'You think?' Jasmin broke off eye contact, struggling to

get the papers back in her case.

'Means of entry in that other one,' he pondered. 'You remember?'

'They told us ground floor window, just like here.' She patted her case. 'There were size twelve footprints found in the front garden, but the eldest son also was a size twelve.'

'You remember a lot.'

'I pulled the file,' Jasmin said. She yawned.

He looked at her. There were dark rings round her eyes. 'How long've you been in?'

But now they'd reached the office. Jeff pushed open the door to a cacophony of noise. He held it for Jasmin and followed her through. Work had apparently been suspended. Sophia wasn't around, but the only other absentee was Brian Hunt, and that was because he was on leave. Advantage of the guv'nor's non-arrival had been taken by Detective Constable Sandra Jones, who was holding court. Zoltan stood to one side and watched, arms folded, the glassy smile on his face suggesting he thought Sandra's bridges were well overdue burning, and if Sophia walked in now he couldn't care less what fate befell her.

Sandra sat behind her desk with her feet on it. She had on a short brown dress and blue tights, and her shoes, kicked off, were deployed at random angles across some half-finished work. The others sat on their desks and listened to her. Jeff booked in and went and parked his backside on his.

The issue under consideration was DC Anne White's leaving do. Anne had just been promoted to Acting Sergeant and was transferring to the Met's Film Unit at Southwark. Next week would be her last with the team. Sandra Jones had been opining for some time that the occasion needed to be marked in a fitting way. The organising of most of the team's social functions was left to Sandra, as she was the only one who seemed to have the motivation. A date had been agreed, and now a heated discussion was taking place as to venue.

'I still think the Casino,' Marie Kirtland said.

'I dunno, I don't like casinos,' Kim Oliver said.

'The Casino's not a casino, it's a club, you brain-dead old witch,' Sandra reprimanded her lightly.

'The amount of dosh changes hands there of a night,' Helen Wallace remarked, 'it might as well be.'

'Drug money?' Larissa Stephenson asked.

'Yep.'

'Not when there's a horde of plods there, surely?'

'Ha ha.'

'Casino's the best club in town,' Marie said.

'No, it ain't,' Kim said.

'All right, Barkeley's, then.'

Jeff said diffidently, 'Does it have to be a club?' To his surprise there were a few murmurs of agreement. Fairly feeble, granted, but he could have sworn one of them came from Anne White herself.

'Well, we're not hiring a hall because it's too expensive,' Marie told him. 'And a restaurant's too civilised.'

'Pub crawl?' someone suggested.

'Could do a pub crawl *and* a club.'

'I just don't want to wear a tie.'

Sandra said to Jeff, 'We all know what you'd have given the choice. Fish and chips and a couple of DVDs round somebody's house.'

'You calling me boring?' He said this rather forlornly, knowing he was no match for Sandra's fire axe wit. But she'd already been distracted.

She was saying, in response to someone's suggestion, 'All right, votes for the Casino?' She put an arm up and counted with the free one. 'Barkeley's?' She looked around. 'Fuck,' she said.

There was a breathless pause.

'That's settled, then,' Anne White said sarcastically, from her corner.

Five of them sat round Zoltan Schneider's desk. A dozen or so files and notes were piled up in front of them, the result of Nina Tyminski's airing of the possible link she and Jasmin had established between two aggravated burglary cases. They didn't make pleasant reading. Zoltan still had his nose in a file. After a while he stopped reading and looked up.

'So?' He peered through the thickest part of his lenses at Nina and then at Jasmin. 'Is someone making a habit of it?'

Nina glanced at the others. 'We've found two other possibles.'

'Which are the ones you've rejected?'

She pointed. There were two piles on the table. Zoltan dumped his folder on the larger one, leaned back and said, 'I'm listening.'

'These stretch back over quite a period of time; possibly why no-one's made the connection before.' Nina reached out and took the folder Larissa Stephenson was holding. She opened it. 'Denise Cole,' she said, 'age at time of complaint twenty-four, single, address Flat 1, 60 Natal Road, Thornton Heath. Crime report's dated the day after the incident. Victim lived alone, came home from the cinema to find two intruders in her living room.'

'Two?' Zoltan cradled his hands and tucked them behind his head.

'They surprised her as she walked in. One of them, described as a very tall man, stood behind the door and grabbed her before she could put the light on.' Nina's eyes flicked back and forth as she skimmed through the witness statement. 'The other man seemed more anxious to get the hell out of it. Said something like, "Come on, you stupid little basket." He didn't take any part in the assault.'

'Stood and watched, though,' Lucky said.

'Yeah, but it was the other one who did the deed. Says here he forced her to strip by the expedient of beating the crap out of her, then penetrated her with a silver trophy she'd won for youth club drama.' She looked up, paler even than usual. 'Which he then nicked.'

'Aggravated assault, then, not actual rape?' Zoltan said.

Nina frowned. 'By the legal definition, no.'

'And no-one was ever found for it?' Zoltan combed his beard with his fingers. 'This accomplice.'

'Apart from him,' Jeff Wetherby spoke up, 'it fits the MO.'

'"You stupid *little* basket,"' the DI repeated. 'But Miss Cole described the rapist as tall?'

'*Very* tall,' Nina said. 'She seems to've been emphatic.'

'Funny way of putting it, then,' Jeff said.

'Figure of speech?' Lucky suggested.

'Possibly something else.'

All eyes turned to Jasmin Winter.

'My English is not that great,' Jasmin said modestly, 'but if a person is very young, don't you say also sometimes he is little?'

They became thoughtful.

'So young but tall,' Zoltan said.

'An apprentice burglar with a sideline as a perv,' Lucky said sharply.

In the next chair, Jeff glanced at her, his hazel eyes neutral. 'Did CSI find any footprints?'

Nina flipped through the file to the scene of crime report. 'First thing Denise did when they'd gone,' she said, 'was springclean the place from top to bottom. That includes hoovering the carpet and curtains, mopping the kitchen floor, wiping down all the surfaces and stuffing everything that would fit into the washing machine. The upshot of which,' she snapped the file shut, 'no forensic.'

There was silence for a moment, then Zoltan sighed. 'No wonder they never got caught.'

'Can't blame her, though,' Lucky said in a small voice.

'No.' He uncrossed his legs, crossed them the other way. 'Let's hear about the other one.'

'Before our time and all,' Nina said. The file was on Jasmin's lap and she passed it over. 'Lisa Harkness, age thirty-three, divorced with a fourteen year old son, of 209 Alton Road, Waddon. Woken by an intruder who assaulted her using a foreign object she thought was a perfume bottle from her dresser, although none of the ones Forensic examined had traces.'

'He took it again,' Jeff said.

Zoltan said, 'Method aside, what links it to the others?'

'Size twelve footprints on the carpet and in the garden,' Nina said, after a glance at Jasmin. 'And means of entry. In all these cases, McMinn and Abernetty included, we've got B and E followed by sexual assault, which is very unusual in itself. Access was through a sash or drop catch window on the ground floor. Plus all the attacks took place in darkness, and all the victims describe a tall or very tall man.'

'Tenuous.' Zoltan lapsed for a few moments into silent thought. 'OK,' he said. 'I'll get on to Records, see if any of this rings a bell. Lucky, stick around and listen in. We need to circulate a request for any knowledge of similar cases. On that note, Nina, Jasmin, start ringing round the women's refuges and rape crisis centres. I know they're confidential but it's worth a try. When that's done you can all have a go chasing up the investigating officers, see if they've anything promising to say.'

'What about the victims?' Jeff asked.

'Only as a last resort,' Zoltan said. 'We don't want to dredge up bad memories if we can avoid it.' He paused. Taking it he'd finished, they started to get up. Over the scraping of chairs he added, 'Let's all keep our eyes open. Chances are there've been other attacks that either weren't reported or haven't been linked.' He stopped and frowned. 'Lucky?'

'Sir?' She was halfway to the corner of Helen's desk where she worked.

'That meant now.'

She stood and stared at him for an instant. She said, 'My biro's run out.'

Zoltan nodded acquiescence and stood. He gave the impression he could wait all day if necessary.

What had seemed the comparatively simple task of locating Luke Benton and informing him of what had happened to his family had proved, owing to the destruction by fire and water of much of the material evidence, to be anything but. There was no other close family, and house-to-house enquiries in Chapel View had failed to yield confirmation that Luke even existed, never mind where he was. It had fallen to a finally filthy Sandra Jones and Anne White to sift through the blackened remnants that had survived the blaze, contact what relatives and friends the search turned up, and confirm that Luke was in Greece, though not the resort nor which hotel he was actually staying at. Having bathed and changed, they'd then had to call every airline that flew there before they were able to track him down to Rhodes, and fax to the UK consulate there a request to put him on a flight home.

A sign of the times, as Sophia remarked, irritated at having to expend so much energy, time and manpower on a routine task - effort which should have gone towards finding the arsonists. The Bentons had lived in Chapel View for five years yet no-one, not even their next door neighbours, seemed to have paid them any more attention than it took to nod when passing in the street.

Sophia considered it her duty to take care of Luke Benton personally, and so it had been she and Sandra who'd met him at Stansted and driven him to Croydon University Hospital to confront the travesty of human dignity that was his younger brother. His college friend Nick, a muscular, quietly-spoken black man, had cut short his own trip to accompany him home, and now sat beside him in the living room of his parents' house in Thornton Heath.

'It's been a tough few hours for you, Luke, I realise that,' Sophia said. 'Maybe you'd like to try and get some sleep before you answer any questions.'

'I couldn't sleep.'

Sophia frowned at Luke. He was a tall youth, light-skinned, with the shadow of a goatee whose successful growth was compromised by his being too young. He slumped in an armchair, bare-chested under a white cricket sweater, red beach pants stained and crumpled from wear and travel. He hadn't rested since being plucked from a nightclub dancefloor at midnight by a policeman who, Nick had told them, he was sure was going to plant something on him. Then the breaking of the news, the escort to the airport and the ten-hour wait for a flight. Finally the return home, to find the nightmare was true, that his mother was dead and that even if he survived, his brother would be disfigured beyond recognition, condemned to a life of helpless pain while Luke, unscathed, tried to get on with his. It was a situation Sophia, with all her experience of the horrors that went with the Job, had never had to face. As a young PC, and then sergeant, she'd sometimes handled something similar as the result of a house fire or a road accident; but never when the next of kin was this particular age, too old to be fostered or taken into care, too young, really, for the awful responsibility that had been thrown upon him; and certainly never when the whole family had been subjected to an attack of such barbarity and when only by chance, perhaps, was Luke not now lying alongside them in the burns unit or on a mortuary slab.

'Fair enough,' she said. 'Let me know if you're finding it a bit much, and we'll stop. We can always come back to it after you've had some rest.'

Nick beckoned her to one side. 'Can't it wait anyway?'

'I think we should get this out of the way as soon as possible,' Sophia said. 'As yet there's no clear motive for the crime. Obviously Robin will be in no fit state to tell us anything for some time. It's possible Luke might have some idea why they were picked on, or even who might have done it.'

Nick sat down beside his friend and said something softly into his ear. Luke nodded bleakly.

'Thank you, Luke,' Sophia said. 'So far we're in a bit of a bind. None of the neighbours seem to have seen anything, despite the fact that someone setting fire to a cross in your front garden would have been pretty hard to miss.'

'I can tell you why,' Luke said.

'Oh?'

'All shit scared, case they get put on the spot. I know who did it and I know why.' He saw his listeners' expressions change. He steepled his fingers and leaned forward, elbows on knees. 'Robin's babysitter knows about it. Debbie Clarke. Talk to her.'

Concealing their surprise, Sophia and Sandra told him about the circumstances surrounding Debbie's disappearance. With much prompting Luke, already distressed enough, was able to clarify why they'd found what they had.

Although Doreen Benton had been left adequately provided for by her late husband, her status as the family's breadwinner had required her, for her own peace of mind, to return to the job market she'd abandoned when Robin was born. His starting school had finally given her the opportunity, and she'd been lucky enough to find a job that corresponded roughly with his school times, leaving only the hour or so afterwards unaccounted for. Debbie Clarke was the latest in a string of babysitters employed through cards put up in Mrs Blissett's shop. She was also the prettiest, and Luke, despite some misgivings about her age, had asked her out.

'She's sixteen, though,' Sandra remarked.

'Yeah, but she acts younger sometimes. She's sort of in the angry teenage phase. I never should've involved her but it's difficult to take no for an answer with her.'

'Involved her in what, Luke?' Sophia said.

He sighed, struggling to marshal his thoughts. 'Long story,' he said. 'I picked her up one night, she was in a right strop. Something on the news about a robbery, and her dad had been spewing his middle class crap about all black men being muggers and rapists. Then of course *we* got dragged into it 'cause Debbie sits for us, and she flew off the handle.'

'Do the Clarkes know about you and Debbie?'

'You joking?' Luke scoffed. 'Bad enough their little girl even being associated with us - working for Sambo. Oh, they never say as much, least not in my hearing. But it's plain enough.'

Sophia nodded. Believable, if Kim's impressions of Andrew Clarke were anything to go by. She said, 'So you think they might have found out?'

'Eh?' He looked puzzled. Then he shook his head. 'No, I'm just telling you how it started. Anyway, she knew I was involved with this pressure group, Justice for Mark Watkins.'

Sophia stiffened. Kim had mentioned a possible link. She'd have to talk to her when they got back.

'D'you remember it?' Luke asked, noticing her reaction.

Sandra, who'd been uncharacteristically taciturn so far, said, 'I was on the investigation.'

Luke and Nick turned piercing stares on her. Luke said, 'D'you reckon it was Carruth?'

Sandra hesitated, conscious of Sophia beside her. 'We were pretty certain he was involved,' she said. 'And we *knew* he didn't act alone. But because he never talked...' She tailed off, knowing as she had known then that it wasn't enough.

Nick made a loud, dismissive noise with his tongue. The tension in the room had risen.

Sandra said, 'A person can't be tried twice for the same crime. That's the law.'

Nick wasn't impressed. He chewed his lip and then said, 'You reckon he had something to do with - ?'

'I checked him out.' Sandra shook her head. 'He's got the perfect alibi. Emigrated to America two years ago and he's in jail in Florida. How he got a green card with his record is anybody's guess, but there you go.'

'He's been spoken to,' Sophia added, 'but he denies knowing anything. I think,' she ventured, 'we've drifted from the point.'

'Yeah, sorry.' Luke scratched his head. 'Debbie started asking me about it. Kept on about how unfair it was. Eventually she talked me into taking her along to a meeting.' He glanced at Nick and then frowned at Sandra. 'I went to the same gym as Mark Watkins, and I'm telling you he was no wimp. I know Carruth's in the clear legally, but like you said, no way he did it on his own. We knew it as well as you lot did. So we formed the group to try and push the police, or the CPS or the Home Office, into reviewing the case properly. But Debbie,' he wiped a hand across his mouth, 'seemed to get the impression we were some sort of vigilante brigade.'

'Why do you say that?' Sophia asked.

'She told me. She was all fired up, wanting to do something. You know how it is: she's sixteen, thinks she can change the world. She was standing up and mouthing off and getting clapped; of course that only encouraged her. Trouble is,' his expression clouded, 'it got her involved with some people.'

'Some people?'

'Far left militants,' Luke said with sudden venom. 'You know the ones: they always turn up in a group like ours and they're always white. We knew they'd be trouble but we can't turn them away because they never actually do anything to justify expelling them.' His anger, fuelled by worry, boiled over and he slammed his fist down on the arm of the settee. 'They used her and I couldn't fucking stop them.'

Sophia waited for him to calm down. 'How did they involve Debbie?'

Luke shook his head, almost out of his reason now with anxiety. 'These guys were after this neo-Nazi outfit they thought was behind Mark's death.'

'Thrall,' Sandra said, her voice pregnant with excitement. 'I remember the name coming up, but we never got close.'

'Explain about Debbie,' Sophia stepped in. 'Are you saying they used her to get at Thrall?'

'The way she went on about it, you'd think she insisted,' Luke said bitterly. 'She was just too scared to say no. She's still so scared,' he raised his voice, 'she won't even tell *me* what she's doing. She stopped going out with me. If I see her in the house when she's babysitting she won't even look at me. I don't know how deep she's in. I fucking don't know.'

He put his face in his hands, then looked up, stared appealingly at Sophia. There was a long silence while the DCI pursed her lips and thought. At last she nodded. He had a right to know.

'The devices that started the fire,' she told him, as gently as possible, 'were set inside the house. They were placed without whoever brought them there having to break in. Besides you and your mother, the only other key we've been able to trace belongs to Debbie.'

Emotions flashed across Luke Benton's face like sunlight and shadow on a time-lapse film. Surprise, betrayal, horror, grief, worry. But finally anger. Impotent anger.

'Oh, God,' he said, and crumpled, head in his lap,

shoulders heaving, as for the first time since they'd met him at the airport he cried. The entire weight of what had befallen his family, befallen him, had finally descended, and Nick, stunned, put his hands on Luke's shoulders and his face close to Luke's and tried to comfort him.

'You don't need telling,' Sophia said at the office meeting she'd called that afternoon, 'that this makes it even more crucial for us to find Debbie Clarke. She alone outside the family had keys, and there are no fingerprints at the scene that haven't been accounted for. Having said that, it does tend to confirm what we already know: it's inconceivable she acted alone. Firstly, the sixteen year old daughter of a building society executive does not have knowledge of incendiary devices and how to place them. Secondly, that cross did not appear out of thin air, however much the house-to-house made it seem so.' She paused for the inevitable wry laughter. 'What Luke's account does throw into question is motive. If he's to be believed, she's passionately anti-racist to the point where she was prepared to try and infiltrate an extreme right wing group. But I think we might be on our way to some answers. Shortly after we fed the name Thrall through the computer, I got a call from DCI Macmillan from the Flying Squad. He's agreed to tell us a bit about who we might be up against.'

There was a stir in the room as the man who'd been sitting behind Sophia's desk got to his feet. He was tall, thin and bloodless, with Brylcreemed grey hair and dark, deep-set eyes. His lean face bore a trace of beard shadow. He moved with a feline fluidity which seemed to have come with his expensive grey suit. He commanded attention effortlessly, startling some of the team who hadn't even realised he was in the room until he'd stood up. The whole effect was almost sinister, like a vampire in an old Hammer movie. They would more readily have marked him down as a spook than a member of the legendary Sweeney.

His speech betrayed his origins at once as the western Scottish Highlands, familiar to many of those present who'd watched *Monarch of the Glen* on TV. But any association the accent might have had with whimsical good humour dissipated swiftly: Macmillan's dark, reedy purr was as unsettling as the rest of him.

He glided over to the board, on which had been written, in large red capitals, THRALL. He looked at it and said, 'If you ask NCIS nicely, they'll tell you that name belongs to an ultra-right wing, white supremacy group. It's an acronym: it stands for Terror Hate Race Alliance. As you may gather from that, they're not overly concerned about respectability.' No-one laughed, for the simple reason that it was very probably not a joke. 'The first indication of them as an autonomous entity is three years back, although it seems they started out some time before that as a faction within the main far right parties. What, you wonder, has this got to do with me?'

He turned and drifted over to the projector he'd set in the middle of the office, signalling as he went to a wretched-looking Jeff Wetherby, who was standing by the blind. As the room darkened, a slide of a slim, balding, fortyish man lit up part of the board. Obviously a surveillance photo, it showed the man turning away from a front door with the number 90 on it.

'This,' the wintry Highland voice floated out of the gloom, 'is Edward Alan Porter, age forty-five. Last known address, 90 Highbury Road, SW12, where this was taken last August. Regarded in the underworld as one of the best blaggers around, largely because he's never been caught.' Macmillan broke off and paced a short way across the floor. 'Word on the street says one secret of his success is that he's found witnesses tend to describe black men, even when the robbers wear masks. Why wouldn't this lead us to look for him? Because Edward Porter is a fully paid-up member of the BNP and the EDL, and generally has a hand in any marches, rallies or concerts of an extreme right or nationalist bent that go on in the London area. Outspoken and an organiser. Not the sort of man to be using black talent on bank jobs. Definitely the sort canny enough to exploit the subconscious racism of the great British public.'

There was a moment of silence, broken only by the faint click of a mouse as Macmillan brought the next slide up. A broad-shouldered, powerful-looking man with a ruddy face and a red crew cut stared out at them, prison slate held defiantly in front of his chest.

'More and more,' Macmillan said, 'we're finding these extremist groups are starting to use some of the same fundraising methods as the Northern Ireland paramilitaries: armed robbery, fraud, extortion *et cetera*. That may be where this guy comes in. Michael Philip Quaife.' He pointed. 'Age thirty-four. Released from Albany Prison on the Isle of Wight in February from a three-year stretch for armed robbery. He's an ex-para and did four tours in Afghanistan and Iraq, where he seems to have picked up some handy tips regarding the practical use of explosives.'

'Is that the link between him and Porter?' someone asked. 'He brought the tactics back from the military?'

The soft whirr of the projector stopped. Uncertainly, Jeff drew the blind back up. Macmillan prowled back to the centre of the room. 'Not that smart,' he answered, 'although certainly he could have rigged the devices that caused your fire. More likely he's the enforcer. The one who actually goes and does the ethnic cleansing while Porter plans.'

'So what you're saying,' Sophia put in, 'is these two *are* Thrall?'

'Porter's the brains. Without him it wouldnae exist. Too subtle. Thrall aren't in the business of claiming credit. They prefer to make the hit and let the rumour mill do the talking.'

Abruptly, he turned away and went and sat down beside Sophia. She stepped forward, the familiar rustle of her tights drawing the team back as if from a trance. It was as if Macmillan had never stirred.

'The point being,' she said, 'Porter's the one we want to be measuring up. His and Quaife's current whereabouts are now a priority. Any questions?'

There were few takers. No-one fancied digging too deeply into Sweeney territory, even if their knowledge was on offer. But Kim stuck her hand up and called out, 'Do we know how big Thrall actually is?'

'Big?' Only Macmillan's lips moved.

'How many are there? Besides Porter and Quaife.'

'They don't publish a membership list.'

This produced a smattering of nervous laughter. Undaunted, Kim persisted, 'You've more or less said Mark Watkins was down to them. I mean there's people in this room who were on that case and know there was way more to it than got to court. He was kicked unconscious, stabbed to death and then bloody tarred and feathered. That wasn't two slags with a baseball bat. Nor was a six foot high flaming cross. Somebody knows their Klan history. Sir,' she added, as Macmillan rose.

He nodded to her. 'What I should have said is that it's

hard to quantify. Thrall is less an organisation than a rallying cry. They've adherents throughout the far right, on whom they call when necessary. Simon Carruth, the man acquitted of the Watkins murder, was one. Makes infiltration difficult, particularly when we're used to impersonating armed robbers, not political extremists.'

There were icicles in Kim's stomach. If the Sweeney couldn't get on the inside of Thrall, what chance did Debbie Clarke have? A thought occurred to her, so momentous it shocked her into standing.

She didn't realise at first. Sophia said, 'Kim?'

The whole room was staring in her direction.

'This is gonna sound daft.'

'Say it,' Sophia ordered, her blue gaze leaving no doubt that she was the one to decide what was daft.

'What if we're looking at this the wrong way?' It seemed to Kim that she was standing to one side, watching herself speak. 'What if Porter found Debbie out? Maybe *she* was the target, not the Bentons.'

'Seems a bit drastic,' Sandra Jones said. 'What's wrong with a spanner and a rubbish skip on a dark night?'

'Then there's the cross,' Helen Wallace chipped in.

'And the no forced entry.'

'I mean, why would she put herself in the frame?'

Kim sat down.

'All valid objections,' Sophia said, looking in turn at their contributors. 'Nevertheless, it's worth bearing in mind. At the moment we can't confirm one way or the other, because there are no witnesses and no evidence. In the meantime, we know we're looking for dangerous people. *Armed* people. Hold that thought.' She clapped her hands together to signal the end of the meeting.

The low chatter, the bustle of backsides transferring from desktops to chairs, occupied the next few moments. When next anyone looked, the seat behind Sophia's desk was empty. No-one had seen Macmillan leave.

Following Kim's contribution there'd been one or two remarks about the grinding of axes, whose perpetrators hadn't taken a great deal of care to voice out of her hearing. Such things she'd long grown used to handling, but not from colleagues she'd come to trust. She felt she was in danger of being marginalised because of her colour, and she didn't like it.

Of course the attacks on Mark Watkins and the Bentons made her angry. They were, in many ways, personal. But it was righteous anger that honed, rather than clouded, her judgement, and it was nothing like the exasperation she now felt. Either you involved black officers and accepted their attitudes, or you didn't, and went on fielding the old accusations about the police being out of touch. There seemed to be an assumption that white coppers didn't feel the same outrage at violence against a black person, and could work more effectively because of the impartiality this gave them. Bollocks, she thought. White or black, the police service would not be doing its duty to minorities until every officer in it looked on racism as an evil to be ground into the dirt, destroyed.

As she pulled up in Ballards Way that evening, she was surprised to see her guv'nor emerge from the Clarkes' house and drive off in her green Saab. Of course, she remembered, Sophia was calling on them daily, keeping them up to date; probably, knowing her, timing the visits to just before Kim or

Nina were scheduled to show up, so as to render them less likely to expect additional police attention. Nothing to worry about. She switched off the engine and settled down to wait.

At a quarter to nine Andrew Clarke emerged from the house and climbed into his wife's VW Golf. He reversed into the street and headed off towards Addington. Kim pulled out and followed him at a distance.

He led her to the Keeper and Wicket in Addington village, where he parked and went into the saloon bar. While she was still debating whether to go in after him he reappeared, got into the car and started back the way he'd come. With a growing suspicion this was all there was to the excursion, Kim followed. If he'd gone to the pub for a drink there was no way he could have finished it that quickly. Maybe he'd bought some cigarettes or bottled beer to take home, but she'd seen nothing in his hands, and there were two off licences in Selsdon, much closer to his house. The only conclusion Kim could come to was that he'd gone there to meet someone. Someone he had reason for not wanting his wife - or the police - to know about.

As expected, he drove straight back to Ballards Way. Kim noted his movements in the log. She saw no further activity that evening.

The duty barman of the Keeper and Wicket wouldn't swear to having seen Andrew Clarke talking to anyone or, indeed, to having seen Andrew Clarke. He couldn't be expected to take notice of every stingy sod who came in and didn't even buy a bloody drink. Bloody rushed off his feet, he'd been.

The fact that it was the quietest night of the week did not shake him from this standpoint. He hovered while Kim finished her half and then ushered her out past empty tables. He hadn't even had to call time.

Detective Inspector Zoltan Schneider remained, six months into the team's operational life, a man of mystery. As such he was the subject of much speculation among his colleagues, generally in pubs after work, when a few adult beverages had enhanced the tendency to gossip. Under such influences most of them had decided that the sarcastic, quietly intimidating exterior hid a lonely, friendless man, with an indefinable something on his shoulder that was not so much a chip as a large log.

One of them knew this to be untrue. Anne White had been going out with him for more than two years. They'd met when Zoltan had been a DS at Richmond, and she a PC on prisoner transport duty. Zoltan had said nothing of this to Sophia Beadle during the setting up of the team. Relationships between coppers who worked together were frowned on. But Zoltan and Anne's personal intimacy seemed to prejudice their work not at all, and they saw no reason, especially now, why it should be anyone's concern but their own.

Zoltan cast a pleasant, relaxed gaze over her as she sat up in bed reading. He sometimes wondered what a girl like Anne saw in him. She was thirty-three, with skin and hair that were fair almost to the point of albino. Too tall for her weight, she maintained by squirrelish eating an enviable, waspish slimness that sat well with her refined, angular face. She looked up and smiled, took off her glasses - all she'd been wearing - and met his kiss with ardent interest. He wasn't fooled.

'Penny for your thoughts.'

'Damn. You guessed.'

'You can tell me, I'm a policeman.' He shrugged, half turning on the way to the bathroom. 'Be with you in a minute.'

For a time there were assorted clatterings through the half-closed doorway, and then Zoltan reappeared, his clothes slung over one arm. He tossed them across the back of Anne's dressing table chair. Still wearing his glasses - he couldn't see three feet ahead without them - he climbed into bed, where he removed them and set them on the night table.

'So what's up?' he said, as she settled into his arms.

'I'm just a bit sad.'

He turned his head and looked down into her face. It wasn't much more than an oval blur, but it pleased him anyway.

'Brought it home to me this morning,' she said, 'all that stuff with my leaving do. I'm actually going.'

'You've only been on the team six months. You can't be *that* attached to us.'

'Special Crime's the best job I've ever had,' she said earnestly. 'I must be mad to leave. Still, a promotion...'

'You said it.' He squeezed her shoulder. 'Besides, Film Unit, a lot of PR, just like most of what we do.'

'I suppose.' She sighed. 'But it's been like a family.'

'The Met's a family,' Zoltan said. 'And you've still got me.'

She said nothing for a while, content to nestle in his embrace. Then suddenly she asked, 'Why don't you move in?'

'Move...?'

'No reason why not, now, is there?'

'No.'

'I love you.'

'And I love you.'

'Two good reasons.' She waited, studying the expression on his face. She decided she didn't like it. She said, 'What're you looking like that for?'

'Looking like what?'

'Like you're expecting something horrible to happen.'

'Was I?'

'Yes.' She poked him in the stomach with a finger.

'Force of habit, I suppose,' he admitted. 'I'm Jewish. It's in the genes.'

'Bollocks,' Anne said succinctly.

Zoltan, with no ready answer to this, sighed.

'Give me a day or two,' he suggested.

'To work out whether the only reason I asked you is to cling onto the team?' she said, only half joking.

'To work out,' he said, 'whether I can fit all my stuff in your cupboards.'

'Pig,' she said.

'Please.' He made a face. 'Something kosher.'

'Another thing about Jews,' Anne said.

'Mm-hmm?'

'Well, one particular Jew anyway.' She ran her fingernails across his chest.

'What's that?' He felt himself stir.

'He's got such an awfully sexy body.'

Zoltan considered himself with mock puzzlement. 'Are you sure that's not bollocks as well?'

'Not all of it,' she breathed, caressing the items under debate, her hair brushing his nipples as she kissed his shoulders. 'Who did you think I meant?'

'Oh, someone I reckon you've been seeing rather a lot of lately.'

'It's a lie.'

'Someone,' he said, 'who's rather good at doing this, for instance?' He ran his hands down her neck, down to the small of her back and along the cleft of her buttocks, a technique of which she was very fond.

'Ah,' she whispered. 'Oh, *him*. That policeman.'

'Got a thing for policemen, have you?'

'Only one particular policeman.'

'You know, that's an astonishing coincidence.'

'Why?'

'Because I find a certain police*woman* of my acquaintance,' he said, still caressing, 'makes me feel like doing certain things that definitely aren't incorporated in the constable's oath.'

'Certain things like what?'

'Show you,' he said.

'Oh, officer...'

They slid deeper under the covers.

FRIDAY

'Mum?'

'Mmm?'

'Would it be all right, d'you think, if I moved into Julia's room?'

'Would you like some more toast?'

'Would it?'

'What is wrong with yours?'

'Nothing, I just don't... It's a bit small.'

'I don't know. Supposing - '

'Julia's not coming back, Mum. She's married now... Well, good as.'

'That is the point.'

'Oh, Jesus.'

'Don't blaspheme, child.'

'Sorry. Look, I just need a bit more space, that's all.'

'Then get yourself husband, your own place.'

'Mum...'

'Look at you, you are twenty-two years old, you are beautiful. It is only matter of time. You will go to all the trouble of changing rooms and then you will find someone and move out.'

'Just because Julia moved out when she was nineteen, that doesn't - '

'In fact I don't understand you at all. You are gorgeous girl, yet you don't have boyfriend, you hardly see your friends. It is not natural. I'm frightened for you. You will grow into lonely old maid.'

'Fine one to talk.'

'What?'

'Nothing. Look, I'm a copper. It's not the greatest job if you want a social life.'

'Then get new job.'

'I don't *want* to. I love what I do and besides, I've only just started with this new posting. Some of us have a career to plan, you know.'

'Career, career! Look at you, Larissa, so tired. It doesn't suit you.'

'Oh, yeah? Four years in the Job and you've only just noticed? ...Oh, look, I'm sorry. Actually it's better in Special Crime; the hours are almost normal. You might even get to see me occasionally.'

'Ha.'

'Mum?'

'Very well. You may have Julia's room. I think it's just waste of time, though.'

'Thanks. Really.'

'But if Julia comes home ever...'

''Course, Mum. Thanks.'

'You know what I think.'

'I'd better get going.'

'Do I have a kiss?'

'Sure.'

'What is this? A hug?'

'I'm not going anywhere, Mum. Not now.'

Debbie Clarke's debit card had been used at nine-thirty the previous evening to withdraw £100 from a Santander cash machine in Mare Street, Hackney E8. Less than twelve hours later Kim Oliver and Marie Kirtland were knocking on the door of a flat two minutes away in Paragon Road. They were here to look for one Philip Meredith. Luke Benton had given this name as that of one of the militants who'd infiltrated the Justice for Mark Watkins pressure group and had cultivated Debbie. A PNC check revealed that a person of that name was currently the subject of a community order for shoplifting. According to his probation officer, he had missed his last two scheduled appointments; this was his current residence.

They knocked, not expecting an answer. These were hardly the most salubrious surroundings in which to wait. They were on the third floor of a massive block of 1950s flats, on the edge of an ugly, sprawling estate of similar buildings. Most of the lights were smashed on the walkways, gang tags covered the brickwork, and the fetid smell of stale piss clung to everything. Across the street stood a row of Victorian terraced houses that had somehow escaped the Luftwaffe and post-war urban redevelopment, but not the harsh economic realities of the new century. Now they were smoke-blackened, boarded up, condemned. Beyond lay more of the same, grimy concrete tenements in every direction, the odd high rise or factory chimney thrusting up between them like giant weeds. Away to the west, half-hidden in the haze, the glass and steel prosperity of the City shimmered smugly on the decay it had helped to precipitate; to the south, the gleaming blue obelisk of Canary Wharf marked where Docklands was rubbing salt in the wound.

It was the sort of place you could kick over a pile of litter and be surprised *not* to find a syringe underneath.

Marie was peering through the letterbox. 'Nobody in. Well,' she sighed phlegmatically, 'it got us out of the office.'

'No, wait a minute.' Kim was in a stubborn mood. 'We ain't come all this way for nothing.'

They stood aside to let an elderly black man pass. He spared them not a glance, eyes fixed on his feet as he shuffled by, as though they didn't exist. In this neighbourhood, two strangers knocking on a door could only mean bailiffs or the law. Paying them heed was putting yourself in line for trouble.

Marie took another cursory peep and said, 'Well, we can't search the place: we haven't got a warrant and we won't get one, not on conjecture.' She straightened up again. 'Hang about, though. If this is a squat - '

'Still gotta have reasonable grounds and besides, it's civil law, not criminal.'

'Maybe we don't need a warrant,' Marie persisted. 'This bloke, he's got previous, right?'

'Am I blacker than Michael Jackson?' Kim said, laughing without mirth. 'All piddling stuff, though. Mostly begging, petty theft, bit of public order, one or two for Class A possession.'

'So we *could* go in there right now, if we ask Hackney for - '

Kim frowned, shaking her head. 'Wouldn't wanna risk it.'

'Come on, Kim, where's your bottle all of a sudden?'

Marie looked both ways along the desolate walkway. 'Look, if we're going to wait,' she said, 'couldn't we talk to some of the neighbours? Least make it look as if we've got business here.'

'We can ask.' Kim gazed towards the old man, who was just disappearing into the stairwell. 'Not sure what answers we'll get.'

'Oh, I reckon on a few,' Marie said wryly.

The occupant of the adjacent flat had probably been following developments with an ear to her front door, for she opened it almost as soon as they knocked. She was a small, stout woman in her eighties, with fine, permed white hair like candy floss. Kim unfurled a toothy smile and held out her warrant card.

'Hello, madam. Detective Sergeant Oliver; this is DC Kirtland.'

'This about them next door?'

'We're looking for Philip Meredith,' Kim said. 'We were given next door as his address.'

The woman frowned. 'Was you now?'

'We know it's a squat,' Kim confided. 'But that's by the by. We're looking for a missing girl, and we think Mr Meredith may know where she is.'

'Yeah, well,' the woman said. 'They may be squatters but they're still me neighbours. Counts for summink in my book.'

'I wish more people felt the same,' Kim agreed. 'Make our job a lot easier.'

The woman craned out of her doorway and looked around. 'You best come in. Ain't wise to be seen talking to the law round here.'

They followed her through to a small, old-fashioned, crumbling but tidy kitchen diner at the back. The woman, who introduced herself as Mrs Brownlie, offered them tea. They accepted.

'Detectives, eh?'

'That's right.'

'I lived in Hackney all me life,' Mrs Brownlie said, pursuing her theme. 'Time was, before the war - before they put these flats up - a detective turning up round here'd be front page news. Only copper we ever seen was the local bobby. We was poor, but we was honest.'

'You had community spirit in those days,' Marie said. 'I think the war did for that.'

'The Blitz.' Mrs Brownlie nodded. 'We was hit hard here, 'cause of the docks. Course I was only a girl at the time, but I do remember everyone pulling together; we had to. Folk as still had homes took in them what didn't. Then after the war everybody had to be rehoused, and all the council could afford was cheap rubbish like this.' She gestured out of the window. 'Can't build no community when you're all stacked up like battery hens. Milk, sugar?'

Kim and Marie supplied their requirements.

'I ain't saying everybody on the estate's bad. Them next door, for instance. Squatters or not, they're nice people, got time for you. Take me washing down the launderette when I'm bad with me arthritis, stuff like that, bless 'em.'

'So you know them quite well?' Kim said.

'Well as you gets to know anybody these days.' She took from a cupboard three teacups on saucers which rattled delicately as she balanced them. Best china for visitors, Kim guessed; her mother observed the same custom. Laboriously she filled the kettle from the sink, plugged it in and switched it on.

'Is one of them called Philip Meredith?' Marie asked.

'Phil, yeah. Didn't know his last name till you told me. Him's what went down the launderette for me.'

'Is he in at the moment, d'you know?'

'Dunno.' She shrugged. 'Ain't seen him for a day or two. Always disappearing off, he is, then popping up again. Trouble with you lot, though he won't own to it. No idea where he goes.'

'Like I said, Mrs Brownlie, it's not actually him we're after,' Kim said. 'We're looking for a girl; she might possibly've come here.'

'Oh, yeah?'

Kim took the picture of Debbie Clarke from her bag and passed it to Mrs Brownlie. 'Have you seen her?'

'The one on the news. The fire in Croydon. Yeah.' She handed it back. 'Yeah, I seen her.' Her visitors looked sharply at one another, not believing their luck. Mrs Brownlie, enjoying their reaction, said, 'Law after her and all?'

Kim decided to evade a bit. 'She's a key witness, but she's gone missing.'

'Well, young lady, you're in luck. So happens she turned up next door - must've been Tuesday evening, at that. Banging on the door, crying, making a shocking racket, that's how come I looked out the window and seen her. Mind you, the rest of 'em... I dunno - they was around yesterday afternoon, come to think of it. But not since then. I *thought* there must be summink up.'

'How d'you mean?'

''Cause you two ain't the first has come asking.'

There was a pause while they digested this. 'Excuse me?' Marie said.

'I assumed he was Old Bill, like you. Right nosey parker, he was.'

Kim asked, 'When was this, Mrs Brownlie?'

'Yesterday evening, round sevenish.' She poured hot water from the kettle into the pot. 'I come back from the senior centre and there he was hanging around outside next door. When he clocked me he started asking if I seen the girl.'

'*The* girl?' Marie leaned forward.

'Yeah. Described her very precise like. Didn't have no photo like you do, mind.'

'What did you tell him?'

'Nuffink. Well, I couldn't, could I? Then later on when I watched the news I realized that was the girl he was talking about. He didn't leave no phone number so I couldn't call him back to tell him. Probably wouldn't've anyway. Didn't like the bugger.'

'Can you describe him for us?'

'Let's see now...' She poured tea carefully through a strainer. 'He was medium height.'

'How so? About my height? Smaller? Larger?'

Mrs Brownlie frowned at Marie. 'Ain't easy to tell when you're sitting down. Bit taller than the both of you, I'd say.'

'Five ten?'

''Bout that.'

Kim wrote it down, with a question mark. 'Go on, Mrs Brownlie.'

'Ooh, right. Er, brown hair - light brown. Going a bit on top. Blue eyes. Quite slim.' She put milk in the tea.

'Age?'

She thought about this while she transported the tea tray over to the table and sat down. 'Thirties?' she ventured. 'I dunno, everybody looks young to me nowadays.'

Kim smiled.

'His eyes.' Mrs Brownlie seemed to tighten up. 'Didn't like 'em. They was... whatchamacallem, *cruel.*' She handed them their tea. 'Help yourselves to sugar.'

'OK, and what was he wearing? Was he casually dressed or more formal?'

'Oh, casual. Brown sort of sports jacket, definitely, and... jeans, I think.'

'Blue jeans?'

'Yeah, but smart ones, not full of holes and pulled down halfway to your knees like all them kids have 'em. And a white button-through shirt.' She watched Kim scribbling all this down. 'I think that's about all I can give you.'

Kim said, 'I know you said his eyes, but did you notice anything particular, anything strange or unusual? I mean like scars, or tattoos?'

'No, nuffink like that. Like I say, just that feeling.'

'Would you recognise him if you saw him again?'

Mrs Brownlie hesitated. 'Yeah,' she answered, clearly not liking the implication of a further police encounter. 'Yeah, I reckon. I can fix him in me mind, yeah.'

'You've been very helpful, Mrs Brownlie, thank you.' Kim, smiling, put down her pocket book and picked up her tea.

'Look, I'll let you have me number. Probably best you ring, rather than come round again. Never know who might wanna smash me windows for talking to the law.'

'Mrs Brownlie,' Kim said two cups of tea later, as they took their leave, 'many thanks for all your help and your time. We'll be in touch if we need you.'

'You'll let me know if you find her, won't you?'

Kim said, 'I'll give you a call. And thanks again.'

'You're welcome,' Mrs Brownlie said, straight-faced, and

closed the door behind them.

They wandered a few yards down the walkway.

'That has to have been Edward Porter,' Marie said, in tones that dared Kim to disagree. 'I just wish we'd fucking brought a photo.'

'Lemme tell you what this looks like to me,' Kim said, serious, gazing at the squat and then turning to lean over the balustrade. Marie joined her. 'It looks like Debbie came here looking for a bolthole. Now if that *was* Porter Mrs Brownlie talked to, means he's found out where Debbie was before we did. He could already've got to her by now.'

'Bloody hell.' Marie, frowning, reached inside her bag for a cigarette. 'If you're right, God help her if he has.'

'Let's go see about that warrant,' Kim said.

Nina Tyminski signed herself out at five and went quickly down to the locker room. Her turn on obbo again tonight, and by rights she should be home changing, eating and, if possible, catching an hour or two's sleep. But the prospect held no appeal. Too many things at home depressed her just now and the Job could be depressing enough on its own without that, thank you. Twenty minutes freshening up, then she'd go down to the canteen or Wagamama or somewhere for a bite and be back by seven to drive over to Ballards Way.

Sooner or later, though, something would have to be done about home.

Nina had met Paul Jackson three years ago when they'd both been working at West End Central, she on the Soho Vice Squad and he as a CID clerk. At the time he'd been engaged to a woman who worked for Westminster City Council, but that hadn't stopped him and Nina hitting it off and falling in love. He'd broken off his engagement, then in due course he'd proposed to Nina and she'd accepted. Shortly before their marriage, Paul had quit his job for a highly paid sales position from which, the idea was, he could put himself and Nina on a solid enough footing to afford the mortgage on a house large enough to fill with the host of children they dreamed of having. Unfortunately, Paul thought tact was what you did to a piece of paper in order to make it stick to a wall. This misconception got him fired within two weeks for casting fluently Anglo-Saxon doubts on the masculinity of the area sales manager after being blamed for the fall through of a vital deal. Nina had gone along with his side of the story, and given him the full support she believed to be her wifely duty and prerogative. But this had all happened over a year ago. Paul, in the intervening time, had managed to land a temporary job in a department store over Christmas - and that had been it. Nina's patience was wearing thin. The entirety of their marriage to date had been spent living at her parents' house. Mr and Mrs Tyminski, in the best Catholic extended family traditions, had welcomed their daughter and new son-in-law with open arms. But the arrangement had serious disadvantages. Lack of space, for one; the guilt of imposing, for another. All this while their sex life, pursued in the uncomfortable knowledge that Nina's parents were the thickness of a wall away, suffered chronic damage that might never heal.

Now it was turning into a race against time. The Tyminskis were used to having the couple as part of the household; the problem, more and more, would be how to sever that bond painlessly. The infuriating thing was that Paul simply did not seem to appreciate the urgency.

Of course, he'd promised her a place of their own - when

they had the money. Nina was seriously wondering whether that promise would ever be fulfilled. She cast sidelong glances at - as it seemed to her - the palatial comforts of Sandra and Neil Jones's maisonette, contemporaries enjoying a lifestyle that should also be *her* right - hers and Paul's. But however much she badgered and nagged him, he still could not land a job. The manner of his leaving his previous employment hadn't helped, but surely *someone* ought to employ him.

And then just lately, the worrying behaviour changes. Little things. Like that business the other night when she'd got back from obbo. Staying out until all hours. The steady disappearance of sex from their relationship, which, even considering... Apart from his shocking sense of timing on Wednesday night, he hadn't touched her for more than a month.

He was slipping away from her. However maddening he'd become, she still loved him; loved him so much it hurt. But this couldn't go on.

The locker room was empty. The relief change had happened an hour ago, and the civil staff and most of the CID were on their way home. Nina walked past the lockers and through the door that led to the toilets and showers. She entered a cubicle, lowered the seat cover and sat down, sliding forward until she was perched on the edge. She leaned back, hands on her lap, sighing deeply, switching her mind back to the events of the day, looking for things she might have missed about the rapist who was out there somewhere.

They'd divided into two pairs. Jasmin and Jeff had started following up the Cole and Harkness cases. They'd left the office in the early afternoon, one bound for Epsom and the other for Ealing, in search of officers who might hold in their memories or notes some clue to the identity of a dangerous sex criminal.

Nina and Lucky had done the donkey work, logging the faxes and emails, the phone calls and voice messages flooding back from all over the Met in response to the APB. It had been a mind-numbing task. Lucky, to her credit, had stuck at it diligently, head down, not stirring except to head off to the kettle when Nina suggested it might be time for more tea. Nina was now feeling a bit guilty about that. But it had paid off. Another five possibles, all south of the Thames, all unsolved, and all involving attacks by an intruder in the victim's home. Already they'd made some calls whose results seemed to strengthen the connection.

A queasy feeling made her look down. With a sense of unreality she realised she'd been masturbating. Her mind having found something to occupy it, meanwhile so had her body. Quickly she brought herself off, then sat back, feeling herself relax, muscle by weary muscle. It had yielded as much sexual gratification as a saucepan full of cold mashed turnips and there were probably better ways of dealing with stress, but she didn't have time for them and this way at least provided an outlet for some of her frustration. It made her ashamed when she thought about it, but it was survival. The alternative was to let it all mount up until she snapped, and she'd lost enough already without her marbles going as well.

She lifted the seat cover, peed, left the cubicle and went back to her locker where she took off her clothes and hung them up. Carrying a towel through to the showers, her pale reflection in a mirror caught her eye. Not for the first time, she wondered if her body could be the cause of Paul's remoteness. There were, she fancied, pinching it between thumb and forefinger, the beginnings of a spare tyre about her middle. She ran her hands upwards and cupped her small breasts in her palms. She had no wish to age into a fat Slavic *babushka*; even so, she envied what she saw as luckier women. Jasmin Winter, for example, whose neat, proud but manageable bust looked great under any clothing and who insisted blithely that it was just a matter of finding the right bra. Nina's, by contrast, all but disappeared the moment she got dressed. If she had to put on weight, for pity's sake, why couldn't it be *there*?

Showers constituted one of the perks of working in a large modern police station. She stood, lathering herself, rinsing off, until the water ran cold and the grime of the day was washed away, and she felt clean and fresh ready for obbo. You learned to find alternatives to sleep in the Job, and a long hot shower was often a good substitute when it came to recharging batteries.

She dried, dressed and gathered her things. She was unaware she was crying until her hand was pulling open the door, when she realised she couldn't see what she was doing for the tears.

Outside she collided with Lucky. Just behind Lucky was Jeff Wetherby, returned from Ealing, on a similar mission to the men's locker room next door.

'You OK?' He frowned at her.

'I'm fine,' she snapped. He recoiled. She succeeded with a struggle in keeping the tremor out of her voice, the desolation she felt from reaching him.

They watched her receding down the corridor, her strange scampering walk even more conspicuous from behind.

'Now what was all that about?'

'Who cares?' Lucky smiled, fleetingly.

Jeff was left staring at the ladies' locker room door.

Hackney's chief superintendent was away at a conference, and it took Kim and Marie some time to track down a subordinate willing to authorize the search warrant. The subordinate wouldn't sign anything without talking to Sophia first, and Sophia had disappeared into a meeting, so it was late afternoon by the time they entered the flat by the same means the squatters had used, knocking out the boarded-up front door to get at the Yale lock. The door opened, and they stepped into the dark hallway.

'Poo!' Marie said, gagging. 'Somebody forgot to flush the bog before leaving.'

Kim switched on the hall light, took a few tentative steps and said, 'Right, we'll start with the obvious. Looks like there's two bedrooms; how about I take a look at them while you do the front room and the kitchen?'

Marie pushed open a door with her fingertips and peered inside. She grimaced. 'You got x-ray vision or what?'

But Kim had already disappeared.

The front room was a tip. Cardboard boxes were stacked floor to ceiling, jostling for floor space with furniture upholstered in 1970s curry powder yellow. Washing up, fast food packaging, lager cans, dirty androgynous clothing and piles of old newspapers and magazines lay everywhere. Marie fished out a bra from under a settee. So there *had* been a woman here. She examined it. 36B. She wished they'd checked the contents of Debbie's underwear drawer more closely when they'd searched her room. Still, from the description it sounded like her size. 'Wish it was mine,' she said wistfully, out loud.

'What?' Kim's voice, from the doorway.

'Oh, nothing.' She turned. Kim was half in the room, arms folded. She looked grim.

'Found something?'

'You could say that,' Kim said. 'Come and look at this.'

Marie followed her into the main bedroom. There was no need for Kim to point out what she wanted her to see. In contrast to the front room, the only furniture was a pine double bed, with slatted head and footboards. It was relatively new, possibly secondhand. It wasn't important. The writing on the wall above it was. Dark red capitals a foot high, dried rivulets running down behind the headboard. They might have been blood, more likely red paint. Whatever the medium, the effect was the same.

The message read:

RACE TRAITOR
NIGGER LOVER
(THRALL)

The CSI was Vietnamese, mid-thirties, with lingering acne and glasses that didn't suit her. Her face behind them was defensive as she stood up and looked at Sophia Beadle. She said, 'Yep. It's blood. Don't ask me if it's human; can't tell that in the field. Could be from a cut of raw steak for all we know at this point.'

She was referring not to the writing on the wall but to a small reddish-brown streak on the mattress. The graffiti, from its chemical smell and from paintbrush bristles left behind in the daubing, had been confirmed as red gloss.

Sophia nodded. 'Get a sample over to Lambeth. Mark it urgent. If it is human and it's Debbie Clarke's, I want to know quickly.'

The CSI glared at her, affronted. 'Was about to,' she said,

and returned to her work.

Sophia turned to Kim. 'Right. What else?'

'Looks bad,' Kim said. 'I mean, she's on the run, right? All she had on her was the clothes she was wearing.'

'We assume,' Sophia reminded her. 'We don't know for certain what was in that bag of hers.'

'Yeah, but we found it. It's got her purse in and some makeup - nothing fancy, just lipstick, mascara, powder: everyday stuff. No change of clothing. Unless, like you say, she'd put it on.'

'You've double-checked the description of what she was wearing against the clothes Marie found?'

'The Clarkes are on their way to Hackney to ID them.'

'What's in the purse?'

Kim shrugged. 'Just some loose change, a condom and an Oyster card. Debit card's missing and no sign of that hundred quid. If there was anything else, it's gone and all.'

'To hinder us, if this is what it looks like,' Sophia said gravely.

'Them bits of rope...'

'Yes.' The DCI nodded. 'Until we get something back from the lab we can't go wildly speculating, but coupled with that' - she waved at the red daub - 'it looks a bit ominous. Is Marie back yet?'

'Guv.'

She was at her shoulder, right on cue.

'I've had another word with Mrs Brownlie,' she said. 'Reckons she can generally tell when the squatters are in or out, 'cause they're not that mindful of being quiet. She had a good think, but she can't remember hearing or seeing Meredith or any of the others since yesterday afternoon, and definitely not since last night when Porter called there. If it *was* Porter.'

Kim said, 'Do they wake her up at night?'

Marie shook her head. 'She's on tablets for her arthritis, says once she's had those, that's her for the night. The Rolling Stones playing live in her bedroom wouldn't wake her.'

'Her metaphor, or yours?' The three of them grinned, grateful for a moment's release from the grim business at hand. 'Now,' Sophia went on, 'I've asked the local CID to tap their informants, and we'll get all the hostels checked, see if that's where Meredith's gone.' She turned to Marie again. 'It would be helpful to have a bit more to work with. Did Mrs Brownlie mention any of the other squatters' names?'

'Aye, she did,' Marie said, pleased to have anticipated. 'There's two other males who've been here besides Meredith. One's called Dermot and she thinks the other one's Bill or Billy. She says there was also a girl turned up from time to time, didn't appear to be a permanent fixture.'

'Debbie?'

Marie shrugged.

'Descriptions?'

'In my pocket book.'

'Get them written up and circulated,' Sophia said. 'Chances are they have some sort of record. How about the neighbours the other side?'

'No luck there, I'm afraid, guv. Saw nothing, heard nothing. All they were interested in, and I quote, "Hope this means those druggie parasites are out of there for good".' A cynical smile. 'No squatters' friends there. Bring down property values, don't you know.'

'There's a laugh,' Kim said, 'round here.'

'Anything else?' Sophia said.

'I was about to go and see if there was any joy from the

house to house.'

Sophia pondered for a moment and said, 'No, leave that. The local bobbies can cover it. I don't think there's much else to be done here; you may as well be off home.'

'Guv?' Kim glanced over at the bed with difficulty. 'In view of this, should I call off the obbo? Least for tonight, seeing as the Clarkes ain't gonna be there.'

'Yes, call and let Nina know she can have an early night. It all depends on what happens when they get here as to how we proceed from then on. I take it,' she added, 'nothing more of interest on that front yet?'

Kim shook her head.

'I still agree with you: he knows more than he's telling,' Sophia said. 'But we shall see.'

We could always go to the pictures, Nina decided, looking at the office clock. It was the second thing she'd done after putting the phone down from Kim Oliver's call. The first thing had been to slam a clenched fist down on the desk and swear very loudly, an action so out of character that Jeff, the only other person still around, had almost fallen out of his chair. He was now staring at her, as aghast as if the Queen had walked into the room and asked if she could bum a smoke.

She stopped short of telling him it was PMS, doubtful he'd be convinced. Six months working in an office full of women, she supposed, you soon got to know when their periods were. She said, to stop him thinking, 'You're a film buff. What's on at the moment?'

His gaze followed hers to the clock. 'Bit late.'

'I was thinking the Warner, Purley Way.'

He nodded. 'Shows all hours there,' he informed her, infuriatingly, because she knew that. He said, 'No overtime tonight?'

'Been a development. Apparently I'm not needed.' She bent down to pick up her bag. 'Oh, well. Better make the most of it. See you.'

'Take care,' he called, making her hesitate in her step as she went out of the door, because if he said any sort of goodbye at all it was a simple grunt - 'Ta-ta' at the most. She told herself to stop being paranoid. He couldn't possibly know anything, unless Sandra had been talking, and if she had Nina would kill her.

Jeff was still bothering her as she drove home. Of course he's going to be curious, she tried to tell herself, if you suddenly start shouting obscenities and assaulting the furniture. He wasn't the sort to pry, but what if he'd overheard something? The canteen was a hotbed of gossip, seldom founded on much more than hints and hearsay, but often conveyed with little regard to volume.

Start thinking like that and she'd go cuckoo. There was no telling what Jeff, or anyone, knew that they kept to themselves. Most likely, she thought with a flash of inspiration, it was this business they were investigating. Rape naturally turned your mind to the wellbeing of those close to you. So stop being a miserable, cynical cow, Nina chided herself, and take his words in the spirit they were intended.

She looked up at the house as she parked, and her heart sank as she saw the front windows were unlit. That meant nothing either. What was the *matter* with her? It was her parents' bridge night, and although her sister had singing lessons on Fridays she was quite capable of cancelling and going out with her friends if they came up with something more interesting to do. Besides, Paul was probably in their room, at the *back* of the house, remember?

Nina, stepping indoors with a lighter heart, decided she wasn't going to take no for an answer. She didn't feel like making a full change just for the pictures but she was washed and brushed up; she might as well redo her face and present Paul with a *fait accompli*. No point looking like Dracula's dinner on top of -

She never knew what made her stop at the top of the stairs. Perhaps something among the tiny, subliminal sounds and smells of the house, alerting her to an alien presence. But there was nothing subliminal about the female giggle she distinctly heard coming from the half-open door next to theirs.

Lucia, she thought, appalled. How could she, in Mum and Dad's room? She crossed herself and edged towards the door, driven by a terrible fascination. It occurred to her that the laugh had sounded nothing like Lucia; it had been shrill, coquettish, where her sister's was a sort of strident bray.

The thought got no further before she froze, ice congealing in her gut.

Through the gap in the door she could see her parents' bed reflected in the wardrobe mirror. The bed was occupied. From beneath the sheets protruded a man's broad, bare shoulders, and on top of the shoulders rested the cropped, balding head of her husband.

Nina recoiled, as though a spider had leapt out at her. For an uncertain time she stood glued to the spot, shivering. Tearing herself free, she plummeted downstairs, snatched her jacket from the hatstand and left, slamming the door so hard she saw the porch shake. Outside it was starting to rain. At the car she stopped, hunched, unable to keep hold of the keys long enough to get in. No, she couldn't trust herself to drive.

There was a sound behind her, someone opening the front door.

She ran.

Sandra Jones, returning home from babysitting for a friend, drew her jacket up over her head and dashed from the car to her front door, shoes splashing in the deluge. Bed and cocoa, here I come, she thought happily, heaving a sigh of relief as she reached the shelter of the porch.

Neil was in the sitting room, watching Channel 4. At the sound of her entry he looked up. 'Nina's not with you, is she?'

'No. Why should Nina be with me?'

'According to Paul she's disappeared.'

'Fucking pissing down out there.' Sandra flopped into an armchair, kicking off her shoes. 'What d'you mean, disappeared?'

'Her mum rang earlier on,' Neil said. 'Apparently she'd called to say she'd be home early because her obbo had been called off.' He smiled self-mockingly, the way he always did when he managed to slip a piece of police jargon into the conversation. 'They went out to play bridge and when they got home at half ten Nina wasn't there.'

'Well, maybe another job came up. Mrs T's being daft. Nina's what, thirty? How can she go missing from her own - ?' A sudden pang lanced through her. Before she could stop herself she said, 'I *knew* it!'

'Knew what?' Neil looked blank.

She sat upright and looked across the room at her

handbag where she'd tossed it on the floor by the door. Her mobile was in there. 'I hope she's OK.'

'Changed your tune all of a sudden.'

She was about to give him a mouthful when the doorbell rang.

Nina Tyminski stood in the porch, umbrella-less and very wet. There was an expression of pain on her face, a ghastly smile that wanted to be a tragic mask.

'What the bloody hell happened to you?' Sandra said, relief disguised as annoyance.

'Been to see a film...' Nina seemed about to burst into tears. Suddenly her features set into an attitude of stern, pale composure. She said, 'Can I come in?'

Sandra stood aside.

Neil, holding a towel, met them at the top of the stairs. He handed it to his wife and said, 'I'll be in the bedroom watching telly if you want me.'

'OK,' Sandra nodded, flashing him a smile. Whatever his many failings, her Neil did have a knack for knowing when his presence was not required.

She sat Nina down in his warm, vacated chair and went to make the promised cocoa (laced with rum). When she came back Nina had wrapped the towel in a turban round her bedraggled head. She took the hot mug and allowed Sandra to take a cold hand between hers.

'Right,' Sandra said. 'What's the bastard done?'

SATURDAY

A large photo of the scene in the bedroom had been tacked to the board. The gruesome graffiti stood out in lurid colour on the freshly-printed image. Sophia had pulled three members of the team in. They all had copies of the surveillance photo of Edward Porter.

'The next door neighbour, Elizabeth Brownlie,' Sophia was saying, 'has now positively identified Porter from this photo as the man who called at Paragon Road on Thursday looking for Debbie. Even more so now, we need to locate him.' The others stole a glance at Kim, but she was looking ahead attentively. 'That is red semi-gloss,' Sophia said, pre-empting any comments. 'This is not.' Beside the photo was another, close-up, of the brown stain on the mattress. 'It's five centimetres across and soaked in to a depth of four centimetres. Lambeth have confirmed it is human blood, and the same group as Debbie Clarke's. CSI also retrieved a number of blonde hairs from the mattress which match Debbie's colour; they'll be able to confirm whether they're hers by Monday.'

'How soon before we get the DNA on the blood?' Kim asked.

'There we have a slight problem. It seems their digital profiling server has gone on the blink.' There were groans. 'As our sample's listed as a priority they've sent it to LCG in Oxfordshire for analysis, but it could take anything up to a week.'

'That's all the blood there was?' Helen Wallace said.

'That was it,' Sophia answered with a nod. 'Which fact gives us some small hope. However, we now have to bear in mind the very real possibility we could be looking at a second murder. These pictures here,' her finger swept up to the board again, 'are of twelve short lengths of nylon clothes line, found on the floor near all four legs of the bed. The lengths vary from eight to thirty-one centimetres. There are human epithelials embedded in the fibres, again, DNA as yet undetermined. As you can see, there are some knots. The rope's been cut in two ways: cleanly, with a sharp-bladed instrument like a craft knife, and elsewhere more ragged, as if someone was in a hurry or didn't have the right tool for the job.'

'The upshot,' Marie Kirtland interrupted her, 'is Debbie was tied up?'

'And then cut free.' Sophia nodded. 'All of which suggests that whoever tied her wrote that' - she tapped the picture - 'and then left her there for Meredith and the others to find.'

'How do we know Meredith didn't tie her up himself?' Larissa Stephenson piped up. She and Jeff Wetherby were also in today, but on other business.

Before Sophia could reply Kim had rounded on Lucky. 'Meredith, the committed leftie and member of an anti-racist pressure group, write "nigger lover" on a wall? Not very likely, is it?'

Lucky looked crushed. 'No, sarge.'

'Returning to the point,' Sophia interjected, 'in all likelihood that blood didn't get onto the mattress because Debbie had a nosebleed. She was injured in some way - whether fatally or not, we can't tell. The fact is Porter knew where to find her, and what he can do once he can do again. If Debbie isn't dead, she's in terrible danger. We have to get to her before Porter does. Or better still, get to Porter.'

Subdued muttering suggested her audience thought this was easier said than done.

'NCIS have come up with a likely list of far right gorillas for us to harass,' she said. 'As we all know, these political encounters can go pear-shaped quite quickly, so we need to be extra careful. In case you were wondering, this is why I asked both the sergeants to give up part of their weekend. And I've arranged some TSG backup in case things get ugly.'

'Personal bodyguards,' Marie quipped.

'One more thing,' Sophia said. 'I'm assured Porter had no idea the Flying Squad were monitoring him. Hopefully he's got no reason to think we're on his tail either. Again, tread carefully. If he gets a whiff of us he's likely to go to ground so deep we'll never dig him out again. Remember, assume Debbie's alive, and don't endanger her.'

'Bog all chance of that,' Kim muttered to Marie a few moments later as they left the room.

'What d'you mean?'

'You know like sometimes you walk onto a crime scene and you get a sort of vibe from it?'

Marie nodded.

'I did history A Level,' Kim said, 'and in the Middle Ages when they caught a traitor, after they executed him they used to stick his head on a pole on London Bridge as a warning to others.'

'Charming.'

'That room,' Kim said simply, 'felt like that.'

It was a surprise to meet Nina Tyminski coming in through the back door as they were on their way out. She looked tired, and had on a blue sweatshirt Kim seemed to remember Sandra wearing on occasion. She stopped Kim with a hand on her arm. 'What happened about Andrew Clarke?'

'Clothes are Debbie's,' Kim said.

'No, I mean the obbo. Is it back on?'

'My turn tonight,' Kim said, trying to be magnanimous.

'I don't mind,' Nina said. 'Fair's fair. Why should I get off?'

'OK, if you're that keen.' Kim grinned. 'One free evening enough for you, yeah?'

'Does *everybody* know?'

Kim was not prepared for being yelled at, nor for the look of undisguised rage that contorted Nina's face. Involuntarily, she took a step back. Nina pushed past and scuttled off at top speed. Perplexed, Kim looked at Marie.

'I'm saying nothing,' Marie said.

Kim's mobile rang. She had a brief conversation and then looked up at Marie. 'Change of plan,' she said. 'You're gonna be riding shotgun with Sophia today.'

'Oh, goody. How come?'

'She's just had Charing Cross on the blower.' Kim smiled. 'Guess what the cat dragged in?'

Philip Meredith had been arrested in Covent Garden the previous evening for being drunk and disorderly. When brought to Charing Cross police station he'd been forthcoming on only two points: his name, and his being of no fixed abode. So forthcoming about his name had he been that he'd attracted the attention of a DC Carter, who was next in the queue with his prisoner, and who read his bulletins assiduously. Meredith became less voluble about his homelessness when confronted with fingerprints taken from a flat in Paragon Road, E8, which matched his own. Told the significance of this fact, he'd since been very quiet; to quote the custody sergeant, pacing his cell so frequently the walls were getting dizzy.

His appearance in the interview room made Sophia and Marie groan inwardly. He was as white as a fresh roll of toilet paper but evidently thought he should have been born in Montego Bay. Gorgonlike red-blond dreads seethed out from beneath a red, yellow and green knitted hat that owed less to religious adherence than a desire to keep warm. There was a Bob Marley tattoo on the inside of his left forearm. He'd evidently made full use of police hospitality and gave off a strong smell of carbolic soap. Seeing two women, his eyes gleamed in anticipation of an easy ride. 'Oh, what's this?'

'Sit down.' Carter pointed to a chair. Meredith sat.

'Morning, Mr Meredith,' Sophia said, expressionless. 'I'm DCI Beadle, this is DC Kirtland. We're from the Special Crime Unit at Croydon.'

'Come a long way to fit me up,' Meredith said. Glancing at the recorder, he added, 'You want to turn that thing on? I've got things to say.'

'Knock it off, Philip,' Carter said wearily.

'I've been in here eleven hours and twelve minutes,' Meredith said, without any apparent frame of reference. 'Now you either charge me or I walk out of here and talk to a solicitor about unlawful detention.'

'You didn't seem too keen to talk to one last night, when you had a nice warm cell to kip in,' Carter remarked.

'That was then.'

Sophia said, 'I'd like to talk to you about Debbie Clarke.'

'Who?'

'A missing witness to a serious crime.'

'What makes you think I know anything?'

'She was last seen at the squat in Hackney where your prints were found.'

Meredith pressed his lips together. He had a plaster on his left hand at the base of the index finger. It was coming unstuck and he was toying with it, as if unsure whether to peel it off or try to stick it back down.

'You're quite welcome to have a solicitor present if you want one.'

'Well, we'll see about that, won't we, lady?' he said. If it was meant to sound ominous, they were unmoved.

'We've been hearing good things about you,' Sophia said. 'Helping the old lady next door with her washing. She was most grateful.'

'I'm a real saint.'

'Mrs Brownlie, isn't it? The neighbour?'

'If that's what she told you.'

'She also told us Debbie turned up there last Tuesday evening, and that you let her in.'

'Now why would I let a complete stranger in?'

'No stranger, Philip.' Sophia was determined that the more obstinate Meredith became, the less she was going to stand for it. 'She's a member of an activist organization called Justice for Mark Watkins. So are you. We understand you get on quite well.'

'Who says?'

'Luke Benton.' Her china blue eyes studied him. 'Does that name mean anything to you?'

He shrugged.

'Don't keep up with the news, Philip?'

'Yeah, well,' he snapped, 'you can't usually hear much when you're watching through the window outside Curry's.'

'What about Billy Scofield?'

'Who?'

'Come on, Philip. You're pals. You've been nicked together about fifteen times. You're well known. Plus the fact his prints were at the squat as well.'

'You're talking horse shit, lady. Billy's cool.'

'Why? Because he wouldn't be seen dead helping us?' Giving him no time to react, she leaned forward. 'Time to stop messing about, Philip. The act isn't impressing anyone.'

'If you're gonna frame me for killing this Debbie what's her name - '

'Did you?'

'Fucking no.'

'Then we won't put you in the frame.'

'What else do I get, lady?'

'Indulgence.' And if he called her lady once more, she decided, he was risking even that.

'Pardon?'

'Who told you Debbie Clarke was dead?'

'You did.'

'No, I said she was missing.'

Phil Meredith was suddenly a different person, a contrite person. 'Look, I didn't kill her.'

'What *did* you do?'

'Nothing.'

'Nothing?'

'No.'

'No, you did nothing or no, you're not telling the truth?'

'I didn't kill no-one. Neither did Billy or Jayne or anyone else who was at the squat.'

She watched him. He looked as if he were about to suffocate.

'I think,' she said, 'before going any further, we could all do with a cuppa. Philip?'

He peered at her hopefully, but he wasn't off the hook. He slumped and nodded. Sophia turned to Marie, who resisted the urge to roll her eyes heavenwards.

'I'll show you where the canteen is,' DC Carter said, getting up with her.

Sophia let Meredith get his breath back. 'OK, Philip,' she said, 'time to indulge you. I'm not going to ask you yet about your relationship with Debbie, what you got her to do for you or whether you were giving her one. I'm going to tell you what I think happened. I think she turned up at the squat on Tuesday looking for sanctuary. I think you took her in, told her to keep her head down and went about your normal business. You, and Billy, and this Jayne, went out as usual doing whatever it is you do. Leaving Debbie alone in the flat.' As she talked, she picked up her bag and took from it a photograph of the bedroom at Paragon Road as Kim and Marie had found it. 'I think you came back on Thursday night or yesterday morning to this.'

She let him study the scene, which although constrained by the dimensions of the photo had as strong an impact as the real thing.

'In a nutshell,' she went on, 'I think the rest of the story is that you panicked, decamped *en masse* and split up. I doubt you even know where Billy and Jayne are at the moment.'

Meredith handed the photo back and shook his head.

'Which brings me to the one gap in my story,' Sophia said. 'We know Debbie was at the squat. The unanswered question is whether she was *still* there when you came back.'

'She wasn't.'

'So what made you all leave in such a hurry?'

'Wouldn't you?' He pointed wildly at the photo. 'Ratty old squat, no-one's supposed to know you're there?'

'Billy Scofield's black, isn't he?'

'Mixed race. What's that got to do with it?'

'Well, a squat isn't the most difficult place to break into, is it? Say if a bunch of racist yobbos from the estate decide to drop by and leave their calling card, what's it to you?'

'Yeah, but that and the blood - '

'It's a *dribble*,' she cut across him. 'You can't be squeamish, surely, not with what you see on the streets every day.'

He looked puzzled, as if this wasn't what he'd expected her to say. He shrugged. 'It was enough.'

The door opened and DC Carter returned, alone. He wore a hangdog expression which suggested, in Sophia's jaundiced experience, that he'd tried it on with Marie and been rebuffed.

'All right, Philip. What did Debbie tell you?'

Meredith picked at his plaster for a moment, composing his words. 'I joined Justice for Mark Watkins about a year ago.'

'Meaning you infiltrated them?'

'Yeah, all right, *Frau Kapitän*,' he said acidly. 'Debbie started coming with this black kid a few weeks after. Wasn't shy about sharing her opinions, sounded promising.'

'As a recruit?'

This time he ignored her cynical interpretation. 'I got talking to her. She wanted to do something concrete. Said she could get in with the Nazis, she'd been following some of their forums online and she knew a few names she could drop. I talked to my lot and they reckoned they could use her as an infiltrator.' He paused, smirking, pleased at having thrown the word back at his interrogator. 'So that's what they did. Took her, trained her up, got her enrolled as a junior member of the BNP.'

'And what happened?'

'She went along to their meetings, joined their discussion boards, kept her ear to the ground, communicated what she heard back to me.'

Sophia stared at him, her expression sphinxlike. It evidently didn't matter to Meredith or his comrades that sooner or later someone on the far right was going to tumble to it being a bit odd one of their youths being openly involved with an anti-racist group and going out with a black man whose family she babysat for.

She said, 'Did you have any idea what was going on before she turned up at the squat?'

'No.'

'Nothing particular she said made you think she might be in trouble?'

'Nope.'

'So that was the first you knew of it?'

'That's right.'

'What did she tell you?'

'Just asked could she hole up there.'

'Did she say why?'

'She was in a right old state. Her boyfriend - '

'Luke Benton.'

'Yeah, the one whose brother she babysits. This Nazi'd told her to help him firebomb their house. She tried to get out of it, but she didn't know how without giving herself away. In the end, apparently, he was waiting outside in a van with some other bloke when she brought the kid home.'

That was how they'd got the cross onto the lawn, Sophia thought. Simple as that. A thumping great van no-one had seen. Three cheers for Neighbourhood Watch. She exchanged a glance with Marie, who returned at that moment with a tray bearing four teas in paper cups.

'He gave her these devices,' Meredith went on, 'right in front of the kid, if you please. All rigged up and ready to blow. Once she left she was supposed to give it five minutes, then ring Mrs Benton from a payphone and warn her to get out. Course by then the fire'd already started. Then cop cars started blaring everywhere, she got spooked and legged it.'

'So you reckon she swallowed it?' DC Carter put in scornfully. 'This crap about the Bentons?'

'Immigrant bashing, wasn't it? Fashionable. People like the BNP, why wouldn't they want to do something like that?'

'Come on, Phil,' Carter insisted. 'A blind moron wouldn't fall for it. All the black families in London, target just happens to be her boyfriend's mum? She'd be off out of it like a shot.'

'She's fucking sixteen!' Meredith snapped. 'How's she supposed to know what to do?'

Sophia, with a warning glance at Carter not to interrupt again – though she had to admit he had a point – passed Meredith two sugar sachets and watched him stir them into his tea. 'All right, Philip,' she said, the stern edge gone suddenly from her voice. 'We've established she took refuge with you. What then?'

'When?'

'While she was at the squat. Any strangers hanging

around? Suspicious happenings?'

'It's an East End estate,' Meredith said. 'How bloody suspicious d'you want?' Her blue eyes held his gaze. He gave in. He said, 'Nothing happened that I know of.'

'Until this.' She tapped the photograph.

He thought carefully and shrugged. 'Pretty much what you said. Debbie stayed in the front room watching DVDs. Then we came back and found that stuff.'

'But no Debbie?'

'She was gone.'

'You checked everywhere?'

He glared. 'Bet *you* fucking did.'

'We found her clothes.'

'Clothes, but no Debbie.' He nodded grimly. 'Yeah, that's what made me finally brick it. I thought fuck, I'm not staying round here. Packed up my stuff and legged it.'

'You didn't bother to warn Billy and Jayne?'

'Fuck, no.' Meredith gave her a sarcastic leer. 'I presume they got the message.'

'When was this?'

'When I got back? About half seven.'

'Debbie's other things,' Marie interrupted. 'Were any of them gone?'

'I didn't stop to take a fucking inventory.'

'But you did stop to go through her purse and help yourself to her cashpoint card?'

'No comment.'

'Right.' Sophia opened her notebook. 'These friends of yours. We'll need to try and track them down if we can.'

'Why?'

'Debbie might have found out where they are, be with them.'

'No chance.'

'Billy Scofield we know. This Jayne, what's her surname?'

'Mansfield.'

She looked at him.

'Seriously,' Meredith said, and turned his attention back to the plaster, which now seemed even less willing to continue adhering to his hand.

'And Dermot?'

He looked genuinely surprised. 'He ain't been around for weeks. Made up with his parents, buggered off back home to Manchester.'

'Surname?' Sophia was careful to convey her irritation at having to prompt him again.

'McCormack.'

Out of the corner of her eye she saw Marie writing it down. 'Anything else you want to tell me?'

'Not particularly. Such as?'

'That plaster. Cut yourself, did you?'

'Broken bottle. Skipping.'

'Must have bled quite a lot.'

'A bit, yeah.' He looked suffocated again.

'Where was this skip?'

'Can't remember.'

'Or maybe you got the injury some other way. Let's say, for example, cutting free a body tied to a bed?'

'No comment,' Meredith said, and the only other thing he said after that was 'yes' when Sophia asked him if he would consent to them taking a cheek swab.

'Next right,' Larissa Stephenson said, slipping the street atlas back onto the dashboard shelf. 'Remind me why we're here again.'

Jeff Wetherby fought an irrational disappointment. Lucky's directions had steered them through the centre of Rye, out onto the Hastings road. Remembering a happy family holiday here long ago, he stole a wistful glance to where a windmill stood at the edge of low, flat pastureland that, centuries before, had been under the sea. Next time he had a free day, and if ever he could persuade some pleasant company, he must find time to revisit properly this beautiful corner of Sussex.

Not that Lucky wasn't good company, but they had a job to do and anyway, she wasn't who he had in mind. But he liked her enthusiasm, her earnest attentiveness, her effortless ability to fill gaps in conversation when he, taciturn, was at a loss. She lacked the cold vanity so often associated with the gift of exquisite beauty.

'That sergeant I went to see yesterday at Ealing,' he told her. 'One of his mates - a DS Nish - overheard us talking and came up with a case that might fit, an unsolved rape when he was at Sutton five years ago. Unfortunately he was only on the periphery, and the DI in charge has since died. Which leaves us with the case file - I trust you found time to read it - and an interview with the victim, who now lives down here and who unlike most of the other women is actually willing to talk to us.' He'd found the street, and was now cruising past a row of neat, new yellow brick houses with white wooden shutters.

'Number 27,' Lucky said, pointing.

Jeff parked in front of an open lawn with carefully tended flowerbeds and a young apple tree. They crammed into a tiny enclosed porch and rang the bell. A man answered. He had on a green cardigan over a grubby blue Fred Perry shirt and jeans. 'Mr Beckett?' Jeff said, showing his warrant card. 'Hello. We're from Croydon police. To talk to your wife.'

'Oh, yes.' The man frowned, then smiled politely and stepped back. 'Come in. She said she was expecting you. Do please excuse the attire,' he added, spreading his arms self-consciously. 'Working from home today.'

They stepped into the cool, quiet hall of a home as immaculately tidy as only other people's houses ever are. A child gate barred the way upstairs, and through a half-open door they glimpsed a box of brightly-coloured toys. The room Mr Beckett led them into was dominated by a Yamaha grand piano in gleaming ebony, making it seem tiny. There were music stands, a bookcase filled with loose and bound sheet music and tuition books, and more music spread crisply across the furniture. A cello case stood propped in a corner. On the walls were framed certificates and photographs of a pretty, smiling girl with long brown hair.

The subject of the photographs sat at a table between the piano and the French windows, immersed in writing what appeared to be a score. Jeff noticed she was several years older than the most recent of the photographs. She didn't react to their entrance until her husband called her name, when she nodded and tilted her head to one side, as though listening to something only she could hear. She jotted on the stave paper, laid down her pen and looked up.

Jeff said, 'Good afternoon, Mrs Beckett. I'm Jeff Wetherby, this is Luck- Sorry, er... PC Stephenson.'

'Larissa,' Lucky said, smiling nervously. Jeff stole an embarrassed glance at her.

Miranda Beckett, *née* Hargreaves, turned to face them, sliding towards the edge of her chair. Her husband hovered. She said, 'Do you mind if we talk in here? I feel more relaxed surrounded by music.'

'Whatever's most comfortable,' Jeff said.

'Do find something to sit on.' She waved a long, willowy arm. 'There are some chairs under that lot somewhere.'

Shifting some of the music, Jeff unearthed one and carried it over to the table. Lucky took the piano stool.

'Thanks for agreeing to talk to us, Mrs Beckett. It must be the last thing you want to recall.'

'I'll manage,' she said, scrutinising Jeff with hazel eyes. 'Though I would have expected another female officer.'

He smiled apologetically.

Mr Beckett was still hovering. He said, 'Would you like me to stay, darling?'

'Yes, please.' She flashed him a desperate smile. 'Only do you mind fetching tea for us first? I'm sure the officers must be a bit parched after the drive down.'

'Sure.' Mr Beckett nodded and went out.

'Nice feller,' Jeff chatted. 'How long you been married?'

His wife smiled proudly. 'Three years.'

'Got kids, I see.'

'Our daughter,' she said. 'Joely. She's fourteen months. Ewan just put her down for her nap, so your timing's perfect.'

Jeff and Lucky smiled.

'So,' Miranda Beckett said, with a sigh that trembled faintly. 'What can I tell you?'

'Would you prefer to wait till your husband comes back?' Lucky asked.

Mrs Beckett shook her head. 'Let's get on with it.'

Jeff said, 'We'd like to go back with you over the night of - '

She interrupted him. 'The night I was raped.'

'If you can.' His face betrayed nothing except - he hoped - reassurance. 'Normally we wouldn't trouble you after all this time, as our boss explained on the phone, but the circumstances are exceptional.'

'I understand. You think they might have... other women.'

He opened his briefcase and took out the faded copy of Miranda Hargreaves's witness statement. He scowled at it. 'You were at home in the shared house where you were living...'

'2 Langley Park Road,' Mrs Beckett said, swallowing hard.

'...when you heard noises in the vacant room next to yours.'

'Yes,' she said. 'Look, do you mind if I try and tell it in my own words? In therapy they teach you that; if you can talk about what happened to you it it's one stage of the battle won.'

Jeff opened his mouth, but it was Lucky who said, rather loudly he thought, 'No. Please go ahead.' He glared at her, but neither she nor Mrs Beckett noticed.

'It was late,' Mrs Beckett said. 'I was in my room reading. That room was empty at the time, at least as far as I knew. I just assumed it had been let and they were moving in.'

Lucky said, puzzled, 'In your statement you said it was half past ten at night.'

'You've obviously never lived in a house share,' Mrs Beckett smiled. 'People move in and out at all sorts of ungodly hours.' Her expression clouded. 'I say it was the next room; really it was the same, one big room, but there was a folding wooden partition dividing it in two. Anyway, they... they tried to get it open. I could hear them moving furniture out of the way and then they started rattling it.' She hugged herself and began rubbing her upper arms, although it wasn't cold. 'Stupid of me, I called out that this was a private room on the other side, and they stopped.'

'Stopped?'

Mrs Beckett took a breath. 'For a while. Then I could hear them whispering.'

'There were two of them?' Jeff said.

'I was frightened, but I didn't cry out because I didn't know if anyone else was home. One of them went out into the hall and started banging on my door. I'd locked it. But... um...'

For a moment it seemed she couldn't go on. Lucky stirred as if to rise. The door opened and Mr Beckett reappeared with tea, milk and sugar on a tray, which he set down on the table. From an unnoticed corner by the French windows he extracted a stool and sat on it beside his wife.

'Thanks. Larissa,' Jeff said, motioning to the tea. 'Could you...?'

Nodding, Lucky got up and poured Miranda Beckett a cup. The lid of the pot rattled. Belatedly, Mr Beckett recovered what he called 'my manners' and served tea to Lucky, Jeff and himself. 'Everything OK, darling?' he murmured to his wife, sitting down again and taking her hand.

Jeff said, 'Are you all right to go on, Mrs Beckett?'

She nodded jerkily. 'I've forgotten where...'

'The banging on your door,' he reminded her gently, trying to make it sound as neutral as possible.

'Yes.' She nodded again. 'They stopped. The other... person... had got the divider part way open - about a foot - and called him back. Then they both squeezed through.'

'Were you doing anything in the meantime?' Lucky asked.

'Trying to find my key to unlock the door and get out of there,' Mrs Beckett retorted, as if this were obvious. 'But I couldn't get my bag open, I was too panicky. Then they were on me.' She crowded close to her husband, who gave her hand a reassuring squeeze.

Jeff nodded carefully and waited.

'Two of them, yes,' she said, belatedly answering his earlier question. 'One grabbed hold of me and pinned my arms while the other one shone his torch around.'

'It was dark?' Lucky asked.

'Yes.'

'Only that was one of the things we weren't clear about.'

'I had the light on, but one of them turned it off as soon as he was in the room. Anyway - '

Lucky was about to ask another question, but her eye caught Jeff's warning glance and she subsided.

Mrs Beckett said urgently, 'I struggled. Don't think I didn't struggle, scream. It didn't do any good. The other one, the one with the torch, he came and took over, it was one of those heavy rubber torches, and he just hit me with it till I stopped. Then he threw me on the bed and said something like, "That's her sorted. She's all yours."' A sob escaped her and her husband, his eyes sharing some of her pain and anger, put his arms round her. She blinked, deliberately, and said, 'He was egging the other one on - the man who'd grabbed me first. I don't think he wanted to... he was hesitating. His friend kept on at him - he was saying, "Go on, it's easy," and getting him to...' She had to stop again, blushing a terrible scarlet. She rummaged on the table for a box of tissues half-hidden under some blank stave paper, grabbed a handful and covered her face, dabbing away tears. Jeff waited. Finally she looked up again, staring past him into space. 'Getting him to take my... clothes off.' She all but swallowed the words.

'It's OK,' her husband whispered.

'The first man still wouldn't do anything,' she went on. 'Until the other one got fed up and got me to tell him where my key was. He went out of the room, I assume to look for more pickings.' She laughed bitterly. 'Some chance, in a place like that.'

Jeff nodded neutrally.

'Well, apparently all the first man was waiting for was no-one watching him,' Miranda Beckett continued, anger fighting now through the tears. 'Because *that's* when he did it. Raped me.'

'Just him on his own?' Jeff asked.

'Just him,' she snarled back, 'would have been enough.' She turned to Lucky, who at once looked down. 'The other one came back just as he was... ejaculating.' The word was bitten off again. 'He hit the roof. I thought he was going to kill his friend - *and* me. He yelled out, "You stupid bastard - don't you know they can get your DNA from that. It's just like a fingerprint." The first... He said, "I thought you wanted me to." The other man said, and I remember this very, very vividly, "Stick anything you like up her, but not your knob." I'll tell you why I remember it vividly, shall I?'

She glared at Jeff, who again nodded.

'I remember it,' she said, crying without restraint now, 'because he found my flute and...'

This time, it seemed, she really couldn't go on. There was no need. Jeff and Lucky waited while Miranda Beckett fought back the nausea, and wept, doubled up, while her husband clasped her heaving shoulders helplessly.

When she'd recovered, Jeff levelled his eyes at her.

'Believe me,' he said, 'we wouldn't've bothered you with this again if we didn't think it was totally necessary.'

'I wouldn't wish what happened to me on my worst enemy,' she said. 'If it helps you catch them, even after so long...'

'I hope so,' he agreed. 'D'you mind if I ask you one or two more questions? Not intimate,' he added hastily, seeing her blanch.

'Ask away.' She poured herself more tea with unsteady hands.

'Now you probably remember helping a police artist come up with some sketches.'

'I told the detectives at the time I wasn't sure. I only caught a glimpse of their faces for a moment before the light went off.' She set her tea down quickly as she realised what he was saying. 'You want me to take another look, don't you?'

As he'd feared, it was a pointless exercise. Her freely admitted flight of imagination bore even less resemblance to her darkened memories, five years later. He moved on. 'You were quite clear on a couple of points. The second man - the one who acted like he was in charge, the one who went out of the room: you told DI Arnold he was tall?'

'Very tall,' she agreed, 'and thin.'

He nodded. 'And both quite young, you reckoned?'

'Oh, yes,' she said bitterly. 'Younger than me. Still at school, I wouldn't be surprised.'

'Sixteen, seventeen...?'

'If that.'

'Couple of other things,' Jeff said, making a note. 'I know this is hard for you. In your statement you never mentioned the second man assaulting you sexually. Now I can appreciate why you didn't. But can you tell me, did they take the flute with them when they left?'

Mrs Beckett nodded and lowered her head, ineffably sad. Jeff saw Lucky swallow, and he understood why. The flute had been Miranda Hargreaves's most cherished possession.

'Can you tell us a bit about it?'

'I inherited it from my gran. It was very valuable... a Böhm eight-key ivory flute, 1866.'

'Many of those about?'

'About fifty in the whole world.'

'How much was it insured for?'

'Ten thousand,' she said. 'And I suspect even that was low. Not that it mattered. I never bought another.'

'Understandable,' Jeff said. He waited for a beat, fighting his own feeling of sickness at what had been done to this woman, what he was doing to her all over again. He said, 'One more thing, and then we'll not outstay our welcome any longer. In the report it says the intruders got in through a ground floor window. Can you remember what sort of window it was?'

'What do you mean, what sort of...?'

'Was it double glazed, or - ?'

'In that place? You must be joking. No, it was an ordinary, old-fashioned front room window, probably the original one.'

'How did it open?' He mimed something.

'That's it,' she said, pointing. 'A sash window.'

Lucky waited until they were back in the car before voicing her thoughts.

'The accomplice,' she said.

'*An* accomplice,' Jeff argued. 'She said specifically they were both kids. In Denise Cole's case the second man was older. Also, he seemed to be the one in charge. This time it was very much other way round.'

'Same person, though?' Lucky said. 'You reckon?'

'Oh, aye,' he nodded, slowing for the turn into the main road. 'I had me doubts before, but there's the MO - sash window, lights extinguished - and now we know about the flute. It's our boy.'

'Right,' she agreed absently. 'Jeff?'

'Mmm?'

'The first guy: the, erm...'

'Rapist.'

'Yeah. Did he use a condom or something?'

'FME's report didn't mention one.'

'Then wouldn't his DNA be on file? If he's a burglar there's every chance he's got a club number, so we might be able to...' She tailed off. Jeff was shaking his head.

'Check the date of the crime report against the date in Miranda Hargreaves's statement.'

She looked puzzled.

'She didn't report it for two days,' he said. 'By then any medical evidence was up the Swannee.'

Beneath her cinnamon skin it was hard to tell if Lucky was blushing, but her head went down and she said, 'Oh, shit.'

'Easy mistake to make,' Jeff smiled. 'Don't worry. Done it myself enough times.'

'Yeah?'

'Aye.' He stared fixedly at the road ahead. Actually he'd made a similar error over dates once, and only once, and it had almost resulted in a hit and run driver getting a free alibi. The bollocking his DI of the time had given him had ensured his unflagging thoroughness in the matter of witness statements ever since. A flash of guilt passed through him for his failure to let rip now, but Lucky deserved a break, and anyway she was keen enough without needing to be bludgeoned into learning this particular lesson.

He said, 'We need to trace that flute.'

'It was five years ago,' she said, astonished. 'How are we supposed to - ?'

'What use'd a couple of burglars have for an antique flute?' he declared with certainty. 'They'll've sold it on or pawned it. Prepare yourself for several hundred pointless phone calls once we get back to the nick.'

They drove on in silence for a while.

'Seems to've put it behind her, though,' Lucky said suddenly, brightly.

'Mrs Beckett?'

'Married, well enough off by the look of it, got a family. House in the country. All since it happened. She's picked up her life.'

'Aye, she has.'

'But?' She'd detected the dubious note in his voice.

'You saw how hard it was for her to talk about it, even after all this time. It'll never not be there. In her case I think she's lucky. Her husband's understanding and supportive, and like she said counselling's helped.' He sighed. Outside the sky had turned warship grey, pregnant with rain. 'Rape gets women different ways. Some come to terms; others, it destroys them and those around them. What you can't do is forget it ever happened.'

'In your experience, at least?' She spoke harshly, seeming to resent him, as a man, making such prognoses.

'Be a remarkable woman who could,' he said, emphasising his experience with a stern glance.

'I - ' She stopped. She frowned and said, 'Oh.'

He waited, but Lucky had lapsed into a cowed silence. The outskirts of Rye gave way to muddy fields. Raindrops mushroomed on the glass. Jeff flipped on the wipers and put his foot down.

Where was he?

The question rattled endlessly around the recesses of Nina's mind like the clickings of bats in a cave. Again she took the mobile phone from her bag to make sure it was on. She knew it was. She'd called Sandra earlier, to see if Paul had rung or turned up there. He hadn't, Sandra had insisted, and there was no message on the machine.

It was stupid. She should be glad. He'd be sitting at home feeling like dog shit, unable to pluck up the courage to call. He'd be sweating, and serve him right. Except that perhaps he wasn't. Perhaps he was unrepentant, out with that... whoever it was; knowing her finding out gave him an excuse to be away.

Why? came the echo. Is it me? Marriage didn't go with the Job. She should have packed it in a long time ago, and it wasn't as if the income was vital, not with Mum and Dad being so... She needn't have volunteered for this pointless exercise, come to that, she decided, thumping the empty seat beside her with the palm of her hand. If she hadn't, Paul wouldn't have brought back that... bitch, and she'd never have known.

Why was she punishing herself? Because this *was* pointless. Even more so now after the information Meredith had provided. She frowned across at the house. Half past nine and still nothing. It looked as if Kim's excursion on Wednesday was all the excitement they were going to get.

Perversely, the front door opened just as she'd resigned herself to this. Nina lowered her head, although she knew she couldn't possibly be seen at this distance. Minus his coat, Andrew Clarke stepped out into the street and looked both ways. He seemed agitated.

Then his gaze settled squarely on the Mini and he crossed the road.

'Shit!'

As if everything else wasn't fucked up, now she'd blown the obbo as well. Helplessly she opened the window, sat and braced herself for the earful which, from Kim and Marie's accounts of the man, she was sure would come.

'Officer?'

It was a diffident voice and she turned her head in surprise. Andrew Clarke was bending down to the window. She nodded.

'I was wondering, could you come with me, please?'

'Sir,' Nina said, 'I'm here on the authority of - '

'I need your advice. I don't know what to do.'

She stared at him, wary.

He sighed and a trace of belligerence crept into his voice. 'Look, my wife's at home. There's nothing for you to worry about.'

'I'd better ring my guv'nor,' Nina said. Mr Clarke nodded and wandered a few steps down the pavement while she called Sophia and left a message. Then, having surreptitiously transferred a can of CS spray from the glovebox to her jacket pocket, she got out and followed him into the house.

Charlotte Clarke was waiting nervously on her feet in the living room. Nina shook hands with her curtly. 'DC Tyminski,' she said. 'Perhaps you'd better tell me what this is about.'

'Sorry to trouble you,' Mrs Clarke said. 'It's this.' She gestured to a low table with a landline phone, an answering machine and three empty coffee mugs on it. She pressed a button. There was a bleep and then a man's voice, sharp and tinny.

'*You'll be pleased to know, Andrew, that I've finally tracked Deborah down,*' the voice said. '*She's been a very silly girl, and she knows that, but she is truly sorry. If you'd care to wait in Thornton Heath, at the southbound bus stop on the corner of London Road and Warwick Road, at about ten past midnight, you can pick her up there.'Bye.'*

In the silence that followed, Nina looked from Andrew Clarke to his wife.

'When did you play the message back?' she asked.

'The call came in about ten minutes ago,' Charlotte Clarke said.

'Why didn't you answer it?'

'He rang earlier and told us not to.'

'Said if he'd talked to one of us live,' Andrew Clarke added, 'we could have strung him along long enough for a trace. So he told us to keep the machine on and wait for him to call.'

'You sound like you know him,' Nina said.

Silence.

'What's his name?'

'Edward Porter,' Andrew Clarke said.

'Should've guessed.' Kim Oliver shoved her hands deeper inside her jacket pockets and looked, once again, both ways along London Road, on a Saturday night busy even at this late hour. 'No wonder we didn't feel right about him.' She glanced across the road to where Andrew Clarke stood under the bus shelter with Sophia.

'Yeah,' Nina said. 'Both in Combat 18 in the nineties. Marches and rallies, football hooliganism with the Chelsea Headhunters. Would you believe he actually *asked* Porter to look for Debbie?'

'You're joking.'

'No.'

'Hey, so we've got an address?'

'No such luck.' Nina shivered in the breeze. 'He got in touch through another old C18 pal.'

'Their fucking network,' Kim said.

'Yeah.'

Kim looked at her watch. 'Nothing's happening.'

'Night bus due in a few minutes,' Nina said. 'That's if a bus is what we're expecting. Just because he said a bus stop.'

Across the road, Sophia Beadle and Andrew Clarke watched in tense silence as it hove into view round a bend in the distance, stopped for some vociferously tipsy teenagers at a pelican crossing, and finally lumbered up to the stop.

'I don't see her,' Andrew Clarke fretted. Sophia, trying to conceal her own anxiety, laid a reassuring hand on his arm.

The rear doors opened. The only person standing inside was a youth of around eighteen, who was talking over his shoulder to some others spread around seats on the lower deck. He climbed down to the bottom step and leaned out. 'You Andrew Clarke?'

Mr Clarke started and said, 'Yes.'

The youth held out a small buff envelope. Andrew Clarke took it and the boy disappeared back inside the bus, whereupon the door closed and it pulled away.

'Mr Clarke,' Sophia said.

Obediently, he stopped his nervous fiddling and put the envelope into her outstretched hand, which had a latex glove on it. She clasped the edges between her fingertips and slit open the flap with a penknife. She used a tissue to extract the contents. Out of the corner of her eye she could see Kim and Nina crossing the road in defiance of the moving traffic. Her frown deepened as she registered the contents of the envelope.

'What is that?' Andrew Clarke demanded in a high-pitched voice, sensing something was wrong. 'I've a right to know.'

'Mr Clarke,' Sophia began, blue eyes seeming a cold grey under the shelter lights, 'I wouldn't advise - '

But, more agitated than ever, he snatched it and looked down. His eyes narrowed, he uttered a strange choking sound and dropped it. Tight-lipped, knowing any trace evidence was now very likely useless, Sophia picked it up and showed it to Kim. Nina crowded over their shoulders.

The thing in the Polaroid photograph was barely recognisable as human. The body appeared to be naked, but there was so much blood it was impossible to be certain. Kim recognised the bed straight away, even without the hateful words painted on the wall. Across the torso and limbs were scores of thick, dark cuts made as if by the slashing of a knife. One arm lay across the midriff, perhaps where it had been lifted in an attempt to ward off blows. The groin, in a mockery of modesty, was covered by a copy of Thursday's *Evening Standard*. Tarpaulin sheeting kept the mess off the mattress. Some of it must have dripped.

'Debbie?' Nina asked in a strangled voice.

'I dunno.' Kim handed her the photo and walked off, shoulders hunched. Nina peered at it. The face was that of a young blonde woman. She'd seen photos, but any doubt as to her identity was dispelled by the sight of Andrew Clarke bent double on the bus shelter seat, face in hands, Sophia next to him with an arm round his shoulders; Kim, leaning against the stop staring at them, unable to bring herself to offer comfort to the grieving father.

WEEK TWO
MONDAY

A busy and frustrating Sunday had brought Sophia, Kim and Nina, at least two of them resentful for the loss of their weekend, little further forward. They'd spoken to Andrew Clarke's C18 friend; he'd been able to tell them that he occasionally ran into Edward Porter but had no idea where he might be now. The contact information he'd given Clarke was an email address which, to their utter lack of surprise, was from a web-based mail service, untraceable.

They'd wanted to talk to Philip Meredith again but Charing Cross, understandably, felt they had better things to do than drag homeless drunks in front of a magistrate, and had released him wth a caution soon after his interview with Sophia.

The first item of business at Monday morning's office meeting was the distribution of blown-up prints of the gruesome Polaroid. Most of the team looked at their copies in grim silence. It was as they'd feared, and the fact that Meredith didn't seem to have added much new was what depressed them most. Nina Tyminski was the first with her hand up.

'This does support his story, doesn't it, guv?' she said. 'When he says there was nobody there when he showed up?'

'Doesn't get us any closer to finding Porter or Debbie though,' Marie pointed out.

'Perhaps not.' Sophia looked at them both. 'We did, however, get some information from Sean Ryder, the mutual friend. He lives in Leatherhead and he told us he runs into Porter in pubs around there occasionally. I think there's a good chance,' she went on, amid stirrings, a sense that they might finally be getting somewhere, 'Porter's gone to ground somewhere in that area. I don't for a moment suppose he's on it, but Kim, if you could get onto Surrey County Council and get them to do a voter's list check for him. And I'll need someone to find out who the local estate agents are. It's not that long since Mr Macmillan's team lost track, so if he's bought or rented property in the area in the last year or two, chances are someone'll remember him.'

Nina put her hand up and Sophia wrote her name against the action on the board.

'I had a meeting with Mr Coleridge first thing this morning,' she announced. 'Because of the sheer size of the task now ahead, we may have to bow to the inevitable and call in MIT, at least in an advisory capacity.'

This provoked a variety of reactions, mostly dismay. Sandra Jones said, 'No disrespect, guv, but we are talking about murder, aren't we? And a cold trail.'

'All we have is a photograph and an answerphone message,' Sophia said. 'On that basis we can't be sure whether Debbie's alive or dead.'

'She looks dead.'

The DCI ignored Sandra. 'The boffins at Lambeth have been analysing the message,' she said. 'There's a ninety-nine per cent certainty the call was made from a phone box on a busy main road.'

'Narrows it down,' Marie said. 'How many phone boxes are there any more?'

'Got the list here from BT,' Nina said in a glum tone. 'More than you'd think.'

'What about the kid on the bus?' Zoltan Schneider said.

'Kim questioned him. "Some bloke" - I quote - walked up to him at a bus stop near the Elephant and Castle and offered him fifty quid if he'd drop the envelope off.'

'Hey, *I* wouldn't ask questions,' Sandra commented.

'Exactly.' Sophia afforded her a brief stare. 'A similar degree of enlightenment on the photo.' She shrugged and raised a hand to the greatly enlarged copy on the board. 'One thing it does explain - we think - is the rope. As you can see, Debbie isn't tied up as we thought she might have been, but look closely and you'll see the sheeting underneath the body is secured to the bedposts by that rope. Best guess, it's a marine tarpaulin with metal rings round the seams for lashing down. The rope goes through four of those holes and around the bedposts.'

Marie Kirtland had her hand up. 'If she wasn't tied up, guv, where did the epithelials come from?'

'Good point; that's been bothering me too. It's possible, I suppose, that somebody handling it at some stage managed to give themselves rope burns. We'll know if the epithelials are Debbie's or not when the DNA comes through.' She hesitated again. 'Don't let's get too excited about the tarpaulin. There was no trace of sea or river water on the bed, or indeed anything much, so it may be new. You're looking at any number of marine supply shops in the London area alone, including one in Croydon. And don't worry,' she paused, anticipating the groans, 'we will be checking.'

'You're very thoughtful-looking,' Marie said.

Kim, who'd been still and quiet throughout the meeting, glanced up and frowned without seeming to see her. She said, 'Sorry. 'Scuse me,' and stood up. She waylaid Sophia at her desk. 'Guv,' she said, 'can I have a word?'

'Yes, Kim?'

'I'm just wondering about the way this is going,' Kim said. 'I mean we started off investigating the arson, right, but that seems to've gone by the wayside.' She stopped. Sophia's blue eyes were fixed on her, and suddenly what she'd been bursting to say didn't seem so urgent.

'What do you mean, by the wayside?' Sophia said.

'We're just like focusing totally on Debbie now,' Kim burst out. 'I mean there's the photo and that, yeah, but we don't even know for sure she's dead, never mind whether she's been murdered.'

Sophia sat and said nothing in an eloquent way. Kim braced herself for the lecture about the unexpected turns major enquiries often took, how a detective should never lose touch of the issue that most concerns her: the eventual apprehension of a suspect, based on the meticulous assembling of evidence.

But all Sophia said was, 'Are you concerned because the Bentons are black and Debbie Clarke's white?'

Kim didn't even have to nod.

'Rest assured,' Sophia said in an expressionless voice, 'I haven't forgotten the Bentons. How could I? I saw them when the paramedics brought them out.'

Kim chewed her lip.

'In fact,' the DCI went on, 'there's a new witness.' She clicked her mouse and pulled up an email. 'Walked into Lewisham nick on Friday and made a complaint of harassment.

Someone tried to warn her off talking to us. Could be nothing, except that the complainant happens to be Mark Watkins's cousin. Go and see what she has to say. Take Marie with you.'

An angry Helen Wallace had drawn Zoltan Schneider's attention with a loud thump to the overnight crime reports. It didn't take him long to understand why she was exasperated, and to share her feelings. Either Croydon had gone insane over the weekend, or the crime desk had. There were things here which were emphatically not Special Crime property. Friday night had seen a spate of burglaries at a sheltered housing scheme, all but one of the flats ransacked while their occupants were on an outing to *Billy Elliot*. The following afternoon a steaming gang had gone on the rampage down South Norwood High Street, leaving a number of cuts, bruises and empty tills in their wake. During a ram raid in the early hours of Sunday morning on a DIY superstore on the Purley Way, a security guard had been tied up and locked in a cupboard with a fire hose for company. All serious crimes, of course, but regular CID's to worry about. In tones that teetered on the edge of a shriek Helen next waved under his nose an attempted rape in Merton, which wasn't even on their ground, for the love of Mike, and goodness alone knew how that had got in there. Added to which was their legitimate quota of two violent attacks on gay men, threatening phone calls to a local imam and the attempted abduction of a teenage girl outside a nightclub.

For all of these last, Zoltan and Helen would have to find the manpower. Trouble was, the manpower seemed to be either absent or otherwise occupied. The balloon had gone up in a major way on the arson enquiry, which no doubt meant more bodies doing other things. Brian Hunt was still off, not due back until next week. Anne was in court, giving evidence in the case of a stabbing at a bail hostel. Across the room Jeff and Lucky were alternately screwing receivers to their ears and bouncing the results of their calls off each other. Possibly he could prise one of them away. If not, it left himself, Helen and Sandra Jones, all of whom had plenty to keep them busy already. Or should have. He could see Sandra raiding the stationery drawer, a ream of A4 in one hand, chatting to Lucky over her shoulder. Zoltan saw light. Excusing himself to Helen, he advanced purposefully towards her.

Sandra said, 'You coming Saturday, then?'

'DC White's leaving do?' Lucky said, grateful for a few moments' respite. 'Am I invited? I mean I don't even know her.'

'Course you are.'

'We've hardly said two words to each other.'

'Listen, if Sandra says you're invited, you're invited,' Jeff grinned, on hold with the phone hooked over his shoulder. 'Anne doesn't have much say in it.'

Sandra ignored him. 'You're team,' she told Lucky. 'All the invite you need.'

Lucky looked unhappy about it. 'Have to see. Could I bring somebody?'

'A date? More the merrier.'

'No, not – '

'Did we say Barkeley's in the end?' Jeff said.

Sandra turned to him. 'Weren't you there?'

'Happen.'

'Well, where did you vote for?'

'It was a tie,' Jeff said, 'I thought.'

'Eyes down,' Sandra said warningly. Jeff's caller came back on and he lifted the phone to his ear. With practised swiftness, Sandra pushed the drawer shut, turned on her heel and sat at her desk, promptly engrossed in the report she was typing. Zoltan wasn't fooled. Smiling at Lucky, who sat transfixed, he stood over her and opened his mouth.

'Don't you just *love* British justice?' a familiar voice said from the doorway.

With an eloquent sag of his shoulders, he headed back across to where Anne White had just entered the room.

'That was quick.'

'Judge threw it out,' Anne said. Tersely, she told him what had happened. Weeks of careful preparation just to get the CPS to take the case to Crown Court. Then at the last minute the young victim, who'd been persuaded at length by Anne to testify against his attacker on the promise of an almost certain conviction should he do so, had changed his mind. Anne knew, and the prosecutor knew, he'd been got at, maybe by threats, maybe by the lure of cash or drugs. But beyond a vain plea for the lad to think about what he was going to have to live with, there was little they could do. The accused had stepped down from the dock with a smirk.

An old, old story. But one Special Crime was supposed to be designing out.

'We can feel his collar again when the time comes,' Zoltan said.

'Be too late for some poor sod,' Anne sighed. 'Oh, well, I'll be long gone. All I've got to worry about now is how to kill time for the rest of the week.'

Zoltan gazed across the office to the three other detectives. Sandra was now genuinely busy, also with a phone call.

'Now you mention it,' he said brightly.

The address was in New Cross, a house in a twenty-year-old estate off Cold Blow Lane that had been built on the site of the old Millwall football ground. A few hundred yards distant, the blue and white stands of the New Den could be seen over railway embankments. Marie parked outside a tiny red brick semi with a neat triangle of front lawn. The house had burnt timber door and window frames, to which someone had begun applying a coat of black paint. A small handwritten notice pinned beside the front door said: BELL OUT OF ORDER - PLEASE KNOCK. Seeing no knocker, Marie rattled the letterbox as loudly as she could. Presently a figure appeared through the frosted glass and opened the door.

They'd been lucky to get hold of Grace Carmichael so promptly. She worked for a publishing firm and had been in an editorial meeting from which, to judge by the white blouse, black skirt and tights she still wore, she'd only just returned. As they introduced themselves she looked at her watch and ushered them inside. They were led into a small living room with a blue three-seater couch, a wicker papasan chair, a pine wall unit from Ikea with an iPod dock on it and no other furniture. A huge cheeseplant had colonised one corner. Drapes, cushions and beanbags in a spectrum of colours softened the bareness of the room. There was a faint but fresh smell of cannabis by which Grace Carmichael seemed wholly unperturbed. Catching the slight wrinkle of Marie's nose, and her quick smile, Kim decided they oughtn't to be, either.

Their host was in her mid-twenties, breezy, businesslike and slightly bossy. She was of a similar height and build to Kim, whose skin was a shade lighter. Her hair was styled in an expensive bob, complemented by bright red lipstick and long, beaten gold earrings. Her gaze swept constantly about the room. She said, 'Will this take long? Only I'm expecting my partner home in half an hour.'

There was a framed photo on the wall unit, Grace Carmichael with a clean-cut looking white man of about the same age. Both wore evening wear and broad smiles. It looked as if it had been taken at a high-end Christmas party.

'He doesn't know we were coming?' Marie said.

'Get you a coffee or something?' Miss Carmichael enquired distractedly, peering this way and that in search of something she'd lost. Kim and Marie both declined the offer, judging shrewdly that it was never likely to materialise. 'He doesn't even know I went to the police, as a matter of fact. Don't want to worry him. He gets a bit steamed up about this sort of thing.'

'About your cousin?' Kim said.

'Funny thing, he never knew Mark.' Grace Carmichael plonked herself down in the papasan and rifled through some papers she'd extracted from a black leather briefcase. 'The campaign needed a lawyer and he said he'd do it. That's how I met him. Don't mind me,' she added as an afterthought, waving the papers about.

Kim nodded, thinking that if they were going to oblige and get this done inside half an hour they'd better get cracking. 'We're here to talk to you about last Friday,' she began. 'The guy who threatened you.'

'What d'you need to know?' Miss Carmichael frowned at something she'd found among the papers, flipped the sheet over to see if it got better on the other side, evidently found that it didn't, and put it back.

'Well,' Kim tried, 'where did this happen and when?'

'I said, you know. To the detective at Lewisham.'

'We realise that, but this is part of a wider investigation now.' Kim, as she said this, felt it sounded limp.

'No problem,' Miss Carmichael smiled, making brief eye contact. 'Just trying to save a bit of time.'

Marie came to Kim's aid. 'As my colleague explained on the phone, it's possible this incident might've had something to do with the arson at the Bentons.'

'It had something to do with it all right.' Miss Carmichael rose and began rummaging through a pile of magazines and other paper on the wall unit. 'Didn't I say?'

Behind her back, Kim and Marie exchanged looks. Why did helpful people always turn out to be such rotten witnesses? From their impressions of her so far, Grace Carmichael's unpleasant experience might well be a nine-tenths forgotten thing already. She was the sort of person, Kim reflected, who left her past breathless in her wake.

'Start from the beginning,' she suggested. 'What happened exactly?'

'This bloke came up to me in the street,' Miss Carmichael said, leaving them suspended. 'Yes!' she exclaimed triumphantly and, to their disbelief, turned from the wall unit clutching a black Mont Blanc fountain pen. She sat back down in the papasan and did absolutely nothing with it.

'What street?' Kim said. 'When?'

'Ladywell Road, eleven o'clock Friday morning.' She seemed to devote her full attention to the interview for the first time. 'Broad daylight, busy road. I even had Diane with me - my sister. She's getting married next month and we'd been to the bridal salon for a fitting. Suddenly there's this big bloke next to me, sort of matching pace with us. I'm trying to take no notice and then he flashes this knife. He had it like backwards up his sleeve; I could just see the handle and a bit of the blade. He mutters in my ear, "Don't talk to the cops about the Bentons or you'll end up like them".'

'Those were his exact words?'

'Exactly. Then he dodged off over the road. This all took probably less than ten seconds. Diane was so excited, rabbiting on about her dress, she never even knew he was there. She was like, "*What* guy?"' Miss Carmichael made a perplexed face. 'Over in a flash. Just as well really. We were meeting my partner for lunch right after. In fact it turned out he was just across the street when it happened. Like I said, I don't like to bother him with this kind of stuff.'

'So,' Kim asked, 'why d'you think this bloke picked on you?'

'No idea. I mean, it's not like I'm the only living member of Justice for Mark Watkins. I do know who he was though.'

Kim and Marie paid keener attention.

'Well, I don't mean actually *know* him. This was after Mark was killed, during the police investigation and the trial and everything. We'd just set up the campaign and it was still all in the news, we had the TV and the press knocking around quite a lot. Anyway, the far right found the office building where we were meeting and we used to get these gorillas hanging around outside, heckling us. This bloke I'm talking about, he was there from the start and he was one of the few who stayed for quite a while after most of them had got bored and given up.' She shrugged again. 'He never used to do much beyond shout and spit and chuck the odd bottle, but he was always *there*.'

'D'you know his name?' Marie said.

Miss Carmichael shrugged. 'Sorry.'

'Not to worry.' Kim made a note. In that sort of public order situation there were bound to have been police about; likely NCIS would know, or be able to make a shrewd guess, who the man was. She said, 'You're sure you can't think of any reason why he'd want to threaten you specifically?'

'Because Mark was my cousin for a start,' Grace Carmichael said. Having stopped trying to work overtime, she was answering them now in a more serious and focused way. 'It's been all over the news you guys think there might be a connection with the Bentons. Maybe he's scared I might remember something that incriminates him.'

'What might that be?'

'Search me.'

''Cause surely by threatening you he's taking *more* of a risk of jogging your memory?'

'Like I said,' she insisted, 'I wasn't there with Mark when he died - I only wish I had been. Maybe he doesn't know who I am. Maybe he just wanted to have a go at somebody connected with the campaign, and he remembered my face same way I remembered his.'

'Too far-fetched,' Marie said outside, turning the ignition key.

'What is?'

'In the whole of London, this bloke just happens to

randomly recognize a face in the crowd from a demo years ago and decides to run up and threaten her in broad daylight?'

'You reckon she was targeted?' Kim said.

'Maybe. What for, I have no idea.'

'Yeah.' Kim belted herself in. 'Let's head over to Lewisham nick. I wanna fax the description to NCIS and talk to that DC, see if Miss Carmichael told him anything she didn't tell us. What's his name again?'

'Cooper.'

As they pulled away, a grey-green Volkswagen passed them and parked in the space they'd just vacated. A man got out and went into the house.

'Must be the boyfriend,' Marie said.

'Reckon he saw us?'

'So much,' Marie sighed, 'for her not wanting to worry him.'

A vexed question, and one Sandra Jones was in no hurry to ask. She'd agreed to do so at the prompting of Neil, who wanted his life back. Sandra had retorted that she supposed he didn't think Nina did too, but she went ahead and broached the subject anyway.

'I need time,' Nina said. They were in the Joneses' bathroom. The hiss of the shower all but drowned out her voice. Sandra dried her hands and glared up at the extractor fan, which wasn't helping.

'Don't you think it's all got a bit daft?'

'Pardon?'

'Don't you think - ? Oh, bugger it.' She raised her voice. 'You're the one stuck at my place while he's sitting pretty at *your* parents'. I mean for fuck's sake, you should've chucked *him* out.'

'If I went back, I'd have to.'

'Why don't you, then?'

There was a long hiatus during which Sandra could all but see Nina's thoughts wafting over the curtain with the steam. Eventually the shower went off and she stuck her head out, dripping over the floor.

'I can't face it. There'll be a scene.' She looked round with a shiver and a sad frown. 'Where did I...?'

In her distracted frame of mind, Sandra couldn't blame Nina for hanging her towel up on the peg *under* her clothes. She extracted it and passed it across.

'Ta,' Nina said, wrapping it around herself. They sat on the side of the bath. She said, 'Mum and Dad, you see. Paul hasn't said anything. I can tell from talking to them on the phone.'

'So they don't know what the fuck's going on, basically?'

'They think the sun shines out of his arse.'

'About the only ones left who do,' Sandra muttered, and instantly regretted it. 'Sorry.'

Nina glared at her. 'Imagine having to go in there and explain to them why I'm giving him the elbow. "Sorry to break up the happy home, but your beloved son-in-law's been using your bed to dip his wick in some slut." I don't know what they'd do.'

Sandra sighed. 'Of all the places,' she said, incredulous still. 'I mean *why*? How dim can you get?'

'Why?' Nina echoed. Her fingers gripped the top of the towel and twisted, pulling it tighter. She said again, in despair, 'Why?'

'I know.' Gently, Sandra laid a hand on her friend's bare, wet shoulder. Imagine what must be going on in her head, the fevered perplexity over what Paul's infidelity was, of what she'd done, or not done, to drive him to it; of whether it was a one-night stand or, as seemed more likely from his recent behaviour, something more serious. Imagine? She didn't have to imagine. She got the inner workings of Nina's head at first hand, every evening.

Suddenly Neil had a point.

She said, 'So why not stop fannying around and do something about it?'

'I will,' Nina muttered, 'in time.'

'That's an excuse.' Sandra lied, 'I've seen it before. With my sister.' Pressing home her advantage before Nina could raise an objection along the lines that Sandra's sister was blissfully married with six children, she added, 'Haven't you at least tried to find out who this bint is?'

'I was going to.'

'Do it!' Sandra harangued her. 'Ask his friends, or better still his friends' wives. You might find out what exactly's been going on, put you out of your misery.'

'Sooner ask him straight.' She stood up, loosening the towel and starting to rub herself dry.

'Then why don't you?'

'If he's still talking to me.'

Sandra couldn't believe her ears. 'If *he's* still...? Christ on a broomstick, Nina, anybody'd think *you* were the one going over the side.'

A horrible thought occurred to her.

'No. All right?' Nina said indignantly.

'That's more fucking like it!' Sandra grinned. 'Go home and talk to him, or phone, even.'

'What if he's with *her*?'

'Listen, he's proved he's stupid. But,' she hoped there was a twinkle in her eye, 'I don't think he's *that* stupid.' Nina didn't answer. 'Just give him a call. What've you got to lose?'

Nina discarded the towel and tugged a pair of dark blue briefs up her legs. Sandra had barely enough time to avert her eyes. 'My marriage.'

'Oh, for fuck's sake.'

'You're right,' she barked, flinging the bunched-up towel at Sandra in a half-hearted way. 'You win. I'll talk to him, you cow.'

She did up her bra, pulled a black t-shirt over her head and scuttled across to the mirror to do her make up. When she was sure Nina wasn't watching, Sandra puffed out her cheeks and let out a long, silent sigh of relief.

'I saw that, bitch.' Nina's reflection glared out at her. But for the first time in days, there was a faint smile there.

TUESDAY

The blown-up Polaroid of Debbie Clarke had been overshadowed - if that were possible - by the return to prominence on the board of the prison photograph of the man who, according to Macmillan, was one half of the engine behind Thrall. Kim found her eye deflected by its subject's baleful stare, and drawn back instead to the picture of Debbie. Something about it bothered her, though she couldn't say what.

'Michael Philip Quaife,' she said to the half dozen members of the team who were present. 'He's just done three years for armed robbery; released on licence four months ago. He's been identified by a Miss Grace Carmichael as the man who threatened her in Lewisham on Friday. Miss Carmichael is Mark Watkins' cousin. She recognised him as a face in the crowd from the time of the murder enquiry and the trial. NCIS have confirmed he was active around that time.' She explained to her audience the nature of Quaife's threat.

When she'd finished Sophia stood up. 'Any questions?'

'*Why?*' Jeff piped up, voicing what everyone was thinking.

'Why draw attention to himself, you mean?' Kim said.

'Me and Marie have been wondering that since yesterday and haven't come up with anything that makes sense. We talked to the DC who took the complaint. He knows Miss Carmichael, or at least he knows her significant other: solicitor, quite often represents people who pass through that nick. Didn't pick up on anything we didn't, though.'

'Is it possible,' Zoltan suggested, 'Miss Carmichael knows something about the fire or about Debbie Clarke? Or Quaife thinks she does?'

'She reckons not,' Kim said. 'Obviously she knows Luke Benton and Debbie, but not well enough, it seems like.'

'What do we know about Quaife's movements since he got out?'

'His probation officer found him a bedsit in Motspur Park,' Sophia said. 'As far as he's concerned he's still there. He was complying with his licence requirements and doing some casual jobs, including, would you believe, a roadie for a heavy metal band.' This got a chuckle. 'I say *was*,' her face clouded, 'because his landlady says he moved out two weeks ago, leaving no forwarding address. And since he's neglected to inform the probation service, it's likely he'll also miss his next appointment with them.'

There were no other questions, so she asked Marie for a summary of progress on tracking down the people from the squat. So far there was precious little. Meredith and his cronies had gone to ground. It was starting to get people down, and the conference broke up in discontent. Nina Tyminski came and stood by Kim's shoulder, following her gaze. She was staring at the two photos.

'What's on your mind?'

'I dunno,' Kim said. She pointed to the picture of

Debbie's body. 'You sent the exhibit in. What did the lab say?'

'Not much.' Nina made a face. 'Bog all to go on, really. Taken indoors, using a built-in flash. The paper's Kodak Instant; similar process but not actually Polaroid.'

'Same result, though.'

'Yeah, and just as common.'

'Not so much these days. Speaking of which, why not use digital?'

'Dunno. Traceable? Too slow?' Nina peered at the picture. 'Twelve obvious wounds that we can see, but without an actual body the pathologist wasn't going to commit himself on what might've made them.'

'I can imagine.' Kim pointed vaguely. 'That many wounds, there should be more blood.'

'Well, it's not set in stone. You know what a crap shoot it is trying to determine what sort of weapon's been used, even when there's an actual body to look at.'

'Something's wrong with this picture.' Kim's face was convulsed in an expression akin to pain as she tried to wrestle the information out of her subconscious.

'You wouldn't give it top marks for composition,' Sandra, who was passing, said flippantly. 'Mind you, with a naked dead girl, be hard to concentrate.'

'Piss off,' Kim said.

Sandra stuck her tongue out at her and left the room. Nina said, 'Only connection I can see at the moment, we've got a big dangerous bastard with a knife out there somewhere and a picture of a corpse with big knife wounds.'

'That's not it, though. There's summink else. Summink about *this* actual photo.' She stabbed her finger at it as if trying to goad it into giving up its secrets.

'I'll chew it over. Maybe if we blow it up more there's a reflection of Quaife in the wet paint or something. But there's no point getting obsessed.'

'No, you're right, I can't stand here worrying about it,' Kim said, staring. 'We've got some neo-Nazis to find.'

When Nina next looked across a few minutes later, she was still standing there worrying about it.

Anne White justified Zoltan's judicious reshuffling at twenty to four, thirty hours after he, who supposedly held her dear above all women, had banished her to the Hades of the phones to free up Lucky for other actions.

'Meadow Music,' a man's voice said in her ear.

'Hello,' Anne said, the effort not to sound mechanical by now almost unbearable. 'My name's Anne White, I'm a detective from Croydon police station. I understand you buy and sell secondhand instruments?'

'We do, yeah.'

'I'm trying to trace a flute that may have passed through your hands. Do you by any chance keep records of transactions like that?'

'Mmm... yeah.' The man sounded worried, as though he were wishing he didn't. 'When are we talking about?'

'This is it,' Anne said. 'Five years ago.'

Silence on the other end of the line. She'd had a lot of that.

She said, 'Hello?'

'Sorry,' the man said, 'you threw me. I'm just thinking, you're lucky it's not longer, because we've only been in business five years.'

'You the manager?'

'Owner.' There was a faint sipping noise. Anne guessed he had a cup of tea. 'A flute, yeah?'

'Yes.'

'When exactly five years ago?'

'February or the few months after.'

'There are a lot of flutes,' the man said cautiously.

'This wasn't just any old flute,' Anne said. 'That's why I was hoping you might remember something.'

'What sort was it, then?' She sensed his interest go up a scale. His was a relaxed middle class voice, the kind of voice you hear at small music venues, discussing authoritatively the merits of obscure indie bands over a pint of real ale.

She gave him the details and the office number and he promised, genuinely hopeful she thought, to look into it and call her back. Two fruitless enquiries later the phone rang before she could start dialling the next number on her list.

'When you told me what it was I thought it rang a bell,' the voice, whose owner's name was Roy Gillam, said. 'I'm astonished it's taken you this long to follow up.'

'How d'you mean?'

'I was suspicious when it was first offered to me,' Gillam explained. 'Böhm eight-key ivory flute, 1866. Beautiful instrument. Bloke who brought it in didn't look as if he knew how to play with himself, never mind a flute. Took cash for it; he was asking... I dunno, five hundred, something ridiculous. Once he'd gone I looked it up and found out what it was really worth; that's when the alarm bells started ringing. So I took it to the police.'

Anne shifted in her seat, the hairs at the nape of her neck stirring.

'They said there was no proof it was lost or stolen, there was no insurance claim, no reward offered, no report of any stolen flute. So they treated it as lost property.'

'Kept it for six months, and...?'

'Nobody claimed it, so it reverted to me. I sold it on at a handsome profit.'

'Would you still have copies of receipts and things?'

'Oh, yeah.'

'I must say,' Anne remarked, 'you've got a good memory, considering how long ago it was.'

'It was only about a week after I opened,' Roy Gillam said. 'First exciting thing that had happened. Plus it was tarnished. Bloody shame, an instrument like that. Spotty, as if it had been in water.'

Or as if, Anne thought, someone had run it under a tap to try and get rid of semen.

'This memory of yours,' she asked, 'wouldn't extend to a description of the man who sold you the flute, would it?'

'I dunno.'

'Tell you what,' Anne said, 'would it be OK if I dropped by? Give you time to think.'

'Yeah, all right.' He sounded bright. 'We close at five.'

'Hopefully I'll see you before then.'

Grinning, she hung up. Several pairs of eyes were staring curiously at her from surrounding desks. Beyond the back of her head, she could feel Zoltan's adding to their number. She suppressed a shiver.

In the heavy afternoon traffic it was touch and go whether she'd make it to Camberwell before Meadow Music closed.

She arrived with ten minutes to spare, but there were double yellow lines outside and she had to drive several hundred yards to find parking. By the time she'd hurried back to the shop Roy Gillam was behind the door, bolting it. He was a handsome man of about her age, similar in stature to Zoltan but thicker set. He wore jeans and a grey sweater over a blue and green plaid shirt. He grinned as she knocked on the glass and displayed her warrant card.

'I had an idea you'd be a blonde,' he said as he let her in. 'Don't ask me why.'

'You look like the kind of person it isn't easy to surprise,' she smiled, once again feeling Zoltan's discomforting presence in her mind. She shut him out with an effort.

'Here you go,' Gillam said, returning from a brief disappearance with a mug of tea and a grubby receipt book. He handed her both. 'Bit of a Luddite, I'm afraid, never been able to get along with Quicken or anything like that. But I do keep transaction records for five years. I can get you the register receipt as well if you want. It'd just mean ploughing through about a million miles of till roll.' He motioned to the book. 'But the details of what I buy and sell are all in there.'

A thick elastic band marked the place. The writing on the carbon was faint, but still just visible. 'What's that?' she said, pointing. 'Pegley?'

'"D. Pegley",' Gillam confirmed, placing his index finger close to hers. Its tip was calloused from guitar playing. 'I don't suppose for a moment it's genuine.'

'Probably not. Did you have any luck blowing away the cobwebs of time for that description?'

He frowned. 'It's difficult,' he said sorrowfully. 'I thought perhaps if you gave me a few suggestions you might jog my memory.'

'OK.' She took her pocket book from her handbag and cast an eye quickly over the amalgamated description of the tall burglar. She settled into her chair and looked him in the eyes. Hazel, she noticed. 'We can but try. People tend to remember what somebody said or did more easily than what they looked like. You said he seemed a bit dim. Does that mean he looked sort of vacant, he had an accent, or what does it mean?'

'It actually means he was too thick to realise he could've sold that flute for upwards of ten times what I paid him for it. Just the way he looked and behaved. I got the impression he wanted to pawn the thing, but didn't really know how to go about it.'

Not an experienced thief, then, she thought, making a note. 'Young?'

'Oh, yeah.' He nodded. 'Late teens. And he did have a London accent, come to think of it.'

'Narrows it down,' she said. 'Good. Right, was he tall?'

'No,' Gillam said, after some thought. 'No taller than me.'

'And you're what? Five nine?'

'Exactly right.' He grinned again. 'How'd you guess?'

'Same way you knew I was blonde,' Anne said.

By a process of deduction, they arrived at a hazy description of the youth. Anne knew she could place no great store on it. Memory plays tricks, fades, jumbles, confabulates, over the course of five years. But it had certainly not been the tall young man described by most of the victims. If it was anyone, it must be the accomplice, the one who'd raped Miranda Hargreaves.

That was something. And she had the receipt, for what it was worth. She looked up the address on her phone and was mildly surprised to find it existed. She closed the map app and speed dialled. 'I'd like a name check, please,' she said to the PNC operator. 'It's Pegley - Papa, Echo, Golf, Lima, Echo, Yankee, initial D-Delta. Possibly an alias.'

'Male or female?'

'Male, IC1, age between, say, 18 and 30.' Might as well leave a margin of error.

'Call you back, yeah?'

She had a few minutes to wait while he ran the details through the computer. Pessimistically she started the car and pointed it back in the direction of Croydon. As she passed Meadow Music Roy Gillam was pulling the shutter down. She tooted, and he looked round, but didn't see her. The phone rang as she drove on.

'Four surname matches,' the operator said. 'Only one D. Pegley. Record for burglary and possession of controlled substances.'

'Can you give me his vitals?'

His name was Darren James Pegley and he was twenty-two. He was white, five feet eight inches tall, slim with brown hair and blue eyes. Distinguishing marks, surgical scars on his left arm from where a break had been repaired with pins. No known tattoos, piercings or other identifiers. 'D'you want his inside leg?' the operator said.

'No, thanks,' Anne said, oblivious to the witticism. It was him. If Roy Gillam's recollection was anywhere close, it had to be. Pegley was the right age, the description and previous fitted. After five years there'd be no trace of fingerprints on the receipt, but there would be a sample of his handwriting on file and that could be compared with the signature. She couldn't believe he'd used his own name. She said, 'What's the last known address?' The operator told her. She couldn't believe that, either.

She'd returned to Croydon in confident mood. It was past seven. Jeff had gone home, but a weary-looking Jasmin was still in the office, as was Zoltan.

'You're that sure it's him?' Zoltan said. 'From a five year old description?'

'I checked again. There are no other stolen Böhm flutes in the PNC, then or since.' Anne said, 'Pegley has form for burglary, his age and build tie in with the rapist's, and his record starts not long after the attack on Miranda Hargreaves. Remember he comes across in her statement as a bit of a novice? Worth giving him a pull, surely.'

'For handling, possibly. No sex offender record?'

'No.'

'We'd be pushing our luck.'

She patted her notes. 'He was born and brought up in Croydon, which places him close to most of the attacks. Also, listen, there's a Michael Bayliss cross-referenced as a known associate. They went to school together; they might still hang out. Bayliss only had a juvenile record, and it's been expunged now he's an adult, but I talked to a DC at Gipsy Hill who remembers interviewing him a couple of times. Bayliss likewise is a burglar, no previous for sex offences, but get this: his MO is ground floor entry, and he looks for low security access, open windows, drop catches. Sash windows.'

'So do most burglars.'

'I know. But,' she smiled, 'how many are six foot four and described as gaunt?'

'What is gaunt?' Jasmin said.

Zoltan told her what gaunt was.

'Tall and thin,' Jasmin said, with suppressed excitement. 'Again and again the victims say this.'

'Where is he now?' The DI stroked his beard.

'There's an address for the family on the Monk's Orchard,' Anne shrugged. 'I checked but they've moved. That's why I reckon we should pick up Pegley. He might be willing to tell us.'

'Did you try here?' His finger tapped the bagged receipt with Pegley's address on it.

She shook her head. 'Camberwell reckon he's moved out. His mum still lives there, though, so I thought I'd better not call round.'

'Good plan. Don't want her broadcasting the fact we're after him. Where's he moved to?'

'Still in Camberwell, flat in Glazebrook Road.'

Zoltan said, 'Well, there's no way he can know we've taken an interest, so at this point it's not worth ruining his evening, or ours. Especially yours, Jasmin. You look all in.'

'I'm OK,' Jasmin said stoically.

Just looking at her made him yawn. He said, 'If Sophia OKs it, we'll pick him up in the morning.'

Jasmin stirred as if to say something.

'Early,' Zoltan said. 'Go home.'

She looked at him as if he'd suggested something obscene.

An adolescent female voice answered the phone. 'Hello?'

'Hi, that Michaela?'

'Yeah.'

'Is Juliet in?'

'I'll go and see.'

The phone slammed down on a hard surface; receding footsteps, labouring as though climbing stairs. The adolescent voice distantly calling a name. A faint, indecipherable conversation; then silence. Time to think; for a thumbtip to hover over the end call button. At last, a rattle as someone picked up.

'Hello?'

'Juliet? It's Larissa. Sorry, your mobile's off.'

'Hang on a sec.' More rattling. 'Got to be careful. I was in the middle of doing my nails. That's better. So how've you been? I haven't heard from you for ages.'

'Yeah, well. Things on my mind.'

'How's being a detective? You started that yet?'

'Last week.'

'So what's it like? Do CID really treat uniform like second class citizens?'

'Not really. This lot I'm with - Special Crime - they're a bit different. Besides, I'm not really a detective yet.'

'No?'

'Trainee investigator.'

'I see. So you make the tea?'

'Not all the time.'

'Yeah, right.'

'No, honest. I've been working on this thing... I'll tell you later. Listen, why I'm ringing - '

'No, I bloody don't!'

'What?'

'Sorry. That miserable child getting under my feet again. Look, *I* don't know - ask Mum.' An exasperated sigh. 'As if I knew anything about ocean currents.'

'Got your geography GCSE, didn't you?'

'That was six years ago.'

'Ha.'

'Anyway, you were saying?'

'Was I? Oh, yeah. I was wondering, you doing anything Saturday night?'

'Don't think so. What's on?'

'Wondering if you fancied going out. It's somebody's leaving do. Kind of a police thing, but they say anybody can come.'

'And you haven't got a date? Come off it, Larissa. New job, CID, *somebody* must want to get their leg over.'

'No. They're mostly women, for one thing.'

'*What?*'

'I know. It feels weird. Anyway, so you wouldn't be out of place or anything. It's just I don't know most of them that well yet, so - '

'Where is it? Anywhere we know?'

'Not sure. They've been having a big debate about it, but I think they eventually decided on Barkeley's.'

'Oh, right.' Juliet sounded brighter. 'Hang on a minute. The nightclub Barkeley's? In Purley?'

'Yeah.'

'Gets raided for drugs every five minutes?'

'Meant to be half the fun, apparently.'

'Oh, great.'

'I didn't mean - '

'No, I know what you mean. Yeah, all right, I'm up for it.'

'Thanks.'

'I'll get myself a book out of the library, though, case you get a better offer.'

'I won't.'

'Doesn't sound like you, Larissa. "I won't."'

'Won't be the chance.'

'Pressure of work?'

'Something like that.'

Suddenly, a note of concern. 'You all right? You sound a bit funny.'

'Do I?'

'Only normally I can't get a word in.'

'Tired, I s'pose.'

'Mmm.'

'Might sound like a contradiction, but it's the not working shifts any more. It's thrown off my circadian rhythms.'

'They'll adjust. Hey, listen.'

'What?'

'If *I* get a better offer, can I bring him?'

Lucky gripped the phone tighter.

'Hello?' Juliet said.

Across town, another phone call.

Nina had wound herself up tighter than the rubber band on a child's toy aeroplane. To hear from her father, when finally she did manage to dial, that Paul had gone that afternoon to stay at his parents', almost snapped her resolve. Tough enough to psych herself up again, without having to reassure Dad first. Among other things, he'd asked whether she, or Paul, had been unfaithful. Fielding his anguished questions, she'd admired

Lucia's restraint; her normally garrulous younger sister was the only member of the family who knew. Such was her state of mind she now wondered whether Lucia's reticence was due to *her* being the object of Paul's adultery. She dismissed the notion with a shudder. This was enough of a mess without turning into a melodrama.

She wiped sweat from her hand and forced herself to hit send. The phone rang once, twice, then was answered. Paul's mother. Her condemnatory silence reverberated down the line. She wondered what Paul had told his parents. Then her husband's voice rang in her ear.

'Nina?'

'Yeah, it's me.'

'Hi.'

'How are you?'

Guarded, flat voices. Like strangers, Nina thought. No: like relatives. Distant, burdensome relatives.

'I'm OK. You?'

'How d'you think?'

'Yeah,' he muttered. 'Don't blame you.'

'For something.'

'What?'

'You must blame me for something, else why'd you do it?'

He hesitated. 'We need to talk. Not like this, over the phone.'

'Why'd you move out?'

'The atmosphere. Your mum and dad worrying and wondering. I'd've caved under the pressure. I needed to get out from under.'

'They deserve to know, Paul.'

'From you.'

He was right. Though if they found out about their bed,

they'd crucify him anyway. 'Fine,' she said. 'I'll tell them. But don't expect me to spare your blushes.'

He said nothing for a moment while this sank in. 'I haven't seen her again,' he said, 'since.'

'I don't give a flying fuck, Paul,' Nina said.

'Honey - '

'But you're right. Let's not talk about it over the phone.' She heard his sigh of relief. 'When can we meet?'

'Saturday.'

'*Saturday*?'

'Give us time to think, get our heads straight. In the meantime I'm going home, and I don't want to see hide nor hair of you till then.'

'OK.' He sounded broken. 'When and where on Saturday?'

'Anne's leaving do, Barkeley's. Pick me up at nine.'

'Jesus,' he said, 'you want to discuss our future in front of a dozen coppers, at a *nightclub*?'

'Take it or leave it.'

'You sound cold,' he said wretchedly.

'I'm nice and warm, thank you.'

'Not what I meant.'

'Saturday, nine p.m.,' she repeated.

'See you then.'

As she hung up, she fancied he'd said something else. Her sudden urge to listen came too late. Sandra, always with that uncanny knack, reappeared bearing coffee. 'How'd it go?'

'All right.'

Her vision blurred suddenly. She reached out. The tissues were already in Sandra's hand. Sandra said, 'D'you want me to call you a cab?'

Nina could only nod.

WEDNESDAY

Jasmin Winter couldn't sleep. She was on call, which always put her on edge no matter how hard she told herself that after all these years in the Job, she ought to be able to cope. What didn't help was a vicious headache that had wrapped itself around her brain like a boa constrictor. She'd downed three Paracetamol before bed but they'd had little effect. She lay in the dark, debating whether to relinquish the relative warmth of the bedclothes for a hot drink and some toast from the kitchen. If her metabolism had some food to occupy it, maybe it would stop bothering her head. As if that would do any good. She'd only start worrying about something else, like what in the name of the Blessed Virgin she was doing in England.

What she was doing was being a guinea pig. It was an officer exchange programme between the Metropolitan Police and the Amsterdame Gemeentepolitie, an experiment to find out how closely the law and order forces of the new improved European Union could work together. Somewhere in the Dutch capital, Jasmin's Met counterpart was working on a similar secondment. Soon, perhaps, as internal borders blurred, as freedom of movement and labour became a reality, such things would be part of everyday life. But this was now, and Jasmin felt acutely the displacement and loneliness of the pioneer.

It was not generally known among the team that half her pay went straight home to her mother, a widow with crippling debts accrued over twenty years singlehandedly raising ten children. As the eldest unmarried Winter, a large portion of the financial burden fell to Jasmin. The accommodation she was subsequently able to afford was a room in a crumbling shared house in Selhurst, by the main line out of Victoria with express trains to and from Gatwick and the coast booming past her window every few minutes. The room was, but for her vain efforts at homemaking, almost slumlike, the walls covered in ancient, mouldy, peeling wallpaper that soaked up damp like a sponge; and often without heat or light because of the seeming pathological obsession of the landlord not to pay the bills. Her fellow inmates at present were the night security guard in the upstairs front, whom she hardly ever saw; a student from Thailand who roomed in the attic, didn't seem to speak English and certainly couldn't speak Dutch; and the elderly RAF pensioner on the ground floor who seldom went out.

'Why the fuck don't you move?' Sandra Jones had once demanded, hearing of all this.

'Too busy,' Jasmin had said.

'Take some time off.' Sandra wasn't put off so easily. 'Use it to find another place.'

'OK, if I find somewhere else, with my money, what would it be?' she'd snapped. 'Another shithole, *ja*? Look, if possible, I would be out of there like a shot.'

Wouldn't she just. She sat up and swung her legs out onto the floor, groping for the bedside lamp. Unimpeded, the cold air slipped easily through her soft cotton nightie, raising goose bumps on her skin. She held a brief and serious debate with herself. Yes, she decided, it would make a lot more sense to get up properly and dress, rather than exhaust herself in a futile attempt to sleep. She didn't know what the new day, with the hoped-for arrest of Darren Pegley, would bring, but there was bound to be a lot more chasing about, whatever happened, and on this schedule she'd have difficulty lasting the pace. She shook off the doubt. Damn it, she was a cop. Long periods without sleep were part of the Job; she could cope, had done many times in the past.

But with Ovaltine and toast prepared she found herself sitting on the bed, wondering what to do with the rest of the night. She wondered if inhaling mould spores was affecting her health. It was probably the cause of her headache, not to mention the nasty gastric bug that had kept her off work for three days last month. She'd contemplated asking the landlord to bring someone in to take a look, but she'd learned that landlords like hers invariably had relatives in the trade who could not, in their expert opinion, find anything to worry about. Really she ought to call someone herself. Environmental Health, for a start. Except that with her luck Mr Aloneftis would probably have a cousin working there as well. Added to which, any resulting work would cost money she was far from sure she had.

Eventually she decided sitting around moping was doing no good, and picked up the copy of *Nostromo* she'd got from the library. Her first language was Dutch and this was a novel in English by a Pole who'd lived in France until his mid-twenties. Not surprisingly it was hard going. After a fortnight of abortive attempts she was on page forty and this was probably not the smartest thing to try and do after twenty hours without sleep and with a head like a ball of barbed wire. But it was about the only thing to do at half past two in the morning.

She was on page forty-five when her mobile rang.

Zoltan Schneider arrived at Camberwell Green police station at seven, just as the local Drugs Squad were starting to assess the haul from their night's work. From a club called the Bluebell, in Denmark Hill, the arrest of Darren James Pegley and one other male, now being questioned by other members of the squad at Peckham. Visual and video evidence of them selling Ecstasy, LSD or similar drugs. When searched, small quantities of tablets, which they claimed to be aspirin, found in their possession; samples sent to Forensic for identification.

From the subsequent raid on a flat in Glazebrook Road, Camberwell, one further arrest for possession of controlled substances. Colleen O'Dwyer, age twenty-three, an unemployed agency nurse from Limerick. No previous, either here or in Ireland. Small amounts of LSD and cannabis resin hidden in a metal bedpost and under the base of an anglepoise lamp in the bedroom. It would be hard to prove anything against her, but they couldn't afford to let up. So when further, substantial, findings of LSD, cannabis, and this time Ecstasy and cocaine had been unearthed from beneath a loose floorboard, and also from the feedpipe and battery compartment of the gas cooker in the kitchen, the detectives had felt justified, their stony intolerance of O'Dwyer's tearful bewilderment vindicated. Anyone daft enough to shack up with a slag like Pegley shouldn't be surprised by a gang of coppers drumming her out of bed at four in the morning.

As if that weren't enough, a DC, availing himself of the loo, had been puzzled by the length of time the cistern took to refill and discovered, in an airtight Tupperware container in the cold water tank, a complete kit of burglary tools, neatly arranged as to use in various small cases and boxes.

Assuming the drugs found in the flat turned out to be from the same batch as those in Darren Pegley's possession, the squad had enough to bury him good and deep. What they were worried about was Special Crime's interest, and whether it was going to sod up their collar. Jasmin Winter had found herself the object of some cold looks.

Zoltan heard this in the Brummie-accented voice of Gareth Beaumont, the DI who'd commanded the raid, as he led the way upstairs. Jasmin walked over when they came into the room the Drugs Squad had requisitioned. Zoltan studied her with a solicitous expression.

'Could've rung me, rather than dragged yourself out of bed,' he frowned. 'Considering how rough you were feeling yesterday.'

'I was on call,' Jasmin said stoically.

He shrugged, unwilling to argue. 'Mr Beaumont's kindly agreed to let me have a go at Pegley before he does,' he said. 'Soften him up.'

'Do you want me with you?'

Zoltan cast a slow gaze over the trestle tables piled high with clear plastic bags containing the exhibits from Pegley's flat, the Drugs Squad officers beginning their task of logging them, preparing them as evidence for court. 'Somewhere among all that,' he said, 'may be the smoking gun that ties in Darren Pegley to one or more of the attacks. I've no more idea than you what that might be, but look anyway. I'd like to have a time bomb ticking while I'm downstairs talking to him.'

Jasmin looked disgustedly round the room. She nodded.

'Come and fetch me,' Zoltan said.

She watched him go, then lowered her head and let out a deep sigh that, before she could stop it, turned into a yawn. Her vision blurred for an instant and she rubbed her eyes to clear it. To stay sharp she wandered over to one of the DCs and offered to help.

Half an hour later something on one of the other tables caught her eye. She waved to get the attention of the DC who'd just buried the object of her interest under something else.

'Can I have a closer look at that?' she said, pointing.

Experience had taught the two men facing each other across the table what they needed to know.

For Detective Inspector Zoltan Schneider, the ability to judge what manner of person he was dealing with was vital in determining his approach to an interview. With a first-timer, often so scared they'd crumble and start babbling under the slightest probing, he need say little. Prompt them where necessary, but let them dig their own hole, or climb out of it. On other occasions his opponent was more formidable, a hardened villain or a sociopath with no remorse or fear of legal sanction. Question, keep at them, wear them down, gradually build up and confront them with the evidence, goad, befriend them, keep working away until they confessed or copped a plea out of sheer frustration or boredom.

Darren James Pegley was about halfway along the spectrum. First and foremost, he was a burglar, with a string of convictions for the offence. He had another string, shorter, for petty drug offences. He was not bright. Faced with interrogation, he knew three things: ask for a brief, keep shtumm, and bow to the inevitable. Let the pigs do the legwork, nail him if they could. Six months in a young offenders' institution had been, in the past, no hardship.

Today was different. For the first time, Darren Pegley had been arrested for dealing Class A drugs. Furthermore, he'd been seen and recorded doing it. To make matters worse, he was now twenty-two years old. No cosy borstal this time. It would be the real McCoy.

Zoltan read the consternation as his suspect realised this copper was not Drugs Squad, nor even regular CID, and was not the slightest bit interested in questioning him about what had gone on in the club. He could picture files riffling through Pegley's memory as he tried to think which undetected offence he was about to be nailed for.

'Mr Beaumont,' he said pleasantly, 'has very kindly agreed to let me talk to you before you sort out this Bluebell business with him.' Tempting him, paying out the briefest length of line.

Pegley's eyes flickered.

Zoltan said, 'Aren't you curious as to what this is all about?'

Sticking to familiar ground, Pegley said nothing. But he was watching Zoltan keenly.

'What I'm trying to do,' Zoltan went on, amiable still, 'is a bit out of the ordinary. There's this piece of property someone lost, very valuable to them. It was stolen, but for some reason they didn't report it. Until now. Even though it's so long ago, we've managed to trace the property. Up to a point, anyway.'

'Speaking of points,' the duty solicitor, Baker, a supercilious, tired man in a tired blue suit, stirred from his note-taking, 'what's yours, Mr Schneider? I don't think any of us are up to riddles at this hour.'

Zoltan gave the solicitor one of his nastiest, most sardonic looks. Making sure Pegley saw it, he transferred it to him, made it pleasant. 'Thing is,' he said, 'this property was last seen sold on by a secondhand shop near here. And they say they bought it from you.'

He was pushing it. In his mind's eye was Anne, hurrying over to Meadow Music to catch Roy Gillam as he arrived to open up. He knew this was a gamble that relied on faded memories; that Pegley would not associate the theft of a musical instrument with another, far more serious crime.

He said, 'I'm talking about a flute, stolen five years ago from a house in Sutton. It was sold shortly after the theft to Meadow Music in Camberwell High Street - just down the road from here. Quite a distinctive flute. Antique. Worth tens of thousands.' He watched Pegley's face. 'Would you, perchance, remember anything about a flute like that?'

Pegley assumed an expression of deep thought that wouldn't have passed muster in the ropiest of amateur dramatic productions. 'No.'

'That's odd,' Zoltan said, 'because what I've got here is a carbon copy of a receipt issued at about that time by Meadow Music for a flute like the one I described.' He pushed it across the table, informing the recording apparatus that he was doing so. Baker intercepted it, studied it with feigned suspicion, then handed it to his client.

'The signature, Darren,' Zoltan said. 'What name would you say?'

'Can't read it,' Pegley said.

'It's no fainter than the rest of the chit,' Zoltan said calmly. 'Try a bit harder.'

'No,' Pegley said at once, 'sorry.'

'Well, the handwriting's not the neatest in the world, I grant you, but I reckon it says "D. Pegley". Bit of a coincidence, wouldn't you say?'

He wouldn't say.

'Especially as the description we've got of the bloke selling the flute,' Zoltan said, 'is you to a T.'

'It weren't me. I never been in there.'

'You can honestly put your hand on your heart and tell me you weren't in Meadow Music five years ago selling a flute?'

'Do I look like I can play the flute?'

'In that case,' Zoltan smiled, 'you won't mind giving me a sample of your handwriting so I can have it compared to the receipt.'

While Pegley was still staring at him, deciding what, if anything, to reply to this, there was a knock at the door and DI Beaumont stuck his head round. Zoltan, after a nod of assent from Baker, stood up.

'Excuse me for a moment,' he said, smiling.

'I am now,' Zoltan happily informed the recorder a few minutes later, 'showing Mr Pegley a long, thin, black leatherbound case, entered as exhibit number 24H.' He watched as first Baker, then a pale Darren Pegley examined the opened, empty case in its plastic evidence bag. 'Ever seen this before, Darren?'

'No,' Pegley said.

'Are you sure?'

'Positive.' Grumpily, he slapped it down into Zoltan's outstretched palm. The DI took it and put it on the table facing him.

'I'm now showing Mr Pegley the inside of the open case lid,' he narrated, and smiled icily. 'Could you see your way clear to reading what the manufacturer's label says?'

'You what?'

'Humour me.'

'It says "B-O-H-M".'

'Now what sort of thing would you say this was designed to hold?'

'Dunno.'

'Take an educated guess.'

'Very long vibrator,' Pegley said, with a leery glance at Baker.

Zoltan waited for their mirth to subside. 'Funny you should say that.'

Pegley stopped grinning.

'Had a proper good look, did you, just now?'

'Yeah.'

'And you, sir?'

Baker nodded and made a noise of assent.

'Better put you out of your misery, then,' Zoltan said. 'We found out what it's supposed to hold. Not burglary equipment, which is what was in it when we found it. That's right, Darren, look relieved. It's for a flute. An antique ivory flute made by Böhm of Germany. To be precise, a flute used by two suspects to assault its owner in Sutton in a five-year-old unsolved rape case, and subsequently stolen by them.' He fancied Pegley was showing signs of disquiet. It was an emotion he often provoked, even in people he wasn't accusing of serious crimes, so he recognised it when he saw it. He pushed the case across the table again. 'Take a look underneath where it says Böhm, Darren,' he suggested. 'See that little faded three-digit number? We've just contacted the woman I told you about and she confirmed that's the serial number of the stolen flute. I'm intrigued,' he pushed on relentlessly, 'because it was that very flute that turned up at Meadow Music. Remember?'

'I'm telling you it weren't me.'

'That's why I'm intrigued, you see, Darren,' Zoltan said, still smiling. 'Because we found this case, with this manufacturer's label and this serial number, hidden in a big plastic box in the cold water tank in your flat. The landlord's given us the names of the previous tenants. None of them has a record for burglary, Darren. But you do. And yet you've never seen this before. Intriguing, isn't it?'

Another knock on the door made Pegley look up with a start. Zoltan thought this was a good place to leave him hanging, so he excused himself again and switched off the recorder.

Outside Anne White greeted him with a triumphant beam. 'Picked him out,' she said, handing him a piece of paper. 'It was Pegley.'

Zoltan raised his eyebrows in mild surprise. 'I thought he was a bit hazy on the details?'

'He's had all night to think about it,' Anne said. 'He's fairly certain.'

'Fairly?'

She shrugged. 'Ninety per cent. But he IDed him straight away from the faces on that page.'

'And this is Mr Gillam's statement to the effect?' Zoltan glanced at the paper.

'Right.'

'Ninety per cent won't be enough for the CPS.'

'I figured it might be enough for you,' Anne said.

Zoltan looked up with a reptilian smile.

'How well you know me,' he said.

'You'll have gathered from the frequent interruptions, Darren,' he said, settling himself back down, 'we've got something else simmering besides you. Well, it's just come to the boil.'

He put down the statement form, pointedly, out of the reach of Pegley and his solicitor, turned to the recorder and pulled out two thumb drives, which he sealed, signed and gave to Pegley to do the same, telling him that one would be his to keep.

'Is that it, then?' Baker said.

'No, it isn't,' Zoltan answered cheerfully, inserting two fresh thumb drives into the recorder. 'The reason I'm doing things this way is that new evidence has come to light, as the saying goes, and because I'm a good boy who follows PACE to the letter. So we'll go again from scratch.' Once more he started the machine and identified the location and those present. 'I'm questioning Mr Pegley with regard to a burglary at 2 Langley Park Road, Sutton, five years prior to the date of this interview, during which the occupant, Miranda Sally Hargreaves, alleges she was raped. I'm bound to tell you, Mr Pegley, that I suspect you of being involved in that crime, so I'm going to caution you again before we continue.'

'Five years ago?' Zoltan noted with satisfaction the paling of Pegley's face, the slackening of his jaw. 'How the bleeding hell d'you expect - ?'

'I must warn you that you don't have to say anything, but it may harm your defence if you don't mention now something you later rely on in court. Anything you do say may be given in evidence. Do you understand?'

'Yeah, yeah.' Pegley was still, desperately, trying to fathom what was going on.

'Now let me tell you what's been happening while we've been in here.' Zoltan settled himself. 'As you know, narcotics officers raided your flat in Glazebrook Road early this morning. They arrested a Miss Colleen O'Dwyer - '

'She ain't got nothing to do with it,' Pegley said, feebly.

' - and found, among other things, the leatherbound wooden case you've previously examined as exhibit 24H. It's very noble of you to try and protect her, Darren,' Zoltan added, underlining that he'd forget nothing Pegley said, 'but I quote from your verbal of last night: "They ain't mine, they're my girlfriend's." Your attack of chivalry's come a bit late.'

He paused, smiling at his own sarcasm, and then frowned.

'This is a copy of a statement,' he announced, placing the form carefully on the table facing Pegley, who sat staring at it as though it were a live frog, 'made a short while ago by a Mr Roy Gillam, who runs a business called Meadow Music. Would you like to read it?'

'May I?' Baker put his hand out to take the document with a glance at his client, who nodded. The solicitor speed-read it, sighed and offered it back. Again Pegley made no move to study it.

'Perhaps you'd like to mull it over for a while,' Zoltan suggested.

'I don't wanna read it.'

'It's in your own best interests, Darren.'

Pegley folded his arms and looked at the wall.

'Here's an idea. I'll tell you what it says.' Zoltan drew the statement towards him and adjusted his glasses. 'Mr Gillam states that having studied a series of photographs from criminal record files, photographs of young men similar in appearance to yourself, he identifies you as the person who sold him an antique ivory flute, subsequently discovered to be stolen. For the record,' he glanced at the tape recorder, 'that flute was the rightful property of Miranda Hargreaves. Now are you sure,'

Zoltan said, pushing the statement over to Pegley's side of the table, 'you don't want to read it for yourself?'

A change had come over his suspect. Slowly, but obviously trying to restrain himself, Pegley took the form and read it carefully.

'You can't prove nothing,' he said at last, tossing it back. 'It was fucking years ago.'

'It certainly seems to have stuck in Mr Gillam's mind.'

'Yeah, I bet,' Pegley grunted.

'Are you saying none of this happened?'

Pegley was saying nothing.

'Did you burgle number 2 Langley Park Road?'

'No.'

'Then how,' Zoltan came back at him, 'did the flute's case, which we found in your flat, and which has your fingerprints on it, come to be there?'

'I bought it.'

'Who from?'

'Can't remember.'

'But you definitely bought it?'

'Yeah.'

'You told me you'd never set eyes on the case, Darren.'

'That was before...' He tailed off.

'Before I told you I suspected you of rape?' Zoltan said with brutal mildness.

Pegley said nothing. Zoltan could see him grinding his teeth.

'I've checked back in our files,' he went on, 'to see if anything else matches. Nothing does. Not for that time period. No other stolen flutes, no other burglars turned rapists. Now I've got Miss Hargreaves's original statement, which I'll give you to look at, and the trouble is her description of the man who raped her sounds a lot like you.'

'So?'

'So there are too many coincidences,' Zoltan said. 'Like the flute being sold shortly after the rape by yet another person who looked like you and who just happened to countersign his receipt with your name and address.'

'It weren't me,' Pegley said.

'Wasn't you who what? Beat that young woman up, forced her to strip, raped her, and then as if that wasn't humiliating enough, stuck her most precious possession, her beloved flute, up her vagina? Who was it, then?'

'Dunno.'

'Do you know a man named Michael Bayliss?'

A flicker of something in Pegley's expression, which Zoltan didn't think was surprise.

'Was Michael Bayliss your accomplice that night? Were you his?'

'I wasn't there.'

'Because if Bayliss committed the rape, how come it was you, Darren, who ended up with the flute?'

'Inspector Schneider,' Baker interrupted, sitting up straight. 'As my client has pointed out a number of times, this alleged crime happened years ago, far beyond reliable memory. Now if you have anything other than some flimsy identification evidence which hasn't the least chance of standing up in court, kindly produce it if you're planning to do anything other than trawl through ancient history.'

'This isn't ancient history, Mr Baker,' Zoltan said. He stared Pegley down. 'Is it, Darren?'

'What are you saying?' Baker demanded.

'There's evidence,' Zoltan explained, still to Pegley, 'linking this rape with at least half a dozen similar incidents. All involving burglary. All involving the use of a foreign object to sexually assault whichever woman was unlucky enough to be in the house at the time.'

Pegley had slid down in his chair.

'Last week an old lady in her nineties, in a retirement community, was attacked in her bed with a nurse sitting at a desk not fifteen yards away. Can you imagine?' Pegley stared. 'Maybe you don't need to. This lady was beaten up and raped with one of her own candlesticks. Ninety years old. What sort of person does that?'

'Mr Schneider,' Baker said, 'I'd like to confer with my client in private for a few minutes. Would that be possible, do you think?'

'Yes, of course,' Zoltan said, as if the request hadn't been rhetorical. 'Interview suspended.'

He found Jasmin in the canteen, slumped beside a plate of scrambled eggs and a half empty mug of cold black coffee. She was asleep, head resting on folded arms, mouth open. Shaking his head, he left her there, bought himself coffee and wandered back upstairs.

Anne looked up from behind a clipboard. 'Sophia wants you to ring her. Let her know the SP.' She peered knowingly at him. 'I gather from your expression Gillam's statement might have done the trick?'

'Possibly.' He gave her hand a quick squeeze while no-one was looking. 'Pegley's closeted with his brief now, no doubt concocting a version of the truth in which he comes out smelling of roses.'

'Is he in the frame, then?'

'He was there all right. But he won't cop to the rape - not as long as he knows we've no forensic. That character Camberwell dug up.'

'Bayliss?'

'Yeah. Pegley got twitchy when I mentioned him. Since he now thinks I'm going to fit him up for the whole series, my money's on him naming Bayliss as the second man. What?' he frowned. Anne was staring at him oddly.

'So,' she scowled, 'in exchange for shopping Bayliss, Pegley gets off scot free on the rape?'

'The price of justice.'

She sighed. 'Well, I'm off out of here in a couple of days, so it's not going to be me that has to tell Miranda Beckett if he does.'

'Quite,' Zoltan said. He looked at his watch, then around the room at the tables piled high with evidence. He said, 'Are you busy?'

Anne shrugged. 'Just killing time, awaiting instructions.'

'Jasmin's flaked out down in the canteen,' Zoltan said. 'Think you could revive her to a sufficient level of consciousness to stuff her in the car and take her home?'

'Sure.'

In the doorway she collided with a uniformed sergeant. 'DI Schneider about?'

Anne looked back to where Zoltan was standing, dialling on his phone. 'You're on,' she called to him.

He opened the door to see Pegley and Baker looking up at him expectantly. He took his seat in silence and, making no move to turn the recorder back on, folded his arms and waited.

'My client,' the solicitor said after a few tense moments, 'is willing to make a statement explaining his part in the, er, events leading up to his coming into possession of the flute.'

Slowly and deliberately, Zoltan nodded.

'In exchange,' Baker struggled on, 'he would like an assurance that you'll take the, er, the mitigating circumstances into consideration.'

'Assurances of any kind,' Zoltan said levelly, 'aren't up to me. What I'm able to recommend to the CPS in the way of reduced charges will depend on what Mr Pegley has to tell me.'

'Darren?' Baker said.

Pegley nodded, tired.

Zoltan switched on the machine, said the necessary and launched in. 'OK, Darren, who assaulted Miranda Hargreaves? You or Michael Bayliss?'

Pegley looked surprised and affronted. He turned to Baker. 'You didn't tell me he was gonna ask that straight off!'

'Mr Baker isn't privy to my interview techniques,' Zoltan said, 'so spare him the grief. All right, let's go back a bit. How do you know Bayliss?'

'Ain't seen him for years.'

Zoltan let it pass. 'You've known him how long?'

'Since school.'

'You used to live in Croydon?'

'Addiscombe. I moved to Camberwell with me mum when her and me dad split up.'

'When was that?'

'Just after GCSEs.'

Zoltan doubted Pegley had ever got near a GCSE, but he dropped the question as irrelevant. 'So at the time this incident took place, you were living with your mum in Camberwell?'

'Yeah.'

'OK, Darren,' Zoltan nodded at him encouragingly. 'Do you now admit that you and Michael Bayliss broke into 2 Langley Park Road, Sutton, on the date in question?'

'We was there.'

'Was that the first time you'd done a job with him?'

As if for confirmation Pegley glanced at Baker, who shook his head.

Zoltan said, 'Who decided to break into that particular house?'

'Nobody really. We was just driving round, looking for somewhere worth doing.'

'So you just happened on 2 Langley Park Road because it looked promising?'

'Yeah, s'pose.'

'Why did it look promising?'

'*I* can't remember, can I?'

'Did the house have any features that made it attractive as a burglary target? Unsecured doors or windows, for example?'

'Can't remember.'

'So, however, you break in. You're inside. What happened?'

'We're in this front room, right? It's dark. I thought the place was empty, but there's this light coming from a partition. Mike seen it too, and he goes, "Somebody in there, let's see who it is, might be some pussy." So he goes out in the hall and tries to get in the room, but it's locked. I wanted to get the fuck out, but Mike's like, "Let's try and get this thing open."'

'Meaning the partition?'

'Yeah.'

'How come,' Zoltan asked slowly, 'he was so keen? For all he knew it could've been a man behind there.'

'I dunno. I was bricking it, expecting somebody to come flying in any minute. I s'pose he figured if it'd been a bloke, he'd've come to see what was going on. Or at least shouted out.'

Zoltan frowned. According to Miranda Hargreaves, she *had* called out. Implausible though it seemed, was Pegley being crafty, knowing that continuing to break through after hearing a woman cry out might, to a jury's mind, constitute proof of intent? More likely, had Baker coached him in what to say? Or was it simply a gap in his memory, five years on?

'Go on,' he said tersely.

'Well, it was locked, but it was pretty flimsy so we managed to force it.'

'You and Bayliss?' Zoltan slipped in, innocently.

'Yeah.' Baker had raised a warning hand, but his client hadn't seen it. 'We got it open just enough to squeeze through, and there's this bird - girl - woman - crouched on the floor, trying to hide under the bed or summink. Mike tells her to give him the key, turns to me and he goes, "She's all yours while I go and check out the rest of the house."'

This, in Miranda Hargreaves's account, was the point at which Bayliss had incited Pegley to rape her.

'What did you take that to mean?'

In spite of himself, Zoltan was impressed. Pegley didn't even need Baker's prompting as he shrugged and said, 'Keep her quiet, I s'pose.'

'Keep her quiet?'

'Yeah.'

'And did she?'

'What?'

'Keep quiet.'

'I reckon.'

'You reckon?'

'Probably too fucking scared not to.'

'So you knew she was scared?'

'Yeah. Wouldn't you be?'

'That's encouraging, Darren,' Zoltan said, smiling his crocodile smile. 'I only wish more villains realised they scared people. Might make some of them think twice. Anyway,' he said briskly, drawing himself back to the point, 'Bayliss left the room?'

'Right.'

'By the way, did you wear masks, balaclavas, anything to conceal your identity?'

'No, never.' Pegley said it as if it were a matter of pride.

'So this young woman could see your faces?'

'No. Mike had the light off soon as we got in there.'

'I see,' Zoltan said. 'Hardly conducive to keeping her quiet, I wouldn't have thought. A young woman alone in a dark room with a burglar.'

'I never touched her.'

'Is that so?'

'I never fucking touched her.'

'So she did keep quiet?'

'Yeah.'

'How did you achieve this?'

'I told her to.'

'You told her to what?'

'Keep quiet.'

'You just told her to and she did?'

'Yeah.'

'You didn't threaten her?'

'No.'

'Slap her around a bit?'

'No, I never.'

'Or else what?'

Pegley looked at him blankly.

'Come on, Darren. "Keep quiet." "Yes, Mr Burglar." She may not have been able to see your face, but she could make out enough to know you were a squeaky, spotty seventeen year old. Hardly inspire dread even now, do you, Darren?'

'No, but Mike Bayliss does. I mean did. I dunno what he's like now, but back then he used to scare the crap out of me, even.'

Zoltan stared at him, thinking, all right, sunshine. Let's listen to your edited version for a while, see how deep you can wade. 'What happened when he came back?'

Pegley swallowed, hesitated.

'He did come back?' A sardonic flicker of Zoltan's eyes. 'Your story does rather seem to depend on it.'

'Yeah, he fucking come back,' Pegley said tartly.

'After how long?'

'I dunno. Few minutes.'

'And what happened?'

'He has a look round, right, and finds this flute. And he goes, "Watch this." And he's like sticking it in her.'

'In her?'

'You know.' Pegley squirmed. In almost a whisper, he added, 'Up her vagina.' He uttered the term as if he had never used it before, which Zoltan reckoned might well be the case. No doubt he habitually employed a shorter word.

'So,' Zoltan said, 'Bayliss went out of the room, came back and sexually assaulted Miss Hargreaves with the flute. Is that right?'

'Yeah.'

'So are you saying now the rape never took place?'

'No.'

'How long was Bayliss out of the room?'

'Not long. Five minutes, tops.'

'So he left you alone with that girl for five minutes and nothing happened?'

'I told you.'

'She didn't scream for help? Plead with you not to hurt her?'

'No.'

'She didn't offer her body in return for not hurting her?'

'No.'

'You both just waited around for Bayliss to come back?'

Pegley nodded.

'So when did she get naked?'

'You what?'

'You told me that all you did while Bayliss was out of the room was sit and wait. How, then, did he have such easy access to her genitalia when he came back if she was still fully clothed?'

'He made her take her kit off.'

'Then why didn't you say that?'

'What d'you – ?'

'You told me Bayliss came back into the room and inserted the flute into Miss Hargreaves' vagina. Not a word about rendering her at least partially unclothed, which would seem to be an essential part of the process.'

'Well, 's obvious, innit?'

'Darren,' Zoltan said heavily, after a carefully calculated pause, 'in the eyes of the law, for it to have been rape there has to have been penetration of the vagina with the penis. Anything else constitutes either attempted rape or indecent assault.' He shrugged, smiling coldly. 'Stupid, but there it is. Be sure of this, Darren: Miranda Hargreaves *was* raped. Brutally, painfully. Or are you telling me she lied about that?'

Pegley stared at his hands, which gripped the edge of the table.

'Why would she, Darren? Why would she go through the humiliation of telling us in excruciating detail about the assault with the flute, which you've just corroborated, and then lie about being raped?'

Still he said nothing.

'Don't get me wrong, you've been very helpful so far. Your account of what happened does tally remarkably well with Miss Hargreaves', considering how long it's been. But it does differ in a couple of important respects. Maybe it's your memory. People do get selective memories when they've something to hide.' He flicked the briefest of sideways glances towards Baker, letting him know he was well aware of what had gone on while he and his client had been conferring privately. 'But Miranda didn't ever forget what happened. When you two broke into her room - she says - she started crying and pleading with you. Bayliss shut her up by giving her a good hiding. *That* is the point at which he forced her to strip and invited *you* to have your way with her while *he* went on a tour of the house. Is that what happened, Darren?'

'No comment.'

'You not remembering the beating worries me somewhat. What worries me more is Miranda's account of what you did while Bayliss was gone.'

'No comment.'

'I didn't ask for your comment,' Zoltan snapped. '"Have your way with her" you took to mean rape her. Which you did. And then when Bayliss came back and found you raping her, he chewed you out for jumping the gun, and took *his* turn using the flute. With a foreign object that wouldn't leave any genetic trace. Is that right?'

'No comment.'

'It's what Miranda Hargreaves says.'

'Her word against mine, then, innit?' Pegley blurted out belligerently. 'You can't prove it was even me there.'

'You've just *told* me it was you, Darren,' Zoltan said. 'It's on tape; it's your statement. I didn't coerce you into it. You made it voluntarily, after taking legal advice.'

'I ain't coughing to no rape. You ain't got nothing to pin it on me.'

'Haven't I?' Zoltan smiled, and leaned back happily in his chair. 'Let me tell you what I have and haven't got. I have got stolen property found in your flat, which has been positively identified as belonging to Miranda Hargreaves. I've got your account on tape of how you and Michael Bayliss got into 2 Langley Park Road, and what you did there. And I've got Miss Hargreaves' version of events, which fits yours like a size eight glove. What I *haven't* got is anything, other than your word, that says it was Michael Bayliss who did that job with you.'

He stopped for a moment to see if the implications were sinking in. Pegley's Adam's apple bobbed gently.

'Supposing we never find Bayliss? Or, more likely, suppose we do and he denies ever having been there? What then? All we've got is your statement. Your word for it; no corroboration. So where does that leave me, Darren? All I have is you.'

Pegley's eyes were dark, shining circles of horror. 'You bastard.'

'You were there when Miranda Hargreaves was raped,' Zoltan went on, mercilessly. 'You've admitted having the case in your possession, and we can quite easily prove it was you who sold the flute on. Don't be under any illusion that I'm not going to charge you with rape, Darren, but if you play straight with me about what happened I might just be able to persuade the CPS to ask for seven years instead of fifteen to life.'

'He fucking told me to!'

The outburst was so unexpected that for a second afterwards there was total silence in the room, apart from the faint echoes of Pegley's cry ringing round the white walls. Zoltan cleared his throat carefully, hoping his surprise hadn't shown.

'Michael Bayliss,' he said, 'told you to rape her?'

Pegley nodded, looking as shocked as either of them.

'Mr Pegley nods to indicate that is what Bayliss said,' Zoltan reported. He shook his head slowly. 'Darren, Darren. Pushing dope for gangs, and now rape by proxy. Do you always do what people tell you?'

'God help me,' Pegley said.

Zoltan watched him inscrutably for a few long moments, noting the way his eyes swivelled to the flashing recording light, as though willing the machine off..

'You've left it a bit late for anyone else,' he said.

'I am awake now.'

Jasmin had ridden back to Croydon with the passenger window open as a measure against the queasiness of the rudely awakened. The cool breeze did, indeed, seem to have revived her, although to Anne's mind the ever muddier areas around her eyes were not lightly to be ignored.

'Look,' she said, 'you can't go on forever, you know.'

'I cannot sleep when I should be working.'

'Come on,' Anne pleaded. 'We've all done it. Besides, you've earned a rest.'

Jasmin made a dismissive noise. She fingered her jumper and scowled. 'I could use a wash. I feel sticky.'

'Well, then.'

'Go to the nick,' she decreed, and folded her arms with a smile of triumph. 'The water is warmer.'

'I did try.' Anne shook her head and braked for a young mother with a pushchair at a zebra crossing. 'All I can say is thank God I'm doing the driving.'

For the time being, Jasmin was right. A hot shower had done much to crank her weary brain up to a sustainable level of awareness. But her body had taken it upon itself to remind her that, whatever her reasons, she was not superhuman. Her limbs felt leaden, and her head able only with a conscious effort to hold itself upright. As she walked into the office she briefly gripped the doorframe for support. In all conscience, she thought, breathing deeply, flooding her bloodstream with oxygen, she couldn't skive off. Tonight, after her shift was done, she'd switch off her mobile, turn in early, and no cold or express trains or mouldy walls or ringing phones would disturb her long slumber.

There was no sign of Sophia, but Helen and one or two of the others were around. Lucky looked up with an anxious smile at Jasmin's approach. 'The DI just called. He says,' she looked away, 'he thought he told you to go home.'

Had Anne ratted on her, or did Zoltan simply know her too well? She said, 'And what else?'

'He's nailed Pegley.'

'Uh-huh?' Making it to her desk, she felt her knees buckle under her and she collapsed with undignified lethargy into her chair. 'For what exactly?'

'Raping Miranda Hargreaves. It was all just about how she told it to me and Jeff. The other bloke was this Bayliss character. Pegley did the rape while he was out of the room.' The words were chattering out of Lucky's mouth, like rapid fire. 'Then when Bayliss came back he was so mad at him for leaving his DNA behind he grabbed the first thing to hand and - '

'The flute?'

'Yeah, and raped her again with that: "Look, this is how it *should* be done."' Suddenly, for no apparent reason, she tore the top sheet off the notepad she'd been referring to, screwed it into a ball and threw it across the room. She sat with her arms folded.

'Are you OK?' Jasmin frowned, startled.

'Yeah,' Lucky said. 'Are you?'

Helen Wallace, who'd been earwigging, looked up from her paperwork. 'That's a point,' she said, studying Jasmin's pouched eyes. 'You don't look as if you've - '

'I had forty winks earlier.'

'Look, go home,' Helen said. 'We'll manage.'

'What I told her,' Anne White said, coming in with two coffees. She put both in front of Jasmin, changed her mind and took one for herself. 'Silly moo won't listen.'

Jasmin said, 'I sign out at five-thirty, right? I am OK till then.'

Helen considered. 'All right. But you stay in the office. Any callouts, I'm sending somebody else. Deal?'

Too tired to argue, Jasmin nodded. Satisfied, Helen turned her attention to what had originally disturbed her. But Lucky had picked up and binned the ball of paper and, with no sign of the petulance that had apparently caused her to throw it, was back at her desk, whiting out a mistake on the form she was filling in.

THURSDAY

In theory, the Special Crime office meeting took priority over anything short of attending your own funeral. In theory, it was the only time Sophia could ever hope to have all her team in one room. In practice, someone was always in court, or attending a call, or out on enquiries. This morning Kim and Marie were absent, chasing a halfway promising lead on Meredith and company at a night shelter in Pimlico; Jasmin, not entirely unaccountably, was also missing.

'First on the agenda,' Sophia began, 'our rape series.' Several heads went up. 'Zoltan, Jasmin and Anne spent most of yesterday grafting away at a probable breakthrough. Where is Jasmin, by the way?' No-one knew. Helen caught her guv'nor's eye; she reckoned she could make a shrewd guess, but it could wait. Sophia nodded and moved on. 'Zoltan.'

The DI stood up. 'A young burglar called Darren Pegley has confessed to being at 2 Langley Park Road and, though he still hasn't said so in as many words, he did rape Miranda Hargreaves. However, I don't fancy him for the other assaults. He has a plausible alibi for Violet McMinn, and anyway none of the descriptions we've been given match Pegley remotely. The one we're looking for is the kid he was with that night.' The palm of his hand patted the photofit Miranda Hargreaves had helped put together. There was some despondent muttering. Even on its own it didn't look convincing. 'His name is Michael Bayliss. He has a record - or perhaps I should say he *did*.'

'Juvenile?' Helen asked.

'How did you guess?' He smiled thinly. 'According to Camberwell's local intelligence officer, who holds the only remaining information we have on him, there are no adult convictions. His last caution was for selling a stolen moped five years ago; nothing further until he attained the age of twenty-one last year, whereupon his juvenile record was expunged and destroyed in accordance with policy.' There were groans. 'If written documentation is to be believed, he suddenly turned over a new leaf at seventeen. Trouble is he no longer lives at the LKA, and no-one there knows where the family went. Pegley also denies knowing his present whereabouts.'

'If he raped Mrs McMinn last week,' Nina Tyminski said, 'bastard's still around somewhere.'

'Exactly. We're looking for a twenty-two year old IC1 male, height six foot four, light frizzy hair, pale complexion, slim, rangy build. He has a distinct...' Zoltan hesitated for an instant. Out of the corner of his eye he thought he'd seen Lucky put her hand up, but when he looked she was busy jotting notes. 'He has a distinct MO. One, he strikes in the victim's own home. Two, he breaks in at ground level through sash or drop catch windows, things that can easily be forced. Three, he doesn't bother concealing his face but relies on darkness as cover. Four, and most significant, he's not a rapist in the legal sense. Since he's apparently motivated by a desire not to have his DNA on file, his method is to pick out some phallic object from among the victim's possessions and sexually assault her with that. He then takes the object away with him. He seems careful not to take anything which might be easily identified; usually something mundane like a kitchen utensil or a cheap candlestick - '

'What about the flute?' Lucky said.

'Ah, yes, the flute.' He looked at her. 'The flute of course is decidedly *not* mundane, and for this we are thankful. It seems he was a bit rattled by Mr Pegley donating his bodily fluids to the cause of forensic science. In a manner of speaking it's his bad luck it wasn't some mass-produced Japanese instrument. My guess is he realised this later, and dumped it on Pegley to get rid of, figuring he'd be too scared to shop him if he got caught.'

'No honour among pervs,' Sandra Jones said.

'Any questions?'

'What bothers me,' Sandra came back, 'is why take Pegley along at all? From what I can see he seems to have done fine on his own apart from that one time.'

The DI shrugged. 'To show off?' he suggested. 'Pegley didn't go into that part of it.'

'And we still don't know who this *other* accomplice was,' Nina said.

'You're talking about Denise Cole?'

'Yeah.'

'That one sounds like an older man,' Zoltan said. 'It's the earliest we know about, so possibly Bayliss was the apprentice there. Could be Denise disturbed them, and because she was a bit of all right Bayliss decided to have some fun.'

A phone rang. Helen picked it up. 'Special Crime, Helen Wallace.'

'The older man doesn't feature in any of the other incidents,' Sophia said.

'Hardly surprising,' Sandra commented.

'Denise's statement did say he seemed disturbed by what Bayliss was doing, yes.'

Sandra said, 'Isn't it worth pursuing? If this bloke's a known villain, maybe he's tried using it as a bargaining chip at some point. Long shot, I know.'

'Good thinking, all the same,' Sophia said. 'Lucky, d'you fancy getting on the wires again, see if - ?'

'Oh, no!' Helen Wallace exclaimed into the phone, much louder than she'd intended. Everyone stared at her. Her face wore a strained expression. She listened, nodded and said, 'OK, then. Come in when you can. Bye.'

She hung up. Sophia said, 'Jasmin?'

'Yeah.' Helen's lips were pursed. 'In private, guv. It's not funny.'

'Why're you laughing, then?' Sandra demanded.

'Mind your own business.'

'What's it worth?' Sandra said, her eyes with a predatory gleam as Helen struggled to keep the corners of her mouth down.

She was aware of banging, of voices, in what seemed to be a fitful abstract dream. A sudden upwards leap of consciousness, prompted perhaps by a particularly loud bang, made her aware of people close by. Someone was speaking in a strange language. No - English, but fragmented, almost pidgin. There was another voice, deeper and more authoritative. 'Who is it, the old boy?' More unintelligible gabble. The banging restarted. 'Hello? You all right in there?'

Jasmin opened her eyes, then screwed them shut again

as light stabbed in. Warily she parted her lids halfway. She could see linoleum, a door; the knocking and the voices must originate on the other side. She had no idea where she was. She decided to open the door and find out. She tried to stand up.

Nothing happened.

Her heart leapt against her chest in panic. She tried again. She realised she was very cold. She was conscious of the commands to move being issued by her brain, but her legs would not respond. She could feel them attached to her body like slabs of frozen, lifeless meat. Something was horribly wrong.

She got a grip and woke up. Look at this sensibly. Slowly she pried open her memory. She recalled signing out just after six, and being at home without remembering how she'd got there. She remembered her despair that sleep had again deserted her, and how she'd sat watching TV half the evening, unable to get her head round anything more challenging. From what her stomach was telling her, it didn't seem as though she'd eaten.

Finally, after *News at Ten*, she'd gone along to the bathroom, deciding maybe the ritual of getting ready for bed would do the trick. It was the last thing she remembered.

This in mind, she took stock of her surroundings. She was still in the bathroom. Relief flooded through her. She would not, after all, be confined to a wheelchair for the rest of her life.

But she'd better say something before her housemates broke the door down.

'Mark?'

'Jasmin? That you in there?'

'Uh-huh,' she answered sheepishly. 'My legs are numb. I fell asleep sitting on the toilet.'

'What?' Mark broke off as the Thai student muttered

something. 'Can you reach the door to unlock it?'

'I will try.'

Legs, when they don't work, are heavy. Jasmin slid off the seat and plummeted to the floor with a crash that knocked the wind out of her. Tears of anger and mortification welled in her eyes. Sweeping up the shreds of her dignity, she managed to wriggle over to the door and, with a quick check to make sure she had her nightie on, reach up to draw the bolt.

As she submitted to Mark and Thien carrying her back to her room, the first pangs of returning circulation shot like period pains through her pelvis and down her thighs. In a way, it was worse than being numb.

Jeff Wetherby already felt as if he'd been kicked by a horse, and Sophia's walking into the office the moment he gave up and answered her persistently ringing phone didn't do much to improve his mood.

'Guv.' Hand over the receiver, he tried not to glare at her. 'Nottingham on the line.' She nodded and took the phone from him. He returned to his desk, still brooding. He caught Marie Kirtland's eye. 'Jasmin OK?' he asked, trying to sound casual. 'Took her coffee, she nearly bit my head off.'

'You not heard?'

'Heard what?'

'It's a classic,' Sandra, who was passing, said.

'Tell me.'

Struggling to suppress a smirk, Sandra told him. He smiled, but she could see in his eyes he didn't find it the least bit funny. She exchanged glances with Marie. Miserable bugger. There was always one.

There was no prophetic dream, no sudden flash of inspiration or intuition. Nina had been right; what was bothering her would occur to her sooner or later. Now, without any detectable method of arrival, the knowledge was in her head. Kim Oliver sat bolt upright and looked across at Marie.

'Ain't got a magnifying glass, have you, by any chance?'

'No.' Marie frowned. 'Why should I have a magnifying glass? I'm not Sherlock Holmes.'

But Kim was already at the notice board, peering at the Polaroid of the blood-drenched Debbie Clarke. There it was, plain as day. It wasn't wishful thinking.

She called Nina over. 'Did Sophia say where she was going?'

'Coleridge's office,' Nina said. 'Not sure how long for.'

'Never mind. Least we know she's in the building.' Kim tapped the photo triumphantly. 'I've cracked it.'

'That thing that was nagging you?'

'Look at her right arm.'

Nina peered. 'Blimey,' she said. 'It moved.'

'Not camera shake, or you'd get a double image,' Kim insisted. 'It's blurred. Her arm moved as the picture was taken.'

'You mean - '

'I mean she ain't dead,' Kim declared, loudly, causing several of the others to stop what they were doing and come over to have a look. 'Least she wasn't at that precise moment.'

'Hang on,' Nina said. 'It might just've slipped.'

'No. See where the right arm's draped across her middle? If it was gonna slip, it'd slip *down*, right? But the blurred edge is at the bottom. She moved it *up.*'

'God help her,' Anne White said, 'if she was still alive then. I mean *look* at her. The wounds, the blood...'

'Not just alive,' Marie Kirtland said. 'Conscious.'

'How d'you mean?' Kim asked.

'No funny remarks,' Marie said, 'but if you were lying there starkers and somebody suddenly pointed a camera at you, what would *you* do?'

'Try and cover myself,' Nina said.

'That's why her arm moved. She's got a newspaper over her fanny, so that's OK, but her tits are exposed. She's trying to cover 'em up.'

'Yeah, but how's any of that possible,' Lucky said, 'with those sort of injuries? Even if you're still alive, you're not gonna be able to twitch an eyelid, never mind - '

'I think I can make a guess at the answer to that,' a voice said.

As a body, they turned. Sophia, grim-faced, was standing behind them. A glance from her sent them shuffling back to their desks.

'Everyone's attention, please,' she called out for the benefit of those few who hadn't been distracted by the commotion. They all stopped work and listened. 'I'm not sure whether this counts as good news or bad. I've just been on the phone to the forensic lab. They've got the DNA result on the epithelials and the blood from the bed. The epithelials are Debbie Clarke's, or at least some of them are.'

She hesitated. She looked angry, or embarrassed, or something. With their guv'nor it was hard to tell. They waited.

'The blood isn't,' she said.

FRIDAY

Ideally, Anne White would have spent her last day fitted with wing mirrors. There'd been rumours a stunt might be pulled - and from past experience that was a certainty, not a possibility - but she couldn't be sure when. Her colleagues were quite capable of keeping her in agonies until Barkeley's tomorrow night. In an attempt to force their hand she'd taken half a day's leave, and would be on her way after that whether they were ready or not.

Their morning's work seemed to have taken most of the team out of the office, chasing halfway promising leads on the whereabouts of Debbie Clarke or her squatter friends. Only Lucky, head down at her desk, and Helen, talking to a social worker, were left. Eventually even the social worker disappeared, and the clock crept nearer to one-thirty: zero hour.

Perhaps the suspense, the emotion of leaving, heightened her sensibilities but the self-contained industry of the others, the almost silent emptiness of the office, now seemed oppressive, and the tedium of clearing her desk, making notes on unfinished cases for handing on to other members of the team, made her impatient. Her head snapped up at the ringing of the phone. It was Bob Price, one of the uniformed sergeants.

'Anne,' he said. 'Got a prisoner down here says he wants to talk to you.'

She groaned. 'Who?'

'He won't say. No ID on him.'

'Got a lot on at the moment, sarge.'

'I dunno about that,' Bob said, 'but it'd make my life a lot easier if you could come down and put a name to the face.'

She thought for a moment. 'What's he in for?'

'Flashing,' Bob said. 'He's in the cells now. Can you imagine, exposing yourself to a shop assistant in Ann Summers? Frightened the life out of her. Won't tell us why, just keeps asking for you. A right arsehole, if ever I saw one.'

'OK, I'll come down,' she sighed, hanging up and mentally kissing goodbye to the last chance of getting her Special Crime affairs in order. She flicked through her memory for likely candidates. A few possibilities, but this one's MO was taking it a bit far. She paused on her way out and took a long look round at what might well be her last view of Special Crime as one of its staff.

Helen and Lucky exchanged glances as the door closed behind her.

'Cell six,' Bob said, unclipping his keys and selecting the appropriate one before handing them to her. 'You know the procedure. Check the Judas hole first, anything looks iffy or you can't see him, come and get me.'

'Right.' Anne nodded and set off down the corridor. It was cool down here after the heat of the office, for which she was eternally grateful. In warm weather, the uneasy truce between a police cell block's two pervading smells of disinfectant and vomit was frequently broken, with invariably the same winner. She remembered well her first such experience as a young probationer, and her subsequent undignified flight to the ladies', pursued by the laughter of male colleagues.

But she'd encountered far more stomach-churning situations in the years since, and nowadays the most unpleasant things in cells tended to be their occupants. Starting next week, she wouldn't even have to put up with prisoners any more.

One for the road, she thought with a wry smile, advancing down the rows of heavy doors. Most were open, unoccupied, and the cell block was quiet, the calm before the inevitable Friday night flood of brawlers and piss artists. Number six, at the far end, was shut. She stood before it, composed her opening line, and slid open the Judas hole.

A nightmare vision filled the opening. What might have been a face was just two pale, hairy half moons, separated by a hellish dark maw, which lunged at her retinas like a bad trip. She yelled, slammed the hole shut and recoiled so fast she lost her balance and fell backwards through the open door of the cell opposite. 'Bastards!' she squeaked, sitting up. Through the door of number six came the sound of helpless laughter.

She scrambled to her feet and went back out into the corridor. Bob Price was standing at the other end, hands in his pockets.

'Told you we had an arsehole in there,' he said, and walked off.

She mustered what she hoped was some semblance of composure and went to unlock number six. Ranged along the bench were Kim Oliver, Marie Kirtland, Nina Tyminski, several uniforms from early turn and, triumphantly clutching an iPhone with a voice memo app, Sandra Jones. To one side were

Jeff Wetherby and Zoltan. Both their trousers were in place but it had to have been one of them. At the sight of her they burst into renewed fits of giggling. 'Bastards!' she spluttered again.

In reply, Sandra played the voice memo back, and she heard herself scream, clear as a bell.

Blushing furiously, she pointed an accusing finger. 'I take it this was your idea?'

Sandra shook her head and indicated Zoltan, who took a step back, cradling his fingers. 'All my own work,' he admitted. 'With help.' Beside him Jeff grinned and tried to cover his face with one hand.

Torn between anger at Zoltan and being a good sport, Anne stood pouting for a long moment. Finally she wagged an ominous finger at her lover and erstwhile DI.

'I'll see you later,' she said.

The Assistant Commissioner had been keen to administer a bollocking to Sophia for, in his words, wasting time and resources chasing wild geese in and out of homeless shelters instead of waiting for the DNA result, and for full effect he had chosen to do so in person as opposed to over the phone. At their meeting, Sophia had refrained from asking him why dragging her all the way to Brixton just so he could see what she looked like standing on his office carpet was *not* a waste of time and resources, partly because the less she said the less likely he would be not to take the investigation away from them, and partly by a desire to curtail the ear-bending so that she could get back to Croydon by half past one if at all possible. It was one-fifteen when she finally made it. Anne was still in the office, but looking eager to get away. She made apologetic noises about the unfinished nature of her paperwork. Sophia waved them away with a rare smile, and rang down to the CAD room to ask them to put out a PA announcement, a presentation to be made to DC Anne White in the Special Crime office, all welcome.

'You don't mind hanging around a few minutes longer, I hope?'

'Course not, guv,' Anne said uncertainly.

Ten minutes later the room was filled with a noisy crowd. Most of the team were present, as far as Sophia could make out, as well as twenty or so other people from uniform, CID and the civilian staff. She fancied they were harbouring some joke; certainly a lot of them were avoiding eye contact. Chuckling to herself, she put the matter aside. In due course she'd hear on the jungle drums about whatever stunt had been pulled to mark Anne's departure.

Sentiment not being her strong point, she called everyone to attention and gave a brief, unembellished but, she hoped, sincere address expressing the team's regard and appreciation for Anne's work over the past six months, their best wishes for her future. Anne blushed crimson throughout this and the subsequent applause. Finally Sophia slid open the bottom drawer of her desk and, to cheers and whistles, took out a large Ann Summers carrier bag.

'Don't need to ask who did the shopping, do I?' Anne said, trying to suppress her embarrassment.

Sophia blinked. She hadn't expected the bag, but then she supposed you were asking for it by letting Sandra Jones spend the money from the whip round and leave the stuff in your drawer.

'Don't worry,' Sandra called out from a safe distance, 'it's not *all* from there.'

'Should hope not,' someone said. 'She'll be knackered.'

The first item Anne unwrapped was an alluring lacy confection in appropriate navy blue, for which she gushed thanks but refused firmly a chorus of male pleas to model it for them. The other presents were more conventional: a Harrods gift card ('I'm going straight up to town to spend this'), Glenfiddich, chocolates and an exercise DVD ('Which you'll need,' Marie said, 'sitting on your arse behind a desk instead of pounding pavements'). The card, supplied and inscribed in best blue ink by Chief Superintendent Coleridge, was suitably vast, and crammed with several dozen messages ranging from the banal to the heartfelt, from the humorous to the downright obscene.

'Thank you all,' she managed to say, surrounded by wrapping paper, wishing she'd prepared better for the dreaded moment someone yelled out, 'Speech!' 'I'm going to miss working here - but not half as much as I'll miss a sergeant's pay if I ever have to come back.' Jeers greeted this remark.

'Gone half one,' Sandra called out dramatically, and it was the signal for the ceremony to end, for urging Anne to make herself scarce before someone found her some more work to do. And so Acting Sergeant Anne White, arms full of gifts, walked on a tide of farewells out of the office, and out of the team.

'Special Crime,' Sophia's voice rang out behind her, suddenly businesslike, 'stay put. It's not quite the weekend yet.'

The last Anne heard before the door closed behind her were the groans as they shuffled back to their desks.

Life for an Anne-less Special Crime Unit lost no time in going on as usual. Jasmin Winter, who had missed both the prank and the presentation because of a previously scheduled appointment, returned looking glum and dove into an impressive pile of paperwork before anyone could engage her in conversation. Zoltan Schneider received a call from DI Beaumont, who informed him that Darren Pegley had just appeared at Camberwell Green Magistrates' Court, charged with rape and several offences under the Misuse of Drugs Act, and had been remanded to Wandsworth pending court dates to be determined. Acting on a tip from an informer, Helen Wallace went to a house in Thornton Heath and brought a 26-year-old man of Turkish Cypriot descent and his two mobile phones in for investigation in connection with a number of anonymous calls placed the previous Sunday to a Mr Muhammad Siddiqi, in the course of which, Siddiqi had alleged, a threat had been made to petrol bomb his mosque. At five-thirty precisely, Zoltan ordered a highly reluctant Jasmin to stop what she was doing and go home immediately. And shortly after that, the forensic laboratory in Oxfordshire rang Sophia to let her know that the previously unidentified DNA of the blood sample from the Paragon Road squat had been matched with the cheek swab taken recently at Charing Cross police station from one Philip Rex Meredith, last known at that address.

Anne flexed her back against the softness of the bed and allowed herself to dwell momentarily on the fact that the man inside her was not Zoltan. Sensing something, he paused and looked into her eyes. But she closed them and, encircling him, drew him closer, bearing down as she drove towards orgasm. She felt him join her in a tight coil of pleasure; then they separated and lay recovering and reflecting beneath the covers.

As always seems the way, she'd found the perfect dress

almost as soon as she'd set foot inside Harrods. The gift voucher accounted for, the rest of the shopping expedition was an anti-climax, and she caught herself wandering up and down Oxford Street thinking despondently that all the shops nowadays were the same as in Croydon, only bigger. Her failure to tie up her Special Crime affairs was still nagging at her, and she decided to shelve a visit to a museum in favour of one task she could still perform.

A courtesy call; that, she insisted to herself on the way to Camberwell, was all it was. Communicating thanks to a helpful witness. But when she reached Meadow Music a strange face was behind the counter. Roy Gillam had taken the day off. He might be at home; his flat was in Greenwich. She thanked the youth and drove there.

Pleasantly surprised, Gillam set aside the accounts he'd been trying to balance and invited her to share a bottle of wine, it being Friday after all. Flirting seemed as easy across his kitchen table as sitting side by side in the shop, ploughing through receipts. The table was small, the brushing of legs a frequent, ultimately deliberate occurrence. Easy, too, to make hand contact under, then over, the table. Not long after, they stood up. They wasted very little more time before moving to the bedroom.

Anne often wondered about this aspect of her nature. It wasn't the first time since she'd been going out with Zoltan that she'd stretched the definition of flirting beyond its limits. Zoltan, she suspected, knew nothing of these dalliances, and would not wish to know. He had her heart; he should not begrudge her lending out, from time to time, her libido. Oddly, the only thing that concerned her now was the million to one chance that next time he sat in her car, he'd notice the extra mileage.

In the warm aftermath of sex she dismissed the notion and snuggled up to Roy, gratified that she couldn't tell what was in his thoughts. In bed, she found the copper's habit of trying to read people's minds a liability. She stopped herself by kissing him. She felt him go hard, and herself wet, and they made love again.

'Better go soon,' she said later, not relishing having to part company with the soft bedcovers and Roy's body.

'Back to your boyfriend?'

It was said not maliciously, but easily, with a benign smile.

She made a face. 'You guessed.'

'The way you talked about him before. Your boss, right?'

'As was until today.'

'Does he know?' Again, Roy spoke with no trace of agitation or jealousy.

'No.'

'Welcome to have a shower before you leave.'

'Thanks,' she said, with a sudden flow of gratitude towards this likeable, thoughtful man. 'Do I have to go yet? *You* haven't got someone coming home too, have you?'

'No, not me. No rush.'

But it was getting late. She rose, bathed and dressed, savouring the familiar glow of satisfaction. Bathrobed, Roy rejoined her as she was brushing her hair.

He said, 'One-off, this, right?'

'Very probably,' she smiled.

'Because I'm a witness?'

'Mmm.'

'Doesn't that bother you?'

'Other people, perhaps.'

'Blimey.' A thought had struck him. She read it before she could stop herself.

'*If* it comes to court,' she said, pre-empting him, 'and assuming you're called...'

Their eyes met and held, and they giggled at their private joke.

'Just try and keep a straight face,' Anne said.

SATURDAY

There is something about the architecture of the motion picture theatre that distinguishes them long after they have been closed down and converted to other purposes. You could still tell, sometimes with the briefest glance, where the old picture palaces of Croydon had once been. Some had become bingo halls, others fitness centres or bowling alleys, theme pubs or thrift shops. One, the old Focus on Crown Hill that had screened mostly soft porn with a side business in Disney films and action blockbusters during the school holidays, was now a Hustler Club. Then there was Barkeley's Discotheque, on the Brighton Road half a mile south of Purley Cross. It had once been the Lyric Cinema, an edifice that epitomised Hollywood's Golden Age. Outside, if you looked beyond the vulgar chrome doors and the huge vertical sign with its gaudy flashing lights, it retained its splendour. It was an entertainment Mecca for the young and young at heart; it couldn't very well fail to be. Apart from a 24-hour Tesco and a couple of characterless pubs, there was precious little else to keep Purley alive once the sun sank behind the roofs of the semis on Woodcote Hill.

Perhaps the word was out that a posse of partying

coppers was on its way. Barkeley's was less than usually packed for a Saturday night, and they had no trouble getting in. Even the doormen, who normally did their level best to provoke a fight, smelled bacon and were gratifyingly subdued. There were, after all, perks to the Job. On the debit side, the doormen would never believe these pigs were off duty and would spread the word to whomever might be interested, then watch them uncomfortably from the shadows all night. The team, for their part, knew this, and knew neither to notice certain people behaving oddly whenever one of them hove into view, nor to draw attention to themselves. At least, not until everyone was having too good a time to care.

The combined stares of Sandra and Zoltan got them a booth. It was still only mid-evening, but Barkeley's already throbbed with noise and humanity. The recipe was deafening trance music, plenty of dry ice and dancing and bar prices that made Lottery jackpot winners wonder why they'd bothered. Some of the party, Paul Jackson along with Lucky's friend Juliet, a thin girl of about the same age with long mousy hair and John Lennon glasses, made straight for the dancefloor. Others took a while longer, settling.

Presently Jasmin Winter descended on Jeff Wetherby. She'd turned up alongside Kim Oliver with a face like a cancelled wedding and, feeling the way he did about her, the apparent lifting of her spirits transmitted itself to Jeff's heartstrings to produce a painfully harmonious twang. He smiled at her.

'Can we wait until something a bit slower comes on?' he said. 'You know what I'm like.'

'Huh?'

They'd been through this before. Jeff danced like a three-legged camel with housemaid's knee. Jasmin nonetheless seemed possessed of a fantasy of turning him into a contender for *Strictly Come Dancing*.

'I will teach you,' she said.

'You tried that.'

'Huh?'

'You *tried*,' he bawled over the din.

'OK,' she relented. 'We wait for a slow one. But I will teach you to dance if it kills me.'

'Brave woman.'

Two tracks later the DJ considered it about time for a slower one, something newish by Armin van Buuren. Jasmin stood up, took Jeff by the hand and tugged. He allowed himself to be towed into the crowd, the merciless giggling of eavesdroppers ringing in his ears.

'This is still a bit fast for me,' he protested.

'What, you want the *Funeral March*?' She coached, 'Just follow my feet and keep time.'

He complied, because it meant he could hold her, and she him. Her warm back stirred under his hands, like the coiled muscles of a cat poised to spring. Her arms round his neck were firm and strong; her fingers left a tingle where they touched him.

'OK?'

'Hope you're ready for bruised toes.'

'I'm used to it.'

Jeff hoped no-one was watching his efforts at grace too closely. For one thing he was wearing a suit, which always made him feel uncomfortable, but it was his balance, or lack of it, that was the main problem. Ideally he liked to see ahead of him, use the horizon as a reference point. Currently Jasmin filled his horizon; not entirely conducive to steadiness. Luckily she appeared to have chosen a spot in the midst of the crowd, away from the main focus of the strobe lights and the view from the team's booth.

'You've perked up a bit.'

'Huh?'

He upped the volume. 'I said you've cheered up a bit.'

'*Ja?*'

'Aye. Only you've been a bit down in the dumps, past couple of days. I heard about the, er...'

She frowned. 'Dance closer and shout in my ear,' she advised. 'It will not fall off, right?'

'No, but your eardrum might burst.' Nonetheless, he followed her advice. Her spicy perfume wafted up his nostrils, down into his chest and tickled his heart. He wondered if she'd consider him forward if he asked her what it was.

She laughed.

'That's better.' He smiled with her.

'What do you mean?'

'Like I said, you've been none too happy. I wanted to ask what's eating you.'

Jasmin opened her mouth, then closed it again. She seemed to ponder a moment. She said, 'You drive here tonight, right?'

He nodded.

'You can give me a lift?'

'Now?'

She tutted indulgently. 'Not *now*. When it's time to go.'

His stomach a tight, burning knot, he said, 'Sure.'

'I'll tell you about it on the way, then.'

He grunted, unsure what he ought to make of this.

He was still thinking about it, in depth, when she said,

'You want to sit down now?'

He looked up, snapping back into the real world. Van Buuren was yielding to something edgy he didn't think he knew, although the way some of these DJs worked nowadays he might easily be listening to a mix of McCartney's 'Yesterday' and not recognize it. Now they were drawing attention to themselves. The floor had almost emptied but for a few engrossed couples gyrating away to one another's more vital rhythms. There was some isolated slow hand clapping from the booth. Separating, gearing themselves for the piss-takes, they went to sit down.

'Sorry,' he simpered. 'Miles away.'

'It's OK,' she smiled at him.

Although Paul was seldom touching base in between forays to the dancefloor, the fact that his wife had barely even spoken to anyone else either hadn't gone unremarked. Both of them seemed edgy and disinclined to be sociable, wary as much of each other as the company. Word was their marriage was on the tramlines. Sandra, who was tighter with Nina than any of them, had a tense look on her sharp face, like someone expecting a balloon to burst. Rather too brightly, she volunteered the opinion that Nina looked fucking miserable and that she was working on a way of forcing her to enjoy herself.

Nina had begun to doubt the wisdom of this evening the moment she'd opened the door to Paul standing hunched in her parents' porch. She'd recoiled, as if from a spider in the bath. He was dressed with ruthless formality and had a weird light in his eyes which she only later recognised as fear when she saw her own reflection in the wing mirror. This was the first time they'd been together since her discovery, and she was desperately trying to work out why he looked so different. A little thinner, maybe some worry lines on his forehead and about his eyes, but that wasn't it.

There'd been precisely three words between them all evening.

'I'm pulling over.'

That had been halfway here, when Paul had no longer been able to stand the icy quiet from his wife. Wordlessly she'd watched him pull into the kerb and switch off the engine. Then she waited. He'd turned in his seat and tried to meet her gaze, but she'd sat rigid, staring blindly out through the windscreen. Whatever words he'd prepared died in his throat. Quite right, too, she thought in sudden wrath. What could he possibly say?

Trouble was, she couldn't think of anything either.

So he'd given up, and they'd carried on to Purley in silence. And in silence, still, Nina sat, an island of unhappiness in a sea of revelry.

'What's with those two, I wonder?' Helen Wallace watched Paul's back as it was swallowed up in the crowd. He'd come back to the booth with Juliet, but had paused only for a few gulps of lager before walking off again. 'Doesn't he know he's got a wife?'

'Major row brewing,' Lucky suggested.

'Or in progress.' Juliet, trying not to stare, took her seat and hunched forward.

'Oh, well,' Helen sighed, 'none of our business, eh?'

'Why not?' Lucky demanded at once.

Helen frowned at her. She seemed irritable tonight, inclined to jump down throats. To the DS, sub-letting to Lucky one end of her desk, she was an enigma. She'd thought she had her figured out that first morning, when she'd found the new trainee to be enchanting company. Lucky had tried hard since then, but somehow her heart didn't seem to be in the sunshine and smiles business as much as its owner would like. It was mystifying, because the obvious explanation - her feeling she couldn't hack it - didn't seem to apply. She'd slogged as hard as any of them and was, as far as Helen could tell, on top of everything that had been dumped in her lap. She made an odd contrast to her friend: Lucky in a dark blue top and Seven jeans, Juliet, ironically, more in keeping with the company in a strap-shoulder white dress of some satiny material. It seemed Lucky had misjudged the dress code again, and perhaps that was what was bothering her. Somehow Helen doubted it was that simple.

'*Should* be our business.' Lucky took a sip of her rum and black and pursued her theme. 'Nina's one of us, yeah? I can't believe you can say that.'

'She's also an old married woman, and that' - Helen gestured towards the Jacksons - 'looks like private business to me. If they want to share, they will.'

'Right,' Lucky said, puzzled, 'and in the meantime don't let it spoil our fun?'

A curly head interposed itself. Sandra Jones had overheard some of their conversation. 'You wondering about Nina?'

'Isn't everybody?' Helen said glumly.

'Bloody right. Wetherby's just opened his great cakehole over there - crafty sod always notices more than he lets on. Chances are this'll boil over later anyway, so I might as well forewarn you.' She stole a guilty glance at Nina, who was staring at the bottom of a Scotch and ginger. 'She walked out on him.'

'What?' Helen's eyes widened. 'Why?'

Sandra explained.

'So what's he doing here, then?'

'Buggered if I know,' Sandra said with a shrug. 'Sit back and watch the fireworks, I would.'

There was a sudden sharp thump of glass on table and Lucky stood up. To Juliet she said loudly, 'I'm going to the bar. D'you want another drink?'

Juliet, given little say in the matter, went off with her. Sandra peered after them, then looked at Helen.

'What's got *her* g-string in a twist?'

'Look, this is pointless. I'm gonna go.'

Paul cracked. Conscience had snared him and he'd come back to the booth to sit down. Grudgingly, Nina had moved up to make room. He was perched on the edge and she was aware of the muscles of his hip tense against hers. She had oppressed him into breaking the silence but she felt too bleak inside even to glory in his discomfort.

'Bye, then,' she said. 'I'll get a cab.'

'This was your idea.'

'Bad idea.'

'Now we're here, can't we at least - '

'What about?'

'What *about*?'

'Two things.'

'What?'

'All I want to know,' Nina said, 'two things. Why you did it, and who she is.'

He looked around. 'Can we move somewhere?'

'No,' she said. 'You've got something to say, say it here.'

'Why are you doing this?'

'Oh, you want me to spare your feelings? Like you spared mine?'

'I can't talk with that lot earwigging,' he pleaded, looking round at the team, some of whom were already casting odd glances in their direction. 'It's none of their business.'

'How do you know?' she said. 'Come to that, how do *I* know? How do I know it's not one of them you've been fucking behind my back?'

He recoiled as if from an electric shock and for a brief instant something sparked. She realised she'd never before used an obscenity to his face.

'Answer me,' she said, pressing it home.

'Nina, do credit me with a bit of common sense.'

'Common sense!' Her eyes shone and her lips puckered in indignation.

'It's not one of your precious team, all right?'

'But I know her.'

'Honey...'

'I know her,' Nina insisted.

'Doesn't matter who she is.'

'I'll be the judge of that.'

'No, listen,' he said. 'You want to know why, I'll tell you.'

'Aha. It speaks.'

'Look, Nina,' he began. Her acid jibe dissolved his response. He tried again. 'Look, it wasn't fair the way it was. That's why I went back to my parents.' It was coming out in a rush. 'I just couldn't face you, you hear? I was ashamed; I couldn't bring myself to phone, in case - '

'No, I *bet* you bloody couldn't.'

'Keep your voice down.'

'Off screwing your bimbo while I'm holed up at Sandra's like a fugitive from my own fucking home!'

Paul leapt up, his face a deep red. 'Shut up,' he hissed, 'and listen.' Angrily he sat down again and turned her round so she was facing him, so the others couldn't see her face. It was a pointless exercise; it would do nothing to distract attention, but he had hers now, undivided. He said, heavily, 'Now you listen. I've ditched her.'

'Ditched her,' she echoed.

'That's right. Given her the elbow. Told her to sling her hook. I am not seeing her any more,' he enunciated with petulant clarity.

Nina said, 'That's supposed to make me feel better, is it?'

'Well...'

'Wipe away the past, let's forget it ever happened?'

'Well, look, I didn't - '

'You clueless patronising bastard,' she said, shaking with fury. 'I bet the moment you heard me slam the door you told her to get dressed, you couldn't see her any more. Have I got that right?'

'About, yeah.'

'Oh, what a saint. So it takes being caught in the act before you realise I'm suddenly too precious for you to lose and it's not right for you to be knocking off some tart on the side!'

'She's not a tart,' he retorted, wishing he hadn't said it as soon as the words were out of his mouth.

'That's right, defend the fucking bitch! Not seeing her, my arse.'

'I'm *not*.'

Her cheeks were wet with angry tears. 'You're going straight to her, aren't you? Tonight? Straight fucking to her and bury your face in her tits and tell her what a nasty frigid bitch I am.' She couldn't stop. Hurling missile after missile, forcing him away.

'You're talking nonsense.'

'Am I?'

'Yes, you are.' Paul glared at his wife. 'I haven't been out all week, OK? Only place I've been is back to my parents'. Ask your mum or dad or your precious sister if you don't believe me.'

Nina sighed, heavily, the sigh turning into a whimper of misery. She said, 'You still don't get it, do you?'

'*Look!*' he said, slamming the side of the seat with his fist. 'I know. It was wrong. If I could make it not have happened I would. OK? But you were never bloody there. And when you were, all you wanted to do was sleep.'

'Oh, so sex is all this boils down to, is it?'

'I give up.' He sprang to his feet, not caring who overheard now. 'I just bloody well give up. I came here, sackcloth and ashes, to try and build some bridges. D'you know how much bottle it took just to ring the doorbell tonight? I came here to eat humble pie and grovel because I wanted to make it up to you. How, I don't know. I was hoping maybe you could tell me. But fine: if you feel our marriage isn't worth saving because of one... mistake, then fine. I might as well be in somebody else's bed. It's your loss.'

'That's right,' she heard herself yell. 'Check out.'

'Why not?' He whirled round. 'You did.'

She sat stunned, open-mouthed, gaze hovering at his chest as he stood over her.

'Actually I'm not gonna check out or go away,' he said. 'You asked me to come, and I'm staying. If you don't want to talk to me, maybe some of your mates might.' He cast his eye around the assembled group, who were all suddenly deep in conversations of their own. He said, 'I'm going for another dance.'

He strode off without looking back. Several pairs of eyes followed his every step until he disappeared in the crowd.

Suspended conversations resumed where they had been broken off, the effect like the spell cast on soap opera addicts, lifted as the episode credits roll. As Nina, stranded, hastily began a conversation with Kim, who sat nearest and slipped into supportive sergeant mode, those out of earshot released held breath.

'Well,' Zoltan said, 'that's got that out of the way. Not sure what was more painful, the row or his mixed metaphors.'

'Brace for more,' Marie said. 'Balloon's well and truly up.'

'So who *is* the other woman, exactly?'

Sandra cut in. 'Does it matter?'

Zoltan shrugged.

'Fucking lousy thing to happen to a marriage,' Sandra said. 'I mean can you imagine?'

'The worst,' Anne agreed.

'What she must be feeling. What *he* must.'

'Oh, I dunno,' Neil Jones said, sounding mildly perplexed. 'How about when I shagged that girl in Corfu?'

Everyone looked at the Joneses. Sandra came as near as she ever did to blushing. 'That's different.'

'How different?' Anne couldn't resist asking.

'Never you bloody mind.'

'She was there at the time,' Neil said cheerfully. 'That's how different.'

Sandra glared at her husband. He'd already had a bit too much to drink, and she knew from experience what fun the canteen cowboys would have if they got hold of this. Some of the faces close by wore grins that bordered on the predatory. 'Shut it now,' she babbled, 'if you want to ever have sex again.'

'Oops.'

'You can't compare that,' she railed at him. 'You just can't.'

Jeff moved closer to Jasmin, who to his dismay had lapsed back into gloom. 'Not quite what we expected, so far,' he remarked.

She made a noise with her tongue. 'I'm sure they do not mean to spoil things.'

'Course not.' He reflected for a moment. 'Everybody seems to be having some sort of crisis.'

She shot him what he took to be an enquiring frown.

'Lucky.' He peered towards the bar, but couldn't see her. 'She is?'

'Well, she's obviously not happy.'

'PMS.'

He didn't look convinced. 'What about you?'

She looked into his eyes full of modest concern, and mustered a smile. 'We are meant to be having fun,' she said. 'I don't want to get people down. Anne will think she is at a funeral.'

She laughed, and her eyes sparkled like gemstones. Jeff started to speak, but thought better of it and ran a pensive finger up and down the bridge of his nose. Something. None of his business, though, he realised with a pang of despair. A reminder, yet again, of how little time was left to him for the impossible pursuit of his feelings.

Lucky was causing light-hearted concern. Although the dancefloor was full of people her age, she'd so far seemed disinclined to join them. She preferred to stay in the booth, launching into energetic chats with whoever was left sitting. Several clubbers, including Neil, had asked, but had been declined with the same polite smile. Though Neil's offer was made at his wife's prompting - he'd been giving her the eye all evening - Sandra put her wary response down to the effect of the three-in-a-bed story. But even Juliet, of whom there'd been precious little sign anyway except when she came in for brief refreshment pitstops, seemed to lack the power of persuasion. Finally, dropping by with Lucky's rum and black, she slapped down the change, said, 'I give up on you, Larissa, I really do,' and was gone into the gyrating multitudes.

'Really, though,' Jeff tried, motivated by an unwelcome compulsion that it was his turn, 'you can't come to a club and not have at least one dance.'

Beside him, Jasmin giggled. Lucky noticed and said, 'Coming from you?'

'I'm serious,' he laboured. 'Not natural.'

'What, because I'm young and pretty?' she retorted. 'I should be out there pulling, not sat in a corner?' He adopted the hangdog expression she'd got to know during their trip to Rye, and she softened. 'No, I'm all right, thanks.'

She picked up her drink and took a deep swig. Casting his eye over the four empty glasses in front of her, Jeff said, 'Can you afford all them on a PC's salary?'

'Asks *DC* Wetherby.'

'Same rank, aye,' he corrected. 'But I get long service. *And* housing allowance.'

'Picky, picky.'

She said this very loudly, and it attracted the attention of a passing tuxedoed young man who appeared, by dint of the name tag on his lapel, to be a member of the club's staff. He stopped and leaned over the booth, looking her up and down with the unabashed nosiness of one used to authority. 'Miss,' he said solemnly, 'how did you get in?'

'I paid,' Lucky said.

Zoltan guessed what was coming and called out, 'It's OK, mate.'

'House policy, no jeans,' the man said. 'Men or women.'

'Piss off,' Lucky said.

'Right.' He made a move for her arm, which she yanked away. 'You're out of here.'

'Mate,' Zoltan said again, louder, 'it's all right.'

The man rounded on him. His scowl froze when he saw the DI's warrant card, brandished in his face like a grenade with the pin out. Without a word he turned and walked slowly away. Several clubbers turned stares in the team's direction.

'Oh, *God*,' Lucky moaned, head in hands. 'I'm sorry.'

'No problem,' Zoltan shrugged, employing his version of a reassuring smile. From him it was a glare, such as a primary school teacher might use as a warning against future bad behaviour.

The scene was over, but a moment later Anne tapped him on the arm and drew him to one side. 'Was that wise?'

He sighed, and put his arm round her. 'Anything for a quiet life.'

'A quiet life?' She raised her eyebrows. 'Now everyone in the room thinks we're here to make a bust.'

The quiet life was a philosophy Nina and Paul had adopted too. Against all odds, albeit influenced by alcohol, they'd agreed a truce. They were, after all, still husband and wife. The wife's attitude to the husband had softened when he left the dancefloor a very few minutes after storming out onto it and crouched down beside her.

'I can't keep up with that lot,' he yelled over the din. 'One of them called me Dad.' He grinned, relieved and delighted to see her laugh, even if it was at his expense rather than at the rudeness of the youth. 'Will you save my ego and dance with me?'

'You've got a fucking nerve.' But the obstinate smile that had commandeered her face robbed the words of their venom. She relented. 'Later. Let me think about it.'

She had thought about it, and decided the hell with it. With or without a husband, she was desperate for a good time, and it might as well be with.

They'd had four dances, and were almost friendly. The DJ had put on Moby, an artist Nina, even when she'd flirted with being a goth before joining the police, had always secretly adored. Moby's music, she and Paul had found during their courtship and the early days of their marriage, had a sensuous effect. As the swirling chords washed over them they'd moved cheek to cheek, then lips to lips. Now Paul's hands were on her bottom, stroking in that way of his that made her want to tear his trousers down on the spot. At that moment she would have done anything for her husband. Why didn't they do this any more?

'I've got to know,' she said suddenly, as the record faded.

He paused in his caressing. 'What?'

'If we're going to dig our way out of this, I need to know

what I've been doing wrong.'

Paul began to protest.

'No, look, I've had a think. There's fault on both sides. I want to know who she is.'

'Nina...'

'I know, I know. Don't worry, I'll let her live. I just need to know, so...'

'So what?'

'So I know what I'm up against.'

'*Were* up against.'

She studied his eyes, but they didn't waver. She said, 'All right. But whatever it is, maybe I can work on it.'

'You really don't want to know.'

'I'll be the judge.'

'You are not,' he tried desperately, 'going to like it.'

'I already don't like it. Just tell me.'

In the split second before the next track began blasting out of the PA, the whole club heard it.

'You *bastard!*'

Nina punched Paul hard in the face and ran off the dancefloor.

'Gawd,' Kim Oliver groaned, as the team watched her headlong flight. 'Here we go again.'

''Scuse me,' Sandra muttered, edging her way out of the booth.

She found Nina outside in the street, minus her jacket, looking wildly this way and that at the passing traffic as if searching for a taxi. At the touch of Sandra's hand on her arm she started.

'Come back inside, Nina.'

'Too hot in there.'

'One way of putting it,' Sandra said.

'I made him tell me,' Nina said matter-of-factly, spotting a black cab and making a move towards the kerb. Sandra hauled her back.

'You can't get a taxi.'

'I've got to.'

'You can't. You left your handbag inside. Come on.'

'D'you think I was asking for it?'

'I dunno,' Sandra said, ushering her back up the steps. 'I wasn't privy to the conversation.'

'I thought I could try and live up to whoever she was, what she had to offer that I didn't,' Nina said, half hysterically. 'But *this*! This takes the fucking biscuit.'

'Do I know her?'

'How the hell am I meant to compete with...?' She tripped on the top step in uncoordinated rage. 'What is it? What's missing?'

'I dunno,' Sandra said again, wishing Nina would make some sense. She pushed open the door and scowled at a doorman who moved to block their path. He stepped aside.

Back at the booth there was no sign of Paul. Somewhere, there was an irritating buzzing noise.

'Well,' Sandra said, 'that one of us or not?'

'It's me,' Nina said, calm again. 'I'm on call.'

Helen picked up Nina's bag and handed it to her. She took it with a cursory nod, rummaged inside, glanced at the mobile and scampered off to find somewhere quiet to talk.

'Saved by the bell,' Zoltan Schneider said.

It took them a few minutes to realise she wasn't coming back. Sandra was sent in search of her. She hadn't checked her jacket out of the cloakroom, but the doorman took great satisfaction in informing her that he'd seen her go outside again. Sandra went out onto the pavement, but Nina wasn't there. She must have found a cab after all.

Cursing, she went back in. Paul was with the team, holding a frosted beer glass to an eye that was well on the way to a world-class shiner. He said, 'Did you find her?'

'Gone,' Sandra grumbled. 'Buggered off in a cab or bus, most likely. Whatever that call was, looks like she's wanted at the nick.'

Strictly speaking, Nina knew, it wasn't her case. Sandra had been in on the original interview, and at the very least she should have rung Sophia at home. But the incident seemed so peripheral, so easily sorted, there was no point ruining Sandra's evening, or disturbing the guv'nor's beauty sleep and dragging her all the way over from Sevenoaks.

So she told herself. Not so deep down, she knew perfectly well why she'd left without a word. What Paul had told her had taken away her last hope of keeping the keel stable. Instead of a goal, she was left with the starkness of rejection.

The call was an opportunity to escape, to cast the ruins of her marriage to the back of her mind for a while. Most immediately, to devote her full attention to sobering up while the taxi drove her home so that she could change and take her own car. Before long she was in the charge room at Croydon nick. Drunken hollers echoed occasionally up from the cells, but apart from a young black man slumped on a bench the room itself was empty. The female custody sergeant was new, and looked up without recognition.

'DC Tyminski,' Nina told her. 'You rang me.'

'Fun night?' The sergeant looked her up and down. Nina realized she must still look a lot more over the limit than she felt. Self-consciously she straightened up. The sergeant gestured towards the figure on the bench. 'That there is Mr Luke Benton. Picked up outside Mayday burns unit.'

Nina frowned at the sleeping youth. 'D and D?'

'Right,' the sergeant said. 'The lads who brought him in thought it was probably the booze talking, but he kept shouting about having some information for DCI Beadle. Mean anything?'

'Maybe,' Nina lied. 'Have you charged him?'

The sergeant seemed to take this as an affront to the way she ran things. She frowned and said, 'He wouldn't be sitting there if I had.'

'I s'pose not.'

'He's got no previous so I gave him a mild ticking off, whereupon he promptly fell asleep.'

'Great,' Nina sighed. 'What d'you want me to do with him?'

'There's a Mr Lynott waiting out front to take him home,' the sergeant said. 'What say you go find him?'

Between them they managed to get Luke mobile, but he was barely conscious. His friend stood up in alarm as they emerged into the front office, but said nothing until he'd relieved the custody sergeant of her burden. Grimacing, she wiped dribble off her shoulder with a hankie and disappeared back into the bowels of the station.

'Mr Lynott?'

'Nick,' the friend said, peering at Luke for some sign of recognition. 'What's happening?'

Nina told him about it and identified herself. 'We haven't met, but I am involved with the investigation. Luke's staying with your folks, is that right?' Nick nodded. 'First thing, we'd better get him home. Have you got transport?'

'No way.' Nick shook his head emphatically. 'I've had four lagers. Wasn't gonna risk it.'

With a twinge of guilt, Nina said, 'All right, sit him down here for a sec. I'll bring my car round.'

A few minutes later they were heading for Thornton Heath. Getting Luke's rag doll body into the back seat of the Mini had proved an impossible task. Nina had finally decided to let him go in the front, and run the risk of him chucking up on her cardigan.

Over her shoulder she asked Nick, 'Any idea how he got like this?'

'He's been moping around the hospital all week,' Nick said, 'and when he ain't been moping around there he's been sitting in his room. Me and a couple of mates decided to take him out for the evening, try and get his mind off his troubles.'

'How much did he have to drink?'

'Dunno.'

'Sev'n pints 'n' two double Scotches,' Luke slurred proudly, and went back to sleep.

'Thanks,' Nina said without blinking. 'So what happened?'

'Said he was going for a piss,' Nick said. 'When he didn't come back and we couldn't find him, we assumed he'd gone home.'

'But when you got back he wasn't there?'

'My parents were in bed. The door to the spare room was shut so I thought he must be and all. Then half an hour later the police rang. Said he'd been running round the hospital, shouting and causing a disturbance.'

'The officers who picked him up said something about him yelling he had information for my guv'nor - Mrs Beadle,' Nina said. 'Any idea what that might've been about?'

'Didn't they tell you?'

'They're back out on patrol. I haven't had a chance to talk to them yet.'

Nick said, 'Luke mentioned a phone call; it'd answer a lot of questions or something, he said. Nearest he got to talking about the fire. We were trying to keep him off the subject.'

'He didn't say who the call was from?'

'Not in my hearing.' She could see Nick's reflection glaring at her in the rear view mirror. 'Why don't you ask him?'

SUNDAY

The endurance of even the hardiest coppers starts to flag, faced at two in the morning by a nightclub filled for the most part with the energetic gyrations of people who seem barely out of the cradle; by a layer of noise from the sound system as thick now as the alcoholic fog that now filled several of the team's skulls. Jeff Wetherby had to crane across the table to Anne to make himself heard.

'As somebody once said,' he yelled, 'I'm getting too old for this shit.'

'Bollocks.' Sandra, omnipresent tonight, stuck her head in between them. 'All in your mind. Look at me.'

'Aye, we all know *you'll* stay till the bitter end.'

'And us,' Anne backed her up, linking her arm in with Zoltan's.

'Wimp,' Sandra said.

'It's not just me.'

'Well,' Sandra leered, 'can only be one other reason you'd want to slope off.'

He paled at the inference and reflexively started to look behind him for Jasmin. 'I only said soon.'

'Long as you're up,' Sandra said, pointing, 'd'you want to do something about that?'

He followed her finger. Lucky had had two or three more rums, and it showed. She'd laid her head on her folded arms on the table, and appeared to be talking volubly about something. Paul was trying to get her to sit up, but from the look on his face she was giving him a hard time.

'Before they try and chuck her out again,' Jeff sighed. 'OK. See if I can find Juliet.'

It took a while, but eventually he prised her away from a young man who seemed to think he was a stag in the rutting season. Passing mention of a nice warm cell got it through to him that Jeff was a copper, and that squaring up wouldn't be a good idea.

'Lucky's a bit the worse for wear,' Jeff explained, as they made their way back to the booth.

'What's she done?'

'Nothing terrible, yet. She's had about six rum and blacks, but other than that - '

'*Six*? Oh, great.'

'Can't hold her drink?'

'Depends.' Juliet quickened her pace. 'I didn't realise she'd... I only saw her have two.'

Paul moved along to make space for her as she clambered over people's legs. 'There you are.' Lucky lifted her head and let it drop again. 'Missed all the fun.'

'I heard,' Juliet said, anxious not to let her embarrass Paul with a full-volume report on Nina's dramatic exit.

'See, what he realises,' Lucky persisted, 'is he can get away with treating us like shit, 'cause we give off all the wrong signals. Women, I mean. Men treat us like shit, and we just go round with our chins on our chests putting up with it, hoping they'll take it as a signal we're unhappy.'

'Larissa,' Juliet said, 'you're pissed.'

'I've never done that. Always had self-respect. Always. Never let anybody treat me like shit. And now I don't know what's happening.'

She turned her head away and buried her face in her arms.

'Loads of people get drunk,' Marie Kirtland called across. '*I* get drunk on occasion. Doesn't make me an alkie.' Lucky didn't move. Marie frowned. 'I think I misunderstood.'

'I'm going to have to take her home,' Juliet said, looking up.

'D'you need a lift?' Neil said.

'We can get a cab.'

'Have to wait hours, this time of night,' Sandra said. 'Somebody can take you.'

'Anyone going New Addington way?' Juliet asked, none too hopefully.

Kim said, 'I can make a detour.'

Juliet looked remorseful. 'Don't want to spoil the party.'

'That's all right. I was about ready to call it a night anyway.'

'Told you,' Jeff said pointedly to Sandra.

Nina left Nick Lynott to put Luke to bed and aimed the car homewards. Passing through the town centre, on an impulse she took the underpass towards South Croydon instead of the left turn into George Street and Addiscombe Road.

In the twilight before dawn 84 Chapel View looked

almost rustic, with little hint of the inferno that had left Doreen Benton dead and little Robin in intensive care, dangling from a fraying thread of life. She parked and stared unedifyingly at it for a few minutes, then drove on, as if summoned, to the Clarkes' house in Ballards Way. She understood what Kim had meant about the Polaroid and why it had been driving her crazy; there was something here as well, something that in her distressed state of mind she'd allowed to escape into her subconscious.

Careful, at this still hour, not to make too much noise with engine or handbrake, she pulled up at the observation point she'd used before. She was surprised to see light shining from a chink in the Clarkes' downstairs curtains. Someone was still up. Everything else seemed as usual: windows closed, burglar alarm on, both cars in the drive.

Then she saw something that hadn't been there. Parked outside the house was a dark blue Vauxhall Astra. Nina had been driving since she was seventeen, and knew about unvarying suburban habits, residents and commuters who parked in the same spot day after day. She'd never seen an Astra there before, and besides, almost all the houses in Ballards Way had garages or driveways.

On a whim, she reached for her phone and dialled the CAD room. The musical Swansea accent of Derek Simons answered her and she smiled. She liked Derek. Unaware of her married status, he'd once asked her out. She felt almost reckless enough to encourage him to try again, but not right now.

'It's Nina Tyminski,' she said. 'Sorry to use the direct line, only I haven't got a PR. I'm on my mobile.'

'No problem. It's quiet tonight. What can I do you for, then?'

'I wonder if you can PNC a vehicle for me?'

'Have to ask you for your warrant number,' Derek said.

She gave him her mobile number as well, and the Astra's colour and registration, cut the connection and waited. It took him only moments.

'Tyminski.'

'Dark blue Astra,' Derek said, reading back the index number. 'Tax and MOT expired. Registered to a Michael Philip Quaife, 33 Carmen Street, SW8. Good one, this, 'cause - '

'I know about his previous,' Nina said. 'Thanks a lot, Derek. I owe you.'

She cut him off in mid-polite disclaimer and sat, heartbeat racing, trying to decide on a course of action. She knew now, thanks to Luke's drunken ramblings, where the attention of the enquiry should be directed; just as clearly as she now recalled what it was about that night in the Clarkes' living room that had so troubled her.

'Only I thought since she's off anyway,' Jeff said, 'you'd be going with Kim.'

'She has enough on her plate right now, don't you think?' Jasmin smiled and pointed to the booth, where Lucky had finally been coaxed to her feet.

'You could be right.' He took a deep breath that did nothing to quell the butterflies. 'OK, then, shall we go?'

'Uh-huh.'

Nearby, further departures were being prepared. Juliet's efforts to persuade Lucky to accept a lift having finally paid off, Kim Oliver found Anne with Zoltan on the dancefloor and exchanged goodbyes that, from both women's points of view, were unexpectedly emotional.

'I feel sorry for you it's been a bit, like, eventful.'

'Not at all.' Anne sniffed and wiped away a tiny tear. 'It could have been boring, and then I wouldn't've missed you all.'

'After all,' Zoltan put in, employing one of his most sardonic grins, 'what would a Special Crime piss-up be without a healthy serving of drama?'

'Quite right,' Anne said, kissing him firmly on the lips. 'I'm having a fantastic time.'

'Probably see you around, then,' Kim said.

'Probably.' Anne broke away from Zoltan and embraced her again. 'Bye... sarge.'

'Sarge yourself,' she grinned. 'Good luck making movies.'

'At a guess,' Jeff said, 'bad news from home.'

'Not exactly.'

'Oh,' he muttered. 'Strike one.'

They drove on in silence for a while, watching the sky lighten to violet.

'Not from home.'

He started. 'You don't have to...'

'I promised I would,' she said. 'I went to Scotland Yard yesterday.'

'What, your exchange review thing?'

'Right.'

'Didn't go OK?'

'Sure, great,' she said bitterly. 'I'm doing real well. Also the Met cop over in Amsterdam. So now they extend the exchange for six months.'

'Ah,' Jeff said, suppressing his own selfish joy and relief with a pang of guilt.

'I was looking forward to be home for Christmas,' Jasmin said sadly.

'You still can,' he said. 'Take time off.'

'It's not the same. I must come back.'

A traffic light glared red. Jeff stopped the car. 'So where's that leave you? In practical terms?'

'What do you mean?'

'I mean like a place to stay. Still in that Arctic room of yours, aren't you?'

A sour expression crossed her face, like a reminder of an unpaid bill. '*Ja*. It's getting a little warmer; I was thinking maybe I can stick it out until December...' She tailed off.

'But now you don't know?'

Jasmin shook her head.

'Have you told Kim?'

'She will just offer me a bunk down at her place, but I don't want to impose. If I tell her, she will insist.'

'Kim's place is very nice.'

'I know. But she is all the way to Penge and I don't have my own car. Also I need my space.'

He pondered. 'Furnished flats,' he suggested. The lights changed and he put his foot down. 'Self-contained. Look on Craigslist, the Gumtree. Might still have to share a bathroom, but basically you're your own boss.' He smiled. 'I could help you look.'

'OK,' she smiled back, 'but how do I pay for it?'

'Do some more overtime.' He regretted the suggestion at once.

'Overtime is killing me.' She didn't need to tell him.

'Look what happened the other day.'

'How about another shared house? One where the heating works.'

'Ach, always there is something with shared houses. If not the heating, then something else, like, the electric meter jams, or your housemates are crazy, or they wish six months of rent in advance, or the landlord is a pervert. I might as well move to a section house.'

'Why don't you?'

'You need to get away from cops sometimes,' she smiled. 'No offence.'

'None taken.'

Too soon, the journey was over. He turned to her. 'Door to door. Can't ask for better service.'

'I can too,' she retorted. 'What about the driver escorts his passenger in?'

'What, *in*, in, or just to the door?'

'Inside, twit,' she said, cuffing him none too gently. Her gruff facade dropped for a moment. 'Anyway, the room is cold and I don't want to be alone yet.'

Jeff killed the engine and applied the handbrake. '"Lead on, Macduff."'

'Huh?'

'Oh, come on. They do have Shakespeare in Holland.'

They got out of the car.

'I don't know this Macduff,' Jasmin said.

'The Scottish play.'

'Huh?'

'Never mind.'

In the darkened hall she groped behind the door until she found the old bicycle lamp the inhabitants used as a torch during the frequent spates of electrical failure that affected parts, or all, of the house. By its guiding light she led the way upstairs. On the landing they stopped outside a door. 'Hold that,' she said, passing him the lamp. She inserted her key in the lock. The door was stuck in the jamb. She shoulder-charged it open, stepped aside and stood by for him to enter.

He'd been in Jasmin's room before, but never on his own. The previous occasion had been following a cinema trip with Kim and Brian Hunt. Afterwards they'd all come back here for pizza and cards. Now, without all the people, it was easy to see why she wore herself out with long hours at work. No-one in their right mind would spend time here willingly, except to sleep. Last time he'd not realised how cold, dingy and plain inhospitable the room was, despite the brave effort she'd made to brighten it up. The brown paint on the skirting boards and the window frame was cracked and peeling. Mould crept carcinogenously up the once rich cream-coloured wallpaper, which adhered to the damp-sodden walls in a way that suggested it only stayed there out of a misplaced sense of loyalty. It lent a pervasive musty odour to the room which Jasmin had tried to counter by deploying a couple of reed diffusers on the mantelpiece. The furniture consisted of a bed, a small, flimsy dressing table, a chair that didn't match, and a deal wardrobe with a hinge missing. Jasmin could have fixed this herself, but where, frankly, was the motivation? Fix one thing, and there would still be another, and another. For a temporary base she spent as little time in as possible, it wasn't worth the effort. Yet this one room, together with an equally soul-destroying, unheated bathroom and kitchen shared with three other tenants, looked like being Jasmin Winter's home address for the next year.

'Best not take off your jacket,' she warned.

'Wasn't going to.'

'Brr!' She had on her only eveningwear, an electric blue, crushed velvet strapless dress with separate sleeves. She dashed over to the bed, grabbed the thick grey wool cardigan she used as a bedjacket and put it on. She kicked off her shoes. 'OK, it looks weird. But I'm cold.'

'Looks fine,' he said. To him it wasn't the clothes that mattered - although as far as bits of him were concerned, they helped. He added, 'That dress looks grand on you.'

She made a face. 'What is the saying? Best of a bad job.'

'Honestly.'

'Thanks.' Her smile was the only warm thing in the house. 'Even though I know it's bullshit, what you say.'

'It's not bullshit.'

Embarrassed, she covered her mouth with a hand. 'I can offer you a hot drink.'

'*Have* to be hot,' he said. 'What's going?'

He followed her downstairs in the dark to the kitchen diner at the back of the house. The drink was, she warned him, conditional on her fellow tenants' practice of intermittently thieving the groceries. They had, as it turned out, been in Jasmin's Ovaltine tin, but there was still just enough left in the bottom. She found some milk that hadn't turned and poured it into a pan to heat.

'So,' she said, searching the cupboards for biscuits, 'a good night out, *ja*?'

'For some.'

'I prefer to remember the fun parts.'

'Best way.' Jeff fingered his collar. He wasn't about to loosen it, though, let the draught in down the front of his neck. He added, 'Think Nina's going to be OK?'

Jasmin shrugged. 'I hope so.'

'Sandra's been putting her up, did you hear her say?'

'Uh-huh.' She hugged herself. 'I wonder what she said to her. Outside.'

'Probably unrepeatable.'

They laughed, full of warmth for their extraordinary colleague. For a moment the cold house seemed less oppressive. 'Sometimes,' Jasmin said, 'I think that if Sandra was not a cop, she would make a good doctor.'

'Dunno about that. Imagine her bedside manner.'

Their Ovaltine ready, they went back upstairs.

'Sit on the bed. I have only this one chair and it's not comfortable.' He sat, pulling himself back so he could lean against the wall. Jasmin said, 'Can I come right up close to you? We will keep each other warm.'

'Be my guest.'

Uncertainly, he extended a welcoming arm. She slipped within his embrace and snuggled up to him, her head resting on his shoulder.

'People would talk, if they saw us,' she said.

'No, they wouldn't. Their teeth'd be too bloody busy chattering.'

They giggled.

'Left our mugs on the mantelpiece.'

'Let them stay there for a bit.' She clutched his waist.

'I think this is as warm as we're going to get,' he hazarded.

'Maybe,' Jasmin said softly.

Given the presence of a car registered to a known violent criminal, Nina knew she should call for backup. But at this hour police vehicles would be heard approaching a long way off; and while marching up to the Clarkes' door now might well bag them Quaife, it could not only rob them of the chance to find any link to Porter, the fire and Mark Watkins, but also endanger more lives.

Besides, she was feeling reckless.

She decided to reconnoitre.

In between several of the houses were alleyways, of the kind that lurk between the back-to-back gardens of suburbia, offering a run to urban foxes and a convenient repository for grass cuttings and weeds. She walked to the nearest one, noting the number of properties between it and the Clarkes', knowing how different houses could look from the back. A few steps took her out of sight of the street, in between high plank fences that smelled of fresh creosote. A smile crossed her face, a sudden childhood memory. Left to amuse themselves in school holidays, she and her sisters as a trio of African explorers, creeping unseen through forbidden places.

At the far end, as she'd expected, another alleyway cut across at right angles, running between the back gardens of Ballards Way and those of the next street. It was still too dark to see far ahead, and she hoped there were enough knotholes and gaps in the fence for her to pinpoint where she was. The path was overgrown with great clumps of bindweed and ground elder, cow parsley and nettles, and she was thankful she'd changed into jeans. In her childhood she would have imagined this a fairytale, she hacking through the undergrowth to free Sleeping Beauty with a kiss.

The Clarkes lived eight houses along. If she stood back she had a clear view of the upstairs windows. There were no lights. She stared at the fence, trying to decide what to do next.

And noticed that, providentially, this garden had a gate.

Warrant? Reasonable suspicion as to the presence of a suspect, she told herself, lifting the latch. If that didn't fly, she was technically already trespassing anyway. As well to be hung for a sheep as a lamb. The gate was not locked. Another thing about these alleyways, they were a godsend for burglars. She slipped through.

Closing it behind her, she inhaled, but never got to let out the deep sigh of relief that went next because something travelling at speed hit her below the ribs and sent her crashing breathless to the ground.

There came a point when the mood between them changed irrevocably, but it was some time before they did anything about it.

Was it Jeff who made the move, lowering his lips to Jasmin's and, elated, felt her respond? Or did she, brown eyes raised, invite him wordlessly to kiss her? If they ever wondered, by that time it hardly mattered.

She sat up to face him and wound her arms around his neck, caressing it and the back of his head with strong fingers. He brought his hands up to her shoulders, easing away the cardigan. Presently it lay spread on the bed behind her, and her bare shoulders were open to his unsteady hands. She sighed and replaced her arms, kissing him still more intensely, her tongue fusing with his, pressing warmth against soft, flexing warmth.

They were long minutes like that. Then their mouths parted; he kissed her chin, on down to her neck and shoulders, while she slipped her fingers under his jacket, her warm hands brushing his chest through the shirt, trembling across to slip the jacket off, then undoing his tie, fingers tangling and touching his chin and throat. She was sighing, short of breath, under his kisses. His hands were trickling down her spine, fumbling fingers finding the tiny hook that took an eternity to undo, and the zip that didn't, as the dress opened and clinging velvet gave way to cold air. And then the dress was being drawn down by gentle but unpracticed hands as his lips and tongue followed, making the goosebumps on her breasts thrill before warming them away.

Moaning, she shifted herself and took the dress right off, allowing him a long glimpse of the body he'd dreamed of experiencing. She'd worn nothing underneath; clad now only in the velvet sleeves she crawled into bed, under the blankets and out of the cold, edging nearer the wall to leave him room.

Watching her watching him, he stood and took off the rest of his clothes. He approached the bed, erect and distended in want for her so much as to be almost painful. Fast. So fast. Uncertain, he checked. He was terrified of making a wrong move, of having misinterpreted whatever it was she meant. Now, after so long, that she seemed to be responding to his feelings for her, it must be right. Ruin it now, and it would destroy him. He was confused, not thinking straight. An inner voice spoke up. Here he was, standing in all his glory in front of a bed containing the woman of his heart, naked and waiting for him. Misinterpret *that*, loverboy. Jeff drew back the covers and climbed into bed with Jasmin.

She came to him, pressing the length of her body against his, breasts moulding themselves to the contours of his chest. Their lips reunited, sliding betwixt and between, discovering all over again. He stroked her back, gliding downwards to the swell of her buttocks which he kneaded, pushing their groins urgently together. Waves of spicy perfume washed up his nose. He wished to draw her whole body inside him where he could keep her forever.

'Oh, my,' she said. She withdrew her hips a little, firmly but very gently so he would not think of rejection. She rolled to him and let a hand coast downwards, velvet-covered arm brushing him, exploring for the shapes and spaces of his hips and groin. Between his legs she went. He cried out in barely controllable ecstasy as her fingers triggered bombs in his lower body. He could bear no more. He had to have her. Driven by this compulsion his hand swept down, coaxing her onto her back. It glided over her belly, combing through the brittle curls of her groin to find the warm, silky dampness of its destination. A cry burst from her. Her squeezing hand left his penis and grasped his hip, fingertips digging into the flesh, tugging him towards her, inviting, demanding.

They were still kissing. He broke away. 'Protection,' he murmured. Eyes half open, lips parted, she nodded.

'Hurry.'

He hurried, stumbling out of bed, grabbing his jacket, dropping it, picking it up again and somehow, after seconds that seemed hours, finding the right pocket. He tore the foil open and stood weak-kneed while she helped to unroll the condom down the length of his erection. It flitted through his mind that Jasmin was a Roman Catholic; not, evidently, something she allowed to get in the way of good sense.

He climbed back into bed and slipped at last in between her thighs. He took a moment to adjust himself. Feeling his difficulty, she reached down and took hold, guiding him. He throbbed at her touch again. He entered her.

And came almost immediately. A climax he'd been

expecting and dreading still took him by surprise with its intensity. With a few frantic thrusts he pushed himself deep inside her, but it was all over so quickly, leaving him released, but unsatisfied.

He groaned with a mixture of rapture and embarrassment. Then, as abruptly as the feelings had come, they were gone, replaced by a surge of shame.

'Shit,' he panted, burying his face in her neck. 'I'm sorry. I really, truly am.'

'Why?'

He screwed up his eyes, which had been tight shut ever since he'd felt himself begin to explode. 'Jeff Wetherby, the one minute marvel.'

'Is that all?' Jasmin said. Her arms were still round him.

A slow sigh escaped him. Useless to say, true though it might be, that it had never happened before. This had been it, she was the one, and he'd blown it.

And yet...

A former girlfriend had once told Jeff women were attracted to him because he was the sort of bloke they felt able to have a crisis at. Choosing to take this as a compliment, he tried grafting it onto the present situation. True, Jasmin was at a low ebb, but it had been an innocent lift home, nothing planned, both of them almost completely sober. One minute they'd been in a chaste embrace; the next, almost without knowing it, they were making love.

But it was more than that. They both knew it.

Because she'd whispered into his ear, with a note of wonder, 'Oh, my.'

At last, he dared to open his eyes. One look at her, at her face glowing with amazement, told him all his fears were unfounded. They understood, and smiled together. Because he'd never fallen in love before, it hadn't occurred to him that the feeling might be reciprocated.

He felt like laughing for joy at the simplicity of it all. Of course he hadn't been able to control himself. It would have been like trying to outrun a tsunami.

Half-stunned, suffocating, stars blotting out her vision. Someone grabbing her arms, dragging her along on her back. Over the roaring in her ears, a voice hissing, 'Handcuffs. In her bag, probably.'

She was hauled to her feet, thrown against something hard and cold, arms twisted behind her. A vicious tug, and she felt the bite of the zip-tie restraints into her wrists. Her legs buckled and she scrambled to stand. She grasped for control of her lungs, took a first laboured, wheezing breath just as another blow, higher between her breasts and not quite so hard, slammed her against the rough surface at her back. There was sharp excruciating pain, a hot, slow trickle down her legs, and the dizzy sickness squeezed her like a fist. Finally the stars cleared. Her head was a dead weight, but she lifted it, and was able to see what, and who, had happened to her.

Dim as the light still was, dim as her vision seemed swiftly to be turning, she knew the face. She'd seen it by proxy through a telephoto lens, as its owner, frozen in time, closed his front door behind him.

'Can't read it in this light.' Edward Porter had her warrant card in his hand and was holding it high, as though trying to catch the first rays of the sun. 'Tym...offski? Bloody Polish, are you?'

She closed her eyes and tried to keep the shake from her voice. 'Police officer.'

'No shit,' he responded coolly. 'Can't even keep Polacks out of the fuzz now. No wonder none of you job robbers ever get deported.'

She swallowed hard, fighting the monster, feeling the hatred of this man for all things not as he was. It gave him strength, the enormity of it; strength, at this moment, directed towards her alone. Opening her eyes again was agony, acute and unexpected, like ripped fingernails. Her joints were trembling, giving way as she struggled to keep upright against the tree she'd been secured to. The blows seemed to have numbed her whole body, so that it would no longer do what she required of it.

'Scream if you like.' Porter spoke with the relaxed, sadistic amusement of a hunter watching his prey die. 'By the looks of you you've probably got, what, a couple of minutes before you black out, so by all means hasten the process if you feel so inclined.' Still rummaging in her handbag, he had found her phone, and now he ejected the battery and hurled it into the next garden.

Dimly she could make out two other people, lurking in the gloom behind. One of them wore pyjamas and a dressing gown, hugging himself, face pale. Others like Andrew Clarke slept in the bedrooms of neighbouring houses, some possibly rising even now, moving to open curtains, to look out at the morning and what it held.

'Doesn't bother me either way,' Porter said, reading her thoughts. 'By the way, don't take this personally, other than the fact that I hate your immigrant guts. In case you were wondering, your job here is to serve,' he hissed in her ear, 'as an example. To someone who needs to know we're going to get to him before the pigs do.'

As if on an unseen signal, the third man stirred and moved forward. Michael Quaife's arms were folded almost carelessly, but she could see the shaped, polished blade he held in his huge fist, one serrated edge glittering in the dawn like dew on a cobweb, and suddenly, in horror, she realised the Bowie knife was what had hit her, and the warm liquid down her legs was not piss. Hail Mary, full of grace -

Porter tilted his head slightly, perhaps expecting her to challenge him, or at least spit in his face, if she still had the strength. But Nina, though mortally afraid, wasn't about to give him the satisfaction. She thought hard of other things, desperate to keep her brain alert, remembering a conversation she'd had with Paul arising from old TV news reports of soldiers captured by the Taliban. Paul had been of the opinion that your best tactic in that situation was to keep silent, give your captors nothing they could twist round and use back at you. It worked for some hardened villains back at the nick, but this wasn't an interview and she wasn't in control. She could forgive Paul a lifetime of betrayals if he'd only appear and be her white knight now.

But he wasn't here. After tonight he never would be. Succumbing to despair, she uttered a terrified whimper.

'Edward, for God's sake.' The quiet, shocked voice, empty now of the bluster that had characterised many of his dealings with the police, belonged to Andrew Clarke.

'Andrew.' Porter spoke mildly, almost avuncularly, turning to him. He started to back away, catching something Porter tossed in his direction. 'Move her car. It's like a bloody signpost. We don't know how she found us here yet.'

Yet.

It wormed through the wound, a gash made far worse in her mind by the fact she couldn't see it, couldn't feel it. It wrapped her heart in icy coils and squeezed. *Yet.*

Quaife laughed contemptuously as Andrew Clarke fled back to the house. 'Tosser.'

'Out of his depth.' They seemed for a moment not to care she was there. 'Good at noticing unmarked police cars at three in the morning, and keeping track of nosy FOB policewomen who go crashing round the backs of houses. Comes to necessary unpleasantness, though, he's not your man and never was.' He looked at Nina now, probing for a reaction to the knowledge she'd been rumbled from the outset. She hoped he saw none.

A car drove by on Ballards Way. Porter looked at his watch.

'I count on you to deal with her,' he said to Quaife. 'Beyond that, as I said, I don't much care.'

Quaife peered at Nina. 'Few more minutes, she's not telling us anything.'

'She's got nothing to tell us I'm interested in hearing,' Porter sighed. 'Nothing to tell *anyone*, as it happens.'

He turned slowly away, then hesitated and stepped right up to her.

'Pretty, for a Polack.' He spoke to Nina rather than Quaife. 'Even racist fascist bastards have weaknesses.'

His hand reached up. She cringed as one finger traced a line down her jaw and under her chin. Her skin seethed with pain where he'd touched it. She cried out. A black curtain descended. Panicking, she escaped it, Nina the heroine struggling free of the thorns round Sleeping Beauty's castle. Reality returned. Porter was gone. She heard the back door close behind him.

Inside the house, someone was watching from an upstairs window. Featureless from here, but she knew all the same she'd been right. There had been *three* empty mugs on the coffee table that night. Three. The clue had, literally, been staring her in the face.

But, as Porter had just suggested and the looming figure of Michael Quaife reminded her, it was a bit late now.

To the despair of environmentalists, Kim Oliver was one of those drivers who invariably choose the straightest line from A to B, even if it means straying far from anything resembling a main road. As a young PC in patrol cars she'd spent so much time down rat runs the relief had nicknamed her Rizzo. Even night's empty highways could not entice her off the back streets, if it meant deviating from her planned itinerary.

Her idea of the quick way to New Addington took them through Purley to South Croydon, then north-east on side streets to emerge onto Croham Valley Road just below the golf course. A quarter of a mile further on Kim turned into Ballards Way.

The plan was to cut across to the top of Gravel Hill, where the main road descended towards Addington. While not consciously thinking about it her choice of route, she realised, was probably influenced by memories of following Andrew Clarke to the Keeper and Wicket. Her surprise, therefore, at seeing what was parked in the space they'd used for obbo was sufficient for her to press her foot down momentarily on the brake.

'What was that?' Lucky, whom fresh air from the open windows seemed to have sobered up somewhat, righted herself from her back seat slump and glanced over her shoulder. 'Fox?'

'Thought I saw Nina's car.'

'Where?'

'Back there. The black Mini.'

Lucky looked again, but they'd rounded a bend. 'Nope.'

'Lot of Minis,' Juliet suggested. 'Probably a different car altogether.'

'Yeah, probably,' Kim frowned. 'I mean we pulled out of there like a week ago.'

The matter closed, silence fell again and they travelled on.

It was difficult to know what was meant to happen next. Jeff withdrew despondently and was about to get out of bed when Jasmin's arm closed round him with the secure grip of a grappling hook. He lay down again and she nestled, head on his shoulder, warm body tight against his side.

'In my bag there are tissues,' she said, stroking his torso with a velvet-clad arm. 'So clean up a bit, huh? And we'll begin again.'

Hardly daring to believe what he'd heard he leaned out of bed for her handbag. He sat up and allowed her to remove the condom and wipe away the residue. His pleasurable moan wavered, like a distorted sound effect, and he closed his eyes, feeling the red rising on his cheeks.

'Huh?' Her breasts swayed as she leaned over, taunting him.

'I've got no more condoms.' Fuck! Where on earth had he got the idea it wasn't classy to carry more than one?

'Don't worry.' She bowed down and, to his astonishment,

kissed him softly on the tip of his dwindling penis. His stomach somersaulted. Smiling, she glanced up. 'I am on the pill.'

He frowned. 'Hardly the point.'

'Is it a problem?'

'Not for me,' he shrugged. 'Got tested a year or so back. Druggie stabbed me in the neck with a needle. All clear though.' He was babbling, and willed himself to shut up.

'I also. So I trust you.' Another smile, then she drew towards him again and kissed him in several places.

He closed his eyes, surprised to feel himself respond so quickly. The climax had released tension, but not fulfilled his greater need. He smiled. 'I'll give it a go.'

'When you thought Debbie was dead?'

'What?' Kim frowned in the mirror at Lucky. They were at the roundabout, waiting to get onto Gravel Hill. To the east the sky was salmon pink above the downs beyond Forestdale. All three women felt the weariness of having been up all night, and now they looked the part as well.

'That's why we called it off, yeah?' Lucky said. ''Cause of that photo. Only now we know she might still be alive.'

The way was clear, but Kim felt a sudden disinclination to move. 'It *was* Nina's car,' she reiterated, certain now.

'She say what that phone call was about?'

'No.' Kim swung the car three hundred and sixty degrees round the roundabout. 'She just took off.'

'You got Nina's number?'

Kim handed over her mobile and Lucky scrolled through the address book, pressed send, waited and disconnected with a shake of her head.

'Voicemail.'

She dialled again from memory and had a terse conversation.

'Apparently they rang the Special Crime duty officer because Luke Benton was picked up D and D,' Lucky reported. 'Dispatch had no idea Nina was up here but she did ring them about half an hour ago for a PNC check on a dark blue Astra. It was registered to Michael Quaife.'

Kim stamped on the accelerator.

Jasmin was right, as she'd known she would be. She'd held him, kissed him, caressed him, offered herself to his gaze and touch. And it had worked. Men's powers of recovery were a lot quicker than many of them cared to recognise.

Her conclusion was based less on practical experience than sound common sense. Most of her relationships had been, as a matter of policy, chaste. She'd intended to be a good Catholic, to remain celibate until the right person came along, and in any case coming to England had been – had seemed to be – a dealbreaker. After all, she'd be in London for a year, maybe less. Sheer madness, then, to seek romantic involvement. Once back home she could take stock of her life and career, make some decisions and, if she felt the time was right, put herself in the market for a man. Common sense.

Only it hadn't happened that way.

Jeff, she knew, had been interested for a long time. He seemed shy, and with a low opinion of himself, but had a quiet inner strength and perspicacity that attracted her. Later, when she caught her body sending signals her conscious brain hadn't authorised, confusion had taken over, not to mention considerable embarrassment. But he had, in her case, proved spectacularly inept at reading body language, and it had become easier and easier for her to suppress thoughts about him that went beyond platonic friendship. Until tonight.

Now she struggled to stop thinking about it, because it was still crazy. Not only was Jeff English and a colleague, but he was a white man. Neither she nor, as far as she knew, her mother or any of her brothers and sisters had ever had a white partner. She had no idea whether it was right, or what they'd say, or what she ought to do now. She was a million miles from home and, to her utter astonishment, in love. It didn't make sense. What was important - what mattered -

What mattered was that, in ways she had no hope of reducing to reason, Jeff Wetherby had just booked his place in the rest of her life. White, English, another cop or not, her heart was in orbit and she wanted him. Once more they rolled and merged and she felt him sliding in, pulsing and expanding as she drew him deeper until he filled her, stretching her as he grew in strength. Gentle, introducing himself with tact and courtesy, confident now, loving, completely right.

Reassured, she closed her eyes and kissed him. His response was to thrust, slowly, shallowly at first, but beginning a sensuous roll of his hips as his strokes lengthened and he found the beat. A wave of fire crackled up from her loins, through her belly and into her breasts, which, just then, he began to caress with his, lifting himself on his elbows and swaying his torso back and forth to their rhythm. Gradually, the pace increased as he went deeper and harder. He gasped by her ear with his efforts, making her scalp thrum. Beyond the sea roar in her ears she heard herself moaning. Wildness took her. Her fingers tried to knead his back. The nails dug in, dragging across and down, leaving red weals, but if there was pain he was oblivious. The pungent smell of pheromones surged from him, rocking her senses. Her sex sprang alive, like a lioness from the grass. She came with an undulating cry she barely heard over the rush of blood, the detonation of a galaxy of light in her mind, a cry that turned slowly into a growl, fading to short, vocal gasps as the climax subsided in a sea of golden syrup. Her legs gripped him as still he worked her, though more slowly now, slowly.

The black Mini was gone. They could see two Astras, but in the improving light it was plain neither was dark blue. Suddenly Lucky's arm lunged out. 'Look!' They followed her pointing finger. There was a man on the pavement, just a silhouette under the streetlights. He'd spotted them, now he was running. 'Go, sarge!' Lucky said. 'We can cut him off.'

'No,' Kim said firmly. 'Got a civilian with us, remember? No offence,' she added, turning to Juliet.

'No problem,' Juliet said.

'Did you see where he came from?' Kim asked Lucky.

'Out from one of the driveways, I think.'

She peered ahead again, but the running figure had gone. 'Definitely nobody else with him?'

'Not that I saw.'

'I don't like this.' Kim unclipped her belt and opened her door. Lucky followed suit, as, a hesitant moment later, did Juliet. Kim stopped her. 'You'd better stay in the car. I'll leave you the keys and you can lock yourself in, you'll be OK.'

'What if I need to come and find you?' Juliet said.

'She's got a point, sarge,' Lucky said over the roof. 'We don't know what the picture is here. She'd do better sticking with us, in case.'

Reluctantly, Kim agreed, with a fierce warning to Juliet to keep at least one of them in sight. As an afterthought, she reached down for the baton she kept under the seat. You just never knew.

Lucky led them to where she'd seen the figure emerge. It was not a drive but a narrow, chalky alleyway, plunging into the gloom under some trees. Ordering Juliet to stay close behind, Kim and Lucky advanced side by side, Kim trying to keep quiet and upright in impractical shoes. Presently they reached a t-junction. Kim indicated that she should explore to the right and Lucky the left, then turned and whispered in Juliet's ear.

'Stay here. We won't go far. Keep both of us in sight and shout if you have to.' Juliet nodded, looking scared. Kim felt able to give her a reassuring smile. In her white dress they, at least, weren't likely to lose her. 'Let's go.'

They stepped out and went their separate ways.

Juliet didn't have to wait long.

'Sarge!'

The taut cry froze Kim's blood. She gripped her baton, turned and ran towards where Lucky was kneeling by a clump of ground elder, stumbling and almost falling as a heel gave way on the chalk. As she approached the spot Lucky glanced up, mobile already to her ear, other hand outstretched towards something on the ground. She looked like a ghost, her cinnamon complexion drained and ashy. Kim realised she was not looking at her but beyond, to where Juliet had followed Kim and was standing, horrified at what she couldn't see but what she, too, knew was there.

'Go back to the street,' Lucky snapped. 'Knock on the first door you come to, get somebody out of bed. Don't take no for an answer, get towels, a first aid kit, anything they can give you.'

Juliet stood and stared. Kim took a step back towards her. 'You'll be all right,' she said. 'Go!'

Juliet went, running. Kim joined Lucky and looked down.

'Jesus Christ.'

It hardly seemed adequate.

The sprawled mass in the weeds was Nina. Kim was standing in a pool of her blood, and it was spreading.

Her eyes saw only coloured light. Her lips, touching, sought out warmth and found it on his neck, his chin, then his mouth which they encircled, searching hungrily. He groaned. He waited until he felt her grip relax and began to increase the rhythm once more, taking his lips away from hers, across her cheek to her ear as her head turned to one side for him. He raised himself up on his elbows and watched her. Her face, an expression of joy, eyes closed and mouth open, seeking out his arms and touching them, tasting the skin stretched over his biceps. He looked down at the firm roundness of her breasts. At the smooth skin of her belly, sequinned with beads of perspiration. The tight, wide hips to hold and caress. The shiny, muscled thighs spread to receive him. The dense black delta of curly fur that decorated the entrance to the heaven of which he was now a part. She was beautiful. Not just, as the saying went, a pretty face but now, her guard down, abandoned to him, in everything. Her closeness, her body, her trust, her love given in return for his. He looked at her. He loved her. All those long months of waiting, watching, listening to her, gearing himself up to speak and then backing out for fear of rejection; hanging on her every word for any clue, any hint she felt towards him the same way as he to her. And now, here she was. Here *they* were. He was making love to Jasmin. He was making love to Jasmin. Surely it was a dream, as it always had been.

He pushed deeper into the dream, building steadily as he fed her his body, his being. And she accepted, whimpering now, wrapping her legs around his back, and she came again with a scream, pulling him down, his hands on her breasts, his body with her body, and her orgasm was his trigger, as all his feelings suddenly canalised, withdrew with an electric purr from his every part and extremity and fed themselves like a lightning bolt out through his groin as his climax detonated, erupting into her womb with a soft warm splash. He cried out after it; then he sank down, exhausted and satisfied at last, into her tender embrace.

He sighed. She kissed his cheek.

'Stay tonight,' she asked.

'All right.'

Hovering on the edge of sleep, they'd no way of telling how long had passed before Jasmin's mobile ruptured their idyll.

'Winter,' she said, nuzzling back into the warmth of his embrace. They grinned in unison at their secret. He put his ear close to the phone but all he could hear was someone squawking. Jasmin said, 'Kim, hi. No, we - I wasn't sleeping. What is it?'

She listened. Then, suddenly, he felt her every muscle tense.

'*Moeder Gods.*' She tore herself free, sat up and crossed herself. 'She is - ? No... slow down.' She turned to him, but he could read nothing behind her deep frown. 'OK. Twenty minutes, we are there.' She rang off and sat bolt upright, clasping a hand to her mouth.

'What's wrong?'

'We have to go in,' she said. She told him why.

'Fuck,' he said. 'What happened?'

'I don't know. Kim found her. That's all she said. Sophia is calling the whole team in.'

For a moment, despite their shock, they pondered the question uppermost in their minds.

Jeff voiced it. 'Should we arrive separately, d'you think?'

'You are kidding?' She threw herself into his arms and held him tight. They were both shaking. 'I'm not letting you out of my sight just now.'

'We'd best get dressed, then.'

'Uh-huh,' she said. 'But it might take some time.' She took one hand from under the bedclothes and held it out, palm down. He put his beside it. They were doing a creditable impression of leaves in a high wind.

Kim had gone with the ambulance, leaving Lucky the keys to her car, instructions to drop Juliet and go on to the nick. Now they were parked outside Juliet's house. Lucky had made no move except to slump forward and rest her forehead against the steering wheel.

'Now I know why you joined the police,' Juliet said, with something approaching awe. 'That was impressive back there.'

Lucky looked up. Her face was pinched, as though on the verge of tears. 'Thanks.' Juliet tried not to notice the vivid, bloody handprint on one cheek, the dark streak on the other where she'd wiped her jaw.

'You OK?'

'I don't know.' She sighed and shook her head. 'I just don't know any more.'

Juliet waited, but Lucky suddenly seemed intent on studying her clothes, which had blood on them as well. It didn't look as if she was going to get any more out of her. She unclipped her seatbelt and opened the door.

'Look, Larissa, I'm your best mate,' she ventured. 'Something's bothering you.'

'Of *course* something's bothering me!' Lucky shouted, smashing her fists down on the wheel, making her friend jump.

'Yep. Right. Sorry.' Cowed, Juliet got out. But she wasn't fooled. Those clenched fists, like a frustrated child's. Shocking though her discovery had been, this wasn't about a murderous attack on a colleague she'd barely met. Juliet bent down to the open window. 'Before you dash off and don't ring me again for a month...'

'I'll ring.'

'I want to know if Nina's going to be all right, whether they've caught that bloke.'

'He might not've had anything to do with it.'

'Yeah, right.' She laid a hand on her friend's arm. 'Not from the newspapers or off the telly. From you, all right?'

'Soon as I hear.' Lucky, impatient to be away, almost smiled.

'Better let you get on.'

'Yeah.'

'Sure you'll be OK? The amount you've had to drink.'

'Look, if *that* didn't sober me up,' Lucky gestured in the rough direction of Ballards Way, 'what will?'

'Just drive carefully,' Juliet said.

'Yes, mum.'

The office looked like a scene from the middle reel of a disaster movie. There were Zoltan, Jeff and Helen, still in their party gear which was starting to look dishevelled. In contrast, Jasmin had changed into a grey sweater and green chinos, and Lucky still wore her top and jeans from last night. A thick silence reigned. On faces the prevailing expression was stunned disbelief; anger had yet to take hold.

All but four of the team were present. Sophia had elected not to tell Sandra Jones or Marie Kirtland, her reasoning being that anything they knew would be likely to filter back to Anne White and, although she was bound to hear eventually, the DCI had no wish to spoil her memories of her farewell knees-up just yet. Her intention was negated rather by putting Zoltan Schneider in charge, but not having been at the club there was no way she could have known about their relationship.

Zoltan, who'd had his back turned, rang off and slammed the phone back on its cradle. 'Right,' he said, 'everyone here?' No-one answered. 'Good. Kim's rung back from Mayday. The verdict's in from A and E, the results of which I've just relayed to the guv'nor.'

He paused, expecting some response, anything but the complete, deathly quiet, the blank faces that stared at him like a Greek frieze.

'At the moment the prognosis seems to be that hoary hospital cliché, too early to say. They've done some running repairs and she's gone to theatre. She's very poorly; someone, to put it bluntly, has had a good go at gutting her like a fish. She's been stabbed four times: once over the breastbone, twice just underneath the ribs and once on the upper right thigh. Three of these wounds are superficial; of greatest concern are the internal injuries caused by the fourth, which looks as if it missed her heart purely by chance.'

'Bloody finishing her off,' Jeff growled, turning to Lucky. 'If you and Kim hadn't - '

'Was she awake at all? Did she say anything?' Helen demanded. 'About who did it?'

'Pardon my French, sarge.' Lucky stood up and indicated her gory clothes. She'd washed her face but not thoroughly; there were still one or two reddish-brown smears. 'Fucking *look* at me! We were wading in this. She arrested when they were putting her in the fucking ambulance. What do *you* think?'

'Sorry.' Helen lowered her head. 'Next question.'

Jasmin voiced what no-one wanted to ask. 'Was she raped?'

'First thing they checked for once they'd stabilised her,' Zoltan said, mustering a faint smile. 'Rest assured, Nina was not raped or otherwise sexually assaulted.'

'He spared her that, at least,' Helen muttered, chin in hand.

'Don't ask me *why* he didn't.' The DI shrugged. 'It seems he had ample opportunity. Perhaps because she was wearing jeans with a sturdy belt. I don't know. Whatever it was, he left her inviolate.'

'Big fucking deal,' Lucky said.

'Nail scrapings we have,' Zoltan continued. 'Dirt. What good it does us I don't know.'

'Skin?' Jeff said. 'She must've put up a - '

'I don't think she got the chance,' Zoltan retorted, finding himself too shocked for his customary sarcasm. 'Although Nina was on call last night and should've had all her service gubbins on her, Kim's been through her stuff and can't find her phone, warrant card or handcuffs. There are marks on her wrists which suggest,' he added heavily, 'she was restrained with them.'

'Bastard,' Jeff muttered in the pindrop silence.

Jasmin had the next question. 'Have we an idea of the weapon?'

'Well, now.' Zoltan had been dreading this one. 'All the FME could tell was that the deepest wound was ragged along one edge. She had trouble observing much more because a paramedic had his fist in it, trying to stop Nina bleeding to death.'

'What the hell was it,' Jeff said, 'a fucking harpoon?'

'For all we know.' Zoltan looked at all of them. 'Or a very big knife.'

He measured it with parallel palms.

'Any more questions?'

There were a million more questions but no-one asked them.

'Good. Save them. All we know from warming our arses here is that Nina is in very bad shape. We don't know who's responsible or what she was doing in Ballards Way. So let's be over there knocking on doors and waking the good citizens from their Sunday lie in. Yes?'

Jeff, his hand up again, said, 'If she was in Ballards Way...'

He tailed off. Zoltan was treating him to one of his stares. 'It's in hand, constable.'

Sophia spotted Brian Hunt's bike secured to a lamppost. Back a few hours from his holiday, jetlag had woken him at half past four, and he'd been fully alert when the call came. Brian was a curiosity to his colleagues. No-one quite believed a detective who employed a bicycle as his preferred mode of transport.

Where the rest of the team used cars for work as a matter of course, Brian cycled. Arguably, in South London traffic he could respond to a call just as quickly.

He emerged from the alleyway as Sophia parked, instantly recognisable, tall, fair and built like an electricity pylon. His cheeks and jaw were adorned with the wisps of one of his periodic attempts at a beard. His shoulders were hunched and his hands thrust into the pockets of a charcoal grey suit jacket. He had on faded blue jeans with one knee out. For Brian, he looked solemn, an opaqueness in his normally affable blue eyes. Sophia got out and looked around. On her instructions, police presence was for the moment being kept low key. The only signs of recent activity were two patrol cars, their crews sitting inside them, and a small van. She frowned at it.

'I hope you haven't let a dog trample all over the place?'

'No, it's OK, guv, they were careful,' Brian said. 'But they did track Nina's scent back to one of the gardens.'

'The Clarkes'?'

'Looks like it. Gate off the alleyway round back.'

'Blood?'

'Some.'

'Have you tried ringing the bell?'

'Thought I'd better wait for you, guv. I've kept an eye on the house: nobody's been in or out. Burglar alarm looks switched on, curtains are closed. On the face of it they're asleep still.'

She nodded towards the alley. 'Is the scene secure?'

'The dog man had some tape. We've cordoned it off.'

Peering past him, she could faintly see a length of blue and white police tape stretched across the far end of the alley. 'Good,' she nodded. 'That'll do until CSI get here. They are on their way, I take it?'

'Any minute, guv.'

'Right.' She rubbed her hands together. 'They'll see where to go, and make a start. What are we waiting for?'

He extended an arm in an 'after you' gesture, and Sophia led the way towards the Clarkes' house. As they approached, she studied it. Brian's assessment seemed correct. Nothing stirred. She wasn't convinced. 'A copper gets stabbed in their garden, ambulance and police sirens wailing right outside their front door, and they sleep through it?' she said angrily, marching up the path. 'Not likely.'

But by her third ring, no-one had answered. The sun was above the roofs now, the air filled with bird chorus. Amidst the clamour it was easy to fancy you heard movement inside. Then, in the street, came the far from imaginary sound of a taxi drawing up. They watched as Andrew Clarke paid the fare, got out and turned in at his garden gate. He stopped dead when he saw them.

'This is DC Hunt,' Sophia said. 'Do you know why we're here?'

Pale, he stood and stared. Behind him, the taxi pulled away. Brian took out a notebook and jotted its number down.

Sophia said, 'May we come in, please?'

He nodded. Fumbling for his keys, he shambled up the path.

'Guv,' Brian said suddenly.

She turned. From behind the door came the sound of locks being unfastened. Then it opened. Brian stepped back. Sophia, face impassive, took a breath.

'Debbie Clarke, I presume?' she said to the girl in the doorway.

Irony piled upon irony, Sophia thought as she took another deep breath preparatory to opening the interview room door. Technically, as Debbie was a juvenile, she must have an appropriate adult present during questioning. With the benefit of hindsight, it had been agreed that for one of her parents to undertake this role would not be wise. It was unlikely Andrew and Charlotte Clarke could profitably be charged with anything more serious than wasting police time, but Sophia had made it clear she was in no mood to give them the opportunity to waste any more.

A social worker, then? Andrew Clarke had reacted with predictable outrage at the very notion. The indignity, if his neighbours should find out, seemed his main objection; those same neighbours who'd seen nothing, heard nothing, either last night or when the Bentons' house had gone up in flames. And so it came down to a lawyer. But the Clarkes had none. In his arrogance, despite his frequent threats, Debbie's father hadn't seen the need. Spurning the duty list, he'd secured the services of one of the City firms he used at the building society. They did criminal work, and had a junior partner who didn't object to driving out to Croydon on a Sunday. It seemed fitting that the interests of the daughter of Andrew Clarke, former neo-Nazi football hooligan, should be represented by a Mr Singh.

Sophia walked in and nodded to Kim Oliver, who'd brought Debbie through from the detention room. Kim leaned over to the recorder and started it as the DCI sat down. 'Recommencing interview with Deborah Clarke,' she announced. 'Persons present are as before. Time is now 17.31. Miss Clarke, I need to remind you you're still under caution.'

Sophia settled herself. 'Feeling a bit better now, Debbie?'

Debbie Clarke nodded. After all that had happened to

her, the experience of police custody seemed to terrify her more than anything. They'd had to suspend the interview three hours ago because of her uncontrollable crying. Hopefully a meal and some rest had calmed her down. She looked pale, shocked, ready to dive down inside the big roll neck of the white wool sweater she wore.

'For the tape, Miss Clarke nods her head,' Sophia said. She asked Debbie, 'I understand the doctor's had a look at you?'

'Yes.' It was a tiny voice. Debbie hugged herself. 'Like I said, there was no need. It was all fake.'

'Scary for you, all the same.'

'Like I said.' She started to shiver again. 'If I hadn't let them...'

And only your father's neo-Nazi past, Sophia mused, gave you a choice. Edward Porter's regard for his erstwhile comrade had, it seemed, saved his daughter's life. Chances were his intentions towards Debbie had indeed been murderous until her father's plea for help had swayed him. Dead fugitives cannot talk. But neither, Andrew Clarke must have pointed out, do the police pursue them. It had been the start of an elaborate deception: the squat laid out like a lynching, the message on the answering machine, the faked Polaroid. The tarpaulin had caught any trace of the theatrical makeup and special effects gore that would have given the game away, and Sophia was kicking herself that she had been led astray by the presence of the blood. It was Meredith's, after all, on a bed in the flat where he lived. The stain could have come from anything, a grazed knee even, and chances were he'd been telling the truth when he'd told them how he'd got the cut on his hand. Andrew Clarke's heartrending cries at the bus stop had been prompted not by grief, but by the shame of seeing his daughter naked before strangers.

There were a couple of things that were still bothering Sophia about Debbie's story, but she would come back to them. Right now, she wanted to get the timeline straight.

'Earlier on,' she said, 'we got as far as Edward Porter taking you down to Leatherhead. You went straight there from the squat?'

Debbie hesitated before nodding.

'Please say yes or no for the recording, Deborah.'

'Yes.'

'Did your parents know where you were?'

'Mr Porter faxed Dad at work. Told him how to get in touch. I talked to him on the phone. He rang from a pub, in case you were listening in on his.'

Sophia glanced at Kim, who nodded. Andrew Clarke's mysterious trip to the Keeper and Wicket.

'How long have you been back home?'

'Since last Saturday.'

'We're not talking about yesterday, are we? This is a week ago?'

'Yeah.'

'And you've stayed hidden in the house all that time?'

'I went into Croydon once, shopping, when Mum was out,' Debbie said. 'Had to. I was climbing the walls.'

'Hardly surprising,' Sophia agreed, with a twinge of resigned annoyance. In a town of three hundred thousand people, no-one had noticed a sixteen year old girl in a crowd. Even one wanted on suspicion of arson and murder. So much for publicity. She asked, 'Why did Mr Porter bring you back?'

'I don't know exactly. I overheard him on the phone to Mr Quaife, shouting something about some lady.'

'Lady?'

Debbie's eyes widened in terror that perhaps she'd told this formidable policewoman something she didn't want to hear. 'That's... that's all I caught.' Sophia nodded slowly, patiently, relaxing her. 'Then he came upstairs and said to me, "Come on, I'm taking you home. We should've done this in the first place."'

'On Saturday morning? So you were home by, when?'

'Afternoon some time.'

'Did Mr Porter bring you home himself?'

'Yeah. Dad flipped. I don't think he was expecting me. He said the police... that you were watching the house. God knows where he'd got that from.'

Inscrutably, Sophia asked, 'But Porter believed him?'

Debbie nodded. 'Said not to worry. He told Dad to put the answerphone on and wait for a message, then do what it said. And make sure the police knew.'

He certainly had us going for a while, Sophia thought. Out of the corner of her eye she saw Kim scribble a note. She said, 'Did you hear from Edward Porter again before last night?'

Debbie shook her head. Sophia frowned. Debbie said, 'No.'

'Do you know why they came?'

Abruptly, Debbie burst into tears again. From his breast pocket, Mr Singh produced an immaculately ironed primrose handkerchief. He said to her, 'Would you like to stop again?'

'Mr Singh,' Sophia said, 'if it's all the same to you I'd rather press on. The quicker we finish, the less upset for your client.'

'That's up to her,' he retorted. 'How do you feel, Deborah?'

'I'm OK,' Debbie said, recovering. She handed back his

handkerchief. 'Thanks.'

'Keep it,' he smiled.

'Debbie, one of my officers is seriously ill in hospital because of what happened last night,' Sophia said gently. 'I don't believe it was anything directly to do with you, but it wasn't just bad luck, either. Porter and Quaife were there at four a.m. for a reason.'

'I know,' Debbie sniffed.

'Was it because you rang Luke?'

'You know about that?'

'We spoke to him this morning.'

'Oh, God.' She buried her face in her hands. 'I tried to tell him I couldn't help it, but he said he never wanted to see me again for what I'd done. He said his mum was on my head, and if Robin died that would be too.' She looked up and sighed. 'But then he's told you that already.'

'Yes, he has. But what's that got to do with Edward Porter being there? Did your dad overhear?'

'No, but I was upset. I had to talk to someone so I told my mum.'

'When was this?'

'Middle of the night.' Fresh tears welled in her eyes. 'It's so stupid. I haven't gone into Mum and Dad's room like that since I was a kid. He was asleep but Mum went and woke him.'

'And he rang Porter?'

'Yeah.'

'And?'

'They turned up about two. I stayed in my room. The three of them just sat downstairs, talking about what to do. I think when the policewoman came they must've figured Luke had talked to her. That's why they did what they did.'

Everyone stared at her.

'I saw it. Out of my bedroom window. Mr Quaife... Mr Quaife hit her with his knife when she came through the gate. They tied her to the tree. Mr Porter talked to her. Then he walked off. Mr Quaife just stood there for a bit, watching. I thought he was waiting for her to bleed to death. She went all limp, like a little doll. I thought, she's dead. She must be dead by now. Then suddenly he stopped and looked round, like he'd heard something. He let her go from the tree and dragged her through the back gate into the alley. He still had his knife, and he... It was like it was happening all over again. Only with the fire I just ran, but this time there was nowhere to run to, because they'd have found me again. I just had to watch... I couldn't make him stop.'

'It's all right, Debbie.' Sophia reached over and laid a hand over a tightly bunched fist. Catching Mr Singh's pleading stare, she nodded. 'It's all right. We'll break for a minute. Interview suspended, 17.48.'

Outside in the corridor, the two detectives stood in thoughtful silence, neither wanting to be the first to speak. At last Kim said, 'Looks like Luke Benton's had a lucky escape, guv.'

'They'd have paid him a visit if he hadn't already been picked up, that's for sure.'

'Instead Nina nearly got herself killed 'cause of him being pissed.'

'Nina nearly got herself killed - ' Sophia began, as near to anger as Kim had ever known her. She sighed, shook her head and said, 'Nina called the CAD room at least half an hour before you found her. Why, in that time, if she knew there might be trouble - ?'

'Maybe she never got the chance.'

'Maybe, but we won't know, will we? Until she's well enough to tell us.'

Kim looked at her watch. 'Shouldn't we've heard something by now?'

'The hospital have strict orders to let me know at once,' Sophia said. 'I want to know exactly where we are before Debbie starts signing statements.' She turned to go, then paused. 'Kim?'

'Guv?'

'Something caught your attention. I saw you writing it down.'

'The photo again,' Kim said.

'Explain.'

'Well, we know it was taken Thursday at the squat, right? But Porter didn't use it till Saturday night, to throw us off. If Debbie's to be believed, all that was last minute. So,' Kim said, 'what'd they *originally* want the photo for?'

Staff Nurse Hamida Aziz (it said on her name tag) told Sandra Jones, 'Yes, she came through surgery very well. Less damage than we first feared.' She said it as if she, personally, had led the operating team.

'She's gonna be OK?'

'Physically, yes.'

Sandra said nothing. She stood and waited. Eventually Nurse Aziz figured it out.

'Oh, yes,' she said, springing to life. 'Second door to your right. But you must remember she is still in recovery. I can only allow you five minutes.'

'Thanks.' Sandra gave her a look that suggested she

was about to experience the longest five minutes of her career, turned and followed her directions.

Even with intensive care beds at a premium, it had to be a good sign that Nina had been moved to a private room on a general ward. While speaking to Nurse Aziz, Sandra had snatched a peek behind her desk, where monitors hooked up to Nina's vital signs waited on constant alert for trouble.

Nina was not alone. In a chair beside the bed a young woman sat reading a paperback. Lucia Tyminski's kinship to her sister was obvious, despite the thickly kohl-lined eyes and bleached gelled hair that clashed oddly with the white ribbed t-shirt and blue sundress she wore. In height and build they were much alike; the more assured way Lucia looked and carried herself was what marked her apart. At the sound of the door she looked up. 'Hi,' she said, recognising Sandra.

Sandra closed the door quietly. 'No Paul?'

'He's been here all day,' Lucia said. 'We sent him home for some kip. My mum and me are gonna take it in turns to do nights. My other sister, too, when she gets here.'

'You'll have Nurse Aziz out of a job.'

'I don't reckon she's in much of a state to talk.' Lucia glanced at Nina, who lay still and silent, eyes closed. A drip fed into her arm, a canula thrust rudely up her nose. Not a mark on her, Sandra thought, startled, looking into the pale face. But she guessed the hospital gown covered a rather nastier truth.

'Has she...?'

'She was awake for a bit when Paul was here. Very groggy, though.'

'Best she sleeps, then,' Sandra said. 'I just came down to see how she was.' Her restless gaze halted once more on the sleeping figure. 'I keep asking myself, should I have stopped her answering that fucking call on her own?'

'It was a drunk, I thought,' Lucia frowned. 'She's handled enough of those in her time.'

'Yeah, but *after* that.'

'You anywhere towards finding out who did this?' Lucia demanded.

'We know who did it,' Sandra sighed. 'It's just catching the bastards. We're all working on it till we drop, I promise.'

Lucia nodded and said nothing for a while, clutching her sister's pale, limp hand.

'I keep asking myself, as well.'

'Asking what?'

'I offered to tag along last night,' Lucia said. 'Police piss-ups aren't really my thing, but Nina was in such a tizzy about Paul that... well.'

'Moral support?'

'Yeah.'

'What could you've done, though?'

'Stopped her blacking his eye, maybe,' she said, shooting Nina a look of poorly disguised admiration. 'You should see it today. It's a real beaut.'

Sandra laughed. 'Attagirl.'

'Mind you, had to restrain myself from socking him in the other one, after what he told me earlier.'

'Oh, yeah?'

Lucia looked dubious at the notion of betraying a family confidence. 'You know why she did it?'

'All I can think, he must've said something pretty spectacular. They seemed to be starting to patch things up.'

'She got him to tell her who he'd been shagging,' Lucia said. 'Only the woman he was engaged to before he met Nina.'

'Shit! No wonder she fetched him one.' It explained a lot of things. Sex, romance, friendship, glamour: Nina had been willing to work on anything to salvage the marriage. Anything within her power. Until she'd found out just how desperate things were.

What a kick in the teeth.

Sandra's arm was getting hot. She stirred. 'Nina's coat,' she said awkwardly, handing it over. 'She left it at the club.'

Lucia took it. 'You going?'

'Better, otherwise we'll have Florence Nightingale on the warpath.'

'I'll tell Nina you came by.'

'Be back same sort of time tomorrow. Will you be here?'

'Somebody will. Me or Mum or my sister. She should be more lucid by then.'

'Hope so.' On impulse, Sandra leaned over and kissed Nina gently on the cheek. To her surprise, it was almost feverishly warm. She stepped back and frowned at her stricken friend. 'Then perhaps,' she admonished her, 'you can tell us what the fuck you were doing in the Clarkes' garden.'

'This is what puzzles me,' Sophia said, glancing up at the clock on the wall. Since Debbie was a juvenile, they could not question her for much longer today. 'I get the rationale behind this tableau, making it look like you were dead, but why do it there? Why bring all that stuff in rather than get you away from the squat immediately?'

Debbie looked disorientated. 'What?'

'Surely there must have been a suitable space in the house in Leatherhead where they could have set all that up in their own good time.'

'How would *they* know about Leatherhead?'

Now it was Sophia's turn to feel as if she had entered an alternate universe. 'You told me Porter and Quaife had taken you from the squat in Hackney to the house in – '

'It wasn't them.'

Sophia sat back. Slowly. 'I'm sorry?'

Debbie said, 'It was Phil, Billy and Jayne who set all that up. They were all at Guildhall Drama School together. Billy Scofield's got a diploma in stage and film makeup. That's how come it looked so convincing.'

WEEK THREE
MONDAY

So far, Sandra's promise was being made good. Everyone was in by eight, the office humming with concern and conjecture, desks strewn with notes, statements and evidence. The mood was bleak, yet underneath lay a determination driven by controlled anger. Faces were creased by care and pale with fatigue. Some of the team had been up all night, scouring and rechecking everything known about the Benton enquiry. For once, it was Sophia who was slightly intimidated by them when she came in, instead of the other way round.

'Right, settle down,' she said, gazing proudly across the debris of her officers' industry. 'I know I'm not the only one anxious to know where we are, and we'll find out a lot quicker than through the canteen grapevine.'

Conversation stopped. One by one, phone calls were ended, receivers replaced and not touched again. She had their undivided attention.

She said, 'First of all, I'd like to thank you for the professional way you've all knuckled down and got on with your work. I had a meeting with Detective Superintendent Heighway last night and we talked about bringing MIT in.' There were some muttered expressions of consternation. 'He's agreed we should keep the case in-house for now, then review the situation again on Friday if we need more manpower.' The discontented sound effects continued, but in their hearts the team knew they were stretched thin; the situation was overwhelming as it was. 'Right. The second piece of good news is that Nina is going to be OK.' Some relieved sighs, no cheering. 'She's awake this morning, and talking to her mother.'

'Did she say anything?' Lucky asked.

'Not about that, no,' Sophia smiled. 'That can wait. Sandra's visiting her tonight.' She glanced at Sandra, who nodded, but remained impassive. The DCI suspected she hadn't been forgiven for not calling her in. She said, 'On to the bad news now, of which there are three main parts. You'll all have heard about Surrey finding Nina's car near Redhill. Forensic have now been over it and found no significant trace of anyone except Nina, her husband, two IC3 males who we assume to be Luke Benton and Nick Lynott, and Andrew Clarke - which confirms his explanation for why he turned up at his front door in a cab. We're still waiting on the Astra, but my bet is that it's in tiny pieces in a breaker's yard somewhere. The PNC check Nina asked for has been followed up: last time anyone saw Quaife or the car at the registered address was before he went to prison. Second piece of bad news,' she modulated her voice carefully to make sure the full implications of what she was about to tell them sank in, 'we are not *only* looking for Porter and Quaife in connection with this investigation.'

'I thought Thrall was just the two of them?' Jeff Wetherby said, voicing the general consternation.

'When I've told you what I'm about to tell you,' Sophia said ruefully, 'you may understand why it is that chief inspectors don't generally do interviews.' She gave them a rundown of Debbie's revelation about the Polaroid. 'Fact is that Debbie Clarke and I spent most of yesterday talking at cross purposes. Me under the assumption that it was Porter and Quaife who'd set up the fake murder scene, her under the assumption that I knew it wasn't.'

Marie Kirtland said, 'Meredith and his mates set it up to make it look like Thrall?'

'To make sure we went after Porter and Quaife and left Debbie alone,' Sophia said. 'She said she went along with it because they convinced her there was no other option.'

'She was compliant,' Kim cut in, 'until Meredith suggested tying her up to make it look more like an execution. They got the ropes onto her ankles and wrists but then she had a panic attack once they tied her to the bedposts. They had to let her free in a hurry 'cause they were afraid Mrs Brownlie next door might hear if she started screaming.'

'Accounts for why the ropes were cut square in some places and frayed in others, yeah?' Lucky remarked.

'Exactly,' Sophia said. 'It also accounts for the blood and the plaster on Meredith's hand. He cut himself getting her loose. Must have dripped some on the mattress as they got the tarpaulin off it.'

'Tell you what it doesn't account for.' Zoltan Schneider had been silent and uncharacteristically grim all morning, but now he spoke up. 'How Porter ended up with the Polaroid if Meredith and his crew took it.'

'That Debbie couldn't tell us,' Sophia said. 'She claims she didn't know Porter had it until her dad got back home after the bus stop stunt and started yelling at her. My best guess is that he found it when he showed up at the squat looking for Debbie, took it; Meredith and co came back later to find Debbie gone, the photo gone, put two and two together, realized there was now going to be a swastika-shaped target on their backs and went to ground.'

'So now we have to find them before Thrall do,' Zoltan sighed. 'Which given our track record of not finding Debbie before they did isn't an encouraging prospect.'

'Although,' Helen Wallace said, 'I reckon three sporadically homeless political activists stroke petty criminals are likely to be a bit better at not being found than a sixteen-year-old kid.'

Zoltan arched his eyebrows at her and shrugged, conceding her point.

'Lots to do on both fronts,' Sophia said. 'Everyone see Kim and Helen after the meeting and they'll give you your actions for the day. Before we do that,' she took a deep breath, 'the third bit of bad news. The house-to-house.'

Groans went up from those who'd spent Sunday knocking on doors.

'Same story as with the fire. At least this time they've all got an excuse.' She saw Kim looking furious and said, 'I don't suppose many of them were awake at four a.m.'

'Have we been asking the right people?' Zoltan said suddenly.

'What do you mean?'

'Who might have been up around that time?' Zoltan said. 'We've been running around looking for shift workers, early gardeners, but maybe we've forgotten about the most likely witnesses.'

He peered at a sea of blank faces.

'What,' he grinned, 'were *we* all doing beforehand?'

Sandra snapped her fingers at him. 'On the razzle.'

'Exactly.' He winked. 'Saturday night, Sunday morning. Half the population of Croydon under the age of thirty out on the tiles till dawn.'

'And we've been mostly talking to older people,' Sophia concluded. 'Sandra, get on HOLMES and run a report on all the households in Ballards Way and the next road with young people aged, say, sixteen to thirty. I especially want to know what happened to the man Lucky saw running away. Where did he go? Was he picked up? *Et cetera*. If someone coming home saw that, find out.' She paused for breath and a sip of water. 'Next. Kim, last night after we finished talking to Debbie you shared something you had on your mind. Do you want to bounce it off people?'

Kim stood up and went to the front. 'Sorry to keep harping on about the Polaroid, but why would *Porter* want to use it? And especially why use it in a way that made sure Debbie's dad was gonna see it, after he'd promised to help them?'

'Doesn't strike me as the sort to get his rocks off that way,' Zoltan commented. 'Quaife maybe.'

'I still think smokescreen,' Jasmin Winter said.

Kim turned to her. 'You mean like for later, but they had their hand forced?'

'I am thinking if they wished to get her out of the country. If we think she is dead, we stop watching the airports.'

'Bloody risky,' Jeff said. 'People might still recognise her face from the telly.'

He had a good point and a pensive silence fell. Eventually Sophia gave up waiting for anything to come out of it. She said, 'OK, next contribution. Helen.'

The DS cleared her throat. 'I've had a call from one of the estate agents we spoke to. Apparently, after we'd left one of his colleagues started acting nosy, asking him what we wanted. Name of Stephen Dollis, which rang a bell, so I checked. He's got previous for GBH, four years back. The victim was Asian.'

'The firm gave us a list of all the properties they've sold in Leatherhead in the past year,' Lucky took it up. 'Dollis sold one to a guy calling himself Webster. Four bedroom semi, like Debbie described. They've faxed us the blurb on a house they've got on the market in the same road, and the room descriptions are very close to Debbie's.'

'Is there a photo?' Sophia said.

'Yes, ma'am.'

Marie Kirtland said, 'Can't Debbie tell us where the house is?'

Kim shook her head. 'She said it was dark when Porter took her there and on the way back he made her lie face down in the back seat until they were well away. Never left the house all the time she was there and he kept the curtains closed.'

'I see.'

'I'll show her the photo anyway,' Sophia said. 'Ten to one there's no-one there now, but it might be worth a look. Good work, you two.' She nodded appreciatively at Helen and Lucky and said, 'Go and pay this Mr Dollis a visit, see what he has to say for himself. Everyone else, keep ploughing through your assigned actions and think hard. Let's see if we can't get a result by Friday.'

PC Tom Walker had experienced his mid-life crisis late. He'd joined the Met at nineteen, and for the next thirty years had patrolled a beat out of Croydon nick, dependable, unassuming, never seeking advancement or promotion. Former colleagues who returned years later were amazed to find him right where he'd always been. Then suddenly, three years ago, he'd decided he wanted a change. The canteen saw him filling in applications left, right and centre until finally his wife, concerned that he was jeopardising his pension by resigning, had persuaded his inspector to get him a transfer. So, aged forty-nine, Tom Walker made his major life change to South East Traffic, based at Catford. It had worked miracles on him. He was a new man.

You still saw Tom around: his patrols sometimes brought him to Croydon with arrests and for refs. So Jeff Wetherby, the only one of the team who'd been there long enough to remember him well, was not overly surprised to see the familiar grey-haired figure walk into the office. He raised a hand and Tom came over, still peering around as if for someone more senior.

'Eh up, mate.'

'Busy in here,' Tom said flatly.

'Aye, well.'

'I'm looking for DC Tyminski.'

Jeff gave him a hard stare. 'That meant to be some sort of sick joke or what?'

'You tell me, mate,' Tom said, looking blank.

Angrily, Jeff told him.

'Shit,' he sighed, sitting on the edge of Jeff's desk. 'Sorry, I had no idea. Me and the missus just got back from Fuerteventura last night.'

'Don't you watch the fucking telly?'

'Not much these days, no,' Tom said. 'Anyway, don't blame me. It was my observer told me I needed to talk to Tyminski. Dozy twat.'

Despite himself, Jeff smiled. The old bugger hadn't

changed that much. Any bobby under thirty was liable, in Tom Walker's system of reference, to be classified as a dozy twat. He said, 'So what'd you want her for?'

'I hear she's looking for a slag called Mike Bayliss.'

Jeff's ears pricked up. 'I've been working on that one.'

'Right, I'll tell you then.' He got up off the desk and looked around. Lucky was out with Helen and astonishingly no-one had pinched her chair yet, so Tom did. He settled himself and leaned forward confidentially. 'You probably know all this already, so shut me up if I'm making a fool of myself. If Bayliss is who I think he is, then I've nicked him a few times.'

'Burglar, ground floor entry, crap locks?'

'That's the one,' he nodded. 'Only he didn't always call himself Bayliss, did he?'

'No?'

'Vicky, that's his mum, was a brass when she was younger, and whenever we nicked her she used to give her maiden name - Bayliss. She married an old lag called Ritchie Prosser, and Mike was the fruit of their loins. Seem to remember they're divorced now.'

'So what you're saying is Michael Bayliss might sometimes give his name as Prosser?' Jeff said, writing 'MICHAEL PROSSER?' on the back of the first piece of paper to hand, which happened to be his gas bill.

'Most of the time,' Tom confirmed. 'But all this must be on file.'

'His juvenile record's been shredded. Three year rule.'

'Bloody red tape.'

Jeff summarised why the team were after Bayliss. Tom nodded and remarked that he wouldn't put rape past him, but was surprised at his use of an accomplice.

'Always did fancy himself a clever bastard,' he said. 'I tell you what this sounds like. Ever read *The Blooding*?'

'Joseph Wambaugh?'

'That's the one. First murder case solved by DNA profiling. Fascinating story, but it's become a sort of sex criminal's bible.'

'The message being if you don't shoot your wad inside your victim, you're in the clear?' Jeff scratched his chin. 'I need to have a word with my DI about this. But if we can find out where he's living at the minute, d'you want in?'

'Doubt I can swing it,' Tom shrugged, 'but keep me posted.'

'Least I can do.' Jeff smiled. 'You might just've helped a dozen-odd women sleep easier at night.'

'My wife'd be a start,' Tom said.

Zoltan was out and Tom had to go back on patrol, so Jeff promised he'd get in touch once he knew what was going on. The DI was expected back around two. Jeff filled in the intervening time with some research.

When Zoltan walked into the office Jeff was waiting by his desk. He told him about Tom's visit. 'I've checked with electoral registration,' he said, 'and there's a Prosser, Michael R., listed on the Handcroft Estate. I'm ninety-nine per cent sure it's Bayliss.'

'How?' Zoltan enquired.

'I went over to the library. They've got back numbers of the voters' lists. This Prosser first appears at that address four years ago, which if he was eighteen then agrees with the age Camberwell have for him. And there's a Victoria Prosser listed at the same address.'

He was taken aback suddenly by one of the DI's fiercest glances, but then Zoltan sighed, took off his glasses and rubbed his eyes. 'Comes to something,' he moaned apologetically, 'when I start viewing an officer's attempts to catch a serial rapist as procrastinating.'

Jeff shrugged. 'That's all right, guv. This business has knocked us all for six.'

'Mmm.' Zoltan looked as if he'd been on his feet since Saturday. Even Jeff, who in his time had slept through the Hertfordshire oil terminal explosion and an earthquake in Turkey, had had a restless night. 'Who's still on this? I can't remember.'

'Hiya.' Lucky came in, brushing by them with a sheaf of statements.

'It was Lucky, you, me, Nina and Jasmin,' Jeff said.

'We can't spare Lucky from the other matter, really.'

'Jasmin's not here,' Jeff said, not having to look.

'And then there were two.' Zoltan grinned sardonically. 'Only question is whether we've got enough to bring him in.'

'We'll know when we see him.' Jeff held out a hand at what he estimated was six foot four.

'Let's do it,' Zoltan said without hesitation.

'Now?'

'Right now.' The DI put his jacket back on.

'Who's nicked my chair?' Lucky plonked her work down and looked around.

'Sorry,' Jeff called across. 'By my desk.' He paused by the door. 'While you're there, could you fetch me my gas bill? May as well pay it on the way over,' he added to Zoltan.

'This it?' Lucky said, bringing it over.

'With some scribble on the back.'

She glanced at the bill, made to hand it to him, and froze. He tried to take it from her but it was gripped tight in her fingers.

'D'you mind?'

'Sorry.' She relinquished it, turned and walked slowly away.

'She looked as if she'd seen a ghost,' Zoltan remarked in the corridor.

Jeff unfolded the bill and read it. His eyes widened. 'Not bloody surprised,' he said.

The Handcroft Estate was a strange example of a 1960s housing development built around existing roads. White-boarded, flat-roofed terraced houses and small blocks of flats seemed to have been dumped beside, or possibly across, the old lanes with little reference to ease of access.

Albion Street twisted around the estate like an angry man elbowing his way through a crowd. Even in broad daylight it was easy to get lost, and subsequently mugged, on the Handcroft and they were glad to be in a car. They parked next to a set of large communal steel dustbins and walked across an overgrown lawn to a green door with 32 on it in dirty white plastic numerals. Zoltan rang the bell. A few moments later a woman with auburn hair opened the door. A look of open hostility was already on her face.

'Vicky Prosser?' Zoltan smiled like a shark and flashed his warrant card. 'Afternoon. I'm DI Schneider, this is DC Wetherby. Is Michael in?'

'He's at work.'

'May we come in?' Grudgingly she stepped aside. 'Thank you. Most kind.'

He walked through into an untidy lounge with a marble effect tiled fireplace. Jeff wandered upstairs. Vicky Prosser followed Zoltan, angry and bewildered. 'What's he done?'

'Where does he work, Mrs Prosser?'

'He ain't been in trouble since he was a kid,' she insisted. 'You check.'

'This Michael?' Zoltan took a framed photo from the mantelpiece and studied it. It showed a tall, skeletal young man with sandy hair, bare-chested and wearing long board shorts. It had been taken on a sunny day and the youth's skin showed up almost as albino. Gaunt was the word.

Jeff came back, shaking his head. Zoltan handed him the photo. He peered at it and said, 'Aye, could be.'

Vicky Prosser found her voice. 'You got a warrant?'

'What for?' Zoltan said innocently.

'Coming in here snooping around.'

'We haven't been doing any snooping. You invited us in.'

'What about him?' She rounded on Jeff, who looked remorseful.

'I needed the loo,' he said. 'Sorry - should've asked first.'

Vicky Prosser snatched back her son's photo and replaced it. 'You bastards tell me what's going on.'

'You tell me where he works, Mrs Prosser,' Zoltan said.

'Carter Engineering, on the Purley Way,' Vicky Prosser spat, as though divulging a state secret under torture. 'Better get over there quick if you want him. His shift finishes at four.'

You'd like that, wouldn't you? Zoltan thought. He smiled at her, lifting his radio and switching it to talk-through. 'All units from DI Schneider. Anyone in the vicinity of the Purley

Way, over.'

'DI Schneider from Zulu three-five,' a male voice came back almost at once. 'We're at Fiveways. That near enough, over?'

'It'll do,' Zoltan said. 'Can you go to Carter Engineering and pick up Michael Prosser, an employee there? Bring him to Croydon for questioning.'

'Will do, sir. What's the beef?'

Zoltan hesitated. He turned away from Vicky Prosser and shifted his grip on the radio. 'Suspicion of rape, Sutton, five years ago,' he said. 'Just bring him in.'

Vicky Prosser's reaction was everything he'd feared, but she went for Jeff instead.

They were out of luck. Fifteen minutes and a cup of possibly poisoned tea later, Zulu three-five radioed back to say that Michael Prosser had skipped the end of his shift. He'd received a brief phone call around the time they were swinging on the doorbell of 32 Albion Street, and when next the foreman had checked he was no longer at his machine. Perhaps Vicky Prosser wasn't as thick as she made out.

A disconsolate trio sat round Zoltan's desk at the back end of the afternoon. There was an APB out on Prosser/Bayliss and the brown Honda Civic that was his current set of wheels, and they could only hope.

'This close,' Jeff grumbled, holding thumb and forefinger together.

'It is him, then?' Jasmin asked.

'Going by the photo?' Zoltan and Jeff exchanged nods. 'Oh, definitely.'

'Look on the good side,' Jasmin said. 'He is wanted for rape. Where can he go?'

'Where indeed?'

Jasmin and Jeff sat up and looked at the DI.

'*Surely* not?' Jeff said.

Zoltan smiled serenely. 'Why do you think I let Vicky hear me on the radio?'

Sandra slid open the gate of the ancient hospital lift and came face to face with Paul Jackson. They stood staring at one another for a moment like two kittens in a drainpipe. He looked so certain she was going to hit him that for a moment she was tempted.

'How's she doing?' she settled for asking instead, biting back the selection of insults that occurred to her.

'Awake,' he said curtly. 'Hurt. Lost. Humiliated. What do *you* think?' His head drooped closer to his chest with every word, as though he were putting it on the block.

'Lucia with her?' she asked. But he pushed past and slammed the gate shut. 'Sod you, then,' she muttered to the descending lift.

In Nina's room Lucia was on her feet, rummaging through her purse for change for the vending machine. 'Hi,' she said.

'She asleep?'

'Drifting.' Lucia shrugged. 'You gonna be all right?'

'Mm-hmm.'

'OK, I'll split.' Gently she reached out, touched Nina's hair. 'Sis? Sandra's here. I'll leave you for a second, but I'll only be outside, yeah?'

After what seemed a full minute, Nina's head moved in

an almost imperceptible nod. Her sister turned to Sandra.

'She's awake. Go easy.' Lucia crept out of the room. Sandra advanced gingerly and sat down.

A tiny, unrecognisable voice croaked, 'It's all right. I won't break.'

'Hey,' Sandra said. 'How are you?'

Nina turned her head on the pillow, opened her eyes and mustered a faint smile. She still had a nasal canula which made her face look puffy. 'Have to forgive me lying here like this,' she wheezed. 'Only it hurts to move.'

'No problem.' Suddenly Sandra was doubting the wisdom of having insisted on this job. Interviewing victims of violent crime in hospital was always a delicate business; when the victim was not only one of your own but also your best mate, it was a potential minefield. She wondered if the guv'nor really was too busy. Maybe even Sophia feared being at a loss in this situation. Nina had always looked fragile, like antique porcelain. But something other than physical damage had happened to her in the Clarkes' back garden. The lustre of her violet eyes, the keen quality in them that marked her down as a copper, was missing, leaving a dull void. It was as if part of her had died.

Sandra reminded herself Nina was tanked up with all kinds of drugs. It didn't do any good. She still wanted to cry, to mourn.

To *mourn*! Ridiculous. Nina was *alive*, for God's sake. She'd pull through. Nice and easy with the questions, lass. No rush.

'They treating you all right in here?'

'Like a baby.'

Sandra leaned forward. 'Mate, I'm sorry, but I've got to ask - '

'I was exp...' Nina's lips kept on going, but her larynx wouldn't co-operate.

'Sorry?'

'I was *expecting*,' she tried again, forcing the word out, 'the guv'nor. Summerfield. Heighway, even.'

'Sophia's had the Commissioner's office on the blower,' Sandra said. 'He wants to come and see you, but he's gonna wait a few days till you've mended a bit.'

Nina scowled. 'Got to look my best for the big guy.'

Sandra shrugged. 'If this is what it takes to get noticed...' She started to smile, but the joke had fallen on stony ground. She slid a hand onto the pillow. 'Nina, I've got to ask. What the fuck happened?'

'I was hoping,' Nina croaked, after what seemed like a great deal of thought, 'you could tell me.'

'You don't know?'

'It's... it's all a blank - like a black cloud...' she muttered. 'I remember, um... running out of the club. And driving Luke home. And then going to Ballards Way. But...'

Sandra waited for her to say something else. She didn't. 'Can you remember why you were there?'

'Debbie's back, isn't she?' Sandra nodded. Nina looked pleased with herself. 'I figured that out. The mugs, yeah?'

Sandra tried to look as if she knew what Nina was talking about.

'How did I end up here?'

'Pure bloody chance,' Sandra said, seized by a sudden impulse to stroke Nina's cheek, prove to herself the miracle had happened. 'Kim was giving Lucky and Juliet a lift.'

'Down Ballards Way?'

'You know what she's like. Anyway, they saw your car.

Thought it was a bit funny, got worried and came back to have a look. Nick of time, as it turned out.'

'God, I must've looked a right mess,' Nina said. She gasped and her eyes screwed tight shut. When she reopened them, they were full of tears that spilled over at once and flowed over her cheeks onto the pillow.

'Nina?'

She shook her head, as violently as she dared. 'When I woke up - I think I sort of just woke up, like - well, it wasn't gradual, put it that way.' Sandra had to lean close to hear. Her voice was little more than a whisper, and kept cutting out like a ropy outboard motor. 'One moment I was, I dunno, *somewhere*; then suddenly I'm awake, aware. All these tubes and machines and... and oh, my God, it was all so *clear*... like I was on speed or something. As God is my witness, I've never had so much clarity in my whole life - like my whole life was all crammed into that single second... And then...' She took in a deep, painful breath. 'Then I just realised all this - all this *junk* was for *me*. Plugged into *me*, like I'm some fucking domestic appliance. Like it was all that was keeping me alive. I kept expecting somebody to come along and - and pull the plug out and I'd be gone, and I couldn't stop them, and that, and...'

'OK,' Sandra whispered.

'And,' Nina said with extreme difficulty, 'I was all alone. Like I didn't have a clue where I was or what was happening and there was *nobody there*. Oh, God, Sandra, I've never been so fucking frightened. Never. Not even when - '

Her mouth slammed shut like a disturbed clam.

'When what?' Sandra prompted.

But all Nina did for a long time was subside into silent misery. By now Sandra could see a large damp patch on the pillow. She snapped out of the semi-daze she was in, took a clean tissue from the box on the bedside cabinet and attempted to stem the flow.

At last Nina spoke.

'Mum and Dad warned me,' she said. 'They've been dreading this since the day I joined up. I'd no right to put them through it. It's my fault. I walked into it.' Her body shook with a violent sob: a moan of agony, or anguish, escaped her.

'What are you saying - you what?' Sandra pleaded. 'Nina, what happened?'

'What happened?' she repeated vaguely, as though the question filtered down to her through a dull, turgid mind. She said, 'I'm done for.'

'You're gonna be fine. Out of here in no time.'

'No.' She looked across at Sandra, and her expression carried such sadness it put a lump in her friend's throat. 'The Job, I mean. I've had it.' She licked her lips. 'I - I - I don't - I don't think I can do it any more.'

'You can't let those bastards win!'

'What bastards?'

Sandra could feel the back of her neck burning in impotent anger. She said, 'We know it was Porter.'

'What?'

'Him and Quaife. We've got eyewitness statements from Debbie and her dad. Every bobby in the country's out looking and the ports and airports are sewn up tighter than an Eskimo's nipple. They're going nowhere.'

'Please don't, Sandra.'

The sudden plea brought her back to her senses with a jolt that snatched her breath away. She stared.

'I don't care,' Nina whispered. 'I don't fucking care.'

Sandra, thinking she understood, closed her eyes and passed a hand over her face. She said, 'I saw Paul outside.'

'Thought you must've.' She tensed. Nina said, 'It's OK.'

'He is your husband.' She didn't know what else to say.

'Yeah. For now, that's enough. I need him. Just concentrate on getting out of here, then worry about...'

There was a sharp knocking. Sandra craned round. Two faces were framed in the glass pane of the door. One was Lucia's; the other, tight lipped and irate, belonged to Nurse Aziz. Sandra nodded irritably and turned back to Nina, who looked exhausted. She said, 'I'm sorry, mate. That was right out of line.'

'Doesn't matter,' Nina said, barely audible. 'I didn't tell you, did I?'

'Tell me what?'

'Who,' she smiled.

Sandra, mystified, shrugged.

'I can see the funny side now.'

Light dawned. 'I've got to admit,' Sandra sniggered, 'that black eye is a fucking work of art.' She was delighted to see Nina's lips twitch.

Nurse Aziz came into the room, followed by Lucia, who appeared to have been attempting to restrain her. She snapped, 'OK, officer, I'm afraid you'll have to leave now.'

'Tell her not to make me laugh,' Nina pleaded. 'It hurts.'

'I was just going,' Sandra grinned. She leaned over to Nina and said, 'You'll be OK, you.'

Nina's lips moved.

Sandra leaned closer.

'Don't forget me.'

'Don't be daft. We're all rooting for you.'

Nina smiled and closed her eyes. Nurse Aziz bent over,

noticed the damp patch and started muttering about fluids. As Sandra went to the door Lucia smiled anxiously and flashed her a tentative thumbs-up sign. Sandra frowned, held her hand out flat and tilted it.

'Nasty?' Jasmin giggled. 'Jeff?'

'He got really nasty,' Zoltan repeated. "'Sorry, I should've asked before using your loo." And glib with it. I didn't know you had it in you, constable.'

'Aye, well.' Jeff wasn't sure he was that keen on Jasmin finding out about his dark side just yet. It was his loss that Zoltan had adjusted the rear view mirror for a better sweep of the road behind, so rendering her admiring smile invisible to him.

'I'm not complaining,' the DI said. 'Even in Special Crime, an occasional bit of old-fashioned, heavy-handed bobbying has its uses. Gave Vicky Prosser the nudge to think she'd put one over on us, anyway.'

'Hopefully,' Jeff sighed, looking at his watch. It was after one and they'd been in Glazebrook Road for two hours without much happening. The flat looked empty, curtains open, windows resolutely black.

'I think still that there is someone in the garden over there,' Jasmin said. Twenty minutes ago she'd reported seeing movement in the shadows behind some railings. They'd watched, but none of them could be certain. Wishful thinking, possibly.

'Sure we shouldn't go and check, guv?' Jeff said.

Zoltan shook his head. 'I want him in the building when we take him.'

'Bang to rights, huh?' Jasmin said, gleeful at a chance

finally to use the phrase.

'We hope.'

'As if we were sure he'll turn up,' Jeff said gloomily. 'What if he knows Pegley's been nicked?'

'They haven't seen one another for years, remember?'

'Pegley says.' He tensed. 'Eh up.'

A car was pulling up outside the flats. The front passenger door opened and a woman got out. They heard the word 'cheers' in an Irish accent.

'Colleen O'Dwyer,' Zoltan said. 'Funny sort of time to be out.'

'She has been working, I think,' Jasmin said, as the car drove off again. 'Those are scrubs she is wearing.' Suddenly she pointed. 'I was right. Look.'

They turned and saw a tall, thin figure emerge from behind the railings and hurry across the road. O'Dwyer, oblivious, had gone indoors. The figure pushed open the door and slipped through.

'He's going to use her to get into the flat,' Zoltan said. 'Right, let's go.'

They got out of the car and followed O'Dwyer and her shadow into the building. Jingling could be heard on the first floor landing, a key being turned in a lock, then shuffling and a startled scream, quickly muffled. By then they were racing upstairs. Jeff, with his long strides, got a foot in the doorway just before it slammed shut. He braced it with his shoulder against efforts to close it from the other side. Shrieks issued from inside the flat, and sounds of a struggle. Zoltan and Jasmin added their weight to Jeff's and the door burst open. In the shaft of light from the landing they saw a man hopping away, nursing his foot with one hand and trying to stop O'Dwyer escaping with the other. Jasmin shut the door and switched on the hall light.

'Let her go, Michael,' Zoltan said. 'She's an impoverished temp. Probably doesn't have anything of value you could use.'

At this moment O'Dwyer did two things. The first was to scream so loudly Jeff felt his eardrums cringing. The other was to kick the tall man very hard in the shin. He yelled and loosened his grip. Jeff moved in and restrained him.

'Who the fuck are you?' Colleen O'Dwyer had fled and was cowering behind the first heavy object she had come across, which was the living room door. Her eyes danced like a chased hare's from one intruder to the next. 'Who's this prick?'

'Good question.' Zoltan stepped round, looked the tall, gaunt, sneering young man in the face and was sure. He said, 'Michael Robert Prosser? You're under arrest.'

Anne White was not surprised to be woken by the sound of Zoltan's key in the door. He was the only man who'd ever been allowed a key to her life, the only one she'd encouraged to consider her flat an open house. She levered up a gummy eyelid and peered at the luminous red digits of the radio alarm. Ten to three. It could only mean they'd booked their prisoner in and were sitting on him until the morning. The buzz of excitement was quickly dulled. Bayliss was no longer her concern. Be that as it may, she couldn't just switch off her interest, especially now. Zoltan was her link to the team. Pretending to be asleep as he tiptoed into the bedroom, she started planning a conversation in her head.

'You with flights of angels?' he murmured.

She grunted sleepily.

'Excuse the hour.'

'Was expecting you.' It was broadly true. Zoltan, in the morning, would have to go and talk to a serial rapist. Recently he'd confided that it was getting steadily easier to come here rather than crash at home. His own flat was starting to look unlived in. Not conducive to preparing his mind for such an interview.

He finished undressing and climbed into bed, his body cool from the London night. 'Sorry,' he said, feeling her tense.

She tutted and drew him close. 'I'm awake now,' she said. 'Mind if we talk?'

'Of course.'

The ambiguity threw her. She said, 'Um...'

'Been meaning to ask anyway,' he said. 'Is your offer still on?'

She felt like laughing. He'd stolen her thunder again. 'About moving in?'

'Yes.'

'Sure,' she squealed, and kissed him in delight. 'Worked out what to do with all your stuff, then?'

'I thought about it,' he said, 'and then I realised most of it's here already. By a process of gradual migration.'

'Cluttering up the place,' she grumbled.

'I could do a car boot sale or something.'

'I was joking.'

'Not entirely, I suspect.'

'Zoltan?' she said. It was the moment of truth.

'Mmm?'

'Before you jump in feet first.'

'I can swim.'

'No, listen. Hear me out before you decide anything.'

'Let's have it.' He ran his fingers through her hair.

'I've got a confession to make.' She felt it coming out in a rush. 'I had sex with Roy Gillam.'

'Was rather afraid you might have.'

Anne struggled to overcome the double take, and groaned. 'I thought I'd kept it really well hidden.'

'I know. That's why I'm a DI and you're a DC.'

'Acting sergeant, thank you.'

'But no longer a detective.'

She let it drop. Something was missing from this conversation. 'You're not angry?'

'No.'

She waited, but it was all he was going to say. She wanted him to rail at her, but then she realised what his game was. He'd keep those feelings to himself, so that she would never know if her sleeping with other men hurt him or not. Especially now they were living together, she would always have to think twice.

She stared at him in the dark.

'You astonishing bastard,' she said affectionately.

TUESDAY

Lucky's journey to work felt like a procession to the gallows. If she was honest with herself, this whole enquiry had been suffused with a dull sense of impending doom. She'd kept it in her head that as long as she could forget, things would be OK. She'd survived crises before. She'd got over Dad's leaving, she'd got over Julia's moving out and she would get over the shock of finding Nina. She would -

But it was the little things, the nagging imps that tormented her, kept knocking her down just as she was struggling upright. How had she even *dreamed* she could be impartial? She'd been all right in herself, but what about all the idle remarks of her colleagues when they discussed the case, the mindless snap diagnoses of a dozen armchair shrinks? What did they know? Several times she'd been unable to stop herself carping back at them, a coded cry, 'Look, this is what it's *really* like.' And no-one had twigged. Not even Juliet, and she'd been bladdered then, for crying out loud.

She'd half-known who they were looking for after they'd spoken to Mrs Beckett, and even before then the victims' consistent descriptions ought to have given her a hint. But the

MO... it was nothing *like*. It couldn't be him. She told herself it would be too much like a sick joke. Even the name was wrong.

But it *was* a sick joke. That had been obvious from the moment she'd seen what was written on the back of Jeff's gas bill. They were on their way to pick Prosser up. When they questioned him he'd tell them, and she would be finished.

No-one said anything when she walked into the office. No-one stared, or asked her if she was OK, and there was no summoning note from Sophia. Everything seemed the same as yesterday, grim faces talking into phones or scowling at computers, persisting despite all the odds with their hunt for Nina's attackers. She felt disorientated.

'Lucky.'

She whipped round as though someone had kicked her. Sophia stood behind her, holding a large buff envelope, and Lucky knew without being told what was inside.

'Ma'am?'

'I'd like you to fax this to Rye,' Sophia said, handing her the envelope, 'then ring Miranda Beckett and warn her there'll be someone calling round with a picture for her to identify.'

'Right,' Lucky heard herself saying. She was shaking like a washing machine on spin and the guv'nor surely must see it. 'We've got a body, then?'

'Zoltan arrested Michael Bayliss last night. He's just about to start interviewing him. The reason we weren't able to find him before is that he's been using the name Prosser.'

She felt her knees go. She grabbed the edge of a desk for support. Then she turned and dashed out of the office, dropping the envelope and trying not to imagine the expression that must be etched on Sophia's face.

Sergeant Bob Price was nearing completion of the tedious forms that were required for DCs Winter and Wetherby to remove Michael Prosser from his cell when the sound of running footsteps distracted all three of them. It is the last sound a policeman who cherishes peace of mind wishes to hear in a cell block because his immediate fear is that it means either a breakout or a death in custody. When he looked up the first thing he saw was Jasmin Winter being barged aside by someone with long black hair, a grey top and blue jeans. Bob didn't remember anyone of that description being booked in and besides, they were running *towards* the cells. Muttering, 'What the fuck...?' he got up and hurried after the figure. 'Oi!' Jeff and Jasmin turned to watch.

Breathing laboured, Lucky shambled down the cell corridor checking names. Prosser was in number three, on the right at the far end. She skidded to a halt and slammed the Judas hole open. She let slip a strange little noise. Bob stepped aside in alarm as she fled past him.

Jeff and Jasmin glimpsed the ghastly look on her face and both had the same thought. They broke into a run and joined Bob as he reached the door, braced himself and peered through the hatch.

Michael Prosser hadn't hung himself, suffocated on vomit or run head first against the wall. He was sitting laughing at them. Bob opened the door.

'That stupid little bitch,' Prosser said, 'thinks I raped her.'

It wasn't hard to tell where Lucky had gone. Jasmin just had to follow the pointing arms. A middle aged civilian clerk was the only visible occupant of the locker room when she walked in.

'Have you seen - ?' The clerk pointed to a closed cubicle. Jasmin said, 'Is it OK for you to leave, please?'

'Sure,' the clerk said, wiping damp hands on her skirt. 'I was just finishing up anyway.'

'Thanks.'

The clerk nodded and went. Jasmin looked around for some way of keeping people out, but there didn't seem to be anything. She'd just have to hope. She cleared her throat, stepped up to the cubicle and knocked on the door.

'Lucky, are you in there? It's Jasmin.' There was no reply, but Jasmin could hear her breathing. She tried again. 'Lucky?' Suddenly the sobriquet didn't seem appropriate. She called gently, 'Larissa, come on. I want to talk to you.'

There was movement, and the bolt was drawn. Cautiously she pushed the door open. Lucky sat on the toilet seat, hugging herself. Jasmin could smell the fear coming off her, like a wind.

'Hi,' she said. Lucky stared at her knees. Jasmin sat cross-legged on the floor in front of her and tilted her head, coaxing her into making eye contact. The hand that finally allowed itself to be taken in hers was cold and trembling. She whispered, 'What's going on?'

'It's him,' Lucky said with a sob. 'Oh, God, it's him.'

The rules state that the supervising officer in an investigation of rape must be of the rank of inspector or above. Even in the 21st century that generally means a man: one who, while he will have been on all the requisite courses and be sincerely sympathetic, will find it difficult even to come close to appreciating what this most humiliating and personal of crimes means to the victim.

For that reason he will find a female officer to talk to her, at least to begin with; an experienced policewoman, not always a detective, but specially trained in the craft of separating facts from the pain, distress and confusion that accompany them in the victim's memory. She will not always succeed, but at the very least she is often the only person who can convince the woman that, in spite of all the cruel questions they must ask, the police are on her side.

It was this principle that was under hot debate in the office of Chief Superintendent Coleridge, the borough commander. Coleridge, on hearing the news, had immediately called in his boss, Assistant Commissioner Parmiter, and it was them, as well as DCI Summerfield, against whom Sophia Beadle was defending her corner.

'Sir, you agreed to let me continue the Benton enquiry even after one of my officers was injured,' she said to Parmiter. 'Why am I considered competent to handle that and not this?'

'DC Tyminski was attacked in the line of duty,' Coleridge butted in. 'She was following up a lead.'

'Nina wasn't on duty.'

'You know what I mean.'

'The point is,' Drew Parmiter raised his voice just enough, 'Tyminski was attacked in her capacity as a copper. PC Stephenson was raped in her capacity as a woman.'

'That's the general idea,' Sophia snapped, and wished she hadn't. 'Look, sir, no-one's even interviewed Lucky - PC Stephenson - yet. We don't know what happened, or why.'

'That's it exactly,' Summerfield said. 'All we know is Prosser sat in his cell and told Bob Price he'd raped Stevens.'

'He said nothing of the kind.'

'He implied it.'

'What he said was, "She *thinks* I raped her." You know as well as I do that consent is the only viable defence against a rape charge.'

'You're too close,' Summerfield said.

'Oh, put your handbags away.' AC Parmiter sat back and unwrapped a stick of gum. In spite of his elevated rank, he still liked to portray himself as laid back, one of the troops. His manner was irritating Sophia; he was acting as if the carpeting he'd given her only four days ago over the DNA result had never taken place. He pushed the gum langorously into his mouth as if it were a square of expensive dark chocolate and looked at them. 'I'm not calling Sophia's ability to conduct an impartial enquiry into question. Point is, through no fault of their own, two of her officers have come a cropper one after the other. Not a good hit rate.'

'So this is down to image, is it, sir?' Coleridge, to both Sophia's and Summerfield's surprise, sounded genuinely outraged by the notion. 'Never mind a young woman's human dignity.'

'Sometimes image is important, Simon,' Parmiter said. 'Within a very few hours I'm going to be fielding cries from inside and outside the service for Special Crime to be disbanded. We all know the circumstances are bad luck, but a lot of people won't see it that way.'

'I see,' Coleridge said. 'Delicate little ladies who shouldn't be exposed to the dangers of high risk policing?'

'There is that to it,' Parmiter replied, unperturbed. 'Of greater concern to me are the implications of Special Crime's existence for Larissa's welfare. Or the welfare of any female officer under my command who's unlucky enough to be on the receiving end of something like this.' He surveyed their uncomprehending faces and smiled. 'Matthew,' he said to Summerfield, 'how many women have you got in CID at the moment?'

'None,' Summerfield said. You don't have to sound so happy about it, Sophia thought angrily.

Parmiter pointed at him triumphantly. 'And Joe Gottlieb up at Gipsy Hill has only got one,' he said. 'These two BOCUs have got fewer women in regular CID than anywhere else in the Met. Why?'

'They're all in bloody Special Crime,' Summerfield said nastily.

'I recruited eight women because eight women were the best people for the job,' Sophia argued. It occurred to her to hope Coleridge or the AC didn't think she was including herself in that number. It further occurred to her that it might be a subliminal way of reminding them the team still wasn't back up to strength. One of her original DCs, Sarah Craig, had lasted barely a month before resigning to move to America with her physicist husband, who'd been offered the job of a lifetime at MIT, and she had never been replaced. They needed another body, and they needed a DC, not – Sophia felt a little stab of guilt for thinking this – another trainee.

'Still looks a hell of a lot like affirmative action,' Summerfield commented.

'Bottom line,' Parmiter said, raising his hand for peace, 'when Special Crime was set up nobody imagined this was going to happen. The specific problem now is we have eight women in Special Crime - counting yourself – '

Damn it, Sophia thought.

' - all trained in handling rape victims, but who all have a conflict of interest. Which leaves us with Marian Southworth from Gipsy Hill...'

'...who Lucky knows from her last posting,' Sophia finished for him resignedly.

'What's wrong with bringing a WPC... someone in from another BOCU?' Summerfield wanted to know.

'Here's what we'll do.' Parmiter puffed happily on his cigar. 'Matthew, d'you think you can take charge of this?'

Summerfield glanced at Sophia before answering. 'It's no secret I don't particularly approve of women police, sir,' he said. 'But I've got two daughters and my younger one's about the same age as WPC Stevens. I wouldn't wish rape on any woman.'

'You'll do an impartial and thorough job, in other words?'

'Yes, sir.'

'Be sensitive about it?'

'Of course.'

'Even if I give you a DC from Special Crime to talk to Larissa?'

Summerfield's reply missed a beat. 'No problem, sir.'

'Three things,' Parmiter said to him, winking at Sophia. 'One, the suspect's already had his collar felt, so you shouldn't need long. Liaise with DI Schneider, who's got him in custody for other offences.'

'Right,' Summerfield grunted, not best pleased.

'Second.'

'Sir?'

'We dropped the W many years ago.'

'I know, sir. Force of habit.'

'And three,' Parmiter said, 'for Christ's sake get the kid's name right. It's Stephen*son*.'

The rape suite was tucked away in a quiet corner of the admin floor, which was populated largely by clerical staff and so well away from the raucous banter of coppers. The surroundings were a world removed from the spartan, regimented rooms and corridors of the rest of the nick. This was tasteful and quiet, done up in pastel shades, floral curtains, pictures on the wall, a three piece suite, a coffee table, a lamp, books, plants; all done with a woman's touch, and striving hard to look like a comfortable domestic scene. It had always struck Jasmin Winter as rather contrived: it was too clean and tidy and cosy, trying slightly too earnestly to put you at your ease.

She couldn't deny, though, that it seemed to work. In this case, Lucky's deliverance into Dr Ticehurst's reassuring hands would probably help a lot. Ruth Ticehurst was a calm, sisterly Jewess in her forties, married to a Gentile and the senior partner of a general practice in Waddon. She'd been a forensic medical examiner for eleven years and a rape specialist for most of those, as well-trained and tactful as any of the team. Depending on circumstances, her examination of a victim could take anything from ten minutes to an hour if running repairs needed to be done prior to the woman going to hospital. Nowadays, standard procedure included tests for HIV, hepatitis, gonorrhoea, as well as advice on contraception and pregnancy. If necessary, she would prescribe the morning after pill.

The door from the examining room opened and Dr Ticehurst appeared, alone. Jasmin stood. 'How is she?'

'Having a bath.'

Jasmin nodded, unsurprised. Most rape victims took up the offer after their examination. After a long soak in a bathroom as luxuriously appointed and homely as the lounge, the woman would find a closet hung with a selection of loose, soft clothing in a variety of tastes, styles and sizes: necessary because her own clothes might be needed for forensic examination. Once dressed, she would be ushered back through to the lounge, where perhaps the worst part of her ordeal awaited her.

Ruth Ticehurst pulled the door to behind her and shoved her hands in her pockets. She looked desultory. 'I'm none the wiser, I'm afraid.'

'Huh?'

'I can't find any medical evidence of assault.'

Jasmin sat down, frowning. Dr Ticehurst sat opposite, where she could keep an eye and ear on the surgery.

'When I say none.' She folded her arms. 'Very, very faint bruises on her upper arms, positioned where they would be if someone had held her down. People heal at different rates, but as Larissa's young and healthy I should say at least a week old. Same goes for the vagina. Old bruising, which is even less conclusive because it could have been caused by just about anything, like a stubborn tampon or even vigorous consensual sex.'

'What else?' Jasmin said, finding she had pen and pad in hand but was writing none of this down.

'I always save the best till last.' Dr Ticehurst smiled humourlessly. 'No trace of semen.'

'What?'

'At all.'

Jasmin shook her head. 'He used a condom?'

'Negative on lubricant and spermicide,' the FME insisted. 'There's nothing. It's fairly safe to say she has not had penetrative sex, willing or otherwise, within the last forty-eight hours.'

Jasmin stared at her. 'Possibly... a foreign object was used?'

'I don't know about that.' Dr Ticehurst unfolded her arms and spread them wide. 'I'm just a medic. It's your job to find the rest out.'

'But you have examined her,' Jasmin persisted. 'You have talked to her. What do you think?'

'Off the record? My impression - and I want to make clear that this is not a medical opinion but the opinion of someone who's seen an awful lot of women like Larissa over the years - she's been assaulted all right.'

'Raped?'

'Assaulted,' Dr Ticehurst looked Jasmin square in the eye. 'But not recently.'

Summerfield went straight from his audience with the AC down to the interview room where Zoltan Schneider was grilling Prosser. Zoltan broke off, and accepted the news that Summerfield was now in charge without surprise. He appraised the DCI of his progress. There'd been very little. To each of the accusations put to him, from Denise Cole to Violet McMinn, Prosser had simply replied by shaking his head. He hadn't yet been tackled on the subjects of Miranda Hargreaves or Lucky.

'He's in there, pleased as punch with himself, as if he knows something. Fixed smirk on his face all morning. I think he's set like it.'

'Trying to wind you up,' Summerfield said.

'Waiting to see if I'll blow my top when it comes to asking him about Lucky?' Zoltan smiled thinly. 'He's in for disappointment, then.'

Summerfield nodded, not doubting it. 'Got the warrant for Albion Street. Wanna come?'

Zoltan shook his head. 'Better keep the momentum going. See if his tune changes when I tell him how Pegley shopped him.'

'Don't forget to let him have a lunch break,' Summerfield sneered.

'What do I look like,' Zoltan shrugged, 'a Nazi?'

At the front desk stood a willowy, fair-haired young woman in a bank uniform. The receptionist smiled at her.

'My name's Juliet Gow. I'm here about my friend.' Behind her round glasses the woman looked anxious. 'Larissa Stephenson?'

When a copper is attacked, even civilian staff regard it as against their own. The receptionist didn't even need to check her message book. She frowned. 'We were expecting a relative.'

'Her mum's at work. Larissa asked for me.'

This time she did consult the book. 'I'll get somebody to come and take you up,' she said, picking up the phone.

'Thanks,' Juliet said.

The team that raided 32 Albion Street was five strong. Summerfield had decided to take Jeff Wetherby, who had a better idea what to look for, one of his own DCs and a uniformed female PC in case Prosser's mother needed sorting. At Jeff's suggestion, the fifth member of the team was Tom Walker. Vicky Prosser knew him of old. 'Thought you'd fucking retired,' she said balefully.

'Afternoon, Vicky,' he smiled as Summerfield handed her the search warrant. 'You've seen one of these before.'

'What's it for?'

'Oh, items from various burglaries. Evidence in six cases of sexual assault and rape. It's all there.' Summerfield pressed the document into her hand and pushed past her.

'You again?' she scowled at Jeff as he crossed the threshold. Jeff smiled and went to join DC Peter Moore upstairs.

An hour later they'd been through almost the whole house and two of them were now up in the loft. A voice echoed out through the hatch and down the stairs. 'Jeff!'

Jeff came out from the kitchen, where Vicky Prosser had been persuaded to lay on more tea. 'Hello?'

Tom Walker's uniform-trousered legs could be seen dangling from the loft hatch. They'd been unable to find a ladder, and Vicky had insisted the space was never used, but Summerfield had been of the opinion that someone of Michael Prosser's height and strength would have no difficulty getting up there without. Tom jumped down and his knees buckled alarmingly before he steadied himself. 'You got that list of stuff that was nicked?'

Jeff took it from his pocket. 'Er, one silver trophy. Brass candlestick. Wooden Welsh love spoon. A plaster of Paris statuette. Possibly some sort of documentation relating to a flute...'

Tom looked upwards. Peter Moore's hands appeared through the hatch and handed him down a cardboard box. 'Look what we found,' he said, coming downstairs.

He carried it through to the kitchen table. Summerfield and Vicky Prosser joined the cluster of heads peering into the box.

'Oh, this,' Summerfield said slowly, 'is choice.'

Even neatly packed and wrapped in sheets of paper

kitchen towel, it was clear that most of the fifteen or so objects in the box were in some way phallic. They got them out and spread them across the table, a feeling of grim triumph rising within the group.

'Gotcha, you bastard,' Jeff muttered.

But there was no trophy and no brass candlestick.

'Keep looking,' Summerfield said.

Lucky was still wearing her grey top and jeans when she finally emerged. She shook off Jasmin's guiding hand and went to sit down next to Juliet, who put her arm round her shoulders. Jasmin sat opposite.

'Do you feel a little better now?' she asked.

'I felt fine before,' Lucky said impatiently.

'You were hysterical, almost,' Jasmin said. 'I mean do you feel OK to talk?'

Lucky pressed her lips together and nodded.

'My God, Larissa, what happened?' Juliet was tearful.

'I got raped,' Lucky snapped. She looked at Jasmin. 'Yes, I know what she's probably told you. So you won't believe me. *I* wouldn't believe me,' she said with a self-contemptuous laugh.

Juliet looked puzzled. 'Who did it?' she blurted out. 'D'you know?'

'Please.' Jasmin tried to calm her.

'That piece of shit down in the cells,' Lucky said. 'Prosser. Michael fucking Bayliss, as known and loved by Special Crime. And the reason Dr Ticehurst couldn't find anything,' she quavered, 'is because it happened thirteen days ago.'

There was a box of Kleenex on the coffee table. Jasmin reached out and pushed it closer to Lucky as cover for some stunned thinking.

'That's right. I'm all eager and anxious to please. My career's just gone into orbit, yeah? I go home at lunchtime to change and that bastard's waiting for me.'

Jasmin's head was in a spin. Two weeks ago. That would have been... What was *I* doing? With a guilty start she realised she'd been too damn tired to notice much of what was going on around her. The arson had happened around then - that was it, the Tuesday - so it must have been the day she and Nina had first linked the McMinn and Abernetty incidents and... good God. It had been Lucky's first day.

There were a million questions. But she must keep a clear head, follow the line. Larissa must be strong to have carried this around for so long, but how close was she to snapping?

'So you know him?'

'Vaguely from school,' Lucky said. 'He didn't have a key, if that's what you're worried about. Got in through an open window.'

'Of course.' Jasmin leaned forward. 'Larissa, I'm trying to think how to say this. For two weeks you knew who he was, but you worked the rape enquiry and still you said nothing. I don't understand.'

'I *didn't* know! I didn't know it was him. I sort of decided it couldn't be.'

'OK.' She waited for Lucky to grab two fistfuls of Kleenex, cover her eyes and leave them there. 'Let's try to figure out - '

'I know what happened.'

'Sure you do.' Jasmin swallowed. 'You were there. Now you came home. Were you alone in the house?'

'Yeah. My mum was at work.'

'Did you notice anything unusual?'

'Just that Mum'd left the bathroom window open.'

'The bathroom, it is upstairs, downstairs...?'

'*Up*stairs.' She bunched her fists, emphasising it. 'Why it didn't connect, right? Our guy had never done upstairs windows.'

'You said he was in your room. That's upstairs also?'

Lucky nodded. A strand of hair snagged on her cheek and she brushed it away.

'So you didn't know he was in the house straight away?'

'You're gonna love this. No, I didn't know he was there. If I'd known he was there,' the bitter edge to her voice grew sharper, 'I wouldn't've stripped off and been prancing about in my best satin undies.'

Jasmin let it go, but she knew Lucky could read in her eyes the mental note she was making. She had to pick up on the point. A defence QC would be guaranteed to.

'I thought I was on my own,' Lucky whispered with a note of pleading. 'I was wearing nice undies because it was my first day in a new job and I felt good. Is that unreasonable?'

'No,' Jasmin said. 'So you did not see him until you went into your room?'

'He was behind the door. I saw him in the mirror.'

'Did you call out, scream?'

'No point.'

'Why no point?'

'Nobody to fucking hear.'

'He wasn't to know...' Juliet began, but tailed off when she saw Jasmin's warning scowl.

'The rest of it's quite straightforward,' Lucky said, trembling with humiliation. 'He raped me, on the bed, and then... left.'

'He raped you?' Jasmin said. 'He really - ?'

'He really raped me,' Lucky cried. 'He didn't shove a brass candlestick or a statue or a flute up there, he really, really did it.'

'So again because of this, you did not think it was him?' Jasmin whispered.

'Because he didn't... use... a foreign object,' Lucky said. 'And the name was wrong too. Everything was wrong. When we were at school his surname was Prosser.' She looked at Juliet, who nodded dumbly. 'Where he gets Bayliss from I have no idea.'

'Haven't seen this guy since school,' Juliet told Jasmin. She looked shellshocked. 'He was in our class. Jesus.'

Jasmin nodded, a haze before her eyes. She was trying to remember her training, trying to imagine herself inside the attack, to empathise and know better when to be gentle with the victim, when to press. This time she couldn't do it. Lucky was one of their own and this couldn't, shouldn't have happened.

'Did he have a weapon?' she said.

'No, he didn't.'

'A knife?' She felt sick. 'A gun? Anything?'

'*Nothing.*'

'Lucky, I must ask this. Did you try to stop him?'

They stared at one another.

'No.'

'Did you say, "Don't," or anything that - ?'

'No,' Lucky said, on the brink of more tears.

'*No?*'

'But, Larissa...' Juliet said.

'But what?'

'You're a copper. You've been trained.'

'Tell me about it.' Lucky blinked desperately and turned

to Jasmin. 'Want to know why I didn't? It should be bleeding obvious.'

'I don't -' Jasmin said, at once aware and furious with herself that this sounded like the waffling it was.

'You don't understand,' Lucky said. 'Nor do I. Two weeks of endless, sleepless nights, asking myself. I've got four years in now, I've faced down G20 demonstrators, street robbers, kids with knives. I can look after myself, I know I can; I've proved any number of times I can. And some sick scumbag breaks into my house and forces me to have sex with him. I did everything wrong, Jasmin. I didn't scream. I didn't fight. I did everything he told me. I lay on the bed when he told me. I even took off my own underwear, can you believe that?' She turned to Juliet. 'You're right. I should've used my training. What I should've done was bite his fucking nuts off. He knew I was Job. I had every bloody opportunity *and I did nothing to stop him!*'

Now she cried. She collapsed onto Juliet and bawled into her neck, her friend's trembling arms trying absurdly to protect her against the nightmare that had already happened. Jasmin felt helpless. This was not discreet, ladylike weeping. This was the howling of a soul in anguish, a flood of tears flung before a burst dam of fear, anger, shame, frustration only Lucky could feel but could make the others shrink from in horror.

To stem the torrent took twenty minutes and the rest of the Kleenex, shared between the three of them. There were damp spots on Jasmin's notebook. Lucky looked ghastly, her eyes and nose red and swollen, whipcords of wet black hair striping her cheeks, thick smudged mascara scarring her face like burns. She looked up with an expression you saw on the faces of beggars outside East Croydon station.

'I get it,' Jasmin said, her voice shaky.

'No, you don't.'

'I begin to.'

'Well, I'm glad,' Lucky snapped, 'because buggered if I do. So tell me, Jasmin. What do I do now? *Tell* me!'

To her despair, Jasmin couldn't answer. She felt terribly that she was letting Lucky down.

She got home at eight with no appetite. Instead she settled down with *Nostromo*, of which she was now in sight of the finish. By ten she was onto the last three chapters and dead beat. She undressed, went and had a bath, poured herself into bed and turned the light out.

Every time she closed her eyes, she could see Larissa Stephenson sitting in the rape suite, saying things she didn't want to hear, things she couldn't bring herself to believe. She tried to tell herself a female cop was at the same risk of attack, remote though that might be, as any other woman. But surely, *surely* a cop ought to know enough to dissuade a potential rapist, or at least put up a fight. Damn it, she'd *seen* Prosser. Sure, he was tall, intimidating, evil-looking if you liked, but there was nothing to him. No way should he have been able to overpower a fit young woman like Lucky without even a struggle.

Yet that was what he'd done to five other women, some who could defend themselves, some who couldn't; more if the reports were true, reports of boxes filled with dozens of objects whose original owners might never be traced. Even without those facts, there was no doubting Lucky's upset, the raw, violated distress as she cried until her lungs withered. She heard the doubts still pitter-pattering at the back of her mind, and felt ashamed. Who could tell how they'd react in a frightening situation? Jasmin, whose attitude had always been that any intruder she disturbed would not remain in possession of his dick for very long, was no longer so sure.

Now wide awake, she listened with raw nerves to the passage of an express train outside her window; to the engulfing, angry silence that surged in its wake.

She swore, got up and got dressed.

The 468 bus stopped two minutes from her front door and ran beyond midnight. One came by with considerate promptness and she rode it to the Swan and Sugar Loaf in South Croydon. Using the map app on her phone, she found her way to a big Edwardian house whose walls were cloaked in Virginia creeper. She pushed open the gate and stepped onto a path through an unkempt front garden. The hall light was on.

Jeff Wetherby seemed only mildly surprised to see her. With the nervous embarrassment of the unprepared host, he ushered her into a large, sparsely furnished room at the back of the house, with original fixtures that even included a disused socket for a bell rope. French windows opened onto a patio, a rockery and a long, large lawn. These, like the front, looked wild, but it was too dark to make out much detail.

Jasmin was speechless. All she had in the world would fit into one *corner* of this room.

'Have a seat,' Jeff offered, 'if - '

But she was still taking things in. 'Big, huh?'

'Oh, aye.'

'Ah! Right,' she said abruptly, his invitation registering. She chose an armchair and flopped into its enveloping depths. With a heavy sigh she leaned back, kicking off her shoes.

A muffled thump from outside made her turn her head to see a flash of orange going past the French windows. Shortly afterwards a distant querulous mewing started up. 'Only Buster,' Jeff smiled.

'Buster?'

'Cat. Better let him in.' He paused in the doorway. 'I was about to heat some soup.'

'I don't want to be trouble.'

'No trouble. I hadn't eaten. Not much of an appetite, last couple of days.'

She nodded to let him know she was in the same mood. 'Then sure. Thanks.'

She smiled, settled deeper into the armchair with a contented wriggle and closed her eyes. With a last affectionate glance, Jeff left the room.

Buster was on the kitchen windowsill, his worried ginger face pressed against the glass. He jumped down when he saw Jeff, who walked over and opened the window. The cat jumped in and landed at his feet. Jeff shook his head wearily. All cats have their idiosyncrasies, and one of Buster's was a disinclination to use the door for going in and out of the house.

He'd been a kitten when Jeff had met him two days after moving in. He'd shown up on the front porch, wearing an expression that said, 'Own me.' There was no collar and Jeff had gone door to door, put up posters, advertised on Craigslist and contacted the RSPCA and the Cats Protection League, all to no avail. Before long Buster was well established, and had been his lodger ever since.

Jeff shovelled cat food into a bowl, washed his hands and put the stock on the stove in a big aluminium pan. He stirred in water, the shredded remains of the chicken, rotelle, chopped vegetables, garlic powder, black pepper and an extra stock cube for body. Twenty-five minutes ought to do it. He turned the gas down and went back to the living room. Jasmin was dozing, but she stirred and looked up as he came in and sprawled out on the settee.

'Comfy?'

'*Ja!*' She closed her eyes and tilted back her head. 'I can't remember last time I could relax in an armchair.'

'How about house calls?'

'That's work,' she said. 'It's not relaxing.'

'True.' He recalled the spartan furnishings of Jasmin's bleak room. No armchair there, no curling up by the fireside on a cold, frosty night. Every waking moment was a quest for constant movement, every muscle coiled against the unrelenting chill. Hardly surprising she looked run down. He wondered when her last decent night's sleep had been.

'It's warm here,' she commented, as though reading his thoughts.

He looked around. 'It's OK, I suppose. Stays nice and cool in here on a hot summer's day. Winter, that's the sod. Trouble is the central heating' - he pointed to an old iron radiator behind the door - 'runs off a coal-fired boiler in the breakfast room, would you believe. There's tons of anthracite in the cellar but it's too much aggro carting enough of it up here. One and only time I ever actually managed to get the thing going it filled the entire house up with soot. So now I just rely on the fires and you should've seen my gas bill yesterday.'

She smiled. 'How long do you live here now?'

'Nearly seven years.'

'How come you have such a big house?'

'It's my dad's,' Jeff said. 'He inherited it from an aunt,

had some vague idea about converting it into flats but never got round to it.' He shifted his position. 'I'd just transferred to the Met, so I moved in here as a sitting tenant, look after the place. Beats the section house.'

'This is expensive, no?'

'Would be if there was a mortgage,' he nodded. 'Auntie Mary's insurance paid that off. I meet all the bills and send Dad rent each month.' He made a face. 'Guess I'm out of pocket a bit, but I can easily get by on what I'm earning.'

Silence fell, the stern knowledge they'd been avoiding for too long the subject at the front of both their minds.

'I heard,' Jeff said.

'How?' She was surprised and horrified. The promise of spontaneous comfort seemed to fade. 'Lucky's statement is passed round the goddamn office now, huh?'

He folded his arms and looked hurt. 'That you'd done the interview, I meant. Is it true?' She looked at him sharply. 'This was two weeks ago?'

'How much of it is out?' Jasmin asked.

'All I know is the bits of Prosser's story I believe. He says two weeks.'

'He admits it?'

'Raping her?' He scowled. 'What do you think?'

'What's his story?'

'D'you really want to hear this?' he sighed. He met her gaze. 'He was never in the house. They bumped into one another outside; she has a hysterical fit, decides he matches the description of the serial rapist and instead of nicking him, threatens to fit him up. *He* says.'

'You're kidding!'

'Oh, no,' he said thickly.

She looked him in the eye. 'You believe him?'

He thought, recognising a test. 'No, I fucking don't. We both saw Lucky's face, and him smirking like it was some big joke. I think he raped her, and I'll stand up in any court and say so.'

But you don't know what I know, Jasmin thought. There's no way it's even going to get that far.

'He knew she was a cop,' she said. 'He was waiting in her room. She has commendations on the walls, her uniform in her closet. I don't get why he was not careful this time.'

'Why he actually raped her instead of using a foreign object?' Sam said. She nodded. 'Beats me. Hopefully Zoltan or Summerfield can wear him down so he'll tell us.'

'Two weeks.'

'Aye,' Jeff said. 'Explains a lot.'

She looked at him in surprise, but he didn't seem inclined to elaborate. She felt a sudden, shameful pang of jealousy.

He said, 'How is she?'

'OK.'

'Bearing up?'

'She bears up for so long, believing that today was never going to happen. I think now that delayed shock is coming.' She spotted his frown. 'Juliet is spending the night with her.'

He looked blank. 'Juliet?'

'Her friend at the club the other night.'

'Don't remind me,' he said, rubbing his eyes to cover the anguished look on his face. He realised what he'd said and paled. 'I didn't mean...'

'No,' she smiled. 'I know.'

'First Nina, now Lucky.' He shook his head. 'God almighty, what's happening to this team?'

For a while neither of them spoke. Jasmin, tilting her head on one side and resting it on a cupped hand, was acutely aware of Jeff looking at her intently.

She said, 'What are you thinking?'

It was her disconcerting habit to ask very direct questions out of the blue, and it nearly always caught him on the hop. Actually he'd been worrying whether her choice of an armchair, rather than the settee, had been deliberate. Under the circumstances, he was ashamed of himself for thinking it. But what *ought* he to say? He plumped for, 'Just wondering how the soup's doing.'

She grinned. 'Go find out, huh?'

He went back to the kitchen and groaned. Buster's idea of table manners was to leave lumps of Felix all over the floor, and he'd excelled himself tonight as a protest at being locked out. By the time Jeff had gathered them all up the soup was ready. He served it up into bowls and onto trays and carried it through. True to form, Buster had sat on their guest's chest and was purring at her adoringly.

'Hop it, you.'

Buster jumped down and went over to the fire.

'He's lovely,' Jasmin said.

'Happen his breath isn't,' Jeff grumbled, remembering the kitchen floor.

'I don't mind.' She brushed ginger fur off her sweater.

Jeff looked admiringly at his cat. 'You're in there, mate.'

She giggled and tasted her soup.

'OK?'

'Great!' She paused and qualified it. 'Maybe less pepper.'

'You're probably right. It's only 'cause I like pepper.'

'Your mom taught you to cook?'

'Not really. It's just I found, living on my own, a constant diet of fish and chips, Chinese takeaway and frozen bung in the oven stuff palls a bit after a while. So I started teaching myself.'

Jasmin said, 'I cook a lot also. Where I live, often the kitchen with the stove on is the warmest place in the house.'

Further talk seemed unnecessary as they set to eating, and thinking. With the soup finished there was a short, awkward spell; then, as is the way of things, they both started at once.

She said, 'Jeff, I have to - '

He said, 'I was wondering - ' He stopped. 'Go on,' he said, anxious.

'I have not forgotten the other night,' Jasmin said.

'Me neither.'

She gulped. 'Don't get me wrong, Jeff. It was... great. Beautiful, a beautiful thing. And now I don't know the answer, what it means.'

'You were lonely,' Jeff said. 'Why I was there, remember?'

'I guess it seems kind of like I have been avoiding you since.'

He shrugged. 'We've been flat out, with what's been happening.'

'It's not that. Ach, maybe it is.'

'Aye.' He frowned. 'I mean when you think Nina must've been lying there bleeding half to death while we were - '

'Falling in love?'

The words were out. She felt her face go warm.

'What's going on?' he said.

She brushed a hand across her eyes. 'I don't know what is right or wrong. Maybe until I've figured that out...'

She stopped, peering at her lap. Jeff thought hard. She was alone in a foreign land, living on the breadline, a cold dank room for shelter, no respite in immediate view. Small wonder a thing so unexpected, unplanned, should throw her into a morass of uncertainty. He understood - he thought - her need for space. Yet as he saw it she was, by her words, leaving the door ajar. He could wait.

He said, 'You want to cool it?'

She nodded gratefully. 'You don't mind?'

'No,' he said, hoping he meant it.

'You are very special, Jeff.' She looked up and smiled in a way that made his heart pole vault. 'Let it be our secret, OK?'

'Aye,' he smiled, 'OK.'

Surprisingly, the idea held great appeal.

He gathered up the dishes. 'Get you owt else? Coffee, cocoa, Horlicks? First class ticket to the Bahamas?'

She yawned.

'You don't need Horlicks,' he chuckled.

'I am fine.'

'Right.' He snapped out of the catatonic trance he'd momentarily been in, realised he was standing there with the empty bowls, and took them out to the kitchen. When he came back she was asleep again, Buster tucked under one arm.

A yawn caught him and he looked at his watch. After half one. He reached out to Jasmin, then hesitated.

It was a quandary. She looked very peaceful. And he didn't want her to go.

He reached a decision. He went upstairs and made up the bed in the second bedroom where his parents stayed on the rare occasions they came down for a visit. He fetched his spare winter duvet from the airing cupboard, took it downstairs and gently placed it over her. Then he wrote a note, downed the fire, turned on the standard lamp and put out the main light.

As he was on his way out she stirred and made a noise, making him turn; but she was pulling the duvet higher over herself and the somniferous Buster. He grinned, and went to bed, sweet thoughts of Jasmin Winter filling his dreams.

When Mrs Stephenson, tearful, had left them alone, after the fifth time of asking, Juliet felt exhausted. Lucky was in for a hard time. Her mother plainly didn't believe her story, wouldn't even accept having left a window unfastened. Magda Stephenson came from a culture which attributed blame first to the woman, and the circumstances surrounding the rape weren't going to change her mind easily. She was bewildered because she could not reconcile what those circumstances told her with her daughter's obvious hurt. She hadn't said as much, but Juliet was afraid she thought Larissa had prostituted herself, and would voice that allegation the first moment they were alone. But that, Juliet was determined, wouldn't be tonight.

They slept as lovers might, cradled together spoonlike, Juliet's arms linked round Lucky's waist like a safety harness. Lucky had complained of being cold but now her body radiated heat like a furnace. Juliet sighed deep and long, trying to cool down but not daring to move away.

'You asleep?' Lucky's voice made a ripple in the gloom, just a table lamp standing sentinel against the night.

'No.' She couldn't see her friend's face, just the back of her head, black hair bunched up against the nape of her neck like unwoven silk. Under her hands Juliet could feel the rise and fall of her breathing, uneven, disturbed.

'Feels weird,' Lucky said, 'having somebody in bed with me.'

'You don't mind?'

'Don't be silly.' She put a hand over Juliet's and squeezed. 'Reminds me of Guide camp, me and Julia sharing a sleeping bag.'

'I never knew you were in the Guides.'

'Must be where my uniform fetish comes from.' Suddenly her shoulders shook. 'Oh, fuck, I'm so confused.'

Juliet let her cry for a while, then spoke. '*That's* why.'

Lucky twisted her head in a vain attempt to look at her. 'What?'

'Barkeley's, you having a go at Nina's husband, banging on about how men treat women. I thought you were talking about him and Nina but you weren't, were you?'

'No,' Larissa said, sniffing.

'The other night,' Juliet said, 'you know Kim? She was as bad as me at first, really freaked. You were the one who kept your head, got me to go for help, did CPR and all that. I think you saved Nina's life. You were absolutely brilliant.' She hugged her closer. 'I told you so afterwards. I couldn't figure out why at the time but you said, "I don't know any more." D'you remember?'

'No.'

'Well, you did. God, you must've felt so fucked up.' She realised what she'd said and winced. 'Everybody else in a flat spin and you just calmly take charge. Like you've been trained for. And then...' She shook her head, feeling tears coming. 'You poor cow. No wonder you're confused.'

'Don't you start,' Lucky said, hearing the tremor in her voice. She craned a hand back and patted Juliet's hip, which was all she could reach.

She sighed.

'*I* dunno.'

Juliet didn't either.

WEDNESDAY

This was the first night she hadn't felt the need for something to help her sleep, so worn out was she from the physical and mental effort involved in keeping pain at bay. They kept insisting so she'd glared at Nurse Aziz until she relented and halved the dose. Now she was out, wandering somewhere in the endless, empty telescope corridors of the hospital. Everything was dark, apart from a few emergency lights casting blurry shadows that shifted and changed shape in the draught.

Something made her stop and turn. Suddenly, out of the black chasm of an unexpected doorway, two hideous monsters, devilish vampire demons so horrible that her eyes, though seeing every detail, failed to form an image her brain could interpret without sending itself mad. They lunged at her rooted to the spot, unable to escape: she could only watch, detached as, slavering fangs and teeth like jackknife blades, one of the creatures bit into her breast with a tearing of flesh, a cracking of bone, and came away with her pulsing, still living heart in its jaws, leaving a geyser of blood, cherry red, spewing from the wound.

An intense light. Hammers in her chest. Unhealed wounds screaming with the agony of the tormented. A strained, tired face, square, unshaven, hair receding, discoloured bruise around one eye, darkly visible against a plain white ceiling.

'What?'

'Don't. Just don't say anything. Bad dreams. All over. Just rest. OK?'

'OK.'

The grasp of clammy hands. A tablet in a small plastic cup. Rest. Silence.

From the doorway Magda Stephenson said, 'It's your boss.'

The moment the doorbell had rung Lucky had known who it was. It didn't occur to her to prepare for the possibility that by 'your boss' her mother might mean Coleridge, or (ha!) the Commissioner, or still more likely Inspector Applewhite, the man Mrs Stephenson had known as her daughter's boss up until a fortnight ago. She let slip a resigned sigh and said, 'OK, Mum.'

The visitor came into the room.

'Hello, guv,' Lucky said.

'Hello, Larissa,' Sophia Beadle said. She turned a polite blue stare on Lucky's mother, who was clutching the open door. 'Mrs Stephenson, would it be possible for me to talk to Larissa alone for a little while?'

'I'll be all right, Mum.'

'Sure,' Magda said frostily, drawing herself up. 'Since I am excluded from my own daughter's life, why not?'

'Mum!'

'It's all right,' Sophia said. 'If you'd rather stay...'

She waited. Magda softened. 'Tea. Would you like tea,

chief inspector?'

'Thank you,' Sophia smiled, with a wink at Lucky. It was a compromise. Tea would remove Mrs Stephenson for a vital few minutes, but not permanently. The DCI watched her go and accepted Lucky's offer of a chair. She eased her bulk down, testing it for gauge. She said, 'How are you?'

'A friend stayed the night,' Lucky said. 'She's gone now. Had to work.'

The non-answer didn't seem to faze Sophia, who smiled wryly. 'I'm not supposed to be here.'

'Guv?'

'Mr Summerfield's the SIO, by order of the AC.'

'Let me guess,' Lucky said, 'I haven't seen you, right?'

Sophia smiled. 'I'm here,' she said, 'but without my warrant card. Understand that. As far as I'm concerned my responsibility for my officers' welfare extends beyond the office.'

'I'm not sure,' Lucky said.

'Not sure?'

'That I do understand.'

Sophia looked thoughtful for a moment. 'There's a lot we don't understand,' she said gently, noncommittally.

Lucky looked away.

'Larissa,' Sophia said, 'why didn't you tell anyone?'

It was the question she'd been dreading. She stalled. 'About what?'

'You carried on for a fortnight without giving the slightest hint of what you were suffering. Why, Larissa?'

Up until half a minute ago, she'd had an answer to that question. Now she just shook her head.

'I haven't been to the office yet,' Sophia said, 'but when I get there I fully expect to find a memo from somewhere on high, the AC or Professional Standards, suggesting you return to Gipsy Hill. I know Mr Applewhite would love to have you back. Help him talk down a few more suicides.'

'Stop it,' Lucky said.

'I thought so.'

'Even without all this shit,' Lucky said, suddenly angry at her guv'nor, 'I failed to report a crime, right? What price my career?'

'I told you the memo would be a suggestion,' Sophia said. 'No more than that.'

Lucky stared at her.

'I had the DI, Helen Wallace and Kim Oliver on the phone one after the other last night. They all know a good copper when they see one, and none of them want to lose you over this. I'll be disappointed if I don't get similar feedback from the DCs.'

'Serious?'

'Zoltan told me as far as he's concerned, if you go Prosser's won,' Sophia said. 'He's been interviewing him.'

Lucky felt faint. 'I thought you said - ?'

'DCI Summerfield may be in charge,' Sophia said, 'but remember Prosser's still in the frame for half a dozen other assaults, and if anyone's going to nail him it'll be Zoltan.' Lucky stiffened and Sophia saw it. 'Do you still want to press charges?'

'What happens if I don't?'

'Then Zoltan's right.'

She felt light-headed. To her great annoyance, she realised she was crying again. 'I really thought - ' She swore and grabbed for a tissue. Sophia waited. 'It's not such a big deal now,' Lucky sighed. 'But it was my first day. I hadn't even had a chance to prove myself, and that bastard...'

'Do you really feel any different?'

'What about the disciplinary?' She felt a sudden rush of despair. 'I was investigating my own rape, for fuck's sake!'

'Is that true, though? You honestly didn't make the connection?'

'It was the MO.'

'MOs change,' Sophia nodded.

'Don't I fucking know it?' Lucky felt like laughing. It was an uncomfortable, frightening feeling. 'Lesson one in the detective handbook. What a fucking way to learn. I'm swearing too much. Sorry, guv.'

'It's your home. Swear all you want.'

'So...?'

'No discipline board.' The DCI smiled. 'I can promise you that. There are plenty of morons who might think you merit one, but no-one wants to be seen as that much of an arsehole.'

Barely daring to, Lucky looked her in the eyes.

'If I have to move heaven and earth,' Sophia said, 'you're staying in Special Crime.'

'Really?'

'As Zoltan might say,' she shrugged, '"you want it written in blood?"'

Lucky found herself smiling. The guv'nor was human after all. She giggled and wiped the corner of one weeping eye with a fist. 'Only I think I might be one of the morons.'

'What do you mean?'

'How can I do the Job when I can't defend myself?' Lucky said. 'Next time it mightn't be just me. Next time somebody else could get hurt because I froze. It's very nice of everybody to back me up but I can't be a passenger and I won't.'

Sophia looked at her for a long while before answering.

'Kim told me about when you found Nina, what you did. That wasn't the act of a passenger.'

'Oh, I get blood on me so I'm a hero?'

'Larissa, I didn't make DCI because of my looks.' Sophia paused and for a giddy moment Lucky was tempted to put in an appropriate response. 'And I didn't appoint you as a trainee for yours.'

'I was paralytic drunk!'

'Not so paralytic you didn't know what you were doing. If you were going to freeze, the alcohol would just have made you do it quicker. But you didn't. Nor did you freeze at the top of that television transmitter.'

'I *know*.' Why did people keep saying these things? Did they think it helped?

'You were a copper on both those occasions,' Sophia said. 'They were both unsettling, even frightening situations, but you kept your cool and dealt with them. I doubt you even stopped to think about it.'

Lucky hugged herself and shook her head.

'But up in your room,' Sophia said softly, 'the rules were different. You weren't doing the Job. Prosser wasn't attacking the uniform. He was attacking *you*. You were in your own home, a place where you should have been, well, safe as houses. You had a shock - a very personal shock. I'm not sure *I* would have kept my head.'

Lucky tried to stare at the guv'nor, but more tears were brimming, blurring her vision like hard rain on a windscreen. Which was ironic, because inside, for the first time in two weeks, she could feel the first faint, warm glimmer of sunlight.

Zoltan looked up to see Summerfield crossing the canteen. He carried two mugs of coffee and placed one in front of him.

'Saw yours was empty,' he said half apologetically, sitting opposite. He pointed. 'Funny thing to have for lunch.'

'What is?'

'Kippers.'

'It's lox,' Zoltan said.

'Oh. Course. Forgot. You're, er...' The DCI thought better of whatever he'd been about to say. Zoltan took the coffee without thanks and sipped.

'Will you be sitting in this morning?'

'Yeah,' Summerfield said. 'Got anywhere yet?'

'He's still adamant.'

'What about?'

'More or less everything,' Zoltan smiled. 'Stonewalling like his life depends on it. He knows I'm holding back about Larissa Stephenson, keeps throwing her into the conversation himself, like it's a big joke.'

'Will he cough?'

'Probably not.' He pushed his half-finished plate of smoked salmon away from him and leaned back. 'He's not denying he did any of the rapes. He's just not saying he did them either. Makes it difficult for us to pin him down to anything.'

'Bastard thinks he's clever,' Summerfield growled.

'How much longer should we try?'

The DCI looked at his watch. 'Thirty-six hours is up, when, two? Give it till then, cut our losses and charge the little shit. We've got enough to throw at him.'

'I want to get him for Larissa.'

'Think *I* don't?' Summerfield glared and for once Zoltan blinked. 'Just with her statement, the way she handled it, I don't think we can.'

'If we can link her to the others...'

'Yeah, *if*. Bastard changed his MO so we couldn't. Just wish I knew why. Why he didn't take anything this time. And more to the point, I wish I knew how he could be so fucking cocksure she wouldn't report it.'

'He did take something.'

'What?'

'Same thing he took from Miranda Hargreaves, and Mrs McMinn, and all the others.' Zoltan took off his glasses and wiped them with a cloth he'd taken from his pocket. 'He took their spirit.'

Summerfield watched him replace his glasses and waited for him to continue.

'Miranda Hargreaves' life was and is music,' Zoltan went on. 'Jeff Wetherby's report, music and musical instruments all over her house. I'll bet you it was the same back when she received the visit from Bayliss and Pegley. It was obvious what was important to her. Bayliss realised that and took the flute.'

'Her most valuable musical item,' Summerfield scowled.

'Mrs McMinn, in a sense, he destroyed her whole life. Didn't matter that she was ninety, fragile, in her twilight years. He was going to assault her anyway.'

'And Stephenson?'

'Uniform,' Zoltan said. 'Hanging up in plain sight. Commendations on the wall. He raped her anyway. Wanted her to know her status as an officer of the law mattered nothing to him.'

Summerfield nodded. 'None of which gets us a conviction.'

'If only jurors possessed my deep psychoanalytical

genius,' Zoltan said sardonically, and took another gulp of coffee as an indication that he was about to change the subject. 'How are you getting along with the Albion Street haul?'

'Twelve complainants going back over six years, we've got either a positive ID on the property or a strong possible from photos.'

'Twelve?'

'Tip of the iceberg, you ask me.'

'How much other stuff is there?'

'Twenty-one bits and pieces from the loft and the garage,' Summerfield said. 'Mostly phallic in some way. Chances are there's more stashed somewhere else.'

'Tip of the iceberg,' Zoltan murmured. He knew the same thought was going through Summerfield's mind. Twenty-one unsolved rapes, minimum, all down to the same man. In this forensics-dominated day and age it was almost inconceivable. He shuddered the thought away. 'Got an inventory?'

Summerfield thrust a hand into his breast pocket and slapped a folded photocopy down on the table. 'Prosser's little trophy cabinet.'

Expressionless behind his glasses, Zoltan read slowly through the list. 'This last but one thing,' he remarked. 'Bit of a stretch to see that as phallic.'

The DCI shrugged. 'Depends how your mind works.'

Zoltan stroked his beard. 'How old is Lucky?'

'Twenty-two,' Summerfield said, puzzled. 'But you know that.'

'I'm being Socrates,' Zoltan said, unsurprised at Summerfield's blank look. 'Youngest of the known victims by a couple of years. Young enough still to be living at home and to have a lot of childhood stuff still knocking around. You may want to direct someone,' he said, 'to get her on the phone and find out if she took pottery classes at school.'

This time the blank look faded quickly. Summerfield pointed to the list and said, 'If she did, can we prove it's hers?'

'Quick call to Human Resources should do it.' Zoltan grinned like a crocodile. 'And I just can't wait to hear what his lordship has to say about this.'

Michael Prosser's legal representative, an articled clerk called Shinners, had been called in only this morning, in his client's own interests but against his wishes. He was busy boning up on the case as the two policemen came in, and seemed hardly to notice them.

'A DI *and* a DCI,' Prosser said, eyebrows raised as Summerfield identified himself for the tape. 'I am honoured. You must want summink tasty.'

'That what you're sitting on, Michael? Something tasty?' Zoltan looked at him askance. Clearly he was going to be as talkative this morning as he'd been taciturn yesterday.

'For you to prove, innit?'

'We have proof.'

'I been in here well over twenty-four hours,' he challenged them. 'Either charge me or I walk.'

'You haven't looked at your PACE code of practice very carefully, have you?' Summerfield said. 'Thirty-six, we've got you for. After that, if you haven't given us the goods, we take you to a JP and ask for a remand. Anything up to, say, a week. Seven days' questioning, Mike. We've got a lot to cover. Feeling up to it?'

'Keep me here seven months if you like,' Prosser said. 'I ain't giving you nothing.'

'I'm not interested in you giving me things, Michael,' Summerfield said. 'You know and I know you raped those women.'

'They wasn't raped.'

'Weren't they?'

'What I hear.'

'It might not be rape in law,' Summerfield said, 'but if using those implements the way you did isn't rape, I'm a Chinaman.'

'What implements?'

'Mr Schneider's been over this with you, Michael,' Summerfield said. 'So far we've found twenty-one mostly phallic-shaped souvenirs hidden in your house and garage. Some of them have already been identified by their owners.'

Twenty-one terrified women, Zoltan thought, all scarred for life because you couldn't just burgle. You had to go on a dominance trip.

'And I know, you know, you can't prove shit,' Prosser countered. 'That stuff's all just junk. You won't find my prints on none of it.'

'No? Bit strange, isn't it? Found in your loft; you're the only man in the household. Don't make your poor old mum go up there, do you?'

Prosser sneered.

'I doubt it,' Summerfield said. 'Because I dare say we won't find her prints either.'

'Maybe not. And you sure as fuck won't find them women's.'

'Because you wiped them off.'

'Shit's been up there since before we moved in. You can't prove none of them women even touched them.'

'We don't need proof, Michael.'

It was Zoltan who spoke. He'd been brooding, nudging the interview on, letting Summerfield build up a head of steam.

'There's a term in law: "beyond reasonable doubt". Ever heard of that? It means even if the prosecution hasn't got hard proof, you can still be convicted on circumstantial evidence. For God's sake, Michael, do you seriously think you can get away with rape just because you didn't do it in front of a hundred witnesses with your name and address tattooed across your bum? So far we've reunited twelve women with items from your collection they say are theirs. You can read their statements. Twelve, so far. More to come, I shouldn't wonder. No jury,' Zoltan smiled and shook his head, 'is going to swallow twelve coincidences.'

'That little lot,' Summerfield added, 'you're looking at life.'

'No remission, if we can match up all twenty-one.'

It was unfortunate that the smirk finally disappeared from Michael Prosser's face at the same moment his legal representative chose to come to life. Shinners told him, 'Mike, this jury exists inside the officers' minds and nowhere else. Don't let them badger you.'

Prosser nodded, his expression thoughtful. 'Mind you, don't want me for them ones, do you?'

'Don't I now?' Zoltan savoured the moment. He'd lost count of how often Prosser had tried to goad him. Well, this time...

'You want me for Stephenson. And you won't get me 'cause I was never there. I told you what really happened. I know what a jury's gonna think, her word against mine.'

'Fingerprints,' Zoltan said. Without warning he deposited a polythene-wrapped lump of crudely shaped, glazed brown clay on the table. 'I don't think you've been formally introduced. Mike, meet Weezle.'

'You what?' Prosser peered at the thing with scorn. 'Think you're gonna find my prints on that, you're – '

'You remember,' Zoltan interrupted him chattily. 'You liked him so much you took him from Larissa Stephenson's bedroom after you'd raped her. Obviously you weren't about to cut off your own penis and frame it, so you chose Weezle because you guessed, rightly, he was precious to her.'

'Get real.'

'This *is* real, Michael.'

'It's a lump of fucking mud. Could've come from anywhere.'

Zoltan picked Weezle up. 'Larissa Stephenson made this with her own hands when she was twelve years old. It doesn't matter a toss whether you wiped off every fingermark and every speck of dirt, because *her* fingerprints are all over this clay where it set hard ten years ago.' Prosser's eyes were cast down. 'Now you can tell us your version of events any way you like. This little chap,' he brandished Weezle one last time before putting him back under the table, 'is going off to Forensic, and if they find prints that match Larissa Stephenson's, it puts you in her bedroom, it renders her account of things more believable than yours, and we'll charge you with raping her.'

He sat back, folding his arms. Prosser didn't move.

'Now,' Summerfield said, 'how about saving us all some time?'

'Fuck off,' Michael Prosser snapped.

It was something HOLMES excelled at, putting two and two together to make five. It was why, as far as Kim Oliver could see, no computer would ever take the place of human detectives on a major enquiry. Real live coppers must use their knowledge, experience and intuition to discern when the electronic sleuth really did have something and when it was in cloud cuckoo land. That said, this particular copper wasn't sure, at the moment, *what* HOLMES was telling her.

She stared at the screen, feeling helpless. Like most of the team, she was finding it hard to focus. Lucky's rape, on top of the attack on Nina, had cast a pall of shock over them all. Rumours of Special Crime being wound up were creeping round the nick. Everyone knew the right body was in the frame but the current whisper was that any charges were far from certain. With AC Parmiter breathing down their necks, they needed a result badly.

Giving up, she clicked print and went to seek higher counsel. Sophia listened patiently while she explained what HOLMES had found. 'I really, really dunno if it's anything. This kid two streets over from Ballards Way, coming home from a night out clubbing, says he saw a bloke get in a minicab and ask to go to Ladyhall Road. And we checked and there's no Ladyhall Road in Greater London so we figured he'd misheard, right? But then Grace Carmichael reported being threatened in Lady*well* Road, Lewisham, yeah? And I've just had a word with Quaife's probation officer. This heavy metal band he's been humping gear for, they're called Ladywell.'

'Did the probation officer tell you anything more about the band?'

Kim shrugged. 'Not even names, guv. Apparently this was just casual work, cash in hand. Till he got summink better, I guess.'

Thoughtful, Sophia examined her fingernails for a moment. 'Do you know of this... Ladywell?'

'No, guv.' Kim was faintly amused that Sophia thought metal might be her bag. 'Thousands of small-time bands like that.'

'Possibly,' the DCI frowned. 'Must be one or two headbangers in this nick who might know.'

Kim couldn't think of any off the top of her head. Police haircuts were a great leveller. She said, 'Brian knows a bit about music.'

He was at his desk. Sophia called his name and beckoned. As he ambled over with his customary half smile, she asked him, 'Ever heard of a metal band called Ladywell?'

'Sounds a bit seventies.' He went blank for a moment, searching his memory. 'Rings a vague bell. Not really my sort of thing.'

'You've heard of them, though?'

'Somewhere, yeah.'

'We're just trying to find names of band members,' Kim said.

Brian chuckled indulgently, as though she were asking for the Holy Grail. 'Have you looked them up on Facebook, MySpace?'

'Yeah. No lineup listings that I could see.'

'You're a bit buggered then,' Brian commented. Then he brightened. 'Tell you what. You could try ringing *Kerrang*.'

'The hard rock magazine?' Kim said.

'Yeah. See if they've heard of them. They might be able to tell you.'

'Good thinking.' Sophia flashed him an approving glance. To Kim she said, 'Get onto it.'

She was in luck. The journalist she was put through to had not only reviewed a Ladywell gig at the Mean Fiddler two issues ago, but also had a list of dates for a forthcoming tour of Germany. If Quaife and/or Porter were in need of a low profile way out of the country, this could be it. The journalist was able to provide a lineup that was complete except for the drummer, whose identity had eluded him in a haze of lager. Grabbing the London residential phone book, Kim looked them up one by one. Beaded plaits are too heavy to stand on end, but she still had a crawly feeling on her scalp when she came to Malcolm Kavanagh, the group's bassist, and discovered a Kavanagh, M. listed at 289A Ladywell Road, SE13.

Her rational mind was still telling her what a stretch this all was when Marie Kirtland walked into the office at half past four, several hours later than she'd been expected back from a court appearance, and headed straight for her, a writeable DVD in her hand. Marie explained that on her way out of court she'd had a phone call from DC Scott Cooper, the Lewisham CID officer who'd taken the complaint from Grace Carmichael. Spurred by the connection to a major investigation of a case that had seemed the epitome of the mundane, he'd been combing through CCTV footage and had found what appeared to be a dreadlocked white man talking to another white male in Ladywell Road at about the same time that Grace had reported being threatened by Quaife there two Fridays hence. After about three minutes, the dreadlocked man had suddenly half spun around as if startled and then sprinted out of shot. Marie had driven over to Lewisham to view the footage. She hadn't needed more than a brief look to identify the sprinter as Philip Meredith. She'd needed a bit more time than that to recognise the other individual, and would need to run the tape past Kim to be definite, but she was pretty sure it was the man who'd been parking at Grace Carmichael's house the other week just as they had been leaving.

So much of the time passed in long periods of shallow sleep that Nina had given up trying to keep track. She woke now and opened her eyes, and there was low early evening sunshine slanting in through the window, and Paul sitting at her bedside, his body turned away from the light so it didn't dazzle the pages of his magazine. She exhaled deeply to let him know she was conscious.

'Hey,' he said.

'What time is it?' she wheezed, furious that it was taking so long to get her voice working properly.

'Half sevenish. Lucia should be here soon.'

A dark thing slithered over her mind, clinging for a moment like oil, and then was gone. 'I had a dream.'

'Mmm?'

'A nightmare. I woke up. Somebody... Was that you?'

'Last night.'

'When?'

'Midnight, bit after.' He yawned.

'How come?'

'I sat in for Lucia. She had a date.'

'A date?'

She'd mustered a croak, but it couldn't convey expression and he misinterpreted her reaction. 'Long standing,' he said.

'Thanks.'

'What for?'

She didn't answer him, but smiled fleetingly and turned

a hand palm upwards. He drew his chair nearer and took it, his free arm resting lightly on the bed.

Nina said, 'You looked after me.'

'You're my wife.'

'Finally he realises it.' She smiled again, the only method she could be sure of to try and show him there was no malice intended. Her arm ached from the IVs and she was hungry. Nil by mouth was getting to be a pain somewhere else.

'Give me the chance,' he said, strained, 'and I'll always - '

'I'm not getting at you.'

'I was off my head,' Paul rambled. 'She's... Anyway, I made a vow to take care of you. Wouldn't blame you if you never forgave me.'

She sighed and squeezed his hand, exhilarated to feel a trace of real power returning to her grip. 'I don't know,' she said.

He waited.

'Had a lot of time to think, lying here.'

'You've been asleep.'

'You reckon.' She grinned and closed her eyes. 'Nothing profound; all I've figured out is I've got a lot more thinking still to do.'

'Yeah,' he said, looking at the floor.

'It can wait till I get out of here.' She squeezed again. 'But I need time. It's not just us I've got to sort out. Don't forget, there's...'

She broke off and tried to swallow. Feeling her shiver, he began to stroke her, soothingly, with his hand on the bed.

'There's Porter,' she said, another surge of triumph as she pronounced the name of her nemesis. 'Still got to decide what to do about him.'

Paul frowned. She didn't know what he thought she meant by the remark. She wasn't sure herself.

She went on, 'There's this Job rehab place. Sophia spent a week there once after she got knocked down by a stolen car. She's going to talk to Welfare Services about getting me in there. You know, convalesce. I think we need some time apart.'

'We've spent enough time apart lately.'

'I mean apart, not separate. Not together-apart. Just some breathing space.'

He nodded glumly. 'Where?'

'Reading.' She saw his expression and added quickly, 'M25 to the M4, hour and a half. You can come and visit me at weekends.'

'Only weekends?'

'Yeah,' she smiled, ''cause during the week you're going to be camped out in the Job Centre till they're so fucking sick of the sight of you they *have* to find you some work.'

He held her gaze, stern. 'Don't.'

'What?'

'Say "fucking",' he mumbled.

'Chance'd be a fine thing.' Her awareness shifted down her battered body, feeling a firm pressure: Paul's clenched fist. 'Mind where you've got your hand.'

He looked at it. 'What, here?'

'Mm-hmm.'

'Sorry,' he said anxiously. 'Does it hurt?'

Surprised, she realised it didn't. Lucia had looked up the weapon, the Bowie knife, tactlessly told her the damage it could do, its extent beneath the entry wound. She'd cried tears of panic, begging to be told her precious ovaries hadn't been harmed. On the consultant's next ward round, he'd assured her they were intact, deep and safe within her body. Suddenly she felt indestructible.

'Now?'

'Eh?' She could feel a soft, back and forth movement, a light pressure. 'Oh.'

'Doesn't hurt?'

'Not much.'

She tried to lift her head to confirm that Paul really was doing what she thought he was doing, but it was still too painful. Far better just to lie there, to concentrate on the nicer feelings, to let... to let...

'You mad bastard,' she gasped. 'If I come, I'll burst my stitches.'

Aghast, she felt him stop. Her arm weighed a ton as she heaved it across herself and pressed it on top of his, the searing spots along the length of her body marking where the injuries were. But not for any amount of pain, now, would she deny them this moment. She was going away, but they both understood that she could not have gone knowing her husband's last sex had been adulterous.

Nina's mute cry of delicious agony was laced with triumph. For the first time in months, she and Paul were on the same wavelength.

THURSDAY

No sooner had Sophia got her team in position in Ladywell Road than Michael Quaife put in an appearance.

'We're not ready.' The terse male voice came over the radio from the green BMW with tinted windows parked in front of Sophia's Saab. It contained Sergeant Rodney Gough and three heavily armed PCs from SCO19. Helplessly, Sophia and Kim watched Quaife, in camouflage jacket and jeans, close the gate of number 289 and head towards them. They ducked down in their seats. He walked by without stopping.

'Shit,' Kim breathed.

'Beadle from OP.' Sandra Jones, coming to the end of her all-night vigil in a flat opposite, sounded tired and irritable. The flat was unoccupied and she'd had just herself and a thermos flask for company, no friendly householder delivering tea and sandwiches at regular intervals.

'Go ahead, Sandra,' Sophia said, grabbing the radio as she sat up.

'That was hairy, guv,' Sandra remarked. The radios were switched to talk-through and she'd have heard what had happened. 'Not to worry too much, though. He didn't look like a bloke about to up sticks and bugger off into the bush.'

'Any thoughts on where he might be going?'

'There's a corner shop five minutes down the road opens at six,' Sandra said. 'Pound to a penny he's just nipped out for a paper.'

'Do you copy that, Sarge?' Sophia asked Gough.

'Got it, ma'am. If DC Jones is right, we'd much prefer to take him on the way back. With any luck he'll have at least one hand full.'

'With luck. Otherwise we'll have to wait until he comes back from wherever he's off to.'

'Who's paying for the overtime again?' Gough wondered.

But Sandra was right. Kim was the first to spot him, climbing back up the hill. She pointed to Sophia's wing mirror. The DCI nodded, checked, and warned everyone by radio.

The next few moments ran like a silent movie. Breath held, they watched Michael Quaife appear in their field of vision and walk past without slowing or showing any other sign he was aware of them. He carried a loaf of bread, a carton of milk and *The Sun*. Reaching the house, he turned and disappeared through the gate.

Kim watched the BMW's rear doors swing open and the SCO19 men in their navy blue flak helmets get out, radio earpieces in their ears, Heckler and Koch carbines in hand, holsters on their belts open with Glock handguns at the ready. They ran lightly to the gate, two hanging back, two either side, one covering while the other pivoted inwards, rifle aimed. He nodded, then dipped through, his colleague following him.

For a moment that seemed longer than it was, nothing happened.

Kim sat up and opened her door.

'Stay,' Sophia snapped. 'Wait for the - '

Out of the corner of her eye, movement. Quaife had just appeared at the top of the wall. How he'd evaded the firearms men, she didn't know. What she did know was that Kim couldn't see him from her side. He vaulted the railing, landing right next to the man Gough had positioned there for just that eventuality and surprising him with a rabbit punch. He crossed the pavement and ducked between two parked cars. Gough stepped out to intercept him.

In the empty flat, Sandra was a helpless spectator. She could see what those on the ground couldn't, the woody old buddleia in the basement garden up whose twisted branches Quaife had swarmed. By the time she'd got on the radio to warn them he was crossing the road, sprinting towards Kim's half open door.

He saw her face and veered straight for her, oblivious to Gough's shotgun trained on him, oblivious to the two PCs who'd now assumed firing positions behind him. Kim froze, half out of the car, one foot on the ground. He still had his groceries but now there was something else in his hand, something that glinted. She croaked a warning, hoping Gough could hear her.

'Armed police!' the shout came, enunciated clearly and firmly. 'Stop or we *will* shoot you.'

Quaife came level with the door, staring with utter hatred into her eyes, and hurled the carton into the gap. It struck the frame and burst with a bang, showering Kim with milk. She screamed. It was an involuntary reaction, but she would regret it all her life.

The morning exploded with noise as the SCO19 men opened fire. Quaife's back erupted crimson in four places and he was thrown forward, his face striking the tarmac with a clear, sickening smack. The knife skittered and disappeared under a parked car.

How long Kim remained in her foetal crouch she didn't know, but eventually she uncoiled at the touch of a hand on her shoulder. Sophia frowned down at her.

'That wasn't wise.'

'I didn't mean to yell out! They wouldn't've fired if I...' She peered questioningly up at the DCI. 'Is...?'

'Yes,' Sophia said. 'Quaife's dead.'

Allowing herself to be helped back up onto the seat, Kim registered the unnatural quiet. Even the birds seemed cowed. The only distinct sound, over the constant London hum, was the approaching wail of an ambulance siren.

For a few reasons, Anne White was starting to wonder if transferring to the Film Unit was the worst career move she'd ever made. Of course, she told herself yet again as she pulled off Blackfriars Road and rolled down the ramp into the subterranean car park, it was nothing more than coincidence that Nina had been attacked the moment she'd left the team, nor was what had happened to Lucky her fault. But she couldn't shake the irrational feeling that she should be back at Croydon, hands on, *doing* something. The reports she got from Zoltan when he dragged himself home late every evening, too tired to go into much detail, just left her feeling stifled, frustrated, stuck on the outside.

She pushed the button for the lift and a couple of office

workers joined her for the wait. They rode up in silence. That was another thing. The Film Unit were the only coppers in the building and she had no idea what her fellow passengers did, not did she have any particular desire to find out. She missed the comradeship, the shared sense of mission and purpose that buzzed through a police station in the early morning and at shift changes. This was the chance to put her acquired skills to new use, from Special Crime to liaising with filmmakers and TV producers, present the Met as a friendly piece of the London scene. As yet, it didn't seem like enough.

The others worked on floors below hers and she was the only one who got off on the ninth. Almost as soon as she'd swiped her keycard to enter her new team's offices she ran into the third reason for her regret. Sergeant Lee Chivers was one of those people who are convinced tales of his and his wife's adventures in re-tiling their fireplace or researching fortnights in Cornwall with the camper van are as riveting to everyone else as to himself. He'd been promoted and transferred in at the same time as Anne, one of the unit's two previous sergeants having been compelled to resign due to leukaemia, coincidentally three weeks after the other had retired. As such the unit had a backlog, and Lee and Anne were more or less training themselves, operations manuals and contact lists and notebooks spread out across their desks, which they'd pushed together in a corner for the purpose. Mind-numbing as their combined project was, it was made more so by Lee's apparently limitless fund of banal stories.

That aside, he had the ideal CV for the Film Unit, his previous posting having been with Surrey Police, piloting a BMW traffic car out of Guildford nick. Anne hoped the producers and movie scouts and the respective film officers of the thirty-two

London borough councils would be able to handle Lee with the same forbearance she felt she was managing.

'Morning!' he said, his pale, round-cheeked southern peasant face blithe and cheerful as always. 'Early start?'

'You and me both,' Anne said and then added, instantly regretting it in case it triggered an anecdote, 'Couldn't sleep much.'

'Cuppa? That'll get you going.'

'If you're having one.' Say one thing about Lee, he did make a decent brew.

He smiled again and pottered over to the small wheeled cart on which they kept their kettle, tea and coffee supplies. 'Been meaning to mention,' he said, and Anne inwardly rolled her eyes in anticipation. 'Taken me a while to put two and two together, but you were on that special unit down Croydon, weren't you? The team that investigated the KKK-style arson? DC that got stabbed this past weekend?'

'Yeah, that's right, I was,' Anne said guardedly. 'Wasn't involved much with what was going on because I was leaving, but yeah.'

'Only those two suspects, the neo-Nazi people: had a run-in with them myself not long ago.'

For the first time ever, Anne was finding him interesting.

Interpreting her leaning forward in her chair as a prompt to continue, he said, 'Before the bulletin went out, of course, or I like to think I would have detained them. Pulled them over near Dorking one afternoon, my last week with Traffic. On the A24, Mickleham bypass. Vauxhall Astra, failure to signal for a lane change, though it turned out their indicator light was broken, so I told the driver – the ex-con, the heavy, odd surname, begins with Q? – told him to get it fixed ASAP and sent them on their merry way. Recognised the descriptions when they were circulated later. No reason to suspect them, both very polite, calm, cooperative.'

'Your last week?' Anne said, an unquantifiable, vaguely horrible feeling starting to creep over her. 'So the week before last?' Despite herself, his account of de-slugging the garden during his week off had somehow become imprinted on her memory.

'Yeah, but like I said, before anyone knew we were after them. Monday, Tuesday, have to check my logs to be sure, which of course I can't as they're locked up back at Guildford somewhere.'

'Afternoon, you said?'

'Pretty sure it was the Tuesday afternoon, thinking about it.' The kettle boiled and switched itself off and Lee set about pouring water on their tea bags. 'Mid-afternoon. Round about school chucking-out time.'

Zoltan listened to Anne's voice on the other end of the line and with his free hand, pulled a notepad towards him and scribbled very precise instructions in what he hoped was a legible fashion. Spotting Jasmin looking more or less in his direction, he beckoned her over and handed her the paper. She read it, nodded, went back to her desk and picked up the phone.

Hanging up, Zoltan immediately lifted the receiver again. Sophia was still at Lewisham so he dialled her mobile number from memory. She waited while he relayed what Anne had told him. After a pregnant silence she said, 'Today just gets better. So if this Chivers is right, which I hope to God he isn't, he's just given Porter and Quaife an alibi for the Bentons?'

'If the day and time are right, no way they could have got from Dorking to Croydon in time to transfer to a van and get over to Chapel View,' Zoltan said.

'No.' There was another long pause. 'So if not them, who in hell did this?'

'I have a feeling you're thinking the same thing I am.'

'Probably,' Sophia sighed. 'And under the circumstances the first thing we need to do, if Jasmin can confirm the timeline, is re-arrest Debbie Clarke.'

'That also,' Zoltan said drily, 'I was thinking.'

An hour later, Jasmin got off the phone with the DC at Guildford who'd been yanked from whatever it was he'd been doing to review the recordings from the dashboard and rear window cameras of the traffic patrol car driven by PC 272 Chivers during the late shift of the Tuesday in question. The DC had confirmed that a stop of a dark blue Vauxhall Astra had been conducted that afternoon, that the index number visible in the video matched Quaife's, and that as far as he could tell, the two men who could be seen in the front seats answered the descriptions of Michael Quaife and Edward Porter. According to the time stamp on the video, the stop had commenced at 3.01 p.m. and concluded at 3.07, around the same time that Debbie Clarke had arrived back at the Bentons' house with Robin.

At eleven o'clock that morning, nine tall men in their early twenties lined up behind a one way glass screen at Gipsy Hill police station. On the other side of the glass, accompanied by a sergeant, Miranda Beckett walked slowly back and forth along the line. After much deliberation she identified man number three, Michael Robert Prosser a.k.a. Bayliss, as one of the youths who'd raped, sexually assaulted and robbed her on that Sunday night long ago.

With Zoltan Schneider in the next room were Mrs Beckett's counsellor, a grey-haired New Zealander called Anne Davies, and Lucky, whom DCI Summerfield had given special permission to attend. When Zoltan had finished taking Mrs Beckett's statement, the three women escaped without him to the restaurant over the road. No-one but themselves ever knew what was said there.

Michael Prosser was driven back to Croydon and formally charged with the rapes of Miranda Beckett, *née* Hargreaves, and Larissa Stephenson. As possible further charges were pending in the cases of Denise Cole, Lisa Harkness, Violet McMinn and two other unsolved sexual assaults, Prosser was taken at once before the magistrates and remanded in custody for a week.

Zoltan was in no hurry. Even if one investigation seemed to be going pear-shaped, a result in another one, on the same day, wasn't to be begrudged.

As soon as the all clear had been given at 289 Ladywell Road, Helen Wallace, Jeff Wetherby, Marie Kirtland and half a dozen bobbies off the early turn at Lewisham had piled in. They'd found Malcolm Kavanagh and his girlfriend in an upstairs bedroom. In one of the downstairs rooms, the one Quaife had been occupying, they found a large Union flag and an army kitbag full of, among other things, fascist literature, some of which Marie had seen copies of before. Kavanagh confirmed that Quaife was booked to accompany the band to Germany and had moved in about a month ago to make things easier. He professed ignorance of the fact that his housemate was on parole and subject to travel restriction, and said he knew he was 'partial to the odd Heil Hitler'. Asked about Edward Porter, he simply looked blank.

A side pocket of the kitbag contained an iPhone on which was very little of interest apart from some texts, received at various times over the last ten days from an unknown number, suggesting where Quaife might be able to find Philip Meredith, Billy Scofield and Jayne Mansfield. At the bottom of the wardrobe, Marie found a plastic bag from B&Q containing a hammer and an opened box of long nails. There was also a receipt showing that these items, together with three metres of timber and two cans of white spirit, had been purchased with a credit card, the last four digits of which did not match the one in Quaife's wallet.

The other downstairs room was full of band equipment and amplifiers. Behind a stack of these they found, propped up in a corner, a man. The long matted hair led one of the uniforms to suggest that he must be a homeless guy who'd found a good place to doss and had then popped his clogs. The first two detectives to enter the room, Helen and Jeff, nixed that theory by pointing out the large knife-induced hole over the man's heart, but it was the third, Marie, who took one look at the Bob Marley tattoo on his left forearm and confirmed that Philip Meredith had finally turned up again.

By noon, a crowd of nearly a hundred neo-Nazis had gathered outside Lewisham police station with placards and chants, accusing the police into any news microphone pointed in their direction of murdering a hero and a patriot. All the police would say in reply was that an official investigation by the Independent Police Complaints Commission was under way.

The news from Croydon University Hospital that Robin Benton had undergone a first successful skin graft operation received a mention at the end of the local lunchtime bulletin.

At one-thirty p.m., officers of the British Transport Police at St Pancras International responded to a report that a man answering Edward Porter's description had booked a ticket on a Eurostar service to Brussels. They boarded the train, but the seat was empty and a thorough search revealed nothing. The train was allowed to depart on time.

By half past four, tension between the protesting neo-Nazis and more recently arrived counter-demonstrators had risen to an ugly pitch. Watching television crews somehow failed to record the first move, but suddenly missiles were being thrown and sections of the crowd were attempting to make rushes at each other. For a long few minutes, the hundred and fifty riot shielded coppers keeping the two sides apart were in danger of caving. The chief superintendent appeared on the steps of the police station with a loudhailer and appealed for calm. Just as abruptly, the counter-demonstrators withdrew behind the cordon. It took another three hours, but eventually the neo-Nazis realised their enemies weren't going to play and dispersed, leaving a dozen diehards to keep vigil at the foot of the station steps. Encouraged by members of Mark Watkins's family, Grace Carmichael among them, the counter-protesters began in their turn to go home, drifting off in the opposite direction down streets full of strobing blue lights and the red glint of the evening sun on helmet visors.

When a police officer shoots a suspect dead, it is proper that a rigorous investigation should ensue. Citizens of a civilised society enjoy the basic right not to be shot by police officers, so when it happens it follows that society demands clear and thorough reassurance that the deed was necessary in the interest of public safety. It is in this same interest that a cop, though his gun may be burning a hole in its holster, must be mindful of the consequences of pulling the trigger.

In Britain, whose police service is one of the few in the world that does not routinely arm its officers, the procedures that swing into motion following a fatal shooting border on the obsessive. The officers concerned, along with any of their colleagues who might have had the remotest sniff of the incident, are hauled in and questioned about events until they can picture them with their eyes closed. The actions of the dead suspect, aggressive and life-threatening though they might have been, are cruelly scrutinised for alternative interpretations. The remotest possibility that lethal force might not have been necessary is brought into the open and left there until its last remnant of plausibility is gone. However murderous the suspect's character or behaviour, it is the police who have taken a life; the officers involved who must answer first for their actions. Any of them who might have passed off lightly the discharging of a firearm will come away from this inquisition with such illusions rudely disrupted.

These, among numerous others, were the reasons why Sophia Beadle's top priority had to wait until the evening. She made it her business to be the one personally to inform Luke Benton of what had happened, but because she'd been present at the death of Michael Quaife she, along with every other member of the team who'd been in Lewisham - even those at the back of the house who'd seen nothing - had been put through the mill by detectives from Professional Standards. Even Sophia's written, signed, witnessed statement had been examined with a fine-toothed comb. She was beginning to appreciate the gruesome canteen talk there'd been of armed operations being routinely videoed, cameras mounted on guns or lapels, just to leave no room for question.

Luke must have watched her park, for he opened the front door as she walked up the path. He wore a nervous smile and an expression in his eyes she couldn't for the moment define. He led the way through to the living room, where a short, cheerful woman in her fifties sat knitting in a chair by the fireplace. She beamed a greeting. Luke introduced her as Nick's mother. She stood and shook Sophia's hand. 'You'll be wanting to talk alone,' she said, and excused herself.

'The Lynotts've said they'll put me up as long as I need,' Luke said when she'd gone. 'They're being really great.'

'No Nick today?' Sophia smiled.

'Upstairs revising,' Luke said. 'Exam tomorrow.'

'Of course. That time of year.' Sophia stopped short of bringing her eldest's first year exams into the conversation. 'How are you managing with yours?'

'Next week, mine start. I'll do 'em, but God knows what grades I'll get. Doesn't seem that important.' He changed the subject, avoiding her eyes. 'Nick's dad's handling the probate for me. Way above my head, all that. He reckons the insurance should be more than enough for us to buy our own place. Me and my brother, I mean, when he gets out of hospital.'

Sophia nodded, sensing the coming shadow Luke didn't want to acknowledge. Robin, when and if he came home, would need constant care.

Luke said, as if reading her mind, 'Not something I really want to think about, right now.'

'You don't expect to be saddled with all this, at your age.'

'Tell me about it,' he said, with sudden bitterness.

He seemed to want to talk about today, but Mrs Lynott came in with tea and biscuits. She fussed around them for a few minutes before withdrawing again. Luke sat anxiously on the edge of his chair.

'I saw what happened on the telly,' he said.

Sophia nodded. 'I gathered you might have.'

'Is it true? What those fascists are saying?'

'That Quaife was killed in cold blood?'

'Some bloke on the news, s'posed to be an eyewitness, said they shot him in the back as he was running away.'

'Luke,' Sophia said, 'the incident's still under investigation.'

'*Sub judice?*'

'In a manner of speaking. I was directly involved, so officially I can't say much at the moment.'

'OK,' he said, 'and *un*officially?'

'Unofficially,' Sophia said with an edge to her voice, 'you deserve the truth. Porter and Quaife, while they have both committed some serious crimes and fully justify the amount of manpower that's gone into trying to apprehend them...'

Luke frowned, seeming to sense that she was about to tell him something he didn't want to hear. 'What?'

'They didn't kill your mother.'

An almost luminous flash of anger crossed Luke's face, superseded by a waxlike blankness.

'Technically, no, I know that,' he said after a long silence. 'But Debbie... they didn't give her a choice.'

'Luke,' Sophia said, kindly but firmly, and told him about the alibi. She also told him about the B&Q receipt they'd found at the Ladywell Road house, the credit card that had been used traced to a stockbroker who'd reported it lost a month ago after a visit to the Royal Ballet in Covent Garden, known to be one of Philip Meredith's preferred panhandling haunts. She told him about Helen Wallace and Jeff Wetherby's conversation that afternoon with Corin Rice-Newman, live-in boyfriend of Grace Carmichael and sometime solicitor providing legal guidance to the Watkins campaign. About how Rice-Newman had admitted exploiting his contacts with other law firms to give Meredith inside information on Michael Quaife and his connection to Edward Porter and Thrall. How the last time he'd seen him was right before meeting Grace for lunch a couple of weekends ago, when Meredith had abruptly broken off their conversation and run away as if the hounds of hell were after him.

She told him about the working theory she, Zoltan and the team had put together, their best educated guess based on what they knew for sure; about how Meredith and his cronies had decided that if they couldn't bring Porter and Quaife to justice for Mark Watkins, they'd create something they *could* bring them to justice for. How Debbie's passionate teenage rhetoric had perhaps inspired them, had given one of them, Billy or Jayne or most likely Philip Meredith, the idea to use her as a stooge. How it had blinded them to the reality that their chosen targets were the very last people they ought to fuck with. It was a blindness soon lifted by the rapidity with which Porter had identified them and tracked them down to the Paragon Road squat, later underlined by the message the attempted murder of Nina Tyminski had sent.

'And Debbie knew about this?' Luke half-whispered.

'She was complicit,' Sophia said. 'We've interviewed her again. She still denies she knew the full extent of what Meredith and his crew were planning. She's sticking to her original story that she was supposed to phone your mum to warn her to get out. But she was well aware that Porter and Quaife were being set up.'

'And they got Meredith back for it? It *was* actually them who killed him and not somebody else again?'

Sophia studied him thoughtfully for a few moments before answering. Natural, perhaps, that Luke should want Porter and Quaife to be guilty of *something*, even if it wasn't his mother's murder. How must he feel now that he knew it was them who'd meted out retribution to her true killer? She said, 'Whether Meredith didn't know where Quaife lived and it was just a coincidence that he'd arranged to meet Mr Rice-Newman in Ladywell Road, or whether he actually was stupid enough to try to stake him out, we'll probably never know. From the CCTV, what it looks like happened is that Quaife saw them talking, almost immediately saw Grace and her sister on the other side of the street, assumed the two must be connected and made the threat. We know Meredith managed to give him the slip, because we interviewed him at Charing Cross police station the following day, but of course they did eventually catch up with him again.' She chose to leave out the part about the large patch of dried blood in the backyard of 289 Ladywell Road, where sometime last week, according to the ME's initial guesstimate, Philip Meredith had presumably met his end in the same way that it had been intended Nina would.

'Jesus,' Luke said, his eyes flicking to the doorway, perhaps in fear that Mrs Lynott, who wouldn't approve of his blasphemy, might be earwigging. 'Debbie's lucky they didn't do her in and all.'

Yes, Debbie Clarke was ironically fortunate, Sophia thought, to have a former neo-Nazi for a dad. A father who had successfully though possibly in ignorance interceded for his daughter's life and safety. Anglo-Saxon blood, as far as Edward Porter was concerned, apparently was thicker than water.

'What's going to happen to her?'

'We don't know yet,' Sophia told him. 'The mastermind of all this, the man we probably would have charged with your mother's murder, being out of the picture, it will depend on what Scofield and Mansfield have to say when we find them.'

'*If* you find them.'

'We will,' she smiled, hoping Luke was more reassured than she felt. 'Being the kind of people they are, they will have gone to ground, but they'll turn up soon enough. The lifestyle they lead, they cross paths with the law quite regularly. And since every police station in the country now has a description of them, it's really just a matter of time.'

Luke said, as if in answer to Sophia's earlier wondering, 'I don't know how to feel about this. I just wish... shit, I don't know *what* I wish.'

Except for my mum to still be alive, was the unspoken qualifier they both knew hung in the air.

'I can't tell you how to feel, Luke,' Sophia said.

'You know what I wish?' he cut across whatever else she might have been about to add. 'I wish you'd tell me he fucking deserved it. To get shot. That those Nazis are wrong.'

Sophia considered. 'I can tell you what I told you before,' she said. 'That trained firearms officers shot Quaife while he was trying to evade arrest, believing him to be a danger to colleagues and to the public.'

'But you were *there*! Can't you give me anything extra?'

'Quaife's dead, Luke,' she said softly. 'Are the circumstances important?'

'They're holding him up as a fucking martyr!' he shouted, flinging a finger at the blank screen of the TV. 'By the time the investigation's finished the truth won't matter. They'll've milked this for all it's worth.' He stood up, shaking with impotent anger. 'Some fucking hero! What about me? What about my family? What about Mark? *We're* the victims, thanks to the likes of fucking Quaife. We matter. That excrement just got what was coming to him.'

'Sit down, Luke.' Her quiet firmness brought him up short. A sad blue stare followed him back to his chair. Sophia said, 'Off the record.'

'What?'

'Quaife had a knife,' she said, 'and he got close enough to one of my officers for her to feel mortally threatened. That's sufficient grounds as far as I'm concerned.' It was indiscreet, but she didn't regret it. Luke Benton had earned more than the playbook. 'That was for your ears only,' she added, making sure he was paying complete attention. 'I'll hold you to it.'

He held her gaze. 'Off the record?'

'Yes?'

'I'm glad he's dead. You know what? I'm glad they're both dead. Him and that fucking loser who reckoned he could help us black people and ended up destroying everything anyway. Glad.' Relaxing, he smiled, and the look on his face as he'd met her at the front door finally had a definition. 'I won't hold you to that,' he said. 'You can tell the world.'

ABOUT THE AUTHOR

IAN MAYFIELD grew up in South London in a house full of books, and made a valiant attempt to read them all, even some of the ones in French. Eventually he developed a desire to convert some of the daydreams these works inspired into his own writing.

As if this weren't enough, he worked for many years as an information technician – well, all right, library assistant. One of the perks of this job was being able to obtain even more books for free when they were impartially deemed by him to be too worn out to continue circulating.

Among his major influences as a crime writer Ian counts Arthur Conan Doyle, Dorothy L. Sayers, Raymond Chandler, Ruth Rendell, William Marshall, Cynthia Harrod-Eagles and John Harvey.

Following his tendency to gravitate to the south of things, he now lives in Southern California with his wife and a cat named Benjamin.

Follow the further adventures of the Special Crime Unit in

TEAM GAMES

Echoes of recent history haunt the detectives of the Metropolitan Police Special Crime Unit as they take on a new caseload. DC Sandra Jones suspects that an old friend may be connected to a number of vicious attacks on night bus passengers; DCs Jeff Wetherby and Danielle Greaves, a newcomer to the team, arrest a high school teacher who has betrayed the ultimate trust; and DCI Sophia Beadle prepares for the extradition of a fugitive who nearly killed one of her own.

As Sophia and her team trace the links between victims, witnesses and suspects through the streets of South London and beyond, investigations that had seemed straightforward spiral into a series of shocking consequences, and they must face up to the possibility that those who survived the violence of the past may not be so lucky this time around.

COMING SOON FROM IAN MAYFIELD